THE

T

THE
PERFECT
LOVER

STEPHANIE LAURENS

HarperLargePrint
An Imprint of HarperCollins*Publishers*

HarperCollins books may be purchased for educational, business, or sales promotional use. For information please write: Special Markets Department, HarperCollins Publishers Inc., 10 East 53rd Street, New York, NY 10022.

FIRST HARPER LARGE PRINT EDITION

Printed on acid-free paper

Library of Congress Cataloging-in-Publication Data

Laurens, Stephanie.
The perfect lover / by Stephanie Laurens.
p. cm.
ISBN 0-06-050571-0 (Hardcover)
1. Cynster family (Fictitious characters)—Fiction.
2. England—Fiction. I. Title. 03 - 242
PR9619.3.L376 P4 2003   HARPER LP
813'.54—dc21   (GALE - LP DIST)
2002032002   3/03
    $22.95
ISBN 0-06-053332-3 (Large Print)

03 04 05 06 07 WBC/RRD 10 9 8 7 6 5 4 3 2 1

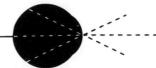

**This Large Print Book carries the
Seal of Approval of N.A.V.H.**

THIS BOOK IS DEDICATED
TO MY READERS NEAR AND FAR
WHO HAVE FOLLOWED THE CYNSTERS
FROM THEIR FIRST APPEARANCE
TO THE PRESENT.

YOU MOST TRULY ARE
THE WIND BENEATH MY WINGS.

LIST OF CHARACTERS

SIMON CYNSTER
friend of James Glossup

PORTIA ASHFORD
in Lady Osbaldestone's train

CHARLIE HASTINGS
friend of James Glossup

LADY OSBALDESTONE (THERESE)
distant cousin to Lord Netherfield

VISCOUNT NETHERFIELD (GRANVILLE)
father of Harold, Lord Glossup

HAROLD, LORD GLOSSUP
present owner of Glossup Hall

CATHERINE, LADY GLOSSUP
Harold's wife

HENRY GLOSSUP
their oldest son

KITTY GLOSSUP, NÉE ARCHER
his wife

JAMES GLOSSUP
second son of Harold and Catherine

OSWALD GLOSSUP
third son of Harold and Catherine

MORETON ARCHER
Kitty's father

ALFREDA ARCHER
Kitty's mother

SWANSTON ARCHER
Kitty's younger brother

WINIFRED ARCHER
Kitty's older sister

DESMOND WINFIELD
pursuing Winifred Archer

GEORGE BUCKSTEAD
close friend of Harold Glossup

HELEN BUCKSTEAD
George's wife

LUCY BUCKSTEAD
their daughter

LADY CYNTHIA CALVIN
connection of the Glossups', widow

AMBROSE CALVIN
her son

DRUSILLA CALVIN
her daughter

LADY HAMMOND
society matron, distantly related to the Glossups

ANNABELLE HAMMOND
her elder daughter

CECILY HAMMOND
her younger daughter

ARTURO
the handsome leader of a band
of gypsies encamped nearby

DENNIS
a younger male gypsy hired as
a temporary summer gardener

BLENKINSOP
the butler

MR. BASIL STOKES
the police inspector sent by
Bow Street to investigate

THE CYNSTER FAMILY TREE

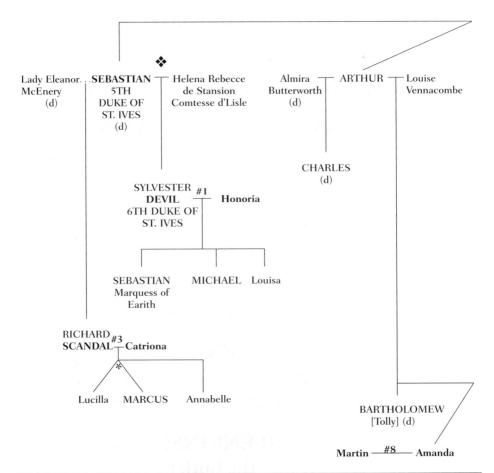

❖

Lady Eleanor. . .**SEBASTIAN** ┬ Helena Rebecce   Almira ┬ ARTHUR ┬ Louise
McEnery   5TH   de Stansion   Butterworth   Vennacombe
(d)   DUKE OF   Comtesse d'Lisle   (d)
              ST. IVES
              (d)

                                                                CHARLES
                                                                  (d)

            SYLVESTER #1
              DEVIL ┬ Honoria
            6TH DUKE OF
              ST. IVES

        SEBASTIAN   MICHAEL Louisa
        Marquess of
          Earith

    RICHARD #3
    SCANDAL ┬ Catriona
              ❖

    Lucilla   MARCUS   Annabelle

                                                BARTHOLOMEW
                                                  [Tolly] (d)

                                            Martin ──#8── Amanda

---

THE CYNSTER NOVELS:

#1 *Devil's Bride*	#4 *A Rogue's Proposal*	#7 *All About Passion*
#2 *A Rake's Vow*	#5 *A Secret Love*	#8 *On a Wild Night*
#3 *Scandal's Bride*	#6 *All About Love*	#9 *On a Wicked Dawn*
❖ *Special—The Promise in a Kiss*		#10 *The Perfect Lover*

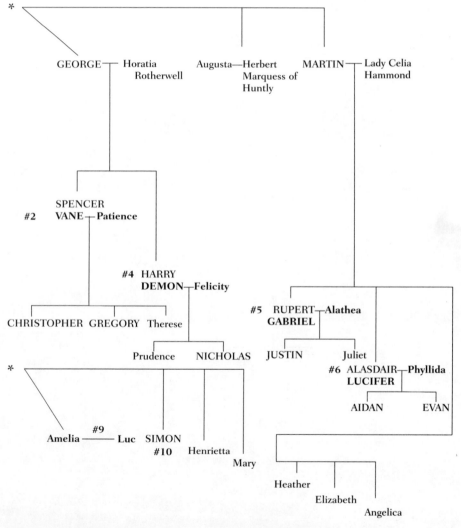

MALE Cynsters in capitals   ★ denotes twins
CHILDREN BORN AFTER 1825 NOT SHOWN

THE
PERFECT
LOVER

CHAPTER 1

Late July, 1835.
Near Glossup Hall, by Ashmore, Dorset.

Hell and the devil!" Simon Cynster reined in his bays, his eyes narrowing on the ridge high above Ashmore village. The village proper lay just behind him; he was headed for Glossup Hall, a mile farther along the leafy country lane.

At the rear of the village cottages, the land rose steeply; a woman was following the path winding up the berm of what Simon knew to be ancient earthworks. The views from the top reached as far as the Solent, and on clear days even to the Isle of Wight.

It was hardly a surprise to see someone heading up there.

"No surprise she hasn't anyone with her, either." Irritation mounting, he watched the dark-haired, willowy, ineffably graceful figure steadily ascend the rise, a long-legged figure that inevitably drew the eye of any man with blood in his veins. He'd recognized her instantly—Portia Ashford, his sister Amelia's sister-in-law.

Portia must be attending the Glossup Hall house party; the Hall was the only major house near enough from which to walk.

A sense of being imposed upon burgeoned and grew.

"Damn!" He'd yielded to the entreaties of his longtime friend James Glossup and agreed to stop by on his way to Somerset to support James through the trials of the house party. But if Portia was going to be present, he'd have trials enough of his own.

She reached the crest of the earthworks and paused, one slender hand rising to hold back the fall of her jet-black hair; lifting her face to the breeze, she stared into the distance, then, letting her hand fall, gracefully walked on, following the path to the lookout, gradually descending until she disappeared from sight.

She's no business of mine.

The words echoed in his head; God knew she'd stated the sentiment often enough, in various phrasings, most far more emphatic. Portia was not his sister, not his cousin; indeed, she shared no blood at all.

Jaw firming, he looked to his horses, took up the slack in the reins—

And inwardly cursed.

"Wilks—wake up, man!" Simon tossed the reins at his groom, until then dozing behind him.

Pulling on the brake, he stepped down to the road. "Just hold them—I'll be back."

Thrusting his hands into his greatcoat pockets, he strode for the narrow path that led upward, ultimately joining the path from the Hall that Portia had followed up the rise.

He was only buying himself trouble—a sniping match at the very least—yet leaving her alone, unprotected from any wastrel who might happen along, was simply not possible, not for him. If he'd driven on, he wouldn't have had a moment's peace, not until she returned safe and sound to the Hall.

Given her propensity for rambling walks, that might not happen for hours.

He wouldn't be thanked for his concern. If he survived without having his ego prodded in a dozen uncomfortable places, he'd count himself lucky. Portia had a tongue like a double-edged razor—no way one could escape being nicked. He knew perfectly well what her attitude would be when he caught up with her—precisely the same as it had been for the past decade, ever since he'd realized she truly had no idea of the prize she was, the temptation she posed, and was therefore in need of constant protection from the situations into which she blithely sailed.

While she remained out of his sight, out of his orbit, she was not his responsibility; if she came within it, unprotected, he felt obliged to watch over her, to keep her safe—he should have known better than to try to fight the urge.

Of all the females he knew, she was unquestionably the most difficult, not least because she was also the most intelligent, yet here he was, trudging after her despite his certain reception; he wasn't at all sure what that said of **his** intelligence.

Women! He'd spent the entire drive west considering them. His great-aunt Clara had recently died and left him her house in Somerset. The inheritance had served as a catalyst, forcing him to review his life, to rethink his direction, yet his unsettled state had a more fundamental genesis; he'd finally realized what it was that gave his older cousins and his sisters' husbands their purpose in life.

The purpose he lacked.

Family—their own branch of it, their own children—their own wife. Such things had never seemed critical before; now they loomed as vital to his life, to his satisfaction with his lot.

A scion of a wealthy, wellborn family, he had a comfortable lot in life, yet what worth comfort against the lack of achievement he now felt so acutely? It wasn't his ability to achieve that was in question—not in his mind, nor, he'd warrant, in any other—but the goal, the need, the reason; these were the necessities he lacked.

Crucial necessities for a satisfying life for such as he.

Great-aunt Clara's legacy had been the final prod; what was he to do with a rambling country house if not live in it? He needed to get himself a wife and start building the family he required to give his life its true direction.

He hadn't accepted the notion meekly. For the past ten years, his life had been well run, well ordered, with females intruding in only two arenas, both entirely under his control. With countless discreet liaisons behind him, he was a past master at managing—seducing, enjoying, and ultimately disengaging from—the wellborn matrons with whom he habitually dallied. Other than that, the only females he consorted with were those of his own family. Admittedly, within the family, they ruled, but as that had always been the case, he'd never felt constrained or challenged by the fact— one simply dealt with it as necessary.

With his active interest in the Cynster investment business together with the distractions of tonnish society, with his sexual conquests and the customary family gatherings to season the whole, his life had been pleasantly full. He'd never seen the need to linger at those balls and parties graced by marriageable young ladies.

Which now left him in the unenviable position of wanting a wife and not having any useful avenue through which to acquire one, not without setting off alarm bells that would resonate throughout the ton. If he was foolish enough to start attending the balls and parties, the fond mamas would instantly perceive he was on the lookout for a bride—and lay siege.

He was the last unmarried male Cynster of his generation.

Stepping up to the top of the earthworks' outer wall, he paused. The land fell away in a shallow sweep; the path continued to the left, leading to a squat, covered lookout set into the earth wall some fifty yards on.

The view was magnificent. Sunshine winked on the distant sea; the silhouette of the Isle of Wight was distinguishable through a soft summer haze.

He'd seen the view before. He turned to the lookout, and the female presently in it. She was standing at the railing, gazing out to sea. From her stance and stillness, he assumed she hadn't seen him.

Lips setting, he walked on. He wouldn't need to give any reason for joining her. For the past decade, he'd treated her with the same insistent protectiveness he applied to all the females of his family; doubtless it was her relationship—the fact she was his brother-in-law Luc's sister—that dictated how he felt about her despite the lack of blood ties.

To his mind, Portia Ashford was family, his to protect. That much, at least, was unarguable.

What tortuous logic had prompted the gods to decree that a woman needed a man to conceive?

Portia stifled a disgusted humph. That was the crux of the dilemma now facing her. Unfortunately, there was no point debating the issue—the gods had so decreed, and there was nothing she could do about it.

Other than find a way around the problem.

The thought increased her irritation, largely self-directed. She had never wanted a husband, never imagined that the usual path of a nice, neat, socially approved marriage with all its attendant constraints was for her. Never had she seen her future in such terms.

But there was no other way.

Stiffening her spine, she faced the fact squarely: if she wanted children of her own, she would have to find a husband.

The breeze sidled up, whispering, coolly caressing her cheeks, lightly fingering the heavy waves of her hair. The realization that children—her own children, her own family—were what in her heart she truly yearned for, the challenge she'd been raised, like her mother, to accept and conquer, had come just like the breeze, stealing up on her. For the past five years, she'd worked with her sisters, Penelope and Anne, in caring for foundlings in London. She'd plunged into the project with her usual zeal, convinced their ideals were both proper and right, only to discover her own destiny lay in a direction in which she'd never thought to look.

So now she needed a husband.

Given her birth, her family's status and connections, and her dowry, gaining such an encumbrance would be easy, even though she was already twenty-four. She wasn't, however, fool enough to imagine any gentleman would do. Given her character, her temperament, her trenchant independence, it was imperative she choose wisely.

She wrinkled her nose, her gaze fixed unseeing

on the distant prospect. Never had she imagined she would come to this—to desiring a husband. Courtesy of their brother Luc's disinterest in pushing her and her sisters into marriage, they'd been allowed to go their own way; her way had eschewed the ballrooms and salons, Almack's, and similar gatherings of the ton at which marriageable young ladies found their spouses.

Learning how to find a husband had seemed beneath her—an enterprise well below the more meaty challenges her intellect demanded . . .

Recollections of past arrogance—of all the chances to learn the hows and wherefores of husband selection and subsequent snaring at which she'd turned up her nose—fed her aggravation. How galling to discover that her intellect, widely accepted as superior, had not forseen her present state.

The damning truth was she could recite Horace and quote Virgil by the page, yet she had no real idea how to acquire a husband.

Let alone the right one.

She refocused on the distant sea, on the sunlight winking off the waves, constantly vacillating. Just as she was, had been for the past month. That was so unlike her, so at odds with her character— always decisive, never weak or shy—her indecision grated on her temper. Her character wanted, nay **demanded,** a decision, a firm goal, a plan of action. Her emotions—a side of herself she'd rarely been swayed by—were far less sure. Far less inclined to jump into this latest project with her customary zeal.

She'd revisted the arguments ad infinitum; there were no further aspects to be explored. She'd walked here today determined to use the few hours before the other guests arrived and the house party got under way to formulate a plan.

Lips setting, she narrowed her eyes at the horizon, aware of resistance welling inside, of a shying away from the moment—so aggravating yet so instinctive, so powerful she had to fight to override it and push ahead . . . but she was not going to leave without a firm commitment.

Grasping the lookout's railing, she tipped her chin high and firmly stated, "I will use every opportunity the house party provides to learn all I can and make up my mind once and for all." That was nowhere near decisive enough; determinedly, she added, "Whoever is present of suitable age and station, I swear I will seriously consider him."

There—at last! She'd put her next step into words. Into a solemn vow. The positive uplifting feeling that always followed on the heels of decision welled within her—

"Well that's heartening, I must say, although of suitable age and station for what?"

With a gasp, she whirled. For one instant, her mind boggled. Not with fear—despite the shadows in which he stood and the brightness of the day behind him, she'd recognized his voice, knew whose shoulders blocked the entrance arch.

But what in all Hades was **he** doing **here**?

His gaze sharpened—a disconcertingly acute blue gaze far too direct for politeness.

"And what haven't you made up your mind about? That usually takes you all of two seconds."

Calmness, decisiveness—fearlessness—returned in a rush. She narrowed her eyes. "**That** is none of your affair."

He moved, deliberately slowly, taking three prowling steps to join her by the railing. She tensed. The muscles framing her spine grew rigid; her lungs locked as something within her reacted. She knew him so well, yet here, alone in the silence of the fields and sky, he seemed larger, more powerful.

More dangerous in some indefinable way.

Stopping with two feet between them, he gestured to the view. "You seemed to be declaring it to the world at large."

He met her gaze; amusement at catching her out lurked in the blue, along with watchfulness and a certain disapproval.

His features remained expressionless. "I suppose it's too much to hope there's a groom or footman waiting nearby?"

That was a subject she wasn't about to debate, especially not with him. Facing the view, she coolly inclined her head. "Good afternoon. The views are quite magnificent." She paused for only an instant. "I hadn't imagined you an admirer of nature."

She felt his gaze slide over her profile, then he looked at the view.

"On the contrary." He slid his hands into his pockets; he seemed to relax. "There are some creations of nature I'm addicted to worshipping."

It required no thought at all to divine to what he was alluding. In the past, she would have made some tart remark . . . now, all she heard in her mind were the words of her vow . . . "You're here for the Glossups' house party."

It wasn't a question; he answered with an elegant shrug. "What else?"

He turned as she drew herself up. Their eyes met; he'd heard her vow and was unlikely to forget . . .

She was suddenly sure she needed more space between them.

"I came here for the solitude," she baldly informed him. "Now that you've arrived, I may as well start back."

She swung toward the exit. He was in her way. Her heartbeat accelerating, she glanced at his face.

In time to see his features harden, to sense him bite back some retort. His gaze touched hers; his restraint was almost palpable. With a calm so deliberate it was itself a warning, he stepped aside and waved her to the door. "As you wish."

Her senses remained trained on him as she swept past; her skin prickled as if in truth he posed some potential danger. Once past him, head high, she glided out of the archway; with a calm more apparent than real, she set off along the path.

Jaw setting, Simon ruthlessly quelled the urge to stop her, to reach out, catch her hand, reel her back—to what end he wasn't sure. This, he reminded himself, was what he needed, her on her haughty way back to Glossup Hall.

Drawing a long breath, he held it, then followed her out into the sunshine.

And on down the path. The sooner she got back to civilization and safety, the sooner his own journey would end. He'd driven straight down from London—he was thirsty; a glass of ale would not go astray.

With his longer strides he could easily overtake her; instead, he ambled in her wake, content enough with the view. The current fashion for gowns with waists that actually fell at a woman's waist suited her, emphasizing the svelte lines of her figure, the slender curves, the very long lines of her legs. The purply blue hue of the light summer walking dress complemented her dramatic coloring—raven black hair, midnight blue eyes, and pale, almost translucent skin. She was taller than the average; her forehead would brush his chin—if they ever got that close.

The thought of that happening made him inwardly, grimly, laugh.

Reaching the crest of the rise, she continued over and on—and only then realized he was following her. She threw him a black glance, then stopped and waited, swinging to face him as he halted before her.

Her eyes like shards of dark flint, she glared at him. "You are **not** going to follow me all the way back to the Hall."

Portia didn't ask what he thought he was doing; they both knew. They'd last seen each other at Christmas, seven months before, but only distantly, surrounded by the combined hordes of their families. He hadn't had a chance then to get on her nerves, something that, ever since she'd turned fourteen, he'd seemed absolutely devoted to doing, if possible every time they met.

His gaze locked on hers. Something—temper? decision?—flashed behind the deceptively soft blue of his eyes. Then his lips firmed; he stepped around her with his usual fluid grace, unnerving in a man so large, and continued on down the path.

She whirled, watched. He didn't go far but stopped a step beyond the fork where the footpath to the village led down to the lane below.

Turning, he met her gaze. "You're right. I'm not." He waved down the path.

She looked in that direction. A curricle—his curricle—stood in the lane.

"Your carriage awaits."

Lifting her gaze, she met his. Directly. He was blocking the path to the Hall—quite deliberately.

"I was intending to walk back."

His gaze didn't waver. "Change your mind."

His tone—sheer male arrogance laced with a challenge she hadn't previously encountered and couldn't place—sent a peculiar shiver through her. There was no overt aggression in his stance, yet she didn't for a moment doubt he could, and would, stop her if she tried to get past him.

Temper, wild willfulness—her customary response to intimidatory tactics, especially from him—flooded her, yet this time there were other, powerful and distracting emotions in the mix. She stood perfectly still, her gaze level and locked in silent combat with his, the familiar struggle for supremacy, yet . . .

Something had changed.

In him.

And in her.

Was it simply age—how long had it been since they'd last crossed wills like this? Three years? More? Regardless, the field had altered; the battle was no longer the same. Something was fundamentally different; she sensed in him a bolder, more blatantly predatory streak, a flash of steel beneath his elegance, as if with the years his mask was wearing thin.

She'd always known him for what he was . . .

Her vow echoed in her head. She mentally shook aside the distraction, yet still she heard . . . recognized the challenge.

Couldn't resist.

Head rising, she walked forward, every bit as deliberate as he.

The watchfulness in his eyes condensed, until his attention was focused exclusively on her. Another tingle of sensation slithered down her spine. Halting before him, she held his gaze.

What did he see? Now she was looking, trying to see past his guard only to discover she could not—

odd, for they'd never sought to hide their mutual dismissiveness—what was it he was hiding? What was the reason behind the veiled threat emanating from him?

To her surprise, she wanted to know.

She drew a deliberate breath, evenly stated, "Very well."

Surprise lit his eyes, swiftly superceded by suspicion; she pivoted and looked down, stepping onto the path to the village, hiding her smile. Just so he wouldn't imagine he'd won, she coolly added, "As it happens, one of my shoes is pinching."

She'd taken only one more step when she sensed him shift, then he was sweeping down on her, moving far too fast.

Her senses leapt. Uncertain, she slowed—

He didn't halt; he bent, and scooped her up in his arms.

"What—?"

Without breaking his stride, he juggled her until he had her cradled, carrying her as if she weighed no more than a child.

Her lungs had seized, along with her senses; it took serious effort to draw breath. "What do you think you're **doing**?"

Her total incomprehension invested every word. Never before had he shown the slightest sign of reacting to her gibes in any physical way.

She was . . . what? Shocked? Or . . . ?

Thrusting her confusion side, she met his gaze as he briefly glanced her way.

"Your shoe's pinching—we wouldn't want your delicate little foot to suffer unnecessary damage."

His tone was bland, his expression guileless; the look in his eyes would even pass for innocent.

She blinked. They both looked ahead. She considered protesting—and discarded the notion in the next thought. He was perfectly capable of arguing until they reached the curricle.

As for struggling, she was intensely aware—far more than she liked to be—that she was physically much weaker than he. The arms supporting her felt like steel; his stride never faltered, powerful and assured. The hand clasping her thigh just above her knee—decently protected by her full skirts—grasped like a vise; the width of his chest and its muscled hardness locked her in. She'd never regarded his strength as anything she needed to consider or weigh, yet if he was going to bring physical contact into their equation, she would need to think again.

And not just on the basis of strength.

Being this close, trapped in his arms, made her feel . . . among other things, light-headed.

He slowed; she refocused.

With a flourish, he set her on the curricle's seat.

Startled, she grasped the railings, out of habit drawing her skirts close so he could sit beside her—noting the equally startled face of Wilks, his groom.

"Ah . . . afternoon, Miss Portia." Wide-eyed, Wilks bobbed as he handed the reins to Simon.

Wilks had to have witnessed the entire performance; he was waiting for her to explode, or at
least say something cutting.

And he wasn't the only one.

She smiled with perfect equanimity. "Good
afternoon, Wilks."

Wilks blinked, nodded warily, then hurried back
to his place.

Simon glanced at her as he climbed up beside
her. As if expecting her to bite. Or at the very least
snarl.

He wouldn't have believed a sweet smile, so she
faced forward, serenely composed, as if her joining
him in the curricle had been her idea. His suspicious glance was worth every tithe of the effort
such sunny compliance cost her.

The curricle jerked, then rolled forward. The
instant he had his bays bowling along, she asked,
"How are your parents?"

A pause greeted that, but then he replied.

She nodded and launched into an account of her
family, all of whom he knew, describing their
health, their whereabouts, their latest interests. As
if he'd asked, she continued, "I came down with
Lady O." For years, that had been their shorthand
for Lady Osbaldestone, a connection of the Cynsters' and an old friend of her family's, an ancient
beldame who terrorized half the ton. "She spent
the last weeks at the Chase, and then had to travel
down here. She's an old friend of Lord Netherfield, did you know?" Viscount Netherfield was

Lord Glossup's father and was presently visiting at Glossup Hall.

Simon was frowning. "No."

Portia smiled quite genuinely; she was fond of Lady O, but Simon, in company with most gentlemen of his ilk, found her perspicaciousness somewhat scarifying. "Luc insisted she shouldn't cross half the country alone, so I offered to come, too. The others who've arrived so far . . ." She rattled on, acquainting him with those present and those yet to arrive, precisely as any friendly, well-bred young lady might.

The suspicion in his eyes grew more and more pronounced.

Then the gates of Glossup Hall appeared, set wide in welcome. Simon turned the bays in and set them pacing up the drive.

The Hall was a sprawling country house built in Elizabethan times. Its typical redbrick facade faced south and boasted three stories with east and west wings set perpendicular to it. The central wing housing the ballroom and conservatory made up the middle stroke of the E. As they neared, sunlight glanced off the rows of mullioned windows and glowed on the tall chimneys with their ornate pots.

By the time he swung the bays into the circular forecourt, Simon felt thoroughly disconcerted. Not a common feeling, not for him; there wasn't much in tonnish life that could throw him off-balance.

Other than Portia.

If she'd railed at him, used her sharp tongue to its usual effect, all would have been normal. He wouldn't have enjoyed the encounter, but neither would he have felt this sudden disorientation.

Rack his brains though he might, he couldn't recall her ever behaving toward him with such . . . feminine softness was the description that sprang to mind. She was usually well armored and prickly; today, she'd apparently left her shield and spears behind.

The result was . . .

He reined in the bays, pulled on the brake, tossed the ribbons to Wilks, and stepped down.

Portia waited for him to come around the carriage and hand her down; he watched, expecting her to leap down in her usual, independent, don't-need-you way. Instead, when he offered his hand, she placed her slim fingers across his palm and let him assist her to alight with stunning grace.

She looked up and smiled when he released her. "Thank you." Her smile deepened; her eyes held his. "You were right. My foot is in an unquestionably better state than it otherwise would have been."

Her expression one of ineffable sweetness, she inclined her head and turned away. Her eyes were so dark he hadn't been able to tell if the twinkle he'd thought he'd seen in them was real, or merely a trick of the light.

He stood in the forecourt, grooms and footmen darting around him, and watched as she glided into the house. Without a single glance back, she disappeared into the shadows beyond the open front door.

The sound of gravel crunching as his curricle and pair were led away jerked him out of his abstraction. Outwardly impassive, inwardly a trifle grim, he strode to the door of Glossup Hall. And followed her in.

"Simon! Capital." Smiling broadly, James Glossup shut the library door and came forward.

Leaving his greatcoat in the butler's hands, Simon turned to greet James.

Relief shone in James's eyes as he shook his hand. "You've arrived just in time to stand shoulder to shoulder with Charlie and me." With a nod, he indicated the drawing room; through the closed doors, the unmistakable hubbub of male and female voices engaged in social discourse reached them. "Charlie went in to reconnoiter."

Blenkinsop, the butler, paused at James's elbow. "I'll have Mr. Cynster's bags put in his usual room, sir."

James nodded. "Thank you, Blenkinsop. We'll join the others—no need to announce us."

An ex–sergeant major, tall, tending toward portly but with a rigidly upright stance, Blenkinsop bowed and departed. James glanced at Simon, then waved to the drawing room. "Come—let's have at them!"

They entered together, pausing to close one door each. Simon met James's gaze as the lock clicked; watching from across the room, Portia suspected both were well aware of the image they presented, strolling in side by side.

Two wolves of the ton; no one with eyes would mistake them for anything else, and seen together, the effect was compounded. They were both tall, lean, broad-shouldered, and loose-limbed, neither overly heavy. Where James's brown hair curled lightly, Simon's once-fair locks, darkened with age to a burnished light brown that still held the promise of hidden gold, lay in silk waves about his head. Simon was blue-eyed and fairer of skin; James had soulful brown eyes he used to good effect.

Both were dressed in the first style, their coats perfectly fitted, the cut bearing the unmistakable stamp of the ton's foremost tailor. Their cravats were pristine white, precisely tied; their waistcoats were exercises in subdued elegance.

They wore the mantle of tonnish grace as if they'd been born to it, as, indeed, they had. They were brothers beneath the skin—rakes of the ton; as James performed the introductions, that was clear beyond doubt.

They were joined by Charlie Hastings, the third member of their crew, a slightly shorter, fair-haired gentleman of the same handsome, devil-may-care ilk.

Portia surveyed the rest of the company, scattered about the large drawing room, grouped about chairs and sofas, teacups in hand. The only guests still to arrive were Lady Hammond and her two daughters, expected later that afternoon.

James led Simon first to their host, his father, Harold, Lord Glossup, a well-built gentleman of middle age, who had made all his guests heartily welcome. Beside him stood George Buckstead, a solid country sort, an old friend of Harold's and in much the same vein. Also of the group was Ambrose Calvin, a gentleman of somewhat different stamp. Ambrose was in his midthirties, and apparently determined on a political career, hence, Portia suspected, his presence here.

Precisely what he hoped to gain she wasn't sure, but she had experience of his type; he was sure to have some goal in mind.

Charlie, already introduced, had hung back; when James and Simon turned, they discovered Miss Lucy Buckstead had captured their friend. Bright, breezy, just twenty, pretty, and dark-haired, Miss Buckstead was delighted to give Simon her hand, but her eyes too quickly returned to James's face.

With an elegant apology, James drew Simon away to continue the introductions; Charlie stepped in to distract Miss Buckstead. Portia noted the glance James and Simon exchanged as they approached the next group.

That contained James's mother, their hostess, Catherine, Lady Glossup. A faded matron with pale fair hair and washed-out blue eyes, she still retained a degree of reserve, a faint echo of a superiority she didn't in fact possess. She was not an unkind woman, but one, perhaps, whose dreams had passed her by. Beside her sat Mrs. Buckstead—Helen—a large, matronly lady whose calm cheeriness declared her quite content with her lot.

Both ladies smiled graciously as Simon bowed; he exchanged a few words, then turned to shake hands with the gentleman standing beside them. Mr. Moreton Archer was a banker, wealthy and influential; the second son of a second son, he'd had to make his way in the world, and had succeeded. The confidence that gave sat like a patina over his person, over the expensive clothes and precise grooming.

Of Lord and Lady Glossup's generation, Mr. Archer was the father of another Catherine, known to all as Kitty, who had married Lord Glossup's eldest son, Henry. It was clear to all that Mr. Archer viewed that circumstance as affording entry into the social circles to which he aspired.

Being introduced to Simon made his gaze sharpen; he would have liked to speak for longer, but James artfully guided Simon on.

The next group included Kitty Glossup, in some respects their secondary hostess. Blond, petite but slightly plump, Kitty had a porcelain pink-and-white complexion and glowing blue eyes; her small hands flitted, her lightly rouged lips were forever in motion, either smiling or pouting or talking. She was never happier than when holding center stage; she was vain, flighty—Portia had found they had little in common, but Kitty was not so different from many others in the ton.

Kitty had been conversing with Lady Calvin and Mr. Desmond Winfield. Cynthia, Lady Calvin, was a severe but well-connected widow, a cool, level-headed lady carefully guiding her two children—Ambrose and her daughter, Drusilla—through life. An earl's daughter, she moved in the same circles as the Cynsters and Ashfords; she smiled regally on Simon and gave him her hand.

Mr. Winfield had arrived only a few hours before; Portia had yet to learn much of him. His outward appearance declared him a gentleman of independent means, sober and rather thoughtful. She'd gathered he'd been invited through the Archers; she wondered if he was intended for their older, as yet unmarried daughter, Winifred.

Winifred herself was in the next group James conducted Simon toward, as were Henry Glossup, James's elder brother, Alfreda Archer, Winifred and Kitty's mother and thus Henry's mother-in-law, and Drusilla Calvin.

As a longtime friend of James's, Simon had visited Glossup Hall frequently and knew Henry well; they shook hands as old acquaintances. Henry was an older, quieter, and more solid version of James, a likable sort on whose shoulders responsibility for the estate had devolved.

Alfreda Archer was effusive; Portia sensed Simon's shields snap into place even from across the room. Mrs. Archer bore all the hallmarks of a matchmaking mama, one keen to use marriage to climb the social ladder. In contrast, Winifred was calm, greeting Simon with a gentle smile and open courtesy, nothing more.

Drusilla barely managed that. She was nearly the same age as Portia, but there the resemblance ended. Drusilla was mousy, retiring, and peculiarly severe for her age. She seemed to view herself as her mother's companion rather than her daughter; she had, consequently, little interest in either Simon or James, and let it show.

The only others present aside from Lady Osbaldestone and Lord Netherfield, beside whom Portia sat, were Oswald Glossup, James's younger brother, and Swanston Archer, Kitty's younger brother. Both were of similar age and attitude; with ridiculously tight, striped waistcoats and coats with long tails, they considered themselves cocks of the walk and strutted accordingly while holding aloof from the rest of the company.

Simon acknowledged them with a curt nod and a look that hinted at disapproval.

And then he and James were approaching the sofa where Lady Osbaldestone and Lord Netherfield had stationed themselves, a little apart from the rest the better to observe and comment without restriction.

Portia rose as the two men neared—not from any sense of proper behavior but simply because she disliked being towered over, especially by two of them at once.

Lady Osbaldestone acknowledged Simon's greeting and bow with a gleeful thump of her cane, and promptly put him in his place by inquiring, "Well, then—how's your mother?"

Inured by long experience, likewise aware there would be no escape, he replied with commendable evenness. Lady O demanded an accounting of his younger sisters and his father; while he satisfied her rapacious curiosity, Portia exchanged a smile with James, and engaged him and his grandfather in a discussion of the prettiest walks in the locality.

Lady O eventually released Simon. He turned to Lord Netherfield with a smile and a few words, renewing their previous acquaintance. That done, Simon, now standing beside Portia, turned back to Lady O—and froze.

Portia sensed it, glanced Lady O's way—and did the same. The basilisk gaze that had terrorized the ton for over fifty years was fixed on them.

Both of them.

They stood transfixed, both uncertain which way to move, how they had transgressed . . .

Awfully, Lady O's brows slowly rose. "You **are** acquainted, are you not?"

Portia felt heat rise in her cheeks; from the corner of her eye, she noted Simon fared no better. Despite being perfectly aware of each other, neither had remembered to acknowledge the other's presence in any socially acceptable way. She opened her lips, but he got in before her.

"Miss Ashford and I met earlier."

If they hadn't been standing in plain sight, she would have kicked him. His cool arrogance made it sound as if their meeting had been clandestine! In an airy tone, she explained, "Mr. Cynster was kind enough to drive me back from the village. I'd walked to the lookout."

"Indeed?" Lady O's black gaze held them for an instant more, then she nodded and thumped her cane on the floor. "I see!"

Before Portia could decide what she meant by that, Lady O continued, "Very well." She pointed to her empty cup on the side table. "You may fetch me another cup of tea, sir."

With an alacrity Portia fully understood, Simon smiled charmingly, whisked up the cup and saucer, and strolled off to where the trolley was stationed at Lady Glossup's side. James was dispatched to perform the same service for his grandfather. Portia seized the moment to excuse herself and drift across the room to Winifred Archer and Drusilla Calvin—the guests she reasoned Simon was least likely to join.

She might have vowed to consider every eligible gentleman present; that didn't mean she had to stand beside any of them while she did so.

Especially not beside Simon.

Especially not with Lady O looking on.

Simon returned Lady Osbaldestone's brimming cup, then glibly excused himself; the old tartar dismissed him with a humph and a wave. Collecting a cup of tea for himself, he joined Charlie and Lucy Buckstead by the windows.

Charlie welcomed him with a grin, but his artful patter didn't falter; he was well launched on turning Miss Buckstead's giddy head. Not that he meant anything by it; Charlie simply loved to flirt. With his curling golden hair, dark brown eyes, and even, fashionable drawl, he was an ornament of the ton greatly sought after by ladies of taste and discernment.

The point ladies discerned, usually with exemplary rapidity, was that Charlie was, in most cases, all talk and no action. Not that he didn't indulge when it suited him; it simply rarely did.

Even Miss Buckstead, naive though she was, seemed quite unconcerned, laughing and parrying Charlie's almost-but-not-quite-risqué comments.

Simon smiled and sipped his tea. Both he and Charlie knew they were safe with Miss Buckstead; it was James she had her naive eyes set upon.

Under cover of the chatter, he surveyed the company. The purpose of the gathering was clearly to acknowledge ties—with the Archers, Kitty's family, and the Bucksteads, old friends, and the Calvins and the Hammonds, useful connections. An entirely normal collection of guests, but with Lucy Buckstead present, Simon could appreciate James's strategy in ensuring a few extra gentlemen attended.

He didn't begrudge James the days; it was, at base, what friends were for. He did, however, wonder what entertainment he himself might find to fill the time until he could safely leave James and continue on to Somerset.

His gaze came to rest on the trio of ladies standing by the other set of windows. Winifred Archer, Drusilla Calvin, and Portia. The latter were of an age, around twenty-four, a few years younger than Kitty, whose giddy laughter reached him over the hum of more restrained conversations.

Portia glanced at Kitty, then returned to the discussion between Winifred and Drusilla.

Winifred had her back to her sister and gave no sign of having heard her shrill mirth. Winifred was older; Simon judged her to be closer to his own twenty-nine years.

He glanced at the group over which Kitty presided and saw Desmond Winfield glance toward Portia. Or was it toward Winifred? Desmond tensed, as if to approach them.

Kitty laid a hand on his sleeve and directed some question his way; he turned back to her and answered quietly.

Nearer at hand, Charlie laughed; Lucy Buckstead smothered a giggle. With not a clue as to what had been said, Simon smiled at them both, then raised his cup and sipped again.

His gaze returned to Portia.

The sun streamed over her, striking blue-black glints from her raven hair.

Unbidden, the fragrance that had risen from her heavy curls, the warm scent that had teased his senses as he'd carried her down the path, returned, sharply evocative. It pricked his memory, and brought back all the rest—the weight of her in his arms, the supple tension in her body, the all-too-feminine curves. The remembered sensations washed over him, and left him heated.

He'd been crushingly aware of her as a woman, a female—something he'd never imagined could be. He'd been stunned, not least by the discovery that some part of his mind had consciously wished he'd been carrying her somewhere else. Somewhere a great deal more private.

Yet at no time had he confused her with any other—he'd known very well who it was in his arms. He hadn't forgotten the sharpness of her tongue, the lash of her temper. Nevertheless, he'd wanted . . .

Inwardly frowning, he shifted his gaze back to Lucy Buckstead. If he wanted a wife, surely she was the sort of female he should be considering— well behaved, docile—manageable. He fixed his gaze on her . . . but his mind kept sliding away. . . .

He set down his cup, conjured a smile. "If you'll excuse me, I should wash off the dust."

With a brief bow to Lucy and a nod to Charlie, he returned his cup to Lady Glossup, smoothly made his excuses, and escaped.

As he climbed the stairs, Portia, that unexpected moment on the path, and her equally unexpected response reclaimed his mind. Glossup Hall had presented him with unanticipated vistas; he had the time—there was no reason he couldn't explore them.

Aside from all else, the challenge of discovering just what one supremely well-educated female had yet to learn about life was well-nigh irresistible.

CHAPTER 2

I never would have thought you a coward."

The words, spoken in a soft, feminine, decidedly provocative drawl, brought Portia to a halt on the landing of the west wing stairs. She'd spent the last half hour with the pianoforte in the music room on the first floor of the west wing; now it was time to gather in the drawing room before dinner—she was on her way there.

By the west wing stairs, not much frequented by the ladies of the party as their rooms were in the east wing.

"But perhaps it's just a ploy?"

The words clung like a caress; it was Kitty speaking.

"It's **not** a ploy!" James spoke through his teeth. "I'm not playing any games—and I never will with you!"

They were out of Portia's sight in the hall at the bottom of the stairs, but James's aversion reached her clearly. Along with a hint of desperation.

Kitty laughed. Her disbelief—or rather her belief that no man, especially not one like James, would not desire her—echoed up the stairwell.

Without further thought, Portia calmly, and firmly, continued down the stairs.

They heard her; both turned. Both faces registered unwelcome surprise, but only James's registered anything approaching embarrassment; Kitty's expression was all irritation at being interrupted.

Then James recognized Portia; relief washed over his features. "Good evening, Miss Ashford. Have you lost your way?"

She hadn't, but Kitty had James backed into an alcove. "Indeed." She struggled to infuse some degree of helplessness into her expression. "I thought I was certain, yet . . ." She waved vaguely.

James brushed past Kitty. "Allow me—I was just heading for the drawing room. I take it that's where you wish to go?"

He took her hand and set it on his sleeve; she met his eyes, and saw the plea therein.

"Yes, please. I would be most grateful for your escort." She smiled easily, then turned to Kitty.

Kitty didn't smile back; she nodded somewhat curtly.

Portia raised her brows. "Aren't you joining us, Mrs. Glossup?"

Beside her, James stiffened.

Kitty waved. "I'll be along shortly. Do go on." With that, she turned and headed for the stairs.

James relaxed. Portia turned and let him steer her toward the central wing. She glanced at his face; he was frowning, and a trifle pale. "Are you all right, Mr. Glossup?"

He glanced at her, then smiled—charmingly.

"Do call me James." With a backward nod, he added, "Thank you."

Brows rising, she couldn't resist asking, "Is she often like that—importuning?"

He hesitated, then said, "She seems to be getting rather worse."

He was clearly uncomfortable; she looked ahead. "You'll just have to cling to other ladies until she gets over it."

He threw her a sharp glance, but didn't know her well enough to be sure of her irony. She let him guide her through the house, hiding a smile at the bizarre twist that had a rake of James Glossup's standing relying on her for, as it were, protection of his virtue.

She caught his eye as they entered the front hall; he was almost certain she was laughing, but wasn't sure about what. The drawing room loomed; she faced forward. Simon would have known.

As they crossed the threshold, she saw him, standing to one side of the fireplace, conversing with Charlie and two bright young things—Lady Hammond's daughters, Annabelle and Cecily. Lady Hammond herself, a warmhearted matron of sunny charm, was seated on the chaise beside Lady Osbaldestone.

Across the room, Simon's eyes met Portia's. James excused himself and went to talk to his father. After pausing to greet Lady Hammond, a friend of her mother's, Portia joined Simon and Charlie, Annabelle and Cecily.

The girls were a breath of fresh air; they were

innocents, yet entirely at home in this sphere and determined to be the life—or lives—of the party. Portia had known them for years; they greeted her with typical joy.

"Splendid! I didn't know you'd be here!"

"Oh, it'll be wonderful—I'm sure we'll have such fun!"

Wide eyes, bright smiles—it was impossible not to respond in kind. After the usual inquiries about families and acquaintances, the talk focused on the expected pleasures of the coming days and the amenities afforded by the Hall and its neighborhood.

"The gardens are extensive, with lots of walks. I read that in a guidebook," Annabelle confessed.

"Oh, and there's a lake—the book said it was not man-made but filled by a natural spring and quite deep." Cecily grimaced. "Too deep for punting. Imagine!"

"Well," Charlie put in, "you wouldn't want to risk falling in. Deuced cold—I can vouch for it."

"Good heavens!" Annabelle turned to Charlie. "Did you? Fall in, I mean?"

Portia caught the glance Charlie sent Simon, and the answering quirk of Simon's lips; she judged it more likely Charlie had been thrown in.

Movement across the room caught her eye; Kitty entered and paused, surveying the company. Henry detached himself from a group and crossed to her side. He spoke to her quietly, head lowered, clearly a private word.

Kitty stiffened; her head rose. She threw Henry a

look of dismissive affront, then replied very shortly, gave him her shoulder, and, with an expression perilously close to a truculent pout, all but flounced off to speak with Ambrose and Drusilla Calvin.

Henry watched Kitty go. His features were tight, controlled, closed, yet the underlying impression was one of pain.

Clearly all was not well on that front.

Portia returned to the conversation still bubbling about her. Annabelle turned to her, eyes eager and wide. "Have you visited there yet?"

She'd obviously missed something; she glanced at Simon.

His eyes met hers; his brows quirked, but he consented to save her. "Portia hasn't visited here before—she's as new to the delights of the Hall as you both. As for the temple . . ." His gaze returned to Portia's face. "I must admit I prefer the summerhouse by the lake. Perhaps a touch too private for some, but the quietness over the water's soothing."

"We must be sure to walk that way." Cecily was busy making plans. "And I hear there's a lookout, too, somewhere nearby?"

"I've walked there." Refusing to meet Simon's eye, Portia did her bit to slake the Hammond girls' thirst for information.

That topic absorbed them until dinner was announced. Once seated at the long table, mindful of her vow, Portia turned her attention to reconnoitering the field.

Whoever is present of suitable age and station, I swear I will seriously consider him.

So whom was she considering? All the males about the table were, at least theoretically, of suitable station, else they wouldn't be present. Some were married and thus easily eliminated; of those left, some she knew better than others.

As they ate and talked, while she attended this discussion, then that, she let her gaze roam, noting each head, acknowledging each possibility.

Her gaze came to rest on Simon, seated across the table two places down. He was struggling to make conversation with Drusilla, who seemed peculiarly reserved, severe, but uncomfortable too. Portia inwardly frowned; regardless of their frequent disagreements, she knew Simon's manners were polished to a high gloss and would never be at fault in a social situation. Whatever the problem, it lay with Drusilla.

There was a lull in the chatter around her; her gaze remained on Simon, noting the glimmer of gold in his hair, his long, elegant fingers curving about his wineglass, the resigned set of his lips as he sat back, leaving Drusilla to herself.

She'd been staring too long; he felt her gaze.

In the instant before he looked her way, she looked down, calmly helping herself to more vegetables, then turning to Mr. Buckstead beside her.

Only when she felt Simon's gaze shift from her did she breathe freely again.

Only then realized how odd was her reaction.

Whoever is present of suitable age and station . . .

By the time the ladies rose and departed for the drawing room, leaving the gentlemen to their port, she'd mentally inked three names onto her list. The house party was clearly destined to be a trial, a testing ground on which she could develop her husband-selection skills; none of the gentlemen present were the sort she could imagine entrusting with her hand, but as specimens on which to practice, they would do very well.

James Glossup and Charlie Hastings were exactly the sort of gentlemen whose attributes she needed to learn to weigh.

As for Simon, just because she'd known him all her life, just because they'd spent the last decade irritating each other—just because she would never have thought to put him on her list if she hadn't made her vow in those precise terms without knowing he'd be present—none of that was reason enough to close her eyes to his marriageable qualities.

Qualities she needed to learn to assess and evaluate.

Indeed, sweeping into the drawing room behind Lady O, it occurred to her that, Cynster that he was, Simon's marriageable qualities might well provide the benchmarks against which she measured all others.

It was a discomposing thought.

Luckily, as the gentlemen weren't present, she

could put it from her mind and allow herself to be distracted by the chatter of the Hammond girls and Lucy Buckstead.

Later, when the gentlemen returned and conversations became more general, she found herself in a group with Winifred Archer and Desmond Winfield. Both were pleasant, a fraction reserved although neither lacked confidence, yet within five minutes, she would have wagered her best gown that there was some understanding between them, or developing between them, certainly. What Winifred's attitude was she couldn't tell, but Desmond, despite his exemplary manners, figuratively had eyes only for Winifred.

Her mental pencil was poised to strike Desmond from her list, but then she paused. Perhaps, given her relative inexperience in this sphere, she should still consider him, not as a potential husband for her, but in defining the gentlemanly attributes ladies like Winifred, who despite her quietness registered as eminently sane, required and approved of.

Learning by observing the successes—and failures—of others was only wise.

The thought had her glancing about. Kitty, in her shimmering aquamarine silk gown, positively sparkled with effervescent charm as she flitted from group to group. No sign of her earlier pout remained; she seemed in her element.

Henry was talking with Simon and James; he no longer seemed concerned or distracted by Kitty.

Perhaps she'd misread their earlier interaction?

Someone loomed at her elbow; Portia turned to find Ambrose Calvin bowing. She bobbed a curtsy.

"Miss Ashford—a pleasure to meet you. I've noticed you at several London events, but never had a chance to make your acquaintance."

"Indeed, sir? Do I take it you spend most of your time in the capital?"

Ambrose had very dark brown eyes and light brown hair; his features were regular, of a patrician cast yet softened by politeness and courtesy enough to be pleasing. He inclined his head. "For the most part." He hesitated, then added, "It's my hope to enter Parliament at the next election. Naturally, I spend as much time as I can following current events—to be close to the source, one must be in the capital."

"Yes, of course." It hovered on the tip of her tongue to explain that she quite understood, being acquainted with Michael Anstruther-Wetherby, the Member for Godleigh, in West Hampshire but the sharpness she glimpsed in Ambrose's dark eyes set a guard on her tongue. "I've often thought that, in these changing times, serving your constituency in Parliament must be highly rewarding."

"Indeed." There was nothing in Ambrose's tone to suggest he was fired by any reformist zeal. "It's my thesis that we need the right men in place— those actively interested in governing, in guiding the country down the correct paths."

That sounded a trifle too pompous for her liking;

she changed tack. "Have you decided where you will stand?"

"Not as yet." Ambrose's gaze shifted to the group across the room—Lord Glossup, Mr. Buckstead, and Mr. Archer. An instant passed, then he refocused on her, and smiled, somewhat patronizingly. "You are likely not aware, but such matters are usually—and best—arranged within the party. I'm hoping for news of my selection quite soon."

"I see." She smiled sweetly in return, the sort of smile Simon would have known not to take at face value. "Then we must hope the news is all you deserve."

Ambrose accepted the comment in the way he wished to hear it; she felt decidedly patronizing herself as they turned to the others about them and joined the wider conversation.

Five minutes later, Lady Glossup raised her voice, asking for volunteers to provide the company with some music.

Before anyone could react, Kitty stepped forward, her face alight. "Dancing! That's just what we need."

Lady Glossup blinked; beside her, Mrs. Archer looked blank.

"Now"—in the center of the room, Kitty twirled, hands lightly clapping—"who will play for us?"

Portia had answered that call so many times over the years, it was all but second nature. "I would be pleased to play for you, if you wish."

Kitty looked at her with surprise tinged with suspicion, almost instantly overlaid by acceptance. "Capital!" Turning, she waved at the gentlemen. "James, Simon—if you would position the pianoforte? Charlie, Desmond—those chairs can go back against the wall."

As she took her seat before the keys, Portia glanced again at Kitty; it seemed nothing bar the simple delight of dancing was behind her actions. Infused by such innocent eagerness, she appeared truly attractive; gone was the siren who'd waylaid James on the stairs, the sultry, disaffected lady who'd first entered the drawing room.

Portia ran her fingers experimentally over the keys; the instrument was in tune, thank heavens! As she looked up, a stack of music books thumped down on the piano's polished top.

Glancing up, she met Simon's steady blue gaze, then he raised one brow. "Hiding behind your accomplishments as usual, I see."

She blinked at him in surprise; with an enigmatic look, he turned and joined the throng sorting themselves into pairs.

Shaking aside the odd comment, she set her hands to the keys and let her fingers glide into the introduction to a waltz.

She knew many; music had always come naturally to her, simply flowed from her fingers, which was why she so often offered to play. She didn't need to think to do it; she enjoyed it, was comfortable sitting at the piano, and could, as she wished, either lose herself in the music or study the company.

It was the latter she elected to do that evening.

What she saw fascinated.

As was customary, the pianoforte stood at the other end of the large room from the fireplace and the chairs and sofas on which the older members of the company sat. The dancers filled the space between; as few imagined the music maker was not watching her fingers, those couples seeking to use the dance for private communication chose to do so while traversing the side of the room farthest from the sharp eyes of their elders. Thus, directly in front of her.

She was quite content to move smoothly from one waltz to the next, mixing in a country dance here and there, giving the dancers only enough time to catch their breath and change partners.

The first thing she noticed was that despite her genuine pleasure in dancing, Kitty was nevertheless pursuing an ulterior aim. Precisely what it was was difficult to discern; Kitty seemed to have more than one gentleman in her sights. She flirted— definitely flirted—with James, her brother-in-law, much to James's irritation. With Ambrose, she was somewhat less overt, but there was still an inviting glint in her eye and a provocative smile on her lips. Although she watched closely, Portia could not fault Ambrose; he gave Kitty no encouragement at all.

With Desmond, Kitty was coy; she still flirted,

but less overtly still, as if modulating her attack for his different character. Desmond seemed to hesitate, to waver; he did not encourage, but neither did he openly dismiss. But when it came to Simon, and Charlie, too, both seemed locked behind positive walls of disapproval. Kitty challenged them, yet her exhibition lacked conviction, as if with them her performance was all for show.

Why she bothered, Portia couldn't imagine; was there something here she was missing?

Yet when Kitty danced with Henry, her husband, she was unresponsive. She made no effort to hold his attention; indeed, she barely said a word. Henry did his best, but could not quite hide his disappointment and a certain sad, resigned disapproval.

Of the others, it became quickly apparent that Lucy Buckstead had set her cap at James. She laughed and smiled with all the gentlemen, but with James, she hung on his every word, her eyes huge, sparkling, her lips parted.

James would have to watch himself, and not just on the Kitty front, a fact Portia suspected he knew; his behavior remained pleasant but cool.

The Misses Hammond weren't interested in any liaisons; they were simply there to enjoy themselves and hoped others would enjoy themselves, too. Their youthful exuberance was something of a relief. Drusilla, in contrast, would have sat out the dances at her mother's side if Lady Calvin had permitted it. Drusilla endured the measures with all the delight of a French aristocrat out for a ride in a tumbril.

As for Desmond and Winifred, there was quite definitely a romance in the air. It was positively instructional to watch the exchanges—Desmond suggesting, never pushing, not diffident yet not overconfident, Winifred quietly responding, lashes falling, eyes downcast, only to raise her gaze again to his face, to his eyes.

Portia looked down to hide a smile as she neared the end of the piece. With the last chord played, she decided the dancers could use a short interval while she searched through the stack of music sheets.

She stood up the better to leaf through them. She was halfway through the pile when she heard the rustle of skirts approaching.

"Miss Ashford, you've played for us so beautifully, but it's unconscionable that in so doing you should be excluded from all the fun."

Portia turned as Winifred swept up on Simon's arm. "Oh, no. That is—" She stopped, unsure how to answer.

Winifred smiled. "I'd be grateful if you would allow me to relieve you. I would like to sit out a few dances, and . . . this seems the best way."

Portia met Winifred's eyes and realized that was literally true. If Winifred simply sat out, some would speculate as to why. Portia smiled. "If you wish."

She stepped out from behind the piano stool. Winifred took her place; together they flicked quickly through the sheets, then Winifred made her selection and sat. Portia turned to the room—

to Simon, who had, with uncharacteristic patience, waited.

He met her eyes, then offered his arm. "Shall we?"

It was absurd, but she'd never danced with him before. Not ever. The notion of spending ten minutes revolving around the room under his direction without their interaction descending into open warfare had not before seemed a possibility.

His gaze was steady, the challenge therein quite plain.

Remembering her vow—hearing it echo in her brain—she lifted her chin, and smiled. Charmingly. Let him make of it what he would. "Thank you."

Suspicion flowed behind his eyes but he inclined his head, anchored her hand on his sleeve, and led her to join the others on the floor as Winifred commenced a waltz.

The first jolt to her equanimity came when he drew her into his arms, when she felt the steely strength of him surround her, and recalled—too well, too vividly—how it had felt when he'd carried her. Once again, her lungs seized, her breath caught, then continued more shallowly; the sensation of his hand, large and strong on her back, distracted her—something she fought to hide.

The music caught them, held them, set them revolving; their gazes touched, slid away.

She could barely breathe. She'd waltzed times without number, even with gentlemen of his ilk; never before had the physical sensations even impinged on her awareness, let alone threatened to suborn her wits. But she'd never been this close to him; the shift and sway of their bodies, her awareness of his strength, her suppleness, the harnessed power, all cascaded through her, bright, sharp, disorienting. She blinked, twice, fighting to focus her mind—on anything except the way they were whirling so effortlessly, on the sensation of being swept away, on the tingles of anticipation streaking through her.

Anticipation of what?

She only just stopped herself from shaking her head in a no-doubt-vain attempt to shake her wits into order. Dragging in a breath, she glanced around.

And saw Kitty waltzing with Ambrose. Her performance, with all its subtle variations, was still going on.

"What **is** Kitty up to—do you know?"

The first thought that had popped into her head, but she'd never been missish, especially not with Simon. He'd been watching her intently; she'd been careful not to meet his gaze. Now she glanced up and, to her relief, saw the frown, the exasperated expression she was used to seeing, form in his eyes.

Reassured, she raised her brows.

His lips thinned. "You don't need to know."

"Possibly not, but I wish to—for reasons of my own."

His frown took on another dimension; he

couldn't fathom what "reasons" she meant. She smiled. "If you don't tell me, I'll ask Charlie. Or James."

It was the "Or James" that did it; he sighed through his teeth, looked up, steered them around the end of the room, then said, his voice low, "Kitty has a habit of flirting with any personable gentleman she meets." After a moment, he added, "How far it goes . . ."

He tensed to shrug, but didn't. His jaw set. When he didn't go on and continued not to meet her eyes, she, intrigued that he hadn't been able to give her the polite lie, evenly supplied, "You know perfectly well how far it goes because she's made improper advances to you, and Charlie, and she's still pressing James."

He looked down at her then, something a great deal more complex than irritation in his face. "How the devil did you discover that?"

She smiled—for once not to irritate but reassure. "You and Charlie exude the most trenchant disapproval whenever you're at all close to her in even a semiprivate setting—like during a waltz. And James because I came upon him in extremis this evening." She grinned. "I rescued him—that's why we came in together."

She sensed a slight easing of his tension and pressed her advantage; she really did wish to know. "You and Charlie have succeeded in convincing her you"—she gestured with her free hand—"aren't interested. Why hasn't James done the same?"

He met her eyes briefly, then replied, "Because James will try very hard not to cause Henry any pain—any more pain than necessary. Kitty knows that—it makes her bolder. Neither Charlie nor I would have any compunction in treating her as she deserves, were she to push us beyond a certain point."

"But she's clever enough not to?"

He nodded.

"What about Henry?"

"When they married, he was extremely fond of her. I don't know how he feels about her now. And before you ask, I have no idea why she is as she is— none of us does."

She saw Kitty across the room, smiling beguilingly up at Ambrose, who was doing his best to pretend he hadn't noticed.

She felt Simon's gaze on her face.

"Any suggestions?"

She looked at him, then shook her head. "But . . . I don't think it's any irrational compulsion—you know what I mean. She knows what she's doing; she's quite deliberate. She has some motive—some goal—in mind."

Simon said nothing. The final chords of the waltz sounded. They stopped and chatted with Annabelle and Desmond, then exchanged partners as the next dance began.

She held to her vow and chatted easily with Desmond; she parted from him thinking Winifred was to be congratulated on her good fortune—

Desmond seemed a thoroughly likable if somewhat serious gentleman. She danced with Charlie, James, and Ambrose, and put her wiles to work with each one; as she wouldn't know how to flirt to save herself, she felt secure in doing so, certain they wouldn't read anything beyond general interest into her artful questions.

Then she danced with Henry, and felt quite dreadful. Even though he made every effort to entertain her, she couldn't help but be conscious of his awareness of Kitty's behavior.

The situation was difficult—Kitty was clever, artful. There was nothing that could be held up as beyond the pale, but her flirting was of the degree, and constancy, that left a very large question in everyone's mind.

Why was she doing it?

Portia couldn't imagine, for Henry was much as Desmond was, a quiet, gentle, decent man. In the ten minutes she spent conversing with him, she fully understood James's wish to protect him, regardless of the circumstances, and Simon's and Charlie's support to that end.

She agreed with them entirely.

By the time they called for an end to the dancing, the question that most insistently nagged was how many others saw Kitty's behavior as she, Simon, Charlie, James, and, most likely, Henry did?

Ambrose and Desmond almost certainly, but what of the ladies? That was much harder to guess.

The tea trolley arrived, and everyone gathered around, happy to rest and take their ease. Conversation was relaxed; people no longer felt the need to fill every silence. Portia sipped, and watched; Kitty's call for dancing had been inspired—it had cut through the rigid formalities and forged them into a group far faster than usually occurred. Now, instead of the shifting currents between various members, there was a cohesiveness, a sense of being here to share the time with these others, that would surely make the following days more enjoyable.

She was setting aside her empty cup when Kitty once again claimed center stage. She rose, her skirts shushing; placing herself at the focal point of the gathering, she smiled charmingly, hands wide. "We should walk in the gardens before retiring. It's positively balmy outside, and so many of the scented plants are flowering. After all that dancing, we need a moment's reflection in peaceful surrounds before repairing to our rooms."

Once again, she was right. The older members of the company who hadn't danced did not feel so inclined, but all those who'd whirled about the room definitely did. They followed Kitty out of the French doors and onto the terrace; from there, they ventured down onto the lawns in twos and threes.

She wasn't surprised when Simon materialized beside her on the terrace; whenever they were in the same party, in situations like this, he'd be somewhere close—on that she could happily wager. Taking the role of reluctant protector had been his habit for years.

But then he broke with custom and offered her his arm.

She hesitated.

Simon watched her blink at his sleeve as if she wasn't quite sure what it was. He was waiting when she glanced up; he caught her eye, raised one brow in a wordless, deliberately arrogant challenge.

Up went her chin; with haughty calm she placed her fingers on his sleeve. Hiding his smile, small victory though it was, he led her down the shallow steps onto the lawn.

Kitty had gone ahead with Ambrose and Desmond, conversing animatedly with Lucy Buckstead so that the damsel was forced to accompany the trio rather than hang back and walk with James as had most likely been her aim. Charlie and James escorted the Hammond girls and Winifred; Drusilla had declined to join them, citing an aversion to the evening air, and Henry had been engrossed in a conversation with Mr. Buckstead.

Reaching the lawns, they stepped out. "Do you have any preference—any sight you wish to see?" He gestured about them.

"By the fitful moonlight?" Portia tracked Kitty's small band as they headed away from the house, toward the dark band of huge rhododenrons that bordered the lawn. "What's that way?"

He'd been watching her face. "The temple."

Her brows rose, faintly supercilious. "Which way is the lake?"

He waved to where the lawn sloped down and away, forming a broad green path wending through the garden beds. "It's not close, but not too far for a stroll."

They strolled that way. The others ambled after them; the Hammond sisters' exclamations over the extensive gardens, the huge shrubs and trees, the numerous walks, borders, and well-stocked beds, rippled an appreciative chorus in the soft evening air. The gardens were indeed lush and dense; the combined scents of untold flowers wreathed through the warm dark.

They walked on, neither fast nor slow, with no vital aim; the moment was goal enough, peaceful, quiet—unexpectedly companionable.

Behind them, the others dawdled, their voices falling to a murmur. He glanced at Portia. "What are you about?"

She tensed fractionally. "About?"

"I heard you in the lookout, remember? Something about learning more, making a decision, and considering all those eligible."

She glanced at him, her face shadowed by the trees beneath which they were passing.

He prompted, "Eligible for what?"

She blinked, her gaze on his face, then she looked forward. "It's . . . just a point of interest. Something I've been wondering about."

"What is 'it'?"

After a moment, she replied, "You don't need to know."

"Meaning you don't wish to tell me."

She inclined her head.

He was tempted to press, but she'd be here, under his eye, for the next several days; he'd have time and more to figure out her latest start simply by watching all she did. He'd seen her taking note of the gentlemen over the dinner table, and when she'd danced with James and Charlie, and Winfield, too, she'd been unusually animated, leading the conversation with questions. He was quite sure those questions hadn't been about Kitty; she might ask him such things, but that was because they were almost family—with each other, they didn't even pretend to the social niceties.

"Very well."

His easy acceptance earned him a suspicious look, but it wasn't in her interests to quibble. He let his lips curve, heard her soft humph as she faced forward once more. They strolled on in easy silence, neither feeling any need to state the obvious—that he would keep watching her until he learned her secret, and that she was now warned that he would.

As they crossed the last stretch of lawn above the lake, he reviewed her behavior thus far. Had she been any other female, he would have suspected she was husband-hunting, yet she'd never been so inclined. She'd never had much use for the male of the species; he couldn't imagine any circumstance that might have changed her mind.

Much more likely was that she was searching for some knowledge—possibly some introduction to or information on some activity not normally open to females. **That** seemed highly probable—exactly her cup of tea.

They reached the lip from which the grassed path ran gently down to the lake. They halted, she to sweep the scene before her, the vista of the wide lake, its waters dark and still, a black pit lying in a natural valley with a wooded hill looming beyond, an informal pinetum on rising ground to the right and, just visible in the weak light, the summer-house on the far left shore, starkly white against a black backdrop of massed rhododendrons.

The sight held her silent, absorbed, head up as she took in the view.

He seized the moment to study her face . . . the conviction that she was seeking a gentleman to introduce her to some illicit experience grew, burgeoned, took hold. In an unexpected way.

"Oh! My goodness!" Annabelle came up, then the others joined them.

"How lovely! Why—it's quite Gothic!" Cecily, hands clasped, bobbed with delight.

"Is it really very deep?" Winifred looked at James.

"We've never found the bottom."

The response drew horrifed looks from the Hammond sisters.

"Shall we go on?" Charlie looked at Portia and Simon. There was a narrow path all the way around the lake, hugging the shore.

"Oh." Annabelle exchanged a glance with Cecily. "I don't think we should. Mama said we must rest well tonight to recover from the rigors of the journey."

Winifred, too, demurred. James gallantly offered to escort the three ladies back to the house. With good nights, they parted. Flanked by Charlie and Simon, Portia headed down to the lake.

They walked and chatted; it was really very easy. They all moved in the same circles; it was a simple matter to fill the time with comments and observations on all that had transpired in the Season just past—the scandals, the marriages, the most scintillating **on-dits**. Even more surprising, Simon did not, as he usually did, comport himself in unhelpful silence; instead, he helped keep the conversation rolling along the generally accepted paths. As for Charlie, he'd always been a rattlepate; it was easy to tempt him into regaling them with colorful tales of wagers gone wrong, of the exploits of the younger bucks.

They paused before the summerhouse, admiring the neat wooden structure, a bit bigger than usual because of its distance from the house, then continued on around the lake.

When they started back up the slope to the house, she felt rather smug. She'd survived a whole evening, and a long night walk with two of the ton's foremost wolves, quite creditably; conversing with gentlemen—drawing them out—hadn't been as difficult as she'd supposed.

They were halfway up the rise when Henry appeared and started down toward them.

"Have you seen Kitty?" he asked as he neared.

They shook their heads. Halting, they all looked down at the lake. The path in its entirety was visible from where they stood; Kitty's aquamarine silk gown would have been easy to spot.

"We saw her when we started out," Portia said. "She and some others were heading for the temple."

Simon added, "We haven't seen her, or those others, since."

"I've already been to the temple," Henry said.

A footstep sounded nearby. They all turned, but it was James who came out of the shadows.

"Have you seen Kitty?" Henry asked. "Her mother wants her."

James shook his head. "I've just been up to the house and back. I didn't see anyone en route."

Henry sighed. "I'd better keep looking." With a bow to Portia and a nod to the men, he headed off toward the pinetum.

They all watched him go until the shadows swallowed him up.

"It might have been better," James remarked, "if Mrs. Archer had thought to speak with Kitty earlier. As it is . . . Henry might be better off not finding her."

They all comprehended exactly what he meant. The silence lengthened.

James recollected himself; he glanced at Portia.

"Your pardon, my dear. I fear I'm not in the best of moods tonight—no good company. If you'll excuse me, I'll go back to the house."

He bowed rather stiffly. Portia inclined her head. With brief nods to Simon and Charlie, James turned on his heel and strode back up the lawn.

The three of them followed more slowly. In silence; there seemed little to say and indeed, some odd sort of safety in not putting what they were thinking into words.

They were at an intersection with a path leading toward the temple on one hand, and on the other curving around to the pinetum, when they heard a light footstep.

As one, they halted and looked down the shadowy path toward the temple.

A figure emerged from a minor path leading down and away from the house. A man, he started along the cross path toward them; stepping into a patch of moonlight, he looked up—and saw them. With no check in his stride, he stepped sideways, onto another of the myriad paths that riddled the dense shrubberries.

His shadow vanished. Leaves rustled, and he was gone.

An instant passed, then they each drew breath, faced forward, and walked on. They didn't speak, nor did they catch each other's eye.

Nevertheless, each knew what the others were thinking.

The man hadn't been a guest, nor yet a servant or helper on the estate.

He'd been a gypsy, lean, dark, and handsome.

With his unruly black hair wildly disarranged, his coat undone, his shirttails loose and flapping.

It was difficult to imagine any innocent reason for such a man to have been up at the house, let alone leaving in such a fashion at such a late hour.

On the main lawn, they met Desmond, Ambrose, and Lucy, like them, heading back to the house.

Of Kitty, they saw no sign.

CHAPTER 3

Well, then, miss!" Lady Osbaldestone sank into the armchair before the hearth in her bedchamber and fixed Portia with a knowing eye. "You may now confess to me what you're about."

"About?" Portia stared. She'd come to assist Lady O down to breakfast; standing in the middle of the room with the light from the window full on her, she found herself transfixed by her ladyship's sharp gaze. She opened her lips to say she wasn't about anything, then closed them.

Lady O snorted. "Indeed. We'll save a lot of time if you just give it to me without any roundaboutation. You usually have your nose so high you don't even notice the gentlemen about, yet yesterday you were not only studying them, you actually deigned to converse with them." Folding her hands on the head of her cane, she leaned forward. "Why?"

Shrewd speculation gleamed in Lady O's ink black eyes. She was old and very wise, steeped in the ton, the relationships and families; the number of marriages she'd seen and assisted in had to be legion. She was the perfect mentor for Portia's new tack. If she chose to help.

If Portia had the courage to ask.

Clasping her hands, she drew breath and chose her words carefully. "I've decided it's time I looked for a husband."

Lady O blinked. "And you're considering those here?"

"No! Well . . . yes." She grimaced. "I haven't any experience in this sort of thing—as you know."

Lady O humphed. "I know you've wasted the last seven years, at least on that front."

"I **thought**," she continued as if she hadn't heard, "that while I'm here, as I've decided I do want a husband, then it would be sensible to use the opportunity to learn how to go about selecting one. How to gather the information and understanding I will need to make an informed choice— indeed, to gauge what sort of attributes I should look for. What in a gentleman is most important to me." She frowned, refocusing on Lady O's face. "I assume different types of ladies would have different requirements?"

Lady O waggled a hand. "**Comme çi, comme ça.** I would say rather that some attributes are central, while others are more superficial. The central ones—the core of what most women seek—is not that different, woman to woman."

"Oh. Well"—Portia lifted her head—"that's what I hoped to clarify while here."

Lady O's gaze remained on her face for some moments, then she relaxed back in her chair.

"I saw you assessing the gentlemen last evening—which have you decided to consider?"

The moment of decision. She would need help, at the very least some other lady with whom to discuss things, a lady she could trust. "I'd thought Simon, James, and Charlie. They seem obvious candidates. And although I suspect Desmond's interest is fixed on Winifred, I thought I'd consider him, too, purely as an exercise in defining suitability."

"Noticed that, did you? How do you read Winifred's reaction?"

"Undecided. I thought I could learn something by watching her make up her mind."

"Except that she's thirty and still unwed." Lady O's brows rose. "I wonder why?"

"Maybe she simply hadn't thought of it before . . ." Portia caught Lady O's eyes and grimaced. "She seems perfectly sensible, from all I've seen."

"Indeed, which begs the question. But what of Ambrose? He's the one eligible you haven't mentioned."

Portia shrugged. "He may be worth considering, but . . ." She wrinkled her nose, searching for words to describe her impression. "He's ambitious, and set on a career in Parliament."

"That should hardly count against him—just think of Michael Anstruther-Wetherby."

"It's not that, exactly." She frowned. "It's the form of ambition, I think. With Michael, he's ambitious to serve, to govern well. To manage because he's good at it, like his sister."

Lady O nodded. "Very perceptive. I take it Ambrose is not driven by such a noble motive? I haven't had a chance to speak much with him yet."

"I think he wants the position purely for itself. Either for the power, or for whatever else it will give him. I didn't sense any deeper reason." She looked at Lady O. "But I might be maligning him—I haven't probed at all."

"Well, you'll have plenty of time while we're here—and yes, I agree, this is a most suitable venue to hone your skills."

Lady O started to rise; Portia went to help her.

"Mind you"—Lady O straightened—"I daresay you'll have your hands full **considering** Simon, James, and Charlie. You likely won't have time to widen your field."

The ghost of a superior smile hung about Lady O's lips as she turned to the door; Portia wasn't sure how to interpret it.

"You may report to me every evening, or every morning if you prefer. While here, you're in my care, no matter how much your brother and you may think the reverse." Lady O slanted a glance at her as they crossed to the door. "It'll be interesting to learn, in this day and age, what you decide are the manly attributes you most desire."

Portia inclined her head dutifully; neither of them was deceived. She would tell Lady O what transpired because she needed help and guidance, not because she recognized any responsibility on her ladyship's part.

Reaching the door, she put her hand to the handle; Lady O pressed the tip of her cane to the door, stopping her from opening it. Portia glanced at her. And met her penetrating gaze.

"One point you didn't explain—why, after seven long years in the ton, have you suddenly decided you should marry?"

There seemed no need for reservation; it was a normal enough reason, surely. "Children. Through helping at the Foundling House, I realized I liked—truly liked—working with young children. Caring for them, watching them grow, guiding them." She felt the need rise up inside her simply at the thought. "But I want my own children to care for.

"Returning to the Chase only reinforced that— seeing Amelia and Luc with their brood, and of course Amanda and Martin visit frequently with theirs. It's a madhouse but . . ."—her lips lifting wistfully, she held Lady O's gaze—"it's something I want."

Perfectly serious, Lady O searched her eyes, then nodded. "Children. That's all very well as an inciting impulse—the spur that has finally compelled you to lower your nose, see what's around you, and consider marriage. Understandable, right, and proper. **However**"—she fixed Portia with a black stare—"that is **not** a suitable reason for marriage."

She blinked. "It's not?"

Lady O drew back her cane and gestured; Portia opened the door.

"But . . ."

"Don't worry." Head rising, Lady O swept down the corridor. "Just follow your plan and consider the eligibles, and the right reason—mark my words—will emerge."

She lengthened her stride; Portia had to hurry to catch up with her.

"Now come on!" Lady O waved to the stairs. "All this talk of marriage has given me an appetite!"

An appetite for meddling, but then she'd always had that. And she was a past master of the art; it was done so subtly, in between passing the toast and marmalade, Portia was quite sure neither Simon, James, nor Charlie realized that the idea to go riding that morning was not originally theirs.

The invitation ultimately came from them; she dutifully accepted. Lucy did, too. To everyone's surprise, so did Drusilla. Winifred confessed she was an indifferent rider; she elected to go for a walk. Desmond immediately offered to accompany her.

Ambrose was engaged in a discussion with Mr. Buckstead and merely shook his head. The Hammond girls, their bright eyes fixed on Oswald and Swanston, had already inveigled them into escorting them around the lake. Kitty was not present, but then neither were the other ladies; all had chosen to breakfast in their rooms.

Fifteen minutes after quitting the breakfast table, the riding party convened in the front hall, and James led them out to the stable.

Selecting mounts took some time; garbed in her deep blue riding habit, Portia strolled with James down the long aisle between the boxes, casting her eye over the mounts, asking him about the more elegant beasts. Was this one of those things that was important to her, that a gentleman should ride well and know his horses?

Most did, but not necessarily to her standards.

"Do you drive your own phaeton in town?"

James glanced at her. "Yes. I have a pair of matched greys, very nice steppers."

"Mr. James . . ." The head stableman called from the door; their horses were ready. James gestured; Portia turned, and they walked back up the aisle.

James's gaze was on her face, not intent but curious. "The greys are in the other wing of the stable—if you like, I'll show them to you sometime."

"That would be nice, if we have time."

He shrugged. "We can make time."

She smiled as they emerged into the sunshine. Into the courtyard where the others were milling. Charlie and the stableman were assisting Lucy and Drusilla into their saddles at the mounting block. Portia headed to where a stableboy held the chestnut mare she'd selected—with James's and Simon's help. Reaching the horse's side, she turned. Waited.

James had paused to pat his own mount, then he looked at the group about the mounting block.

Portia focused her gaze on him, waiting for him to realize and lift her to her saddle.

"Here—let me."

She turned as Simon appeared at her shoulder.

He frowned; his hands fastened about her waist. "We haven't got all day to stand around staring."

He hefted her up with ridiculous ease; once again she lost her breath. He set her safely in the saddle, then released her, pushed her skirts aside, and held the lower stirrup. Gathering her scattered wits, she settled her boots into position, then rearranged her skirts. "Thank you," she said, but he was already moving away.

She watched as he took the reins of his mount from a groom and swung up to the animal's back with lithe ease. Why was he frowning? It wasn't so much a lowering of his brows as a hardness in his blue eyes. Mentally shaking her head, she retrieved her reins from the stableboy and nudged the mare into a walk.

James saw she was ready, mounted his gelding, and joined her under the stable arch. Simon shepherded Lucy and Drusilla along, his gaze raking their postures, assessing their abilities. Charlie scrambled into his saddle and followed.

With Portia beside him, James led the way out, at a walk, then a trot. Rutlandshire-born and -bred, she'd ridden with the hunt in earlier years; while she was no longer quite so wild, she still loved to ride. The little mare was skittish and playful; she indulged her just so far, drawing her patiently back into line until she settled.

James had wanted to give her a docile grey mare; she'd opened her mouth to protest, and would certainly have done so, but Simon had intervened and suggested the chestnut instead. James had accepted Simon's assessment of her abilities with a raised brow but no comment; she'd bitten her tongue and thanked both of them with a smile.

Now James was watching her, gauging, assessing; Simon, she realized, wasn't. A quick glance around showed him, still with that frown in his eyes, watching Lucy and Drusilla. Charlie, his mount trotting easily beside Drusilla's, was chatting with his usual facility. Drusilla, as always, was quiet, but she seemed to be listening, or making an effort to listen . . . Portia wondered if it was at her mother's insistence that she'd joined them.

Lucy kept darting glances ahead—at her and James. Facing forward, recognizing that in all kindness she should yield her position to Lucy shortly, she smiled at James. "I love to ride—is there much hunting in these parts?"

As they rode down the leafy lanes, he answered her questions readily; she gradually steered them in the direction she wished—to what his life was like, his preferred activities, his dislikes, his aspirations. All subtly, of course.

Despite her best efforts, or perhaps because of them, by the time they reached the outliers of

Cranborne Chase, the ancient royal hunting forest, a puzzled, curious, but somewhat cautious look had taken up residence in James's brown eyes.

She smiled airily. They reined in and waited for the others to come up before venturing into the rides between the towering oaks. Seizing the moment to yield her position to Lucy, she set her mare to trot smartly beside Charlie's grey.

Charlie brightened; he turned to her, leaving Drusilla to Simon. "I say—meant to ask. Did you hear about the scandal with Lord Fortinbras at Ascot?"

He rattled on happily; somewhat to her surprise, despite his readiness to talk, she found it difficult to direct his attention to himself. At first, she thought it was simply his natural, outward-looking character, but when he time and again slid around her carefully posed questions, when she caught a flicker of his lashes, and a sharp, far-from-innocent glance, she realized his patter was a shield of sorts—a defense he deployed, all but instinctively, against women who wanted to get to know him.

James was more sure of himself, therefore less defensive. Charlie . . . in the end, she smiled at him, perfectly genuinely, and dropped her inquiries. They were little more than a game—a practice; it would be unkind to set him on edge, to spoil his enjoyment of the house party, purely to sharpen her skills.

She looked around. "We've been terribly restrained so far—dare we gallop a little, do you think?"

Charlie's eyes widened. "If you like . . . I can't see why not." He looked forward and whooped. James looked back. Charlie signaled they were going to ride on; James slowed, nudging his and Lucy's mounts to the side of the path.

Portia sprang the mare. She passed James and Lucy with the mare stretching into a gallop. The ride was wide, more than enough space for two horses abreast, but she was well in the lead as she reached the first bend. A long stretch of turf lay ahead; she let the mare have her head and raced, the thud of hooves behind drowned beneath the relentless beat of the chestnut's stride. The steady pounding, the reaching rhythm, slid through her, echoed in her heart, in the flash tide of blood through her veins, the giddy rush of exhilaration.

The end of the turf drew near; she glanced back. Charlie was some yards back, unable to overtake her. Behind him, the other four were coming along, galloping, but not racing.

With a grin, she faced forward, and swept down the track as it constricted; twenty yards on, it opened onto another glade. Joy in her heart, she flung the mare into it, but halfway along started to rein in.

The thud of hooves behind was growing fainter. No matter how much she enjoyed the speed, she wasn't fool enough to race ahead along rides she didn't know. Still, she'd had her moment; it was enough to tide her over. As the trees drew closer and the track once more narrowed, she eased the mare to a jog, then a walk.

Finally, at the very end of the glade, she halted. And waited.

Charlie was the first to join her. "You ride like a demon!"

She met his gaze, ready to defend herself—only to realize he wasn't scandalized. The look in his eyes was quite different, as if her being able to ride so well had started some line of thought he hadn't previously considered.

Before she had a chance to ponder that, James and Lucy rode up. Lucy was laughing, chattering, eyes radiant; James exchanged a glance with Charlie. With his usual smooth smile and easy address, he displaced his friend at Lucy's side.

Simon and Drusilla joined them. They all stood milling for some moments, regaining their breath, letting the horses settle, then James spoke to Drusilla and they moved off, leading the way back to the Hall.

Lucy followed immediately, but was forced by Charlie's gentle persistence to give him her attention. By the simple strategy of holding his horse back, he kept Lucy safely away from James.

Portia hid a grin, and fell in in their wake; she barely registered Simon's presence beside her. Not outwardly. Her senses, however, were perfectly aware of his looming nearness, of the controlled strength with which he sat his mount as it ambled beside hers. She expected to feel something of her usual haughty resistance, precursor to irritation, yet . . . the faint prickling of her skin, the tightening of her lungs—these were not familiar.

"Still a hoyden at heart, I see."

There was a hardness in his voice she hadn't heard before.

She turned her head, met his gaze, held it for a pregnant moment, then smiled and looked away. "You don't disapprove."

Simon grunted. What could he say? She was right. He **should** disapprove, yet there was something in him that responded—too readily—to the challenge of a woman who could ride like the wind. And with her, knowing she was nearly as assured in the saddle as he, there was no niggling concern to dim the moment.

He was irritated because he hadn't been able to ride with her, not because she'd ridden as she had.

Their mounts ambled on; he glanced at her face—she was smiling lightly, clearly thinking, about what he had no idea. He waited for her to question him, talk to him, as she had with James and Charlie.

The horses plodded on.

She remained silent, distant. Elsewhere.

Finally, he accepted she had no intention of pursuing whatever she was after with him. The suspicion he'd been harboring darkened and grew. Her reticence with him seemed to confirm it; if she was set on gaining some illicit experience, the last man she'd apply to was him.

The realization—the flood of emotions it unleashed—made him catch his breath. A sharp stab of regret, the sense of something lost—something he hadn't even realized he might hold dear. . . .

Mentally shaking his head, he dragged in a breath, glanced again at her face.

He wanted to ask, to demand, but didn't know the question.

And didn't know if she would answer, anyway.

After exchanging her riding habit for a gown of green-and-white twill and re-dressing her hair, Portia descended the stairs as the clang of the luncheon gong reverberated through the house.

Blenkinsop was crossing the front hall. He bowed. "Luncheon is served on the terrace, miss."

"Thank you." Portia headed for the drawing room. The ride had gone well; she'd acquitted herself quite creditably in the "chatting with gentlemen" stakes. She was learning, gaining confidence, exactly as she'd hoped.

Of course, the morning had been free of the distraction of Kitty and her antics. The first thing she heard on emerging through the French doors onto the terrace flags was Kitty's seductive purr.

"I've always had a **great** regard for you."

It wasn't James but Desmond Kitty had backed against the balustrade. The woman was incorrigible! The pair were to her left; turning right, Portia pretended she hadn't noticed. She continued to where a long table was set with serving platters, glasses, and plates. The rest of the company were gathered around, some already seated at wrought-iron tables on the terrace, others descending to the lawns where more tables were set in the shade of some trees.

Portia smiled at Lady Hammond, seated beside Lady Osbaldestone.

Lady O gestured to the cold salmon on her plate. "Wonderful! Be sure to try some."

"I will." Portia turned to the buffet and picked up a plate. The salmon was displayed on a large platter set at the back; she would have to stretch.

"Would you like some?"

She glanced up, smiling at Simon, suddenly beside her. She'd known it was him in the instant before he spoke; she wasn't entirely sure how. "Thank you."

He could reach the platter easily; she held out her plate and he laid a thick slice of the succulent fish upon it, then helped himself to two. He followed her along the table as she made her selections, doing the same.

When she paused at the end of the buffet and looked around, wondering where to sit, he stopped again at her shoulder and waved toward the lawn. "We could join Winifred."

Winifred was sitting alone at a table for four. Portia nodded. "Yes, let's."

They crossed the lawn; she was conscious of Simon beside her, as if he were shepherding her, although from what he might think to protect her she couldn't fathom. Winifred looked up as they neared; she smiled in welcome. Simon held out the chair opposite and Portia sat, then he took one of the seats between them.

Within minutes, Desmond joined them, taking the last chair. Winifred, who had smiled up at him, looked at his plate, and frowned. "Aren't you hungry?"

Desmond glanced at the plate on which resided one slice of salmon and two lettuce leaves. He hesitated for only an instant, then replied, "First course. I'll go back once I've finished this."

Portia bit her lip and looked down. From the corner of her eye, she could see Kitty standing on the terrace at the end of the buffet, staring their way. Portia shot a glance at Simon; he met it—even though his expression remained utterly bland, she knew he'd noticed, too.

Clearly James was not the only gentleman running from Kitty's embrace.

Mrs. Archer waved and called Kitty to her—to the table where she and Henry and Kitty's father were seated. Kitty's reluctance was transparent, but there was little she could do to avoid joining them. To everyone's relief, she did so with some semblance of grace.

Everyone relaxed and started to talk. The only one who showed no sign of relief was Winifred— indeed, she'd given no sign of being aware of her sister's behavior at all.

Yet as they chatted and ate, Portia, surreptitiously studying Winifred, found it hard to believe she was ignorant of Kitty's designs. Winifred spoke softly; she was naturally quiet but not at all shy or hesitant—she declared her views calmly, always courteous but never submissive. Portia's respect for Kitty's older sister grew.

Sherbet and ices ended the meal, then they all rose and mingled on the lawn, in the shade of the large trees.

"It's the ball tonight—I'm so looking forward to it!" Cecily Hammond all but bounced with excitement.

"Indeed, I think every house party should have one. It's the perfect opportunity, after all." Annabelle Hammond turned to Kitty as she joined them. "Lady Glossup told me the ball was your idea, Mrs. Glossup, and that you've done most of the organizing. I think we must all thank you for your foresight and industry on our behalfs."

The perhaps naive but glowingly sincere praise had Kitty smiling. "I'm so glad you think it will be diverting—I truly believe it'll be a delightful night. I do so love dancing, and felt sure most of you would feel the same."

Kitty glanced around; a general murmur of agreement ensued. For the first time, Portia glimpsed a real eagerness, something almost naive in Kitty—a real wish for the glitter and glamor of the ball, a belief that in it she would find . . . something.

"Who will be attending?" Lucy Buckstead asked.

"All the surrounding families. It's been over a year since there was a major ball here, so we're assured of a good turnout." Kitty paused, then added, "And there's the officers stationed at Blandford Forum—I'm sure they'll come."

"Officers!" Cecily's eyes were round. "Will there be many?"

Kitty named some of those she expected. While the news that military uniforms would grace the dance floor that evening was met with interest by the ladies, Portia noted the gentlemen were not so enthused.

"Dashed bounders and half-pay officers, I'll be bound," Charlie muttered in an aside to Simon.

It was on the tip of Portia's tongue to retort that such guests would doubtless keep them on their toes, but she swallowed the words. No sense doing anything more to trigger Simon's usual protectiveness; it would doubtless surface tonight without any further prodding. She would have to beware, perhaps try to avoid him. The last thing she'd need tonight was a chaperon.

A major country ball promised to be an excellent venue at which to further polish her, not to put too fine a point on it, husband-hunting skills. Many of the gentlemen she would meet she would assuredly never meet again; they were perfect examples on which to practice.

All young unmarried ladies fell over themselves

to attend balls; she supposed she'd have to develop the habit. For now, as they stood in loose groupings and conversed beneath the trees, she listened and took note of the reactions of the other ladies—of Winifred's quiet enthusiasm, Drusilla's reserved acceptance, the Hammond girls' thrilled excitement, Lucy's romantic expectations.

And Kitty's genuinely keen anticipation of delight. For a lady who'd been married for some years, who had presumably attended her fair quota of balls, the fervor with which she looked forward to the evening was unexpected. It made her appear younger, even naive.

Odd, given her other recent actions.

Mentally shaking aside the confusion that was Kitty, determined to make the most of the ball, Portia carefully noted all that the other ladies let fall of their preparations and gowns.

She shifted from group to group, intent, absorbed; it was some time before she registered that Simon was either hovering close by or else watching her.

He was presently standing with Charlie and James, a little beyond the group she was engaged with. Lifting her head, she looked directly at him, expecting to see an expression of bored irritation, his customary expression when he was watching over her because of his compulsive protectiveness.

Instead, when her eyes met his, she could detect no hint of irritation. Something, yes, but something much harder, more steely; his whole expression reflected it, the austere angles of cheek and brow, the squared and determined jaw.

Their gazes locked for only mere moments, yet it was enough for her to see and know. To react.

Hauling in a breath, she turned back to Winifred, nodding as if she'd heard what had been said; her only clear thought was that whatever impulse was driving Simon to watch her, it wasn't protection he had in mind.

The younger ladies were not the only ones enthused by the prospect of the ball. Lady Hammond, Lady Osbaldestone, even Lady Calvin were very ready to allow themselves to be thus entertained.

It was summer; there were precious few other events at which they might exercise their talents.

Portia did not immediately preceive the source of their interest; when, however, in midafternoon, Lady O demanded her assistance in going upstairs and settling for her nap—only to insist they go via Portia's room—understanding dawned.

"Don't stand around gawping, gel!" With her cane, Lady O thumped the gallery floor. "Show me the gown you intend wearing tonight."

Resigned, wondering if any good might come of it, Portia ushered her to the chamber she'd been given in the east wing. It was a largish room with a good-sized armoire in which the maid had hung all her gowns. After installing Lady O in the armchair before the hearth, she went to the armoire and set the doors wide.

And hesitated. She hadn't really thought about what she would wear; she'd never truly bothered about such things. Courtesy of Luc and the family's excellent finances, she had pretty gowns aplenty, yet until now, she'd taken them, and her appearance in general, for granted.

Lady O snorted. "As I thought—you haven't the vaguest notion. Well, then, let's see what you've brought with you."

Dutifully, she paraded the evening gowns she'd packed. Now she thought of it, she favored one in deep green silk, and said so.

Lady O shook her head. "Not at this point. Leave the dramatics for later, once you're sure of him. That's when they'll have the most useful effect. For tonight, you need to appear . . ." She waggled her hand. "Less certain, less sure. Think strategy, gel!"

Portia had never considered the color of gowns in such a light; she resurveyed the gowns she'd left draped on the bed, thinking anew . . .

"How about this one?" She extracted a gown of soft pearl grey silk—an unusual color, especially for an unmarried lady, but with her dark hair and eyes, and her height, she could carry it well.

"Hmm." Lady O gestured. "Hold it up."

Portia did so, smoothing the bodice over her bosom, draping it so Lady O could see the clever cut. The underbodice was fitted silk, with very fine silk chiffon of the exact same shade draped loosely over it, disguising the décolleté neckline, making it seem much less daring.

A slow smile spread over Lady O's face. "Perfect. Not innocent so much as not quite attainable. Have you shoes to go with it?"

She had, along with a fine, dark grey beaded shawl and matching reticule; Lady O nodded her approval. "And I thought I'd wear my pearls."

"Let me see them."

She fetched the long strand of creamy pearls from her jewel casket and draped them about her neck. The strand was long enough to reach nearly to her waist. "I've drop earrings to match."

Lady O gestured to the necklace. "Not like that—try it wound once round your throat, then let the rest dangle."

She raised her brows, but obliged.

"Now hold up the gown again . . ."

She did as she was told, smoothing the bodice into place. Turning to the cheval glass in the corner, she surveyed the unexpected effect. "Oh. I see."

"Indeed." Lady O nodded with satisfaction. "Strategy! Now!" She heaved herself out of the armchair; Portia left the gown on the bed and hurried to help. Once upright, Lady O headed for the door. "You may now help me to my room and onto my bed. You will then return here, lie down on your bed, and rest."

"I'm not tired." She'd never rested before a ball in her life.

The shrewd look Lady O shot her as she stepped

into the corridor said she suspected as much. "Be that as it may, you will please me by returning here and lying down upon your bed until it's time to dress for dinner and the ball." When she opened her mouth to argue, Lady O silenced her with an upraised hand. "Aside from the fact that no lady wishful of appearing her best should attend a ball other than well rested, what else, pray tell, had you planned to do?"

There was enough sharpness in the question to give her pause. She considered as they walked down the corridor, then confessed, "A walk in the garden, then maybe a survey of the library."

"And do you imagine, given the composition of this party, that you will be able to accomplish that while remaining alone?"

She grimaced. "Probably not. Someone's bound to see me and come to join me—"

"Not **someone**—some gentleman. All the other ladies will have the wit to rest, of that you may be sure." Lady O stopped outside her door and set it swinging wide; Portia followed her in, closing the door behind them.

"One or other gentleman—even more likely more than one—will join you." Lady O set her cane aside, hitched herself up on her bed, and fixed Portia with a sapient eye. "Now think! Is this wise?"

It was like being tutored in an art she had no previous training in; she guessed. "No?"

"Of course it's not!" Lady O fell back on her pillows, and settled herself comfortably. She squinted at Portia. "You've spent all morning and half the afternoon with them. Giving them a steady diet of your company is unlikely to lead to any hunger. Now—the next hours until the ball—is the time to deprive them of sustenance. Then, later, over dinner and at the ball, they'll come more readily to your hand."

Portia couldn't help but laugh; leaning forward, she kissed Lady O's cheek. "You're a **terrible** schemer."

"Nonsense!" Lady O closed her eyes and composed her features. "I'm an experienced general, and I've fought—and won—more battles than you can count."

Smiling, Portia retreated. She was at the door when, without opening her eyes, Lady O ordered, "Now go and rest."

Portia grinned. "Yes, sir!" Opening the door, she slipped out.

And, for once, did as she was bid.

CHAPTER 4

Now remember—think strategy!"

With those rousing words, Lady O swept into the drawing room, leaving Portia to follow rather less forcefully in her wake. Head high, she glided in—and was immediately aware of heads turning.

Even more interesting, while the female heads, after the briefest of comprehensive glances, turned back to their conversations, the male heads remained turned her way for significantly longer, some until they were recalled to their surroundings by some comment.

She knew well enough to pretend not to have noticed. With unimpaired serenity, she curtsied to Lady Glossup, who inclined her head with a regal smile, then continued on to join Winifred, who was talking to Desmond and James.

The admiration in both Desmond's and James's eyes as they greeted her was marked. She blithely accepted it as her due and slid into the usual social patter.

Inwardly, she frowned. Had she changed? Was she somehow different just because she'd decided to seek a husband—did it show in some way? Or, given that previously she'd never bothered to notice how people, gentlemen especially, reacted to her, had she always excited such responses and never noticed?

As she circulated, exchanging greetings here and there, she became increasingly sure the latter was the case. A lowering thought in some respects; Lady O had been right—she must have had her nose very much in the clouds. Yet the realization boosted her confidence; for the first time she realized she had something—some weapon, some power—she could use to attract and attach a husband.

Now all she had to do was learn how to chose the right gentleman and learn to wield that weapon.

Simon stood chatting with the Hammond sisters and Charlie; she passed by with a cool nod. He'd been watching her consistently since she'd entered the room. His expression was hard, rocklike; she couldn't tell what he was thinking.

The last thing she wanted was to encourage his protectiveness; she glided on to join Ambrose and Lady Calvin.

Simon watched Portia smile and charm Ambrose. The muscles of his face set even harder, the better to suppress his scowl. Why he felt as he did—what the emotions roiling within him were—he was in no mood to consider. Never in his life had he felt this way—more than driven. Goaded.

The fact he didn't know why, didn't understand,

only increased the pressure. Something had changed, but he couldn't free his mind of its overriding obsession long enough to identify what.

This afternoon, he'd lain in wait for Portia to come down after seeing Lady O to her room. He'd wanted to talk to her, to inveigle her into revealing just what she was seeking to learn.

She hadn't appeared—or rather, he hadn't found her, which raised the question of where she'd gone, and with whom.

He could see her from the corner of his eye, a slender figure in soft pearl grey, her dark hair piled high, higher than he'd seen it before. The style left her nape exposed, drew his attention to the graceful curve of her neck, the fine bones of her shoulders. The pearl necklace she wore . . . one strand circled her throat, the other loop hung low, dangling beneath the gauzy edge of her bodice, disappearing into the shadowy valley between her breasts. Taking his imagination with it. His senses remained riveted even when he looked away; his palms tingled.

She still moved without consciousness or guile; the way she conversed hadn't altered. Yet something within him recognized beyond doubt that her intent had changed.

Why that should affect him he didn't know—he only knew it did.

A stir near the door had him glancing that way. Kitty had joined them. She was resplendent in white satin liberally bedecked with silver lace. Her pale hair was intricately dressed; diamonds winked on her breast and in her lobes. Seen by herself, she was an enchanting sight, not least because she was flown with delight—it showed in her face, in her eyes, made her skin glow.

She very correctly spoke to the older members of the company, then took Henry's arm and started to stroll, stopping by each group to pay and receive compliments.

Simon looked back at Portia. When Kitty paused beside her, the result was as he'd guessed; against Portia's subtler, more intriguing beauty, Kitty appeared tawdry. She did not linger but moved on, then she was beside him.

They only had time to exchange a few words before the butler entered and announced that dinner was served.

He led Lucy in, hoping against hope . . . but no, the seating was organized, and he suspected Kitty had done the organizing. Lord and Lady Glossup took the chairs at the table's ends; Kitty had seated herself in the middle along one side with Henry directly opposite, entirely appropriately. Desmond was on her left, Ambrose on her right. Portia was toward one end, between Charlie and James; he, Simon, was at the far end on the opposite side of the table, flanked by Lucy and the all-but-silent Drusilla.

If matters had been different, he would have had no reason to complain—Lucy was bright and cheery, even if her gaze strayed rather too often

James's way, and Drusilla required no more than the occasional polite word to be content. As it was, throughout the meal, he was forced to endure the sight of Portia being artfully regaled by Charlie and James.

Normally, he wouldn't even have thought to watch her, not in this sphere; prior to today, her attitude to gentlemen had been nothing short of contemptuously dismissive. Neither Charlie nor James would have had the least chance of making any headway with her; the thought of her responding to their practiced wiles wouldn't have entered his head.

All through the courses, he covertly watched her; at one point, he noticed Lady Osbaldestone's eye on him and became even more careful. But his eyes had a will of their own; he couldn't hear anything of their conversation but the way Portia smiled, the quick, alert, interested glances she lavished on both James and Charlie locked his attention on her.

What the devil was she up to?

What did she want to learn?

Even more importantly, did she have any idea what was going through James's and Charlie's heads?

He did. It bothered him more than he wanted to admit, far more than he wanted to think about.

Lady O's head swung his way. Lowering his lashes, he turned to Lucy. "Have you heard of any plans for tomorrow?"

He bided his time; luckily Lucy was as eager as

he to head for the ballroom. The instant Lady
Glossup rose and shooed them in that direction, he
offered Lucy his arm, leaving Drusilla to follow
with Mr. Archer.

Having been nearer the doors, Portia, on Charlie's arm, was some way ahead of them. In the
front hall, they had to skirt the local guests who
had started to arrive; the houseguests went directly
down the hall to the ballroom. It was clear from
the throng already in the foyer that the ball would
be well attended; Simon swept Lucy straight on,
intent on catching up with Portia before the developing crowd engulfed her.

Stepping into the ballroom, they saw James, just
ahead of them, surveying those already present,
scanning the heads.

Simon knew without question that James was
seeking Portia; with Lucy on his arm, he paused.

Kitty swept up to James; she was there before he
realized. Placing one hand on his arm, she stepped
close—too close. James stepped back but she followed; he was forced to allow her to lean familiarly
against him. Her smile was pure seduction; she
spoke softly.

She was a small woman; to hear her, James had to
lower his head, creating a tableau that suggested a
relationship somewhat closer than family ties.

Beside him, Simon felt Lucy stiffen.

James straightened, lifted his head; an expression
close to panic flitted over his features. He saw
Simon; his eyes widened.

No friend could ignore such a plea.

Simon patted Lucy's hand. "Come—let's speak with James."

From the corner of his eye, he saw Lucy's chin rise. Determinedly, she stepped out beside him.

Kitty saw them coming; she fell back a step, so her body was not quite touching James's.

"My dear Kitty!" Lucy spoke before they'd halted; they were now all on first-name terms. "You must be quite thrilled with the turnout. Did you expect so many?"

Kitty took a moment to change mental tracks, then she smiled. "Indeed, it's very gratifying."

"I'm surprised you aren't standing with your mama-in-law to greet them."

Simon bit his lip, inwardly applauding Lucy's gumption; her eyes remained wide, her expression innocent, yet she'd swiftly put Kitty in an uncomfortable spot.

Kitty's smile turned brittle. "Lady Glossup doesn't require me to assist her. Besides"—she turned her gaze on James—"this is the best moment in which to make one's arrangements to be sure one enjoys the evening to the fullest."

"I believe just that was in a certain gentleman's mind." Simon lied without compunction. "He was asking after you as we passed—dark-haired, someone up from town."

"Oh?" Kitty was instantly diverted. "Did you recognize him?"

"Not to name." Simon glanced at the area inside

the doors, now filled with guests streaming in. "Can't see him at present—perhaps you'd better circulate that way and see if you can come up with him."

Kitty hesitated for only an instant, then smiled—intently—up at James. "You will save that waltz for me, won't you?"

James's face set like stone. "If we happen to be near at the time, and not otherwise engaged . . ." He shrugged. "There are many guests it's our duty to entertain."

Kitty's eyes flashed; her lips pressed tight on an unwise rejoinder. With Lucy and Simon looking on, she was forced to incline her head. She looked at Simon. "Dark-haired, you said?"

He nodded. "Average height, good build. Good hands. Excellent tailor."

That summed up the attributes one gentleman was likely to notice about another; Kitty swallowed the bait whole—with a brief nod, she left them.

James met Simon's eyes; his relief was transparent.

Between them, Lucy brightly remarked, "I hadn't realized you had so many neighbors in the district." She glanced at James. "Perhaps we could stroll, and you would be good enough to introduce me?"

James hesitated for only an instant, then smiled and offered his arm. "If you wish, I would be honored."

Simon was not surprised at the glance James,

straightening, shot him over Lucy's head. Another plea—this one not to leave him alone with Lucy. Swallowing his own urgency—Portia was unlikely to do anything rash, after all—he consented to stroll and chat, making them a threesome; he could sympathize with James's desire not to encourage Lucy to imagine there was anything personal developing between them.

"Thank you." James clapped him on the shoulder as the first dance commenced, and they stood watching Lucy whirl down the set with the young squire who had earnestly solicited her hand. "Now you can see why I was so keen to have you here."

Simon humphed. "I wouldn't worry overmuch about Lucy—she might be enthusiastic, but she knows where the lines are drawn. Kitty, however . . ." He glanced at James. "Do you intend remaining here after the houseguests have left?"

"Good God, no!" James shuddered. "I'm leaving in the same hour you are—I think I'll go visit old Cromer. Northumberland ought to be far enough to outdistance even Kitty."

Simon grinned and they parted. While socializing with James and Lucy, he'd surreptitiously quartered the room and located Portia. She was presently standing along the opposite wall, near the French doors open to the terrace and the balmy evening outside. Charlie flanked her, along with an officer in dress uniform; both were fully engaged, attentive to the exclusion of all else about them, ignoring the glitter and swirl of the ball.

Understandable, for Portia was sparkling. Her dark eyes were alive, her hands gestured gracefully, her face was alight. Even from a distance, he felt the tug. Her attention was wholly given to whichever man was speaking with her; such devotion was guaranteed to fix—transfix—any healthy male.

In any other woman, he'd have labeled such behavior flirting, and been right, but Portia was, he was still prepared to swear, constitutionally incapable of that art. He circled the room, gauging his approach; his gaze on the three, he studied their faces, and doubted even Charlie and her latest conquest, whoever he was, mistook her behavior for the customary invitation.

It was something else. Just what, the mystery of what she was about, only lent her greater charm, made her attraction even more potent.

He was mere yards from her when a hand descended on his arm and gripped with surprising strength.

"There you are!" Lady Osbaldestone grinned evilly up at him. "You haven't any sisters or cousins present, so you can't be employed. Just come with me—there's someone I want you to meet."

"But—" He resisted her tug; she wanted to lead him away from Portia. The damn ball had been going an hour, and this was the closest he'd got.

Lady O glanced at his face, then around him—at Portia. "Portia? Pshaw!" She flicked her fingers. "No need for you to concern yourself there—and anyway, you don't even like her."

He opened his mouth to refute at least the former.

Lady O shook her head. "Not your problem if your friend Charlie supplies her with one too many glasses of champagne."

"What?" He tried to turn and look.

Lady O held on to him with a viselike grip. "So what if she gets a mite tipsy? She's old enough to know what's what, and strong enough to hold her own. Do her good to have her eyes opened a trifle—silly chit's twenty-four, after all." Lady O snorted, and yanked. "Now come along. This way."

She waved ahead with her cane; suppressing his welling panic, he conceded. The fastest way to freedom was to fall in with Lady O's plans. At the first opportunity, he'd escape—and after that, **nothing** would get in his way.

Portia saw Lady O lead Simon off, and inwardly sighed, whether with relief or disappointment she wasn't sure. She didn't want him hovering in his usual, arrogantly disapproving manner, yet that might not have been his intention. If the look in his eyes earlier was any guide, his attitude to her had changed, but to what she didn't know, and hadn't yet had a chance to divine. Regardless, she wanted to try out her new weapon on him. He was one of the three she'd elected to "consider," and while she was doing quite well with Charlie and James, she'd yet to take a tilt at Simon.

Still, Charlie and Lieutenant Campion were interesting enough, and sufficiently susceptible to her wiles to count as practice.

She fixed her gaze on Lieutenant Campion's face. "So you spend most of the year here in Dorset. Are the winters very cold?"

Campion beamed and replied. With little encouragement bar her rapt attention—her gaze fixed on his face, her mind cataloging all points of note he let fall—he was happy to divulge a great deal about himself, enough for her to guess his relative wealth, his family's standing and properties, his enthusiasms both military and personal.

How very amenable gentlemen were, once one learned the knack. Comments made by her elder sisters regarding managing their husbands replayed in her mind.

Not that Lieutenant Campion would do for her; he lacked a certain something. Challenge, perhaps; she was quite sure she could wrap him about her little finger—curiously, that didn't appeal.

Charlie, who had drifted away, returned, bearing yet another glass of champagne. He offered it with a flourish. "Here you are—you must be parched."

She took the glass, thanked him, then sipped. The temperature in the ballroom was rising; the room was now crowded, the heat of bodies combining with the sultry heat of the night.

Charlie's gaze had remained on her face. "That was an excellent set of plays at the Theatre Royale this last season—did you get a chance to see them?"

She smiled. "The first two, yes. The theater's under new management, I heard."

"Indeed." Lieutenant Campion fixed Charlie with a steady gaze. "I understand . . ."

It occurred to Portia that Charlie had hoped to exclude the lieutenant with such a question; he hadn't known Campion spent part of each Season on leave in town. Her lips twitched; the lieutenant continued, expounding at some length.

Charlie bore the reverse with grace, but seized the opportunity to solicit her hand the instant the musicians resumed playing.

She accepted, and they waltzed, with vigor, verve, and quite a bit of laughter. Charlie's earlier reticence had flown; although he was still cautious about letting her know much about himself, he was much more intent on learning all he could of her.

And her intention. Her direction.

Well aware of that last, she laughed, gave him her eyes, her attention, but kept her thoughts to herself. Males of Charlie's and James's ilk seemed much more interested in learning just where she wished to lead them—what she truly wished to know—presumably wondering if they could assist her in the knowing . . . she smiled and wielded her wits to keep all such answers to herself. She saw no reason unnecessarily to lose what she was starting to suspect was a large part of her new-found allure.

The most engaging aspect of mentally fencing with gentlemen such as Charlie was that they understood the rules. And how to get around them.

When the last chord of the waltz faded, and they whirled to a halt, hot, exhilarated, and laughing, he smiled with dazzling charm. "Let's recoup on the terrace—it's far too stuffy in here."

She kept her smile in place, and wondered if she dared.

Nothing attempted, nothing gained; she'd never know if she didn't try.

"Very well." She let her smile deepen, accepting the challenge. "Let's."

She turned toward the terrace—and nearly collided with Simon.

Her nerves leapt; for one instant, she couldn't breathe. His eyes met hers; his expression was hard but she could read none of his usual disapproval therein.

"We were about to adjourn to the terrace." The pitch of her voice sounded a fraction too high; the champagne, no doubt. "It's grown rather warm in here."

She used the excuse to wave a hand before her face. Her temperature had certainly risen.

Simon's expression didn't soften. He looked at Charlie. "I've just come from Lady Osbaldestone—she's asking for you."

Charlie frowned. "Lady Osbaldestone? What the devil does the old tartar want with me?"

"Who knows? She was, however, most insistent. You'll find her near the refreshment room."

Charlie glanced at her.

Simon's hand closed about her elbow.

"I'll escort Portia out for a stroll—with luck, by

the time you're finished with Lady Osbaldestone, we'll be back."

The suggestion sounded straightforward, yet Charlie wasn't all that sure; the look he sent Simon said as much. But he had little choice; with a graceful bow to her and a nod to Simon, he headed for the far corner of the room.

Simon released her; turning, they strolled toward the open French doors.

She glanced at his face. "Did Lady O really want Charlie? Or are you just being your usual pompous self?"

He met her gaze for an instant, then waved her through the door. "It'll be fractionally cooler outside."

She stepped out onto the flags. "You made it up, didn't you?"

He ushered her along; she swung around and stared at him.

He searched her face. His eyes narrowed. "You're tipsy. How many glasses of champagne have you had?"

Again, he moved her on, his long fingers closing about her elbow as he steered her along the shadowy terrace. There were couples and groups strolling on the terrace and the nearby lawns, availing themselves of what relief there was in the fresher night air.

"That's beside the point." She was quite certain about that. "I've never been tipsy before—it's quite pleasant." Realizing how true that was, she plucked her elbow from his grip and twirled. "A new experience, and a perfectly harmless one."

The look on his face was odd—patronizing, but also something else. Something more taken. A frisson of hope ran through her; would her wiles work on him as well?

She fixed her eyes on his face, and smiled winningly. Then she laughed and turned to walk on beside him. They were heading away from the bustle and the ballroom into less frequented areas; they could converse freely.

How silly, now that she thought of it. "No point getting you to talk about yourself—I know all about you already."

The end of the terrace loomed near. She felt his gaze on her face.

"Actually"—his voice dropped to a deep murmur—"you know very little about me."

The words slithered across her nerves, tantalizing, tempting; she merely smiled and let her disbelief show.

"Is that what you're after—learning about gentlemen?"

She couldn't recall hearing that peculiarly beguiling tone from him before; tilting her head, she considered. Her mind wasn't, in truth, operating with its customary facility. "Not about gentlemen in general, and not just about them." They turned the corner of the terrace and continued on; no one else was strolling on this side of the house. She drew in a breath, let it out with, "I want to learn about all the things I haven't learned about before."

There—that should hold him.

"What things?"

She whirled and stopped, her back to the house wall; some instinct warned her they were straying too far from the ballroom. Yet she smiled, openly delighted, at him, letting the happy confidence welling inside her show. "Why, all the things I haven't experienced before." She flung out her arms, her gaze locking with his. "The excitement, the thrills. All the things gentlemen can show me that I haven't bothered with, until now."

He'd halted, facing her, studying her eyes. His face was in shadow.

"Is that why you were so keen on strolling out here with Charlie?"

There was something in his tone that alerted her, that had her wrestling her wits back into place. She held his gaze steadily, and answered with the truth. "I don't know. It wasn't my suggestion—it was his."

"Hardly surprising, given your wish to learn. And you did come out here."

The accusation in his voice focused her wits wonderfully.

She lifted her chin. "With you. Not him."

Silence.

The challenge lay between them, implicit, understood.

Their gazes remained locked; neither shifted, broke the spell. The heat of the night intensified and closed about them. She could have sworn things swayed. She could feel the blood beating under her skin, at her temples.

He was only a foot away; she suddenly wanted him closer, could sense some primal tug.

So could he. He shifted fractionally nearer, then froze; his face remained in shadow, his eyes unreadable.

"If it had been Charlie who brought you here, what would you have sought to learn?"

It took a moment to form an answer; she had to moisten her lips before she could say, "You know him much better than I—what do you think, given this moment, given this setting, I might have learned?"

Time stretched; her heartbeat made it seem forever. His eyes remained locked on hers, then he shifted, closed the distance. Slowly lowered his head.

One hand rose to touch her face, long fingers tracing, then cradling, her jaw, tipping her face up.

So his lips could settle, warm and strong, on hers.

Her lids fell; her lungs seized. Her senses swam as her body came to sensual life.

She had nothing to compare it with, that first precious kiss. No man before had dared to step this close, to take such a liberty. If any had, she'd have boxed his ears.

Simon's lips moved on hers, warm and pliant, seeking; her fingers gripped the stone behind her, tight.

All her senses condensed until the gentle, beguiling pressure was all she knew, all she cared about. Her lips throbbed. Her head spun, and it wasn't from the champagne.

She'd forgotten to breathe, even now didn't care. She kissed him back, hesitant, not knowing . . .

He shifted, not away but closer yet. The fingers about her jaw firmed; the pressure of those beguiling lips increased.

She parted her own as he seemed to want her to; his tongue slid between—her knees quaked. He seemed to know—how she couldn't guess; the caresses slowed, slowed, until each touch seemed drenched with languor, with unhurried appreciation, with simple shared pleasure. The dizzying shock of the novel intimacy faded.

The certain knowledge that she'd never been kissed before rocked Simon; the powerful urge to seize that raced through him in response shocked him to his core. He shackled it, refused to let it show—not in his lips, not through his fingers, not through the slow, mesmerizing play of his tongue.

She tasted of nectar, of warm peaches and honey. Of summer and goodness, fresh and untouched. He could have happily kissed her for hours, yet . . . he didn't want to stop at just a kiss.

He'd backed her against the wall; he leaned one forearm on the cool stone, muscles bunching, fist clenching as he fought the urge to take advantage. To step closer yet, to press against her, to feel her silk-clad curves against him.

She was tall, long-legged; the impulse to confirm

how well they would fit, the driving desire to soothe his aroused body with at least the touch of hers burned hot and strong. Along with an urgent need to fill his palms with her breasts, to duck his head and with his lips follow the tantalizing trail of her pearls to their end.

But this was Portia. Not even in the heady instant when he tried to break the kiss and she straightened, following his lips with hers, wanting more, and he sank back into her mouth, now freely—unreservedly—offered, did he forget who she was.

The conundrum was there, from the very first clear in his mind, mocking, jeering at the desire that rose so swiftly for her.

Every minute he indulged—indulged her, indulged himself—sent the price he would pay for ending the interlude soaring.

But end it he must. They'd been gone from the ballroom too long.

And this was Portia.

The effort to end the kiss and lift his head left him reeling. He lowered his hand from her face, lowered his arm, simply stood, waiting for the desire thundering through his veins to subside to a safe level. Watched her face as her lids fluttered, and rose.

Her eyes glittered darkly; a flush tinged her pale cheeks—it wasn't a blush. She blinked, searched his eyes, his expression.

He knew she would read nothing—nothing she

would know to recognize—in the graven lines of his face. In contrast, he could see the thoughts tumbling through her mind, mirrored in her expression.

No shock—he hadn't expected it; surprise, curiosity, a thirst to know more. An awakened, intrigued awareness.

He drew a deep breath, waited a moment more until he was sure she was steady on her feet. "Come—we have to get back."

Taking her hand, he turned and drew her with him, back around the corner, onto the main terrace.

There were two couples at the far end, but otherwise the terrace was deserted. He set her hand on his arm; they continued toward the ballroom in silence.

The French doors were near; he was thanking his stars she'd been sufficiently distracted to hold her tongue—he wasn't up to any discussion, not at that moment—when he heard voices.

Portia heard them, too. Before he could stop her, she stepped to the balustrade and looked over, down to the path below.

He tugged, but she didn't move. Something in her stillness alerted him. He moved to her side and looked down, too.

Hissed whispers floated up to them. Desmond stood with his back to the terrace wall. Kitty stood before him, clinging, her arms wound about his neck.

Desmond, rigid, was struggling to put her from him.

Simon glanced at Portia; she met his gaze.

They turned and strolled back into the ballroom.

What Kitty was up to, what she hoped to achieve with her outrageous behavior, Portia could not fathom; it was simply beyond her. She put it from her mind—she had far more important matters to ponder.

Such as the previous evening's kiss.

Her first loverlike kiss—hardly surprising it so fascinated her. As she walked the gardens in the cool of the morning, she replayed the moment, relived the sensations, not just of Simon's lips on hers but of all that had risen in response. The prickle of her nerves, the rush of blood beneath her skin, the welling urge to indulge in much greater physical closeness. No wonder other ladies found the activity addictive; she could almost kick herself for her previous disinterest.

She had certainly wanted more last night; she still did. And despite her inexperience, even despite his experience, she couldn't help suspect— feel—that Simon had felt the same. If the opportunity had been there . . . instead, they'd had to return to the ballroom.

Once back among the dancers, they'd exchanged not a word about the interlude, or indeed, much else; she'd been too consumed with thinking about it, and he, presumably, had seen no reason to comment. She'd eventually retired to her bedchamber, her bed; the remembered sensation of his lips on hers had followed her into her dreams.

This morning, she'd risen, determined to embrace the experience and go forward. But rather than face Simon over the breakfast table before she'd had a chance to decide on her direction, she'd elected to take breakfast with Lady O in her room.

Lady O's blithe comments on the propensity of gentlemen and their natures, peppered with elliptical allusions to the physical aspects of male-female relationships, had only made her more determined to sort out her own mind on the subject and decide how to go on.

Which was why she was walking alone in the gardens.

Trying to decide on the importance of a kiss. On how much significance to attach to her response.

Simon had given no indication that he found kissing her any different from kissing another. She wrinkled her nose as she headed down one of the lawn walks; she was too realistic not to acknowledge that he had to be an expert, that there were sure to be legions of ladies he'd kissed. Yet . . . she felt fairly certain he would kiss her again, if the opportunity presented.

That much, she felt comfortable with, reasonably sure. The path to the temple lay ahead; without conscious thought, her feet took her in that direction.

Her own route ahead was much less clear. The more she thought of it the more she felt at sea. Literally, as if she'd set out on a voyage on some fathomless ocean and then discovered she had no notion how to navigate, no map.

Would the next time she was kissed feel the same? Or had last night's reaction been because it was the first time? Would she have felt the same if another gentleman had kissed her? If Simon were to kiss her again, would she feel anything at all?

To get right to the heart of the matter, was how she felt when a given gentleman kissed her even relevant?

The answers were hidden beneath a miasma of inexperience. Straightening her shoulders, she lifted her head—she would simply have to experiment and find out.

Decision taken, she felt much more positive. The temple appeared before her, a small marble folly with Ionic columns. It was surrounded by lush flower beds; as she started up the steps, she noticed a gardener, a youngish man with a thick thatch of black hair, weeding one of the beds. He glanced up at her; she smiled and nodded. He blinked, looking rather uncertain, but politely nodded back.

Portia stepped up to the marble floor of the temple—and immediately realized why the gardener had looked uncertain. The temple was filled with words—an altercation. If she'd been paying attention she would have heard it before she climbed the steps. The gardener would be able to hear every word. In the quiet of the garden, he could hardly help it.

"Your behavior is **unconscionable**! I did not bring you up to comport yourself in such a manner. I can't **conceive** what you think to achieve by such appalling displays!"

The melodramatic tones belonged to Mrs. Archer. The words rose up from where Portia assumed a seat was set on the outside of the temple, overlooking the view. Within the temple, the words echoed and grew.

"I want excitement in my life!" Kitty declared in ringing tones. "You married me to Henry and told me I'd be a lady—you painted the position of his wife in glowing colors! You led me to believe I'd have everything I'd ever want—and I haven't!"

"You can't possibly be so naive as to imagine all in life will be precisely as you dream!"

Portia was glad someone was saying what needed to be said, but she had absolutely no wish to overhear it. Silently, she turned and went back down the steps.

As she gained the path, she heard Kitty reply in hard, harsh tones, "More fool I, I believed you. Now I'm living the reality—do you know he wants us to live **here** for most of the year? And he wants me to give him **children**?"

The last was said as if Henry had asked her to contract the plague; stunned, Portia hesitated.

"Children," Kitty went on, scorn dripping. "I'd lose my figure. I'd bloat and swell and no one would look at me! Or if they did, they'd shudder and look the other way. I'd rather be **dead**!"

Something close to hysteria screamed in the words.

Portia shivered. Refocusing, she saw the gardener; their gazes met. Then she lifted her head, drew breath. The gardener returned to his bedding plants. She walked on.

Frowning.

Reemerging onto the main lawn, she saw Winifred, like her, idly ambling. Thinking it wise to ensure Winifred did not amble to the temple, she changed course and joined her.

Winifred smiled with easy welcome. Portia smiled back. Here, at least, was someone she might learn from.

After exchanging greetings, by mutual accord they turned toward the lawn walks leading to the lake.

"I hope you don't think me unforgiveably forward," she began, "but I couldn't help noticing . . ." She glanced at Winifred's face. "Am I right in assuming there's some degree of understanding between you and Mr. Winfield?"

Winifred smiled, then looked ahead. After a moment, she said, "It would perhaps be more realistic to say we're considering some degree of understanding." Her lips curved; she glanced at Portia. "I know that sounds very timid, but, indeed, I suppose I am that, at least when it comes to marriage."

Portia saw the chance and seized it with both hands. "I know just what you mean—indeed, I feel the same." She caught Winifred's gaze. "I'm at present considering marriage—in general at this point—and have to confess there's much I don't understand. I've left it late for entirely selfish reasons, because of my absorption with other things in life, so now I find myself somewhat at a loss, and not as informed as I ought to be. However, I imagine you've had much more experience . . . ?"

Winifred grimaced, but her eyes were still easy, her expression gentle. "As to that, indeed, I have had more experience, in a way, but I fear it is not the sort to assist any other lady in understanding." She gestured. "I'm thirty, and still unwed."

Portia frowned. "Forgive me, but you're well-born, well dowered by my guess, and not unattractive. I imagine you've had many offers."

Winifred inclined her head. "Some, I grant you, but not many. I have not encouraged any gentleman to date."

Portia was at a loss.

Winifred saw it and smiled wrily. "You've favored me with your confidence—in return I will give you mine. You do not, I take it, have a very lovely younger sister? In particular, a highly acquisitive younger sister?"

Portia blinked; an image of Penelope, spectacled and severe, rose in her mind. She shook her head. "But . . . why . . . ? Kitty has been married for some years, has she not?"

"Oh, indeed. But, unfortunately, marriage has

not dampened her desire to seize whatever might come to me."

"She"—Portia searched for the word—"**poached** your suitors?"

"Always. Even from the schoolroom."

Despite the revelation, Winifred's expression remained calm, serene—resigned, Portia realized.

"I'm not sure," Winifred continued, meeting Portia's eyes, "that in truth I shouldn't be grateful. I would not wish to marry a gentleman so easily led astray."

Portia nodded. "Indeed not." She hesitated, then ventured, "I mentioned Mr. Winfield—he appears to have remained constant in his regard for you despite Kitty's best efforts."

The glance Winifred threw her was uncertain; for the first time, Portia glimpsed the lady behind the quiet mask who'd suffered consistent disappointment at her sister's hands. "Do you think so?" Then Winifred smiled, wry again; her mask slipped back into place. "I should tell you our history. Desmond met the family in London some years ago. At first, he was greatly taken with Kitty, as most gentlemen are. Then he discovered she was married, and transferred his attentions to me."

"Oh." They'd reached the end of the walk. After standing for a moment, looking down toward the lake, they turned and headed back toward the house. "But," Portia continued, "doesn't that mean Desmond's been pursuing you for some years?"

Winifred inclined her head. "About two." After a

moment, she somewhat diffidently added, "He told me he retreated from Kitty as soon as he'd drawn close enough to see her for what she is. Only later did he learn she was married."

Fresh in Portia's mind was the scene she'd witnessed below the terrace the night before. "He does seem . . . quite stiff with Kitty. I've seen no indication that he would welcome the opportunity to further any interest with her—quite the opposite."

Winifred looked at her, studied her face, her eyes. "Do you think so?"

Portia met her gaze. "Yes. I do."

The emotion—the hope—she glimpsed in Winifred's eyes before she looked away made her feel unexpectedly good. Presumably that was what Lady O felt when she meddled to good effect; for the first time in her life, Portia could see the attraction.

They walked on. She glanced up; the sight of the two male figures coming toward them abruptly recalled her to her own situation.

Simon and James strolled up. With their usual polished charm, they greeted both her and Winifred. Surreptitiously, Portia studied Simon, but could detect no change in his demeanor, sense nothing specific in his attitude toward her—no hint of what he thought about their kiss.

"We've been dispatched to fetch you," James said. "There's a picnic on. It's been decided luncheon will taste much better in the ruins of the old priory."

"Where is this priory?" Winifred asked.

"To the north of the village, not far. It's a pretty place." James gestured expansively. "A perfect place to eat, drink, and relax in the bosom of the countryside."

CHAPTER 5

James's words proved prophetic; the priory was every bit as accommodating as he'd intimated. Located on an escarpment, the ruins were extensive; while the views were not as good as those from the lookout, they were nonetheless very pleasant.

The stretch of ancient, overgrown lawn where the picnic was set out afforded a pleasant vista over valley and fields merging into a blue-grey distance. The day was warm, but the sun remained hidden by light cloud; a wafting breeze stirred the leaves and set the wildflowers nodding.

Once the food and wine were consumed, the older members of the party were content to sit back and swap tales and opinions on society and the world. Everyone else dispersed to explore the ruins.

They were as romantic as any young lady might wish, the tumbled stones well settled, not dangerous, in parts overgrown with creepers. Here and there an arch remained, framing a view; in other places walls still stood. A portion of the cloisters provided a sunny nook in which to take one's ease.

Since seeing her walking in the gardens that morning, Simon had been unable to shift his attention from Portia. Even when she was not directly in view, he was aware of her, like the caress of silk across naked skin—her presence now affected him in precisely the same way. He watched her, helpless not to, even though he knew she was aware of it. He wanted to know—**had** to know—couldn't let go of the possibilities that unlooked-for kiss on the terrace had raised.

He hadn't intended it; he knew she hadn't either, yet it had happened. Why such an interaction, so minor in the scheme of such things, should so grip his interest was a riddle he wasn't sure he needed solved.

Yet he couldn't leave it, couldn't shake aside the insane idea that had rushed into his mind on a torrent of conviction and taken up implacable, immovable residence. The idea that had kept him awake half the night.

Regardless of his impluses, he knew better than to crowd her or to make their awareness of each other public knowledge. When, with the others, she happily rose and set out to explore, he ambled along some distance behind, with Charlie and James supposedly keeping a general eye on proceedings.

The Hammond girls went quickly ahead, hallooing and giggling. Oswald and Swanston, clinging to spurious superiority, followed, but not too fast. Desmond walked beside Winifred; they parted from the other ladies, taking a different route into the ruins. Drusilla, Lucy, and Portia strolled on, Portia swinging her hat by its ribbons.

Henry and Kitty had remained with the elders— Mrs. Archer, Lady Glossup, and Lady O had all felt the need to engage Kitty in conversation. James, therefore, was relaxed and smiling as they walked through the arch into what had once been the church's nave.

Simon, too, smiled.

It took him fifteen minutes to lose James to Drusilla Calvin. When she paused to rest on a fallen stone, urging Lucy and Portia to go on, Simon paused, too, frowning, communicating his thoughts to James without words; James felt obliged to remain with Drusilla, entertaining her as best he could.

Charlie was a more difficult proposition, not least because he, too, had his eye on Portia—quite why, and with what aim, Simon was certain Charlie himself didn't know. Considering his tactics, with Charlie beside him he lengthened his stride, closing the distance to Lucy and Portia, eventually joining them.

Both turned and smiled.

He addressed himself to Lucy. "So are the ruins all you'd hoped for?"

"Indeed, yes!" Face alight, eyes shining, Lucy spread her arms wide. "It's quite wonderfully atmospheric. Why, one could easily imagine a ghost or two, even a sepulchral company of monks slowly making their way up the nave, censers swinging. Or perhaps a chant, emanating through the mists when there's no one there."

Portia laughed. Simon looked at her, caught her eye; distracted, she didn't utter the response she'd been about to make.

Leaving Charlie to say, "Oh, there's many more possibilities than that." He flashed Lucy his most engaging smile. "What about the crypt? Now **there's** a place for imaginings. The tombs are still there, guaranteed to send a shiver down your spine."

Lucy's eyes had grown round. "Where?" She swiveled, looking around. "Is it near?"

Her gaze returned to Charlie, eager and appreciative; as usual, he responded in his customary way.

"It's on the other side of the church." With a flourish, he offered his arm, totally distracted from his earlier aim by the giddy enthusiasm in Lucy's eyes. "Come—I'll escort you there. If you're a lover of atmosphere, you won't want to miss it."

Lucy happily slipped her hand in his arm. Over her head, Charlie arched a brow at Simon and Portia. "Coming?"

Simon waved him on. "We'll stroll on a little way. We'll meet you in the cloisters."

Charlie blinked, hesitated, then inclined his head. "Right-ho." He turned back to Lucy; they started on their way. "There's a story about a sound heard on dark and moonless nights . . ."

Simon turned back to Portia in time to see her smile, then she caught his eye; her smile faded.

Head rising, she studied his face, his eyes. He studied hers, and couldn't tell what she was thinking.

He waved, directing her on along the old paved path that wound down and around to the priory's kitchen gardens. She turned, stepped out.

"You knew about the crypt, didn't you?"

He followed close behind her, coming alongside as the path evened out. "Charlie and I have visited often over the years."

Portia smothered a grin and dutifully strolled on. He had a habit of not specifically answering questions he would rather not, questions whose answers revealed more of him than he wished to have known. Yet she was more than content to spend some time alone with him; she had no real interest in the ruins, but there were other matters she wished to explore.

They walked on in silence, oddly companionable. The sun briefly broke through, warm, but not too strong; she didn't feel obliged to put on her hat—aside from anything else, it made conversing with tall gentlemen difficult.

She could feel his gaze as they walked, feel his presence, and something more, a facet of his behavior she'd noticed years before, but which had only become clear in recent days. The constant flirting—Kitty, James, Charlie, Lucy, even the Hammond girls—had sharpened the contrast; Simon never flirted, never extended himself to engage, unless he had a purpose—unless he acted with intent.

He prowled beside her now, long strides lazy, the disguised power that invested every movement never more apparent. They were in an ancient place, alone. Whatever they said, whatever happened between them here would not need to conform to any social requirements. Only their own.

Whatever they wished, whatever they wanted.

She drew a deep breath, aware of her bodice tightening, aware that he noticed. A tingle of anticipation tickled her spine. They'd reached the kitchen gardens, originally walled, but now the walls were crumbling. The ruined kitchens lay to one side, the remains of the prior's house beyond them. She stopped, glanced around. They were out of sight of everyone, essentially private. She turned to face Simon.

A scant foot lay between them. He'd halted and was waiting, watching—waiting to see what tack she'd take. Knowing she wouldn't be able to resist taking—doing—something.

She lifted her chin. Fixed her eyes on his.

Couldn't find the words.

His eyes narrowed, searched hers, then he raised a hand, slowly, placed the tip of one finger beneath the angle of her jaw, just beneath her ear, and traced forward, tipping her face up. The simple touch sent sensation skittering through her, left her skin tingling.

She was tall, but he was a good half head taller; his fingertip beneath the point of her chin brought their faces closer.

"I assume you're intent on learning more?"

His voice was deep, hypnotic. She kept her gaze locked with his. "Naturally."

She could read absolutely nothing in his face, yet the sense of being considered, like prey, grew.

"What did you have in mind?"

The invitation was blatant—and exactly what she wanted.

She raised her brows, faintly haughty, knowing the challenge would not escape him—and he would not escape it. "I'd imagined the next step."

His lips curved, just a little; now that she knew what they felt like, she found them fascinating, both visually and in the expectation of how they would feel . . .

"And just what had you imagined that to be?"

She watched the words form on his lips; they took a moment to penetrate her brain. Then she hauled her gaze up to his eyes, blinked. "I'd imagined . . . another kiss."

Calculation flashed through his eyes, enough to tell her she might have answered differently, that there was more yet she could have learned . . . if she'd known to ask for it.

"Another kiss? So be it"—his head lowered, her lids followed—"if that's all you really want."

The last words drifted into her mind, pure temptation, as his lips settled on hers, warm, firm, more definite this time, more sure, more commanding. She knew how to respond now and did, parting her lips, inviting him in. His hand shifted, long fingers sliding to cup her nape, his thumb remaining beneath her chin, holding her steady as he angled his head and—as she'd demanded—took the kiss further.

Deeper, into some realm that was hotter, more exciting. More intimate.

She felt it in her bones, felt her senses unfurl like petals under a sensual sun. And went forward with eagerness and delight.

Lifting one hand, she lightly touched, lingeringly traced his cheek. Drew breath from him and kissed him back—shyly testing, trying, mimicking— growing more assured when she sensed, not only his acceptance, but beneath his expertise and his strength, an elusive, beguiling need.

Caught in the deepening intimacy of the kiss, in the slow tangle of their tongues, the long moments of disguised but insistent plunder, she was nevertheless aware of his arm closing around her, of his other hand spreading over her back, supporting her, trapping her, easing her nearer, tempting her closer yet.

His strength was a palpable force surrounding her; she was tall and slender while he was taller, broader, infinitely stronger. She felt like a reed to his oak, not that he would snap her, but that he could, and would, bend her to his will . . .

A shiver raced through her, an echo of what must have gone through some other woman, centuries before, when she'd stood, caught, in some long-ago Cynster's embrace. Just because time had passed didn't mean anything had changed; he was very much that earlier conqueror, disguised only by a veneer of sophistication. Scratch him, and the roar would be the same.

She knew it, yet the knowledge didn't stop her from inviting more. Indeed, the implicit challenge only made her bolder. Bold enough to close the distance between them until her bodice brushed his coat, until her skirts tangled with his legs and covered his boots, to rest her forearm on his shoulder and spear her fingers, slowly, experimentally, through his soft hair.

Simon felt his control quake; he locked every muscle against the rampant urge to draw her fully against him. To give his clamoring senses that much ease at least, to feel her lithe body molded to his. Cleaving to his as she would, sometime . . .

But not yet.

He could feel the compulsion rising within him and fought to suppress it, let it find expression only in his increasingly ravenous plundering of her mouth.

Soft, warm, she offered and he took, flagrantly claiming, guiding her deeper into the intimacy, until her lips, tongue, the succulent recesses of her mouth were his to savor as he wished.

He wanted much more. Wanted the promise of the body in his arms—wanted to claim it, to dictate her surrender, to have her soft body offered up as appeasement to the hardness of his.

A second kiss—that was all she'd asked for. Even though he knew in his conqueror's soul that she

wouldn't complain if he took their interaction further, he knew her. Far too well to make the mistake
of giving her more than she'd haughtily requested.
She was foolish to trust him, him or any man, as
she was, yet he was too wise in her ways not to
abide by the letter and intent of her trust.

He intended to build on it, and so gain a great
deal more.

Drawing back to safe ground was an effort,
accomplished step by step, degree by reluctant
degree. When their lips finally parted, they
remained for an instant, heads close, breaths mingling. Then he lifted his head, and she did the
same, blinking up at him. Realizing, as did he, as
her eyes searched his, that the landscape between
them had altered. New vistas had opened up, ones
neither had previously imagined might be. She was
enthralled . . . as was he.

She realized his hands were about her waist;
dragging in a breath she stepped back. He let her,
his fingers releasing, reluctantly sliding from her.

Her eyes were still locked on his, but her mind
was racing. She was still short of breath, suddenly
uncertain. She looked lost.

He smiled—charmingly. Reaching out, he tucked
a stray curl back behind her ear. Raised a brow,
faintly teasing. "Satisfied?"

She wasn't deceived, but recognized his tack—
his offer of an easy way back to the world they'd
left; he saw her understanding in her eyes. Along
with her hesitation.

But then she straightened and inclined her head,

haughty as ever. "Indeed." A smile flitted about her lips; abruptly she turned away, toward the path that would lead them around and back to the others. "That was perfectly . . . satisfactory."

He hid a grin as he fell in on her heels. Farther along, he took her hand to help her over a jumble of tumbled stones, and kept it. When they approached the cloisters, he wound her arm in his; they strolled on, outwardly easy, in reality all aware.

By unspoken agreement they would hide that last, but continue to explore it in private.

Reaching the cloisters, they heard the others' voices; he conducted her in, watching her still but with a new and quite different intent. He needed to ensure she remained comfortable with him, that she felt no qualms about approaching him, being with him, ultimately asking more of him.

He was perfectly prepared to teach her all she wished—all she would ever need to learn. He wanted her to turn to him for her next lesson. And the next.

Holding her in his arms, feeling the strength of the compulsion she evoked, sensing her reaction, had been enough to answer the question in his mind.

His insane, wild, previously inconceivable idea wasn't such a crazed notion after all.

He wanted her as his wife—in his bed, bearing his children. The scales had shattered and fallen from his eyes with a resounding crash. He wanted her by his side. Wanted her. He didn't truly understand why—why her—yet he'd never felt so certain of anything in his life.

The next morning, lounging against the frame of the open French doors of the library, Simon kept watch over the terrace doors of the morning room, the downstairs parlor, and the garden hall, the doors through which Portia might emerge to go walking in the gardens.

He'd known her for years, knew her character, her personality, her temper. He knew how to deal with her. If he pushed, overtly steered her in any direction, she'd either dig in her heels or go the opposite way on principle, regardless of whether that was in her best interests.

Given what he wanted of her, what position he wished her to fill, the fastest way to achieve all he desired was to lead her to think it was her idea. That it was her leading and him following, not the other way around.

An added benefit of such a plan was that it made redundant any declaration on his part. There'd be no need for him to admit to his compulsive desire, let alone the feelings that spawned it.

Tactics and carefully guarded strategy would be his most certain route to success.

The morning room doors opened; Portia, in a gown of blue muslin sprigged with deeper blue, stepped through, shutting the doors behind her. Strolling to the edge of the terrace, she looked across the lawn toward the temple, then she turned and went down the steps, heading for the lake.

Pushing away from the doorframe, taking his hands from his pockets, he set out in pursuit.

Reaching the stretch of lawn above the lake, she slowed, then she sensed his approach, glanced back, halted, and waited.

He studied her as he neared; the only signs of consciousness, of her recollection of their last moments together alone, were a slight widening of her eyes, a hint of color beneath her fine skin, and, of course, her rising head and uptilted chin.

"Good morning." She inclined her head, as ever faintly regal, but her eyes were on his, wondering . . . "Did you come out for a stroll?"

He halted before her, met her gaze directly. "I came to spend time with you."

Her eyes widened a fraction more, but she'd never been missish; with her he would stand on firmer ground if he dealt with her openly, honestly, eschewing social subtleties.

He waved toward the lake. "Shall we?"

She glanced that way, hesitated, then inclined her head in acquiescence. He fell in beside her; in silence, they walked to the edge of the lawn, then on down the slope to the path around the lake. By unspoken consent, they turned toward the summerhouse.

Portia strolled on, glancing at the trees and bushes and the still waters of the lake, struggling to appear nonchalant, not at all sure she was succeeding. This was want she wanted—a chance to learn more—yet this was not an arena in which she had any experience, and she didn't want to founder, to put a foot wrong, to end over her head, out of her depth.

And between them, things had changed.

She now knew what it felt like to have his hands locked about her waist, to sense his strength close, closing around her. To know herself in his physical control . . . her reaction to that still surprised her. She never would have thought she would like it, let alone crave it more.

Over all the years, in all that lay between them, there never had been any physical connection; now that there was, it was surprisingly tempting, enthralling . . . and its existence had shifted their interaction to an entirely different plane.

One she'd never been on before—not with anyone—a plane on which she was still very much feeling her way.

They reached the summerhouse; Simon gestured and they left the path, crossed a short stretch of lawn and went up the steps. The area within, a room open to the breezes, was unusually spacious. Instead of a single point to the roof, there were two, supported by columns flanking the central section, in which two large cane armchairs and a matching sofa were arranged around a low table. The sofa faced the entrance and the lake with the armchairs to either side, all fitted with chintz-covered cushions. Periodicals sat in a cane holder beside the sofa. A window seat ran around the walls, beneath the open arches.

The floor was swept, the cushions plumped, all ready for the enjoyment of whoever ventured in.

She turned just inside the threshold and looked back at the oval lake. Simon's earlier comment about the privacy of the summerhouse replayed in her mind. From this position, there was no evidence of a house anywhere near, not even a glimpse of a sculpted bed or a stretch of tended lawn. It was easy to forget, easy to believe there was no one else in the immediate world. Just them.

She glanced at Simon and found him watching her. Knew in that instant that he was waiting for her to give him some sign, some indication that she wished to learn yet more, or alternatively that she'd decided she'd learned enough. Casually at ease, blue gaze steady, he simply watched her.

Looking again at the lake, she tried to ignore the sudden leaping of her senses, the distracting conviction that her heart was beating faster and harder.

The other ladies had gathered in the morning room to talk and take their ease; the other gentlemen were either collected in groups, discussing business or politics, or out riding.

They were alone, as alone as the surroundings promised.

Opportunity knocked. Loudly. Yet . . .

She frowned, walked to one of the wide arches, set her hands on the sill, and looked out. Unseeing.

After a moment, Simon stirred and followed her; despite not looking, she was aware of his prowling grace. He joined her at the arch, propping his shoulder against its side. His gaze remained wholly on her.

Another minute slipped past, then he murmured, "Your call."

Her lips twisted in a grimace; she lightly drummed her fingers on the sill, then realized and stopped. "I know." The fact didn't make things any easier.

"So tell me . . ."

She would have to. He was only just over a foot away, but at least she didn't have to meet his eyes, nor speak loudly. She drew breath, drew herself up. Gripped the sill. "I want to learn more, but I **don't** want you to get the wrong idea. To misconstrue my intentions."

The dilemma she'd woken to that morning and come out to the gardens to think through.

He was silent for a moment; she could sense him trying to follow the tack her mind had taken.

"Why, exactly, do you wish to learn more?"

His tone was so even she could read nothing from it; if she wanted to know what he was thinking, she would have to look into his eyes, yet if she was to answer his question, she couldn't afford to.

She kept her gaze on the lake. "I want to understand, to experience enough so I can comprehend all that exists between a man and a woman that would encourage a woman to marry. I want to

know, not be forced to guess. **However**"—she placed ringing emphasis on the word—"my interest is academic. Totally and completely. I don't want you to . . . to . . . get any incorrect impression."

Her heart **was** beating faster, but she'd said it, got the words out. She could feel heat in her cheeks; she had never felt so uncertain in her life. Unsure, unconfident. **Ignorant**. She hated the feeling. She knew absolutely what she wanted, knew what, if her conscience hadn't raised its head, she wanted from him. But she couldn't, absolutely could **not** ask it of him if there was the slightest chance of his misinterpreting her interest.

She didn't imagine him to be readily vulnerable—she knew his reputation too well—but things between them **had** changed, and she wasn't sure how or why; feeling her way as she was, she couldn't be certain—as absolutely certain as her heart and honor demanded—that he wouldn't develop some sudden suceptibility and come to expect, in return for his teachings, more than she was prepared to give.

She was absolutely certain she couldn't bear that.

Simon studied her profile. Her revelation—her intention, her direction, so reckless and unconventional—was so Portiaesque, it did not evoke the slightest surprise; he'd long been inured to her ways. Had she been any other unmarried lady he'd have been shocked; from her, it all made perfect sense.

It was her courage and candor in stating it, in seeking to make sure he understood—more, in seeking to make sure he did not leave himself open to any hurt—that evoked a surge of emotion. A complex mix. Appreciation, approbation . . . even admiration.

And a flare of something much deeper. She cared for him at least that much . . .

If he chose to go forward and accept the risk, however small, that he might fail to change her mind and persuade her into matrimony, he couldn't claim he hadn't been warned.

By the same token, informing her that he had decided that she was the lady he intended having as his wife was clearly out of the question. At least for the present. She wasn't thinking in those terms—that was the challenge he had to overcome, deflecting her mind and her considerable convictions onto the path to the altar. However, given their previous history, given all she knew of him, if at this delicate point he mentioned he intended making her his bride she might well run for the hills.

"I think we need to talk about this—get the situation clear."

Even to him, his tone sounded too even, almost distant; she glanced briefly at him but didn't meet his eyes.

"What," he asked, before she could respond, "**specifically** do you wish to learn?"

She fixed her gaze once more on the lake. "I want to know"—the color in her cheeks deepened, her chin rose a notch—"about the physical aspects. What is it about their times with their beaux that the maids titter over on the backstairs? What do women—ladies especially—gain from such encounters that inclines them to indulge, and most especially prompts them to marriage?"

All logical, rational questions, at least from her strictly limited point of view. She was patently in earnest, committed, or she wouldn't have broached the subject; he could sense the tension holding her, all but quivering through her.

His mind raced, trying to map the surest way forward. "To what . . . point do you wish to extend your knowledge?" He kept all censure from his voice; he might have been discussing the strategies of chess.

After a moment, she turned her head, met his eyes—and glared. "I don't know."

He blinked, suddenly saw the way—reached for it. "Very well. As you don't—logically can't—know what stages lie along a road you've never traveled, if you're truly serious in wanting to know"—he shrugged as nonchalantly as he could—"we could, if you wish, progress stage by stage." He met her dark gaze, held it. "And you can call a halt at whatever point you choose."

She studied his eyes; wariness rather than suspicion filled hers. "One stage at a time?"

He nodded.

"And if I say stop . . ." She frowned. "What if I can't talk?"

He hesitated, well aware of what he was committing himself to, yet he felt compelled to offer, "I'll ask your permission before every stage, and make sure you understand, and answer."

Her brows rose. "You'll wait for my answer?"

"For your rational, considered, definitive answer."

She hesitated. "Promise . . . ?"

"Word of a Cynster."

She knew better than to question that. Her expression remained haughty, but her lips eased, her gaze softened . . . she was considering his proposition . . .

He held his breath, knew her far too well to make the slightest move to press her—battled the compulsion—

She nodded, once, decisively. "All right."

Facing him fully, she held out her hand.

He looked at it, glanced briefly at her face, then grasped her hand, turned and towed her deeper into the summerhouse.

"What . . . ?"

He stopped a few feet before one of the columns. Looked back at her and raised a brow. "I assumed you'd want to progress to the next stage?"

She blinked. "Yes, but—"

"We can't do that by the arch, in full view of anyone who might wander by the lake."

Her lips formed an O as he drew her past him, twirling her to face him. Freeing her hand, he lifted both his to frame her face, tipping it up as he stepped closer and lowered his head.

He kissed her, waited only until the steel went from her spine and she surrendered her mouth, then he backed her, slowly, step by deliberate step, until the column was at her back. She stiffened with surprise, but when he didn't press her against the wood, she relaxed, bit by bit, gradually let herself become engrossed in the kiss.

For long moments, he did nothing more—simply kissed her and let her kiss him back. Sank into the softness of her mouth, with lips and tongue caressed, enticed, then let her play. Let her sense and grow accustomed to the give and take, to a slower, less overwhelming rhythm.

To the simple familiar pleasure.

She was taller than the average, a fact he appreciated; he didn't need to tip her face so far back, could stand with her comfortably. The column behind her merely delineated their space, providing something she could later lean back against . . . assuming she agreed to their next stage.

The thought sent heat sliding insidiously through him. He angled his head, pressed the kiss deeper, made her cling to the exchange. Releasing her face, he reached for her waist, spanned it with his hands, then slid them around, over the fine muslin, feeling the silky shift of her chemise between the gown and her skin.

She made a soft sound and pressed nearer; he met her lips, met her tongue—and eased her back, gently, until she stood against the column. She relaxed against it; her hands, previously resting passively on his shoulders, shifted, slid up, back, around. Spreading her fingers, she speared them slowly through his hair, let it fall.

Then she twined her arms about his neck and stretched up against him, meeting his lips with increasing ardor, her lithe body bowing.

Inwardly, he smiled, let his hands slide over her back, tracing the long line of the muscles framing her spine, up, then down. He kissed her deeply, sensed the heat rising beneath her skin, felt the soft mounds of her breasts, pressed to his chest, firm.

Her perfume rose and wreathed through his mind, teased his senses. He held to the kiss, letting his hands do no more than caress the firm planes of her back, over and over.

And waited.

More. Portia knew she wanted more than this. Kisses were all very well, exceedingly pleasant, heady and intoxicating, sending warmth sliding through her, bringing her senses alive. And the feel of his hands, cool and hard, and the unstated promise in their steady, deliberate stroking, sent shivers of anticipatory delight down her spine. But now expectation crawled along her nerves; her senses were avidly agog. Waiting. Ready.

For the next stage.

He'd said he'd show her. She wanted to know, to learn of it. Now.

She drew back from the kiss, found it required real effort; when their lips finally, reluctantly, parted, she didn't move back, only lifted her suddenly heavy lids enough to meet his gaze from beneath her lashes.

"What's the next stage?"

His eyes met hers; his seemed darker, a more intense blue. Then he answered. "This."

His hands shifted, leaving her back to slide forward to her sides. His thumbs cruised, brushing the sides of her breasts.

Sensation streaked through her; her senses abruptly focused—followed, hungrily, greedily, as he stroked deliberately again. Her knees quaked; she suddenly found a use for the column behind her, leaned back against it. He followed her lips with his, brushed them as his wicked thumbs circled lightly, tantalizingly—just enough for her to understand . . .

He lifted his head, met her eyes. "Yes? Or no?"

His thumbs circled again, too lightly . . . if she'd had the strength she'd have told him what a stupid question it was. "Yes," she breathed. Before he could ask if she was sure, she drew his lips back to hers, certain she would need that much anchor to the world.

She felt his lips curve, but then his hands shifted again and she forgot—stopped thinking—about anything else bar the delicious delight that flowed from his touch, from the languid, repetitive caresses, alternately firm then teasingly insubstantial. Increasingly explicit, more openly sensual, more overtly possessive.

Until he closed his hands, slowly, firmly about her breasts, until he took her tightly budded nipples between his thumbs and fingers, and squeezed.

Fire lanced through her.

Gasping, she broke from the kiss. The pressure about her nipples eased.

"No! Don't stop."

Her voice surprised her—a sultry command. She cracked open her lids, glanced at his face. His eyes met hers. There was something—some expression—she'd never seen in them before. His face was hard, very angular. His lips, thin yet mobile, were not quite straight.

Obediently, he squeezed again; once again, sensation speared, spread and tingled beneath her skin. Warmth followed, rushing through her, washing her inhibitions away.

She let her lids fall on a pleasured sigh.

"Do you like it?"

She tightened her arms and drew his lips back to hers. "You know I do."

He did, of course, but he hadn't wanted to miss hearing her admission. It pleased him—a consolation prize given the limitations of their present engagement.

The severe limitations—the open ardor of her response more than warmed him; it was a spur to which he couldn't react.

Yet.

She was warm and alive beneath his hands; her breasts filled them, hot, firm, swollen. Her delight, her pleasure, was there in her kiss, in the eagerness investing her supple frame.

When he closed his hands more definitely and

kneaded, she made a sound deep in her throat and kissed him back, flagrantly demanding . . .

It was suddenly a battle to stay exactly where he was and not press closer, not trap her against the column, mold her to him, ease his pain against her softness. He drew breath, felt his chest swell, grappled, and hung on to his control—

Clang! Clang!

The sound was off-key, sufficiently grating to distract them both.

They broke the kiss; he hauled in a breath, hands sliding to her waist as he turned.

Clang! Clang!

"It's the luncheon gong." Portia blinked, slightly dazed, up at him. "They're ringing it outside. There must be others wandering the gardens, too."

He hoped so, hoped it wasn't just they being so specifically summoned. He stepped back, reached for her hand. "We'd better get back."

She met his gaze briefly, then nodded. Let him take her hand and lead her down the steps.

As they walked quickly back up the lawns, he made a mental note to reinforce his reins before her next lesson. To prepare himself for the temptation, the better to resist it.

He glanced at her, walking steadily beside him, her stride longer than most women's. She was absorbed, thinking—he knew about what. If he made a mistake, let his true intent show, he couldn't rely on her naïveté to blind her to it. She might not see the truth immediately, but later, she would. She would analyze and dissect everything that passed between them, all in the name of learning.

Looking ahead, he inwardly grimaced. He was going to have to ensure she didn't learn more than was good for her.

Such as the truth of why he was teaching her.

CHAPTER 6

Portia sat at the luncheon table and let the conversations flow past her. She was sufficiently adept to nod here, murmur there; no one realized her mind was elsewhere.

She longed to discuss what she'd learned, but there was no one present suitable for the role of confidante. If Penelope had been here . . . then again, given her younger sister's views on men and marriage, perhaps it was as well she was not.

Assessing the other ladies, she mentally ticked them off on her fingers. Not Winifred—she didn't want to shock her—and certainly not Lucy or the Hammond girls. As for Drusilla . . .

Kitty, brittlely vivacious as she teased Ambrose and James, seemed the only possibility—a lowering thought.

Portia cast a glance at Lady O, then looked down at her plate. She had a sneaking suspicion that, far from being shocked, Lady O would baldly tell her she'd merely scratched the surface and there was a lot more she'd yet to learn.

She didn't need further encouragement. Curios-

ity was eating her from inside out; she didn't dare
catch Simon's eye in case he guessed. One point
they hadn't discussed was the frequency of her lessons; she didn't want to appear too . . . "forward"
was the word that leapt to mind. She had a deep-
seated conviction it wouldn't be wise to let him
know how fascinated and enthralled she was. He
possessed quite enough arrogant pride; she didn't
need to add to it, to give him any reason to feel
superior.

Consequently, she rose with the other ladies and
went out onto the lawns to sit and idly gossip in the
sunshine. Simon watched her go, but he gave no
sign; neither did she.

An hour later, Lady O summoned her to help her
upstairs.

"Well, then—how are your deliberations pro-
gressing?" Lady O slumped back on her bed and
let Portia straighten her skirts.

"In a positive but as yet inconclusive manner."

"That so?" Lady O's black eyes remained on her
face, then she humphed. "You and Simon must
have walked for miles."

She shrugged nonchalantly. "We went down to
the lake."

Lady O frowned at her, then closed her eyes.
"Well, if that's all you have to report, I can only
suggest you look lively. We've only so many days
here, after all."

She waited; when Lady O said nothing more, she
murmured a good-bye and left her.

Slowly, she walked back through the huge house, wondering . . .

How many days would she need to learn all? Or at least enough? Reaching the long gallery, she turned into one of the deep embrasures and sat on the window seat. Staring, unseeing, at the sunbeams dancing on the wood paneling, she opened her memory, let her senses slide free . . .

And felt again, carefully mapped the limits of her learning, the frontier beyond which lay so much she'd yet to feel. To know.

She had no idea how long she'd been sitting there, no idea how long Simon had been watching her; as she drew back from her thoughts, she sensed his presence, shifted her gaze, and saw him leaning against the outer edge of the embrasure. Met his blue eyes.

A moment passed, then he raised a brow. "Ready for your next lesson?"

Did it show? She lifted her chin. "If you're free."

He had been for the last hour. Simon bit back the words, coolly inclined his head, and straightened.

She rose, her soft skirts falling about her, sheathing her long legs. He reached out, took her hand, fought not to seize it. Calling on every ounce of his expertise, he wound her arm in his and turned down the corridor.

She glanced at his set face. After a moment, she asked, "Where are we going?"

"Somewhere we won't be disturbed." He heard the harshness in his voice, knew she'd heard it, too.

Nevertheless, he couldn't resist adding, "Incidentally, if you wish to progress through the various stages to any reasonable conclusion, you'll need to make yourself available for the purpose."

She blinked, then faced forward. "I often go to the music room in the afternoon—to practice. I was thinking of going there now."

"You're accomplished enough on the piano—you can afford to be distracted for once. Or twice. We'll only be here for a few days more."

Halting, he opened a door, set it swinging wide, and ushered her into a small parlor attached to a bedchamber; neither room was presently in use. He'd chosen the room from memory, knowing what it contained.

Portia stopped in the middle of the room, looking about at the lumps of furniture all swathed in Holland covers. He locked the door, then joined her; taking her hand, he drew her toward one of the long, curtained windows. The room faced west, overlooking the pinetum. He swept the curtains wide; sunshine streamed in.

Turning back, he reached for the sheet covering the large piece of furniture facing the window. With a flick, he drew the sheet aside, revealing a wide and lushly cushioned daybed, now bathed in golden light.

Portia blinked. Dropping the sheet, he reached for her. Giving her no time to think, he lifted her and fell, taking her with him, into the cushioned comfort.

They bounced; she giggled, then sobered as her

eyes met his. He shifted, propping his shoulders against the daybed's padded side, settling her alongside him, half over him, within the circle of his arms.

The sun poured over them. Her gaze drifted to his lips. She licked hers, then her eyes flicked up to his. "What now?"

One dark brow rose fractionally; her dark blue eyes remained steady on his. He had absolutely no doubt she was willing.

He smiled, insensibly relieved; lifting a hand to her face, he drew it to his. "Now we play."

They did—he couldn't for the life of him remember any interlude like it. Whether it was the simple word or the sunshine warming them, or the silence of the deserted rooms around them, even the anonymity of the shrouded furniture surrounding them, that infused those first moments with a giddy, reckless pleasure he couldn't tell, but they were both susceptible, both quickly infected with a heady lightheartedness that freed them from the world, left them both focused, not on propriety but on needs—he on hers, she, it seemed, on his.

Within seconds of their lips meeting, she'd relaxed into the kiss, yet her body remained, not stiff, but tensed, like a deer not yet sure of its safety, poised to retreat. He drew her deeper into the kiss and she came readily, offering her mouth, eagerly responding when he took, claimed; he did nothing more, simply waited, let her learn for herself, come to her own conclusion.

He had long ago learned that this particular con-
figuration was most useful for easing a skittish
lover; with her in his arms, protected yet not
threatened by his weight, by his strength, the illu-
sion of being in control rather than being controlled applied. As with others before, it worked;
gradually that telltale tension flowed away, and she
sank, warm, supple, vibrantly alive, against him.

His hands on her back stroked, soothed; it was
she who shifted back, gave him access to her
breasts, flagrantly encouraged him to fondle.

To gradually, inch by inch, wind her tight.

As before, she ultimately broke from the kiss,
lifting her head, dragging in a breath, her breasts
swelling under his hands. This time, he didn't
stop, let his hands and fingers continue their artful
torture.

She opened her eyes and looked down, sucked in
another breath as she watched him pander to her
senses. Then she lifted her heavy lids and, with her
usual directness, met his eyes. "What's next?"

He held her gaze, tightened his fingers about her
nipples, watched her concentration fade . . . her
lids droop. "Are you sure you want to know?"

She opened her eyes; the look she pinned him
with would have been imperious, but for the curve
of her lips. "Quite sure." She tried to straighten
her lips and failed; she couldn't have been kittenish
if she tried, nor yet played the coquette—she simply didn't have it in her—but he sensed—could
almost feel—the gaiety welling within her, the
thrill, the excitement, the anticipation.

It was as if they were exploring something, some unknown landscape between them, all on a personal dare. She had not an ounce of fear in her; she was eager and sure of him, sharing the moment even though she didn't know what would come . . .

She trusted him.

The knowledge crashed through him—not just the realization that she did, but all that it—so totally unexpectedly—meant to him.

How he felt.

He drew in a deep breath, fighting the constriction locked about his chest. She'd glanced down, watching his hands knead the tight, heated mounds of her breasts; when she glanced up at him, raising her brows, he had to clear his throat, and surreptitiously shift beneath her.

"If you're sure . . . ?"

The look she threw him told him to get on with it; he found it impossible not to smile. Her bodice was closed with a row of tiny buttons from neckline to waist; releasing her breasts, he set to work easing the tiny nubs free of their holes.

She blinked, but made not the slightest move to stop him. However, as his hands pressed between them and her bodice gaped, a frown gathered in her eyes; light color rose in her cheeks.

The instant the last button slipped free, he reached for her face, curled one hand about her nape and drew her back down. Caught her gaze in the instant before her lids fell. "Stop thinking."

He kissed her, long, deeply, claiming her senses

in truth for the first time, something he'd been careful, previously, to avoid. She hadn't needed to know he could kiss her witless, yet if he didn't deprive her of her considerable wits now, just for a few minutes, she might well draw back . . .

He was not in the mood to cajole, let alone argue; he no longer possessed sufficient coolheadedness, not where she was concerned, to ease her trepidation with words. And it was that—trepidation, not fear. Simply a hesitation on the brink of the unknown.

Ruthlessly, with the gentlest of touches, he drew her over the edge, over the threshold of her— their—next discovery.

When he let her surface, his hand cupped her breast, skin to silken skin. Their lips parted, but she didn't draw back; their eyes met briefly from under lowered lids. He continued to touch, trace, felt her shiver. Felt something within him shudder in response.

He was hard, aching; he wanted her with an urgency that stole his breath. He lifted his lips, closing the half inch that separated hers from his, wanting, needing, succor.

She gave it; how she knew, he didn't know but she kissed him, framed his face, angled hers and pressed deep, then invited, incited—dared him to take. As ravenously as he wished. She met him, matched him, followed, then led.

Eventually drew back as the brief flare between them faded. She made no demur when he pressed her bodice wider, so he could fill both hands and touch, caress, knead. Her breath caught, hitched, then came again, faster. Beneath his palms, her skin burned.

Portia felt giddy—with delight, with a sense of illicit awareness so sharp she could barely breathe. His touch was pure pleasure, more golden than the sunshine that played over them, warmer, more real.

Infinitely more intimate.

She should be shocked—she knew it. The thought floated through her brain. And out.

There was too much to take in, to absorb, to learn. To feel. No missish sentiment, no modesty was strong enough to distract her from the sensuous delight of his fingers, the strength of his hands, the pleasure they conjured.

Fascination was too weak a word for all she felt.

From under her lashes, she glanced down at him, sensed, within herself, a change, a shift, a wish to give him as much pleasure as he was lavishing on her. Was that how it happened? Why sane women made the decision to accept a man's need and pander to it?

Her mind couldn't give her the answer; she let the question slide away.

He was looking at her breasts, at his hands upon them; he glanced up, caught her gaze.

Heat welled, and a tide of emotion swept through her; she smiled, deliberately, equally deliberately leaned low, ignoring the press of her breasts into his hands, and kissed him.

Felt him still, drag in a huge breath . . . then he shifted, tipped her back, and turned so he lay beside her; one hand remained on her breast, the other framed her face. He kissed her—ravished her mouth, sent her senses spinning once more, then slowly, gradually, drew her back.

When he lifted his head they were both breathing raggedly; their gazes met briefly, their lips throbbed. Her fingers were sunk into his shoulders, clutching tight. They both held still, caught in the moment, both aware of the heat, the beat of their hearts—the almost overwhelming yearning.

The moment passed.

Slowly, very slowly, he bent his head and their lips met again in a gentle, clinging, soothing kiss. His hands left her skin; he tweaked her bodice closed, then slid his arms about her and held her— simply held her.

Later, as they left the parlor, Portia glanced back. The daybed lay swathed again; there was no sign that anything dramatic had occurred in the room.

Yet something had happened; something had changed.

Or perhaps been revealed.

Simon drew her out and shut the door; she could read nothing in his face, yet she knew he felt the same. As he twined her arm with his, their gazes touched, held. Then they faced forward and walked back to the gallery.

She needed to think, but the dinner table and the company surrounding it were no help at all. Portia cast an irritated glance at Kitty; she wasn't the only person thus employed. The woman was a vacillating nitwit; that was the kindest conclusion Portia could reach.

"I hear we're to have a major luncheon party tomorrow." Beside her, Charlie raised his brows, then slanted a glance up the table at Kitty. "Apparently she's organized it."

Distrust, not to say suspicion, rang in his voice.

"Don't borrow trouble," she advised. "She was perfectly reasonable over lunch today. Who knows? Maybe it's only in the evenings that she . . ."

"Transforms into a femme fatale, and a peculiarly unsubtle one at that?"

She nearly choked; lifting her napkin to her lips, she bent a frowning look on Charlie.

Unrepentant, he grinned, but the gesture wasn't humorous. "I'm desolated to disappoint you, m'dear, but Kitty can behave atrociously at any time of day." He glanced up the table again. "Her attitude seems entirely at whim."

She frowned. "James said she'd grown worse—worse than she used to be."

Charlie considered, then nodded. "Yes. That's true."

Kitty had started the evening badly, openly flirting—or trying to—with James in the drawing room. Charlie had tried to intervene, only to bring Kitty's wrath down on his head. Henry had come up and tried to smooth things over, resulting in Kitty's flouncing off, sulking.

They'd come to the table with Mrs. Archer agitated, as if her nerves were giving way. Others, too, showed signs of distraction, of awareness, reactions they would normally cloak with well-bred ease.

It was, Portia thought, as the ladies rose to repair to the drawing room, as if the genteel facade of the house party was fracturing. It hadn't cracked and fallen away, but ignoring Kitty's behavior was proving too great a strain for some.

Like the Hammond girls; confused by it all—hardly surprising, for no one understood—they clustered around Portia, eager to chatter brightly and forget all the black looks. Even Lucy Buckstead, rather more up to snuff and with greater self-confidence, seemed subdued. Portia felt forced to take pity on them; she encouraged them to dwell on the prospects for tomorrow—whether the officers with whom they'd danced at the ball would ride over for the luncheon party, whether the quietly handsome young neighbor, George Quiggin, would attend.

Although her efforts were sufficient to distract Annabelle, Cecily, and Lucy, she could not rid herself of the irritation Kitty evoked. Glancing across the room, she saw Kitty talking airily to Mrs.

Buckstead and Lady Hammond. Despite her occupation, Kitty's eyes were fixed on the doors.

The doors through which the gentlemen would return.

Portia stifled a disgusted humph. An oppressive sense of impending social doom seemed to be spreading outward from Kitty. She, for one, had definitely had enough—and she absolutely **had** to find some time, and some better place, to think.

"If you'll excuse me?" With a nod, she stepped back from the three girls and walked to the French doors open to terrace.

Without a single glance right or left, she glided through—into the sweet coolness of the night.

Beyond the light cast through the doors, she stopped and dragged in a huge breath; it tasted delicious, as if it was the first truly free breath she'd managed in hours. All frustration fell from her, slid like a cloak from her shoulders. Lips lifting, she strolled along the terrace, then descended the steps and set out across the lawns.

Toward the lake. She wouldn't go down to it, not alone, but the new moon rode high, and the lawns themselves were bathed in silvery light. Safe enough for her to wander; it wasn't that late.

She needed to think about all she'd learned, of what she could make of things thus far. Her hours spent alone with Simon had certainly opened her eyes; what she was seeing was both more and surprisingly different from what she'd expected. She'd assumed the attraction, the physical connection, that occurred between a man and woman would be something akin to chocolate—a taste pleasant enough to wish to indulge in whenever it was offered, but hardly a compulsive craving.

What she'd thus far shared with Simon . . .

She shivered even though the air was warm and balmy. Walking on, her gaze fixed on the clipped grass five feet ahead of her, she tried to find words to describe what she felt. Was this desire—this urge to do it again? More, to go further? Far further.

Possibly, but she knew herself—at least some of herself—well enough to recognize that mixed in with the purely sensual compulsion there was a healthy vein of curiosity, of her usual determination to know.

Along with the desire, that, too, had grown.

She knew what she wanted to know, what, now she knew it existed, she would not be able to leave be until she'd examined it fully and understood.

There was something—something totally unexpected—between her and Simon.

Walking slowly down the lawns, she considered that conclusion and could not fault it. Even though in this sphere she was untried and inexperienced, she trusted her innate abilities. If her faculties were convinced there was something there to be pursued, then there was.

What it was, however . . .

She didn't know; she couldn't even hazard a guess. Courtesy of her heretofore sheltered life, she didn't even know if it was normal.

It certainly wasn't normal for her.

But was it normal for him? Something that occurred with every lady.

She didn't think so. She was sufficiently familiar with him to sense his moods; toward the end of their interlude lolling on the daybed, when she'd sensed that curious shift between them, he'd been as taken aback as she.

Rack her brains though she did, she couldn't recall anything specific that had caused the moment—it was as if they'd suddenly simultaneously opened their eyes and realized they'd reached a place they hadn't expected to find themselves in. They'd both been, not to put too fine a point on it, enjoying themselves—neither had been paying attention, neither had been steering their play . . .

It **was** something special because he hadn't expected it to happen.

She was definitely going to find out more. Discover, uncover, whatever it took. The obvious place to start was to return to the same place, the same spot—that same odd plane of feeling.

Luckily, she had an inkling how to get there. They'd been totally focused on the physical delight, engrossed as only two people who knew each other so well could be. Neither had been watching the other in the sense of gauging the other's honesty or character; if he'd wanted to say or do anything, she trusted absolutely that he would have said or done it. He viewed her in the same light; she knew that without thinking.

That was the key—they hadn't been thinking. With each other, they didn't need to bother; they'd concentrated completely on the doing.

The sharing.

She'd reached the end of the lawns above the lake. It lay ahead and below, dark and fathomless, inky black in its hollow.

No matter how hard she stretched her imagination, she couldn't—could not—imagine sharing those moments with any other man.

Like a touch, she sensed his presence, felt his gaze. Turning, she watched him come down the lawn toward her, hands in his pockets, shoulders wide, his gaze fixed on her.

Halting beside her, he looked out over the lake, then returned his gaze to her face. "You shouldn't be out here alone."

She met his eyes. "I'm not."

He looked away but she caught the quick lift of his lips.

"How was it"—she waved back at the house— "in there?"

"Ghastly. Kitty's skating on thin ice. She seems bent on attaching Winfield, despite the fact he's running the other way. After the earlier fracas, Henry's retreated, pretending not to notice. Mrs. Archer's horrified but impotent; Lord and Lady Glossup are increasingly distracted. The only light relief was provided by Lord Netherfield. He told Kitty to grow up."

Portia smothered an unladylike snort; she'd been consorting with Lady O for too long.

After a moment, Simon looked at her. "We'd better go back."

The thought didn't entice. "Why?" She glanced at him. "It's too early to retire. Do you really want to go back in there and have to smile through Kitty's performance?"

His look of haughty distaste was answer enough.

"Come on—let's go down to the lake." She intended to look in at the summerhouse, but didn't feel obliged to mention it.

He hesitated, looking not at the lake, but at the summerhouse glimmering faintly at its end. He did, indeed, know her well. She set her chin and looped her arm in his. "The walk will clear your head."

She had to tug once, but, reluctantly, he went with her, eventually settling to stroll by her side as they turned onto the path around the lake's rim. He steered her toward the pinetum, away from the summerhouse; head high, she glided along, and said not a word.

The path circumnavigated the lake; to return to the house without retracing their steps, they would have to pass the summerhouse.

Lady O had, as usual, been right; there was a great deal she had yet to learn, to explore, and not over many days in which to do it. In other circumstances, three lessons in one day might be rushing things; in these circumstances, she could see no reason not to grasp this opportunity to pursue her aim.

And to ease her curiosity.

Simon knew what she was thinking. Her airy demeanor deceived him not at all; she was fantasizing about the next stage.

So was he.

But, unlike her, he knew a great deal more; his attitude to the subject was equivocal. It didn't surprise him that she would seek to rush ahead—indeed, he was counting on her reckless enthusiasm to carry her far further. However . . .

He could have used a little time to come to grips with what he'd glimpsed that afternoon.

A little time to reorient himself.

And to think of some way to reinforce his control against her temptation—a temptation all the more potent because he knew she wasn't even aware she possessed it.

He was certainly not fool enough to tell her; the last thing he needed was for her to set out deliberately to wield it.

"You know, I can't understand what Kitty's thinking. It's as if she doesn't consider others, or their feelings, at all."

He thought of Henry, of what he had to be feeling. "Is she really that naive?"

After a moment, Portia answered, "I'm not sure it's a question of naïveté so much as true selfishness—an inability to think of how others feel. She acts as if she's the only one who's truly real, as if the rest of us are"—she gestured—"figures on a carousel, twirling about her."

He grunted. "She doesn't seem close to even Winifred."

Portia shook her head. "They aren't close—indeed, I think Winifred would rather they were even more distant. Especially given Desmond."

"Is there an understanding there, do you know?"

"There would be if Kitty would let be."

They walked on in silence. Eventually, he murmured, "It must get very lonely at the center of her carousel."

A few seconds passed, then Portia tightened her hold on his arm briefly, inclined her head.

They'd strolled around most of the lake; the summerhouse loomed out of the darkness. He allowed her to steer him across the lawn to the steps; he made no demur when she let go of his arm, picked up her skirts, and went up. He cast a quick glance around the lake path, then followed her.

She was waiting in the dimness. In the shadows, her face was a pale oval; he had no hope of reading her eyes. Nor she his.

He halted before her. She raised a hand to his cheek, lifted her face, guided his lips to hers. Kissed him in flagrant invitation. Locking his hands about her waist, glorying in the feel of her supple, slender form anchored between his palms, he accepted and took. Without quarter.

When he finally raised his head, she sighed. Then asked, perfectly equably, "What's next?"

He'd had the last half hour to formulate the right

answer. He smiled; in the darkness, she couldn't see it.

"Something a little different." He walked forward, step by slow, deliberate step backing her.

He sensed the skittery excitement that flashed through her. She tensed to glance around, to see where he was steering her, but inherent caution overcame her—she didn't take her gaze from his face.

The backs of her legs hit the arm of one of the deep chairs. She stopped. He released her, caught her hand, stepped past and around her and sat, reaching for her, pulling her down, perching her on his knees, more or less facing him.

He could feel her surprise. They were now in dense shadow; the moonlight didn't reach this far.

But she was quick to adjust; he didn't need to draw her to him. Unbidden, she leaned close, and kissed him.

Invitingly. He was deep in the exchange, caught, captured, before he realized. Not a kitten, not a coquette, but she could, it seemed, when the mood was on her, be a temptress of a different sort.

One infinitely more attractive to him.

He could feel his hunger rise; he fervently prayed she never realized how easily she could conjure it. Call it, lure it, like some beast of prey coming to her hand.

Ready to feast.

His hands, until then spread over her back, over the fine silk of her evening gown, slid forward.

She sat up—he assumed to give him better access to her breasts. Instead, she broke the kiss, raised her head.

"I have a suggestion."

Wariness flooded him, not least because her voice had changed. The tone was lower, richer, as sultry as the night that wrapped about them and screened her eyes, her expression. He could read neither, had to gauge their play—her state—from other things.

Far less accurate things.

"What?"

He saw her lips lift. She set her forearms on his upper chest, leaned in and kissed him lightly. "An addendum to our last lesson."

What on earth was she about? "Explain."

She laughed softly; the sound sank into him. "I'd rather show you." She caught his gaze. "It's all perfectly reasonable—and only fair."

It was then he realized she'd undone his waistcoat; his coat had already been open. Before he could react, she shifted on his chest and set nimble fingers to his cravat.

"Portia."

"Hmm?"

Arguing would get him nowhere; he lifted his hands and helped her untie his cravat. In a gesture of triumph she sat up and drew it free, went to fling it away. A sudden vision flashed across his brain; he caught the cravat and laid it on the chair arm.

She'd already lost interest—hers had focused on

the buttons closing his shirt. He shifted, letting her draw the front free of his trousers, then she had it fully open, spread the halves wide—and stopped, staring down at what she'd uncovered.

He would have given an arm to see her face clearly. As it was, he drank in her stillness, her absorption, the sense of fascination that held her as she slowly released the shirt, spread her fingers, and touched.

For a full minute, she simply traced, explored—learned. Then she glanced at his face, registered his reaction, the fact he'd stopped breathing. Her hands stopped for a moment, then touched more boldly.

"You like this." She moved her hands slowly, sensuously caressing across the wide muscles banding his chest, then down, fingers lightly touching, only to return to spear through the crinkly thatch of brown hair.

He dragged in a breath. "If it pleases you."

She laughed. "Oh, it pleases me—even more because it pleases you."

He was in pain, acute pain. The tenor of her voice, sultry, warm, and so oddly mature—so knowing of him and confident of herself—was the most potent siren's call he'd ever heard. Her weight, warm and femininely alluring, across his thighs, only added to his torment.

Portia stroked, caressed, drank in the sheer delight of touching him, and knowing that, for at least these few minutes, she had him in her thrall.

His skin was warm, almost hot, the steely resilience of the muscles beneath utterly fascinating. She was enthralled, but even more, she was thrilled to learn that she, with her touch, could pleasure him as he had her.

Only fair, as she'd said—fair to them both.

At last, he drew a deep, not quite steady breath, and reached for her. He didn't push her hands away, but urged her to him. Leaving her hands spread on his chest, she eagerly leaned down and gave him her lips, her mouth, her tongue.

The kiss deepened into blatant intimacy, then extended into some arena they'd not before explored; her fingers sank into his flesh, and she pressed her burning palms to his bare skin.

She felt his hands on her back, his fingers busy with the line of buttons down her spine. He undid them all, all the way to where the gown's opening ended in the small of her back.

The night air was warm; it lay heavy all around them, barely stirring as he urged her up, to sit up and let him draw her gown down.

A shiver, not of modesty but of sheer awareness, shook her. He'd caressed her bare breasts before, but her gown had been there, largely shielding all he'd touched from his sight. But now he drew her gown down and she let him, with only the slightest hesitation freed her arms from the sleeves. The gown collapsed about her waist. She looked at his face as, almost lazily, he reached for the ribbon straps of her chemise.

He didn't ask permission, but simply tugged them free, perfectly sure he had the right.

She was very glad she could not see his expression; only the fact that they were cloaked in shadows allowed her to sit still and let him peel her chemise down.

The air was warm. Her skin felt hot, her nipples already tight and aching. She felt his gaze on her, roaming, cataloging; she thought his lips lifted, but it wasn't in a smile.

Then he raised a hand and touched her. Her lids fell, suddenly heavy; she swayed. He closed both hands about her breasts, and she shuddered.

Closed her eyes and gave herself up to feeling, her senses focused on each caress, each knowing touch, the escalating torture. Her skin seemed even more sensitive than before, her nipples so tightly ruched they hurt. An odd hurt that, every time he squeezed, transmuted to heat, to washes of feeling that flooded through her, pooling low in her body.

She cracked open her lids enough to look at his face. Did he know what he was doing to her?

One glance was enough; of course he did. Had he planned the darkness so she'd be amenable? No—she'd been the one to lead him to the summerhouse, but he'd capitalized—was capitalizing—on her plan.

The notion pleased her; one made a move and the other took it further. That seemed right. Encouraging.

As was his touch, the way he kneaded her flesh. She caught her breath and glanced down—watched his hands, dark against the whiteness of her breasts, play, possess.

The heat within her swelled, grew.

"Do you want to go on to the next stage?"

She glanced at him. She didn't know—couldn't guess—what the next stage was. Didn't care. "Yes."

Simon heard the decision in her voice, could just detect a firming of her jawline. Enough to let out a small sigh of relief.

Forcing his fingers to leave her swollen flesh, he reached for his cravat. She blinked, watched as he smoothed the yard-long strip, folding it to a narrow band. Drawing it tight between his hands, he met her eyes over it. "A suggestion of mine."

He'd gone along with her suggestion; she could hardly demur at his. She did, however, frown, yet . . . placing her hands on his chest, she leaned forward and let him tie the blindfold in place.

"Is this really necessary?"

"Not absolutely, but I think you'll prefer it."

Her silence screamed that she wasn't sure how to interpret that. Cinching the knot at the back of her head, he grinned. He released it and she tensed to sit up.

"No." He slid his palms over her naked back, felt something tighten deep within him in response. "Stay just as you are." With one hand, he drew her lips to his. "You don't need to do anything, other than feel."

Their lips met; he drew her back into the heat, into the familiar intimacy. Her hands, braced on his chest, kept their bodies apart—just as well as this point. He drew her deeper, trapped her senses—seized the moment first to absorb the fact that she was naked to the waist, sitting, waiting, on his knee, then to set the final touches to his preparations.

The darkness she'd handed him was an unexpected boon, the blindfold an added benefit; it would have assuredly taken him longer, otherwise, to find a way, a suitable setting, in which to introduce her to this, the next stage, without risking evoking an instinctive reaction, a wariness, a deep-seated reluctance to be in any man's control—an instinct with which he knew her to be very well endowed. She'd handed him herself on a platter; of course, he was going to feast.

He eased her up, sitting up himself, his hands sliding over her smooth skin, glorying on their way to cup her breasts anew. The intensity of the kiss increased, pouring heat and fire through them both. He was happy to let it happen, knowing what was to come. When her kisses turned urgent, when her breasts where heated and tight again, he broke the kiss, nudged her head back, set his lips to cruise the long line of her throat.

Her hands slid up, one locking on his shoulder, beneath his shirt. The other slid to his nape, stroking, then spearing into his hair as he bent and laved the pulse point at the base of her throat, then set his lips to it.

Head back, she caught her breath on a soft gasp.

Drawing his lips from her skin, he cupped one breast, lifting the ruched peak—bent his head and took it into his mouth.

The sound she made was a shattered cry of delight; it streaked through him and urged him on. He drew the tortured peak deep, suckled and laved, until she cried out again. He paused only to transfer his attentions to her other breast. He feasted like a conqueror with her his slave, offered up to him. As she was. Not once did she draw back—if anything, she urged him on, wordless in her entreaties, effective nonetheless. He knew every nuance, could interpret and understand every little gasp, every soft moan.

Her fingers sank into his shoulder, clutched tight on his skull. She held him to her, begged him to take. And give.

He did. He fed the conflagration mercilessly—let her sense, know, learn all she wished—but then ruthlessly, determinedly, even against her wishes reined them back, both of them, drew them back from the brink of the furnace, from the scorching flames of desire.

That time was not yet.

They were breathing raggedly when he finally slumped back, and she followed, collapsing on his chest. She murmured, then shifted, sinuously abrading her brutally sensitized breasts against the roughness of his chest. He let her, drew her lips to his, and kissed her, but softly. Let her ease back in her own way.

Finally accepting, she sighed, and sank into his arms, then reached up and pulled off the blindfold.

She looked up at him. Even in the dimness, he would have sworn her eyes glittered. She looked at his lips, licked hers, then met his eyes.

"More."

Not a question—a demand.

"No." It hurt to say it. He drew breath, felt desire's vise locked about his chest. "Be patient."

Foolish words. He knew that the instant he uttered them, saw a definite flash in her eyes—and reacted instantly, before she could.

He kissed her. Shifted her in his arms, then ravaged her mouth. Simultaneously, deliberately, slid his hands down, over the long planes of her back, down, sliding beneath the back of her gown, down over her flushed skin, over the curves, tracing, learning. Mapping what, one day soon, would be his.

She murmured deep in her throat—not a protest but pure encouragement. He ignored it, but could not draw his hands away, not yet. Not until he'd satisfied some undeniable inner craving to know that much, at least, of her. To know, absolutely, that she would be his—sometime.

Soon.

When he finally raised his head, she opened her eyes, and met his. Fearlessly, without guile or guilt.

She was lying in his arms, bare to the hips, her naked breasts pressed to his bare chest, his hands caressing her bare bottom, her skin dewed with desire.

Desire itself lay naked between them.

Both of them recognized it.

It was an effort to draw breath, but he did.

"We have to go back."

She studied his face, understood what he meant. Eventually inclined her head.

Going back took time. Letting their senses settle, righting themselves, rearranging their clothes. He didn't bother retying his cravat but left it about his neck, trusting they'd encounter no one while returning to the house.

They set off, her hand locked in his, walking through the deepening shadows. The moon had sunk low; the gardens were dark.

The house loomed ahead. Portia frowned. "The lights—I would have expected most would still be downstairs. It can't be that late."

In truth, she had no idea of the time.

Simon shrugged. "Perhaps, like us, they fled Kitty's court."

They walked on; Simon steered her in a different direction to their usual route, she assumed so they could slip into the house unseen. They were still some way from the walls when they heard the thud of footsteps, then the rustle of leaves drawing nearer.

Simon halted; perforce she did, too, in the black shadows thrown by a tree. Silent and still, they waited.

A figure emerged some yards away, cutting down

the narrow paths heading away from the house. He didn't see them, but as he passed from shadow to shadow, they saw him.

Recognition was instant; as before the gypsy continued through the gardens as if he knew every inch of them.

When he was gone, and Simon urged her on, she whispered, "Who the devil is he? Is he really a gypsy?"

"Apparently he's the leader of a band of gypsies that spends most summers camped nearby. His name's Arturo."

They'd nearly reached the house when Simon stopped again. She peered ahead, and saw what he had—the young gardener standing under a tree to their right, near a corner of the mansion. He wasn't looking their way—he was watching the other face of the house, the one out of their sight. The one the gypsy, Arturo, had most likely come from.

The same wing of the house that contained the family's private rooms.

Portia glanced at Simon. He looked down at her, then waved her on. The path they were on was lawn, as were most of the paths in the garden, perfect for moving along silently.

They rounded the corner they'd been making for; Simon opened a door and ushered her into a small garden hall. The instant he shut the door, she asked, "Why do you think the gardener's boy's out there?"

Simon looked at her, then grimaced. "He's not a

local—he's one of the gypsies. Apparently he knows his plants—he often works here through the summers, helping with the beds."

Portia frowned. "But if he was keeping watch for Arturo, why is he still there?"

"Your guess is as good as mine." Taking her arm, Simon propelled her to the door. "Let's get upstairs."

They emerged into one of the minor corridors. No one was around. They strolled nonchalantly, but silently along. Both were used to country houses, to the subtle signs of where people were, the hum of distant conversation; all were presently lacking.

They came upon a candle left burning on a side table. Simon stopped. "Keep watch."

He swiftly retied his cravat into something that, in the dim corridors, would pass muster if they met anyone.

They went on, but didn't. When they reached the front hall, she murmured, "It really does look like everyone's gone up."

Which seemed odd; a clock they'd passed had given the time as not quite midnight.

Simon shrugged and steered her to the main stairs. They were halfway up when voices reached them.

"It'll cause a scandal, of course."

They both stopped, exchanged a glance. It was Henry who had spoken.

Simon moved to the balustrade and looked over; she moved to his side and did the same.

The library door was ajar; inside the room, they could see the back of an armchair, the back of James's head, and his hand, resting on the chair's arm, gently swirling a crystal glass holding amber liquid.

"The way it's shaping, you'll risk a far greater scandal if you don't."

Henry humphed. After a moment, he replied, "You're right, of course. I just wish you weren't, that there was some other way . . ."

His tone told them what—or rather who—was being discussed; as one, she and Simon turned and silently continued up the stairs.

In the gallery, he kissed her fingertips and they parted—no need for words.

Reaching her room without encountering anyone, she wondered what they'd missed. What Kitty had done to send everyone to bed early, and leave Henry and James discussing the relative merits of scandals.

CHAPTER 7

She really didn't want to know. Portia had too much on her own plate; she felt no need to burden herself with knowledge of Kitty's shortcomings. Each to their own—live and let live.

For herself, she was fired with a zeal to live—to the fullest. To a degree, a level, she hadn't before realized was possible. The events of the previous evening should have left her scandalized. They hadn't. Not in the least. She felt exhilarated, eager, very ready to learn more, to sip from the cup of passion once more, to taste desire again, and this time drain the chalice.

The questions consuming her were when and where?

With whom didn't rate a thought.

She tacked through the crowds thronging the lawns; Kitty's luncheon party was in full swing. From the alacrity with which the surrounding families had attended, she deduced the Glossups had not entertained much in recent times.

Purposely eschewing the other houseguests, she wandered, stopping to chat with those to whom she'd been introduced at the ball, meeting others.

Accustomed to the role of young lady of a great country house—her brother Luc's principal seat in Rutlandshire—she was entirely at ease chatting with those who would, were they in London, be her social inferiors. She'd always been interested in hearing of others' lives; only via that avenue had she come to appreciate the comfort of her own, something that, like most ladies of her station, she would otherwise have taken for granted.

To give her her due, Kitty, too, did not hold aloof; she was very much in evidence, weaving among her guests. While searching for possibilities—for some inkling of an opportunity through which to pursue her fell aim—Portia noted that, along with Kitty's mood du jour, a joie de vivre that was, she would have sworn, quite genuine. Smiling, laughing gaily, flown on excitement, Kitty might have been, perhaps not a new bride, but one of short standing thrilling to her first social success.

Watching her greet a buxom matron with transparent good humor, and exchange comments with the woman's daughter and gangling son, Portia inwardly shook her head.

"Amazing, ain't it?"

She whirled and met Charlie's cynical gaze.

He nodded toward Kitty. "If you can explain that, I'll be in your debt."

Portia glanced again at Kitty. "It's too hard for me." Looping an arm through Charlie's, she turned him about; with a quirk of his lips, he accepted her decree and fell in by her side. "Perhaps it's like charades—she behaves as she thinks she should—**no!** don't state the obvious!—I mean that she has a mental image of how she **should** be, and acts like that. That image may not, in every situation, be what we, or others like us, would think right. We don't know what Kitty's view of things might be."

Steering Charlie on, she frowned. "Simon wondered if she was naive—I'm starting to think he may be right."

"Surely her mother would set her straight? Isn't that what mothers are for?"

Portia thought of her own mother, then thought of Mrs. Archer. "Yes, but . . . do you think Mrs. Archer . . . ?" She left the question hanging, not quite sure how to phrase her reading of Kitty's mother.

Charlie humphed. "Perhaps you're right. We're used to our own ways—to people like us and how they behave. We expect them to know what's acceptable. Perhaps it really is something along those lines."

He glanced around. "Now, minx, where are you taking me?"

Portia looked ahead, then stood on her toes to see past various people. "Somewhere over there is a lady who knows your mother—she was eager to speak with you."

"What?" Charlie stared at her. "Thunder and turf, woman! I don't want to spend my time doing the pretty with some old harridan—"

"You do, you know." Having sighted their goal, Portia towed him on. "Just think—if you speak with her now, in the midst of all this crowd, it'll be easy to exchange a few words, then move on. That'll be quite enough to satisfy her. But if you leave it until later and she catches you, with the crowd more dispersed, you might find yourself trapped for half an hour." She glanced at him, raised her brows. "Which would you prefer?"

Charlie narrowed his eyes at her. "Simon was right—you're dangerous."

She smiled, patted his arm, then delivered him up to his doom.

That good deed done, she returned to her consuming passion—identifying somewhere and somehow to legitimately, or at least without drawing any untoward attention, get Simon to herself for an hour or two. Or perhaps three? She had no real idea how long the next stage along her path to understanding would take.

Skirting a group of officers resplendent in their scarlet with an easy but distant smile, she considered the point. At her age, the accepted strictures deemed twenty minutes in private to be no great scandal, but more than half an hour to be beyond redemption; presumably half an hour was sufficient. However, from what she'd heard, Simon was an accredited expert, and experts never liked to be hurried.

Three hours would probably be wise.

She surveyed the crowd. Until she came up with

a plan there was no sense seeking Simon out, no sense spending too much time in public by his side. It wasn't as if they were courting.

She chatted to a major, then to a couple who had driven over from Blandford Forum. Leaving them, she circled the gathering, strolling along a high hedge. She was about to plunge into the throng again when, to her left, she saw Desmond with Winifred on his arm.

They were standing where an alcove in the hedge hosted a statue on a pedestal. Neither was looking at the statue, nor at the guests. Desmond held Winifred's hand; he was looking down at her face, speaking quietly, earnestly.

Winifred's eyes were cast down, but a slight, very gentle smile was just curving her lips.

Suddenly, Kitty was there. Like a small whirlwind she erupted from the crowd and latched on to Desmond's arm. The look she cast Winifred as her older sister looked up in surprise was frankly triumphant. Then Kitty turned her eyes on Desmond.

Even from fifteen yards away, Portia could feel the brightness of the smile Kitty beamed on Desmond. She artfully pleaded, fully expecting to lead him away.

She'd misjudged; that much was obvious from the abrupt, curt dismissal Desmond, his face set like stone, handed her.

As surprised as Kitty, Winifred looked at him, Portia thought with new eyes.

For one instant, Kitty's face was a study in surprise, then she laughed, set herself to cajole.

Desmond stepped between Winifred and Kitty, forcing Kitty to step back; winding Winifred's arm in his, he spoke again—brutally short. With a brusque nod to Kitty, he walked off, taking an amazed Winifred with him.

Portia lost sight of them as they merged with the crowd; her attention returned to Kitty, to the stunned, somewhat lost expression that showed briefly on her face. Then Kitty blinked, and her smile returned. With a light laugh, she turned back to the crowd.

Curious, Portia headed in the same direction, but was distracted by a friend of Lord Netherfield's. It was twenty minutes later before she again sighted Kitty.

In her bright yellow gown, she stood like a stamen in the center of a poppy—a circle of scarlet coats and gold braid. Her bright, breezy charm and tinkling laugh were very much in evidence, yet to Portia, standing a few yards away chatting with a group of older ladies, Kitty's performance now contained a brittle note.

Increasingly obviously, Kitty encouraged the officers. They, as such men were wont to do, returned the favor in jocular and correspondingly audible vein.

Portia noted the glances directed Kitty's way, the swift exchanges between local ladies.

Lady Glossup and Mrs. Buckstead were some

yards distant; they'd noticed, too. They excused themselves from the couple with whom they'd been conversing; arm in arm, they bore down on Kitty.

Portia didn't need to watch to know the outcome; three minutes later, Kitty left the officers and was swept away by her mama-in-law and friend.

Relaxing, feeling as if some disaster had been averted, Portia focused on the short, sweet-faced older woman beside her.

"I understand you're staying here, my dear." The old lady's eyes twinkled up at her. "Are you Mr. James's young lady?"

Portia quelled her surprise, smiled, and disabused the lady of that notion. A few minutes later, she wandered on; the crowd was now partaking of delicate sandwiches and pastries served by a small army of helpers. Taking a glass of cordial from a footman, she sipped, and strolled on.

Was there any chance of her and Simon slipping away?

Deciding to gauge how dispersed the crowd had become, she headed for the far side of the lawn. If guests had ambled as far as the temple . . .

Nearing the crowd's edge, she looked toward the entrance to the path. It was blocked. By James.

Kitty stood before him.

Still within the crowd, Portia stopped.

One glance at James's face was enough to gauge his state; his jaw was clenched, as were his fists, but his eyes kept flicking to the crowd. He was furious with Kitty; words were burning his tongue, but he was too well-bred to create a scene, not with half the county looking on.

Portia suddenly wondered if Kitty realized that **that** was why James didn't repulse her advances outright, that his reluctance to tell her to go to the devil was not an indication of susceptibility.

Whatever the case, James needed rescuing. She drew herself up—

Lucy appeared from the opposite direction; smiling sweetly, she walked up and spoke to Kitty, then James.

Kitty's reply was polite, but dismissive. Even a touch contemptuous. She turned back to James.

Faint color rose in Lucy's cheeks, but she lifted her head, held her ground, and at the first break in Kitty's words spoke again to James—asking about something.

With an impatience no true hostess would ever own to, Kitty swung around to point—

James drew breath, smiled at Lucy, and offered to show her. Offered her his arm.

Portia grinned.

Lucy accepted with a pretty smile.

The look on Kitty's face was . . . stunned. Disbelieving.

Almost childlike in its disappointment.

Portia's levity faded. She shifted in the crowd, not wanting to get trapped in any conversation. There was something very wrong with Kitty's view of things—her perceptions, her expectations, her aspirations.

She'd thought she was moving away from Kitty, but Kitty must have swung on her heel and stormed off. She was still storming when Portia nearly ran into her; she saw her just in time and changed tack.

There was too much color in Kitty's cheeks; her blue eyes glittered. Her soft, pouty lips grimly set, she strode on with unladylike vigor.

Looking away, Portia saw Henry leave a group of gentlemen and move to intercept his wife. Feeling like someone about to witness an accident and incapable of preventing it, compelled, she moved to the edge of the crowd.

Twenty feet away, Kitty all but walked into Henry. There were others near, but all were engrossed in their conversations; Henry grasped Kitty's arm, firmly but not with anger, as if both to steady her and to recall her to her surroundings.

Face set, Kitty looked up at him. Her eyes flashed, she spoke—even without hearing the words, Portia knew they were vicious, cutting, intended to hurt. Henry stiffened. Slowly, he released Kitty. He bowed, speaking low, then he straightened. A moment passed; Kitty said nothing. Henry inclined his head, then stiffly moved away.

Fury—the anger of a child denied—roiled in Kitty's face, then, as if donning a mask, she composed her features. Drawing in a breath, she swung to face her guests, called up a smile, and moved into the crush.

"Hardly an edifying spectacle."

The drawled words came from behind her.

She looked up and back, over her shoulder. "There you are."

Simon looked down, read her eyes. "Indeed. Where were you going?"

He must have seen her earlier, heading doggedly this way, one drawback of being rather taller than the average.

She smiled, turned, and linked her arm with his. "I wasn't going anywhere, but now you're here, I would like to stroll through the gardens. I've been talking for the past two hours."

Others, likewise, were starting to amble, taking advantage of the extensive walks. Rather than head for the lake, as most were, she and Simon turned toward the yews and the formal gardens beyond.

They'd reached the open lawn beyond the first row of trees when he offered, "A guinea for your thoughts."

He'd been watching her, studying her face. She flicked him a glance. "Do you think they're worth that much?"

They paused; he held her gaze, then his attention shifted to the black curl that had come loose and now bobbed by her ear. Lifting a hand, he caught it, tucked it back behind her ear; his fingertips lightly brushed her cheek.

Their eyes met.

He'd touched her much more intimately, yet there was a quality in the simple caress that conveyed so much more.

"I want to know your thoughts that much." His gaze didn't waver.

Studying his eyes, she felt something inside her quiver. It was an admission of sorts, one she hadn't expected. One she wasn't sure she was reading correctly. Yet . . . letting her lips curve, she inclined her head.

Arm in arm, they walked slowly on.

"I intended to avoid Kitty and all her doings—instead, I've been tripping over her at every turn." She sighed, looked ahead. "She's betrayed Henry, hasn't she?"

She felt him tense to shrug, knew when he stopped, reconsidered.

He nodded curtly. "That seems fairly certain."

She would have wagered her best bonnet they were both thinking of Arturo and his nocturnal visits to the house.

They ambled on; Simon's gaze returned to her face. "That wasn't what you were thinking about."

She had to smile. "No." She'd been pondering the basics of marriage—the relationship, what it must mean in fact as distinct from any theory. She gestured. "I can't imagine—"

She'd been going to say that she couldn't see how Kitty and Henry could continue in their marriage, but such a statement would be unbelievably naive.

Many marriages rolled along quite reasonably with nothing more than respect between the partners.

Drawing breath, she reached for her real meaning. "Kitty's betrayed Henry's **trust**—she seems to think that trust doesn't matter. What I can't imagine is a marriage without it. I can't see how it could work."

Even as she spoke, she was conscious of the irony; neither of them was married—even more, both had avoided the subject for years.

She glanced at Simon; he was looking down as they walked, but his expression was serious. He was thinking of what she'd said.

After a moment, conscious of her gaze, he looked up, first at her, then ahead, over the manicured lawn. "I think you're right. Without trust . . . it can't work. Not for us—people like us. Not with the sort of marriage you—or I—could countenance."

If anyone had told her, even a week ago, that she would be having such a conversation about marriage with Simon Cynster, she would have laughed herself into stitches. Yet now it seemed nothing more than right. She'd wanted to learn what lay between a man and a woman specifically with respect to marriage; the scope of that study had broadened further than she'd foreseen.

Trust. Marriage really was very much about that.

It was also at the heart of what was growing between her and Simon; that wasn't trust itself, but whatever it was had only grown—presumably could only grow—because trust, real trust, had already existed between them, nascent, untried.

"She—Kitty—will never find what she wants." She suddenly knew that beyond doubt. "She's searching for something, but she wants to be given it first, and then decide whether to be worthy of it—whether to pay the price. But with what she wants, she's putting the cart before the horse."

Simon thought about it, not just her words but the ideas behind them; he felt her glance, and nodded. He did understand, not so much Kitty but what Portia was saying; it was she who commanded his thoughts, who inhabited his dreams.

Her view of marriage was vitally important to him. And what she'd said was corrrect—trust did come first. All the rest, all that he wanted of her, all he wanted her to want of him, all of which was only now becoming clear—all that was like a tree that could grow strongly, well rooted and secure, only if solidly planted in trust.

He glanced at her, walking, thinking, by his side. He trusted her completely and absolutely, far more than he trusted any other living soul. It wasn't just familiarity, being able to rely on her, knowing with unquestioning confidence how she would think, react, behave. Even feel.

It was knowing she'd never intentionally hurt him.

She'd prick his ego without compunction, defy him, irritate, and argue, but she'd never seek to truly harm him—she'd already proved that.

Drawing breath, he looked ahead, suddenly aware of how very precious such a trust was.

Did she trust him? She must to some extent, but exactly how far he wasn't yet sure.

A moot point. If—**when** he prevailed on her to trust him far enough, would that trust survive if she later discovered that he hadn't been completely open, completely honest with her?

Would she understand why? Enough to be lenient?

She was an open book; she was and always had been too direct, too self-confident and assured of her own station, her own abilities, and her indomitable will, to bother with deceit. It was simply not in her nature.

He knew exactly what she was seeking, what she looked to gain through her interaction with him. The one thing he didn't know was how she would react when she realized that, in addition to giving her all she sought, he was determined and intent on giving her a great deal more.

Would she think he was trying to capture her, saddle her with responsibilities, hem her in— imprison her? And react accordingly?

Despite all he knew of her—indeed, **because** of all her knew of her—that was impossible to predict.

They reached a long, wisteria-covered walk leading back toward the house. Turning under the wooden arches, they strolled along in easy silence. Then Portia slowed.

"Oh, dear."

He followed her gaze to the adjoining lawn. Kitty stood at the center of a group of officers and youthful sprigs, a glass in her hand, laughter on her lips. She was talking, gesturing, excessively gay; they couldn't make out her words but her tone was too high-pitched, as was her laugh.

One of the officers made a comment. Everyone laughed. Kitty gestured wildly and responded; two gentlemen steadied her as she wobbled. Everyone laughed even more.

Simon halted. Portia did, too.

A flash of lavender skirts had them glancing down the lawn. Mrs. Archer came hurrying up.

They watched as, with some argument and many weak smiles, she succeeded in extricating her daughter. Arm in arm, she marched Kitty back to the main lawn, where the majority of guests had remained.

The officers and gentlemen re-formed into groups and continued to talk. Simon led Portia on.

They met and conversed with a number of other couples strolling in the opposite direction. Finally regaining the main lawn, they stepped into the still-considerable throng, and immediately heard Kitty.

"Oh, **thank** you! That's exactly what I need." She hiccupped. "I'm so **very** thirsty!"

To their right, the young gardener, roped in to help as a waiter, stood by the hedge bearing a salver with glasses of champagne. In his borrowed black clothes, tall and rather gangly, with his shock of black hair and dark eyes, he possessed a certain dramatic handsomeness.

Kitty certainly thought so; standing before him, she ogled him blatantly over the rim of the glass she was draining.

Portia had seen, and heard, enough; her hand on Simon's arm, she pushed—he moved as she wished and they strolled away into the crowd.

They spent the next twenty minutes in blissfully pleasant conversation, meeting with Charlie, then later the Hammond girls, both flown with success and happiness over the youthful swains they'd met. Chattering, teasing, they'd all relaxed, imbued with good feelings, when a stir by the terrace steps had them turning, looking.

Along with all about them.

What they saw transfixed them.

At the bottom of the steps, Ambrose Calvin stood with Kitty draped upon him. She'd wound her arms about his neck; her face, uptilted to his, was filled with laughing, openly sensual delight.

No one could make out what she was saying— she was attempting to whisper, yet the words were loud, slurred, her tongue tripping.

She dragged heavily on Ambrose while he, rigid and pale, fought to put her from him.

All talking stopped. Everyone simply stared.

Absolute silence descended. All movement ceased.

Then a guffaw, quickly smothered, shattered the

frozen tableau. Drusilla Calvin left the crowd; coming up behind Kitty, a much smaller woman, she reached around and grabbed her arms, aiding her brother to free himself.

The instant he did, Lady Hammond and Mrs. Buckstead swooped on the trio; all sight of Kitty was lost in the ensuing melee. There were calls for cold water and orders flung at the staff; it quickly became clear they were saying Kitty was ill and had been taken faint.

Portia met Simon's eyes, then turned her back on the fracas and engaged the Hammond sisters, picking up their comments where they'd broken off. The girls, although momentarily distracted, were too well-bred not to follow her lead. Simon and Charlie did the same.

Everyone tried not to look at the group by the terrace, now swollen by Lord and Lady Glossup, Henry, and Lady Osbaldestone and Lord Netherfield. Lady Calvin had sailed up, too. Heads turned again as Kitty, a drooping little figure, was helped inside, supported by Lady Glossup and Mrs. Buckstead with Mrs. Archer, fluttering ineffectually, bringing up the rear.

At the base of the steps, those who hadn't gone in exchanged glances, then turned and, easy smiles on their faces, returned to their conversations in the crowd.

There was no denying the awkwardness, no dispelling the questions raised, ones of impropriety if not outright scandal. Nevertheless . . .

Lady O stumped up, her lined face relaxed, no

hint in her eyes or her bearing that anything untoward had occurred.

Cecily Hammond, greatly daring, asked, "Is
Kitty all right?"

"Silly female's taken ill—no doubt extended herself too far organizing today. Excitement, too, I
don't doubt. Had a dizzy spell—the heat wouldn't
have helped. No doubt she'll recover, just needs to
lie down for a spell. Young married lady, after all.
She ought to have more sense."

Lady O smiled brightly into Portia's eyes, then
her gaze passed on to both Simon and Charlie.

They all understood—that was the tale they were
to spread.

The Hammond sisters didn't need to have it
explained. When Portia suggested they should part
and mingle, Cecily and Annabelle were perfectly
ready to flutter off like butterfiles and spread the
word. Charlie went one way, Portia and Simon
another. They exchanged a glance, then dutifully
set themselves to do what they could to help
smooth things over.

The other houseguests were doing the same;
Lady Glossup took charge of the arrangements
and sent the footmen into the crowd bearing ices,
sorbets, and cakes.

All in all, they were moderately successful. The
rest of the afternoon—the following hour or so—
passed in reasonably comfortable style. That, however, was all on the surface, in the faces people
showed to the world. Underneath . . . significant
glances were exchanged between friends, although

no one was so outré as to put their thoughts into words.

As soon as it was possible to do so without giving offense, people started leaving. By late afternoon, the last guests were wending their way down the drive.

Lady O clomped up to where Simon and Portia stood. She poked Simon's leg with her cane. "You may give me your arm upstairs." She turned her black gaze on Portia. "You can come, too."

Simon obeyed; they turned to the house. Portia walked on Lady O's other side, taking her other arm when they reached the main stairs. Lady O was not young; for all her ferocity, they were both deeply fond of her.

She was breathing stertorously when they reached her room; she pointed to the bed and they helped her to it. They'd barely got her settled, sitting propped high on her pillows as she'd commanded, when there came a knock on the door.

"Come!" Lady O called.

The door opened; Lord Netherfield looked in, then entered. "Good—a confabulation. Just what we need."

Portia quelled a grin. Simon met her gaze briefly, then turned to set an armchair for his lordship close by the bed. Lord Netherfield accepted Simon's help into the chair; like Lady O, he, too, walked with a cane.

They were cousins, Portia had been informed, although several times removed, much of an age, and very old friends.

"Right, then!" Lady O said, the instant he was settled. "What are we to do about this nonsense? Horrible mess, but there's no sense in the whole company suffering."

"How did Ambrose take it?" his lordship asked. "Will he prove difficult, do you think?"

Lady O snorted. "I should think he'll be glad if nothing more is ever said. Shocked to his toes—he went white as a sheet. Couldn't get a word out. Never seen a would-be politician so lost for words."

"I should think," Simon said, propping a shoulder against the bedpost, "that this would be a case of least said, soonest mended."

Portia perched on the edge of the bed as Lord Netherfield nodded.

"Aye, you're most likely right. Poor Calvin—no wonder he was in such a state. Last thing in the world he'd want at present, to take up an intrigue with a female like Kitty. Here he is, trying to get her father's support for his cause, and there she is, flinging herself at his head!"

Lady O looked from one face to the other, then nodded. "We're in agreement, then. Nothing of any great moment occurred, nothing need be said—all is perfectly normal. No doubt if we stick to that line, the others will, too. No reason Catherine should have to weather having a disaster of a house party just because her daughter-in-law's lost her wits. Hopefully, that mother of hers will straighten her out."

Decision made and judgment delivered, Lady O

sank back on her pillows. She waved at his lordship and Simon. "You two may take yourselves off. You"—she pointed at Portia—"wait here. I want to talk to you."

Simon and Lord Netherfield left. When the door was once more closed, Portia turned to Lady O, only to discover she had shut her eyes. "What did you want to talk to me about?"

One lid rose; one black eye glinted. "I believe I've already advised you against spending all your time in any man's pocket?"

Portia blushed.

Lady O humphed and closed her eyes. "The music room should be safe enough. Go and practice your scales."

An imperious wave accompanied the order. Portia considered, then obeyed.

Their plan to keep the house party on an even keel should have worked. Would have worked if Kitty had behaved as they'd all expected. However, instead of being sunk in mortification, quiet, careful of her manners, especially careful to toe every social line and transgress no more, she swept into the drawing room and proceeded to give a command performance in the role of "the injured party."

She didn't utter a single word about the afternoon's debacle; it was the set of her face, the tilt of her chin, the extraordinary elevation of her nose that communicated her feelings. Her reaction.

Sweeping up to Lucy and Mrs. Buckstead, she placed her hand on Lucy's arm, and inquired solicitously, "I do hope you met some entertaining gentlemen this afternoon, my dear?"

Lucy blinked, then stammered a vague answer. Mrs. Buckstead, made of sterner stuff, inquired after Kitty's health.

Kitty waved, limpidly dismissive. "Of course, I did feel let down. However, I do think one should not let such wounding behavior on the part of others overwhelm one, don't you?"

Even Mrs. Buckstead didn't know how to answer that. With a smile and glittering eyes, Kitty moved on.

Her high-handed, arrogant behavior overset everyone, left them off-balance, totally unsure what to do. No one could understand what was going on. What were they witnessing? Nothing made any kind of social sense.

Dinner, far from being the agreeable, soothing if quiet affair they'd all hoped for, was subdued to the point of discomfort, all laughter in abeyance, talk suppressed. No one knew what to say.

When the ladies removed to the drawing room, Cecily and Annabelle, along with Lucy, encouraged by their mothers, retired early, claiming tiredness after the long day. Portia would have liked to leave, too, but felt compelled to remain in support of Lady O.

The conversation remained stilted. Kitty continued to play the martyr; Lady Glossup was at a loss to know how to deal with her, and Mrs. Archer, all but visibly wringing her hands, starting every time anyone directed a remark her way, was no use at all.

It soon became apparent that, far from coming to rescue them, the gentlemen had decided to leave them to their fate. And Kitty.

It was difficult to blame them; if the ladies—including Lady O, who sat openly frowning at Kitty—could not fathom what was going on, the men must be completely at sea.

Accepting the inevitable with true grace, Lady Glossup called for the tea trolley. They all remained just long enough to do justice to one cup, then rose and retired.

After seeing Lady O to her room, Portia retreated to her own chamber, high in the east wing. The window overlooked the gardens; she paced before it, frowning at the floor, oblivious of the silvered view.

She'd told Simon she believed that Kitty did not understand or value trust; she'd been speaking of trust between two people, but the performance they'd just witnessed had confirmed her view, albeit in a different context.

They all felt—they'd all reacted—as if Kitty had broken a social trust, that she'd betrayed them by refusing to follow any of the patterns they recognized. The patterns of social commerce, of civility, the underlying structure of how they related one to the other.

Their reaction had been quite profound, the gentlemen's refusal to return to the drawing room a very definite statement.

An emotional statement—indeed, they'd all reacted emotionally, instinctively, deeply disturbed by Kitty's breaking the social code they all held in common.

Portia stopped, stared out at the darkened gardens, but didn't truly see them.

Trust and emotion were closely linked. One led to the other; if one was prodded, the other responded.

Frowning, she sat on the window seat; after a moment, she crossed her forearms on the sill and rested her chin upon them.

Kitty wanted love. In her heart, Portia knew that was so. Kitty was searching for that which so many other ladies looked for, but in Kitty's case, with her unrealistic expectations, love was no doubt highly colored, a passionate, overpowering emotion that rose up and swept one away.

Unless she missed her guess, Kitty subscribed to the idea that passion came first, that highly charged physical intimacy was the path, the gateway to deep and meaningful emotional attachment. Presumably she believed that if the passion was not sufficiently intense, then the love she imagined would ultimately arise from it would not be sufficiently powerful—powerful enough to hold her interest, to satisfy her craving.

That would explain why she did not value Henry's gentle devotion, why she seemed bent on raising an illicit and powerful lust in some other man.

Portia grimaced.

Kitty was wrong.

If only she could explain it to her . . .

Impossible, of course. Kitty would never take advice from an unmarried, virginal, near-apeleader-cum-bluestocking on the subject of love and how to secure it.

A soft breeze wafted through the window, stirring the heavy air. It was silent outside, dark but not black, cooler than indoors.

Portia rose, shook out her skirts, and headed for the door. She couldn't sleep yet; the atmosphere in the house was oppressive, uncertain, not at peace. A walk in the gardens would calm her, let her thoughts settle.

The morning room doors were still open to the terrace; she walked through and out, into the welcome softness of the night. The scents of the summer garden wreathed around her as she strolled toward the lake; night stock, jasmine, and heavier perfumes mingled and teased her senses.

Moving through the shadows, she glimpsed a man—one of the gentlemen—standing on the lawns not far from the house. He was looking out into the darkness, apparently lost in thought. The path to the lake took her nearer; she recognized Ambrose, but he gave no sign of noticing her.

She was in no mood for polite conversation; she was sure Ambrose wasn't either. Keeping to the shadows, she left him to his thoughts.

A little farther on, while crossing one of the many intersecting paths, she glanced to her right, and saw the young gypsy-cum-gardener—Dennis, she'd heard Lady Glossup call him—standing absolutely still in the shadows along the minor path.

She continued on without pause, sure Dennis hadn't seen her. As before when she and Simon had seen him, his attention was focused on the private wing of the house. Presumably, he'd retreated deeper into the gardens because of Ambrose's presence.

Quelling a frown, she pushed the matter from her mind; it left a lingering distaste. She didn't want to dwell on what Dennis's nocturnal vigil might mean.

The idea naturally brought Kitty to mind—she bundled her out of her thoughts, too. What had she been thinking about before?

Trust, emotion, and passion.

And love.

Kitty's goal, and the stepping-stones to it that she was quite sure Kitty had scrambled. Kitty was approaching them in the wrong order, at least to her mind.

So what was the right order?

Letting her feet lead her down the last stretch of lawn to the lake, she considered. Trust and emotion were linked, true enough, but people being people, trust came first.

Once trust was there, emotion could grow—once one felt safe enough to let emotional ties, with their consequent vulnerability, develop.

As for passion—physical intimacy—that, surely, was an expression of emotion, a physical expression of an emotional connectedness; how could it be anything else?

Engrossed, she took the path to the summerhouse without thought.

Her mind led her inexorably onward in characteristically logical fashion. Walking through the deep shadows, her gaze on the ground, she frowned. By her reasoning, with which she could find no glaring fault, the compulsion to physical intimacy arose from an emotional link that, logically therefore, must already exist.

She'd reached the steps of the summerhouse. She looked up—and saw in the dimness within a tall figure uncurl his long legs and slowly come to his feet.

In order to feel the compulsion to intimacy, the emotional link must already be there.

For a long moment, she stood looking into the summerhouse, at Simon, waiting, silent and still in the dark. Then she lifted her skirts, climbed the steps, and went in.

CHAPTER 8

The crucial question, of course, was what emotion was it that was growing between her and Simon. Was it lust, desire, or something deeper?

Whatever it was, she could feel it rising like heat between them as she walked across the bare boards—straight into his arms.

They closed around her; she lifted her face and their lips met.

In a kiss that acknowledged the power shimmering through them, yet held it at bay.

She drew back, looked into his face. "How did you know I'd come out here?"

"I didn't." His lips twisted, perhaps wrily—she couldn't tell in the shadows. "James and Charlie decamped to the tavern in Ashmore. I wasn't in the mood for ale and darts—I cried off, and came here."

Simon drew her closer until her thighs met his. There was no resistance in her, yet she was watching, thinking . . .

He bent his head and took her lips, toyed with them until she threw aside her distance and answered him, kissed him back, taunted him. Then surrendered her mouth when he responded, wrapped her arms about his neck, and clung as he devoured.

And they were there, once again, at the center of a rising storm. Desire and pure passion licked about them, sending heat across their skins, feeding a yearning in their souls.

They broke from the kiss only to gauge the other's commitment, eyes meeting briefly from under heavy lids. Neither could truly see in the darkness, yet the touch of a gaze was enough. To reassure, to have her pressing closer, to have his arms tightening before he angled his head and their lips met again.

Together, they stepped into the furnace. Knowingly. He didn't need to urge her; her hand metaphorically in his, she stepped over the threshold at his side. They both welcomed the fire, the flames that caressed, that flared and grew.

Until they were both heated, burning, hungry for more.

He stepped back, taking her with him. The edge of the sofa met the back of his legs; he sat, sweeping her onto his lap, their lips parting for only a second before coming together again.

Her hand touched his cheek, caressed, cradled as she pressed a blatant invitation upon him. Where others might be reticent, she was bold, direct. Definite.

Sure. She sighed with satisfaction when he slid

her loosened gown from her shoulders and laid her breasts bare, urged him on when he bent his head, set lips and hands to the swollen mounds, and feasted.

Her skin was unbelievably fine, so white it almost glowed, so delicate his fingertips tingled as they traced. Tightly puckered, her nipples beckoned; he took one in his mouth and suckled deeply, deeply, until she cried out, her fingers clenching tight on his skull.

Her breathing was rapid, fractured, when he lifted his head. Their lips met, brushed. From under heavy lids, their gazes met in a fleeting touch; their breaths mingled; heat lapped and wrapped about them.

"More." Her whisper was like a waft of flame against his lips, through his mind.

His body was already tight, muscles rigid with desire, locked by his will against the all but over-powering need to seize, to take. To claim.

But not yet.

He didn't bother asking if she was sure. Setting his lips to hers, he drew her back into his arms, sank back into the sofa, drawing her with him, across his lap. Her knees were curled alongside his thigh; lying back, holding her to their kiss, he sent one hand stroking down her back, over the swell of her hip, tracing down the long line of her legs.

Drew her down into the heated darkness, step by small step drawing her deeper into the realm where passion and primitive wants held sway.

Where the need to be touched grew and swelled to a compulsion, where the compulsion to be intimately known became an overriding need.

When he drew her skirts up and slipped his hand beneath, the only murmur she made was one of encouragement. He fought the urge to send her wits spinning, to befuddle her until he had captured her; with her, he was following a different script, one designed to capture more than just her body. He wanted her mind and her soul as well.

So he kept their kiss light, enough for her to be aware, to know, not just what he was doing, but every touch, every caress, every intimate liberty. And to know he knew it, too.

She was wearing silk stockings. His fingertips traced her calf, then trailed upward; he cupped the back of her knee, then slowly stroked higher, finding her garter, circling it with his fingers.

He felt the shudder that went through her when he reached higher and touched her bare skin. Like her breasts, fine, delicate, warm with desire. He traced, and knew she was with him, that her awareness was focused on the shifting connection between his hand and her thigh.

The edge of her chemise trapped his fingers; he flicked them free, slid his hand beneath the fine silk, cruising over the bare skin of her hip, over her bare bottom, over skin that heated and dewed at his touch.

She shuddered and clung to the kiss, for one moment shaken; he soothed with his lips, with his tongue, with his hand slowly, possessively, stroking, then, when she eased, more explicitly exploring.

She shivered, but stayed with him—followed and felt as he wished. Experienced the thrills, both his and her own, as they took the next step into intimacy.

When they'd both had their fill, he traced forward, over her hip, splayed his fingers over her bare stomach. Felt again the shudder of pure awareness that racked her, sensed her sudden tensing.

Felt forced to breathe against her swollen lips, "You're sure?"

She dragged in a breath, her breasts swelling against his chest. "Touch me—touch me there."

He didn't wait for further direction, needed no detailed instruction. Taking her lips again, taking her mouth, he waited only until he sensed her awareness join with his again before sliding his hand lower, tracing the sweet curve of her stomach down to the profusion of soft curls between her thighs.

Stroking slowly, deliberately, through them, he touched her, set his fingers to her softest flesh and traced, explored, learned. And still she was with him, sharing every sensual moment, every single tactile impression . . . never before had he been so aware of a woman beneath his hands.

The knowledge of what that would translate to once he had her beneath him, body to body, skin to naked skin, sent a shaft of pure heat to his groin.

He was aching, had been since she'd walked so confidently into his arms; pure torment was only a heartbeat away.

Yet the moment held the power to command him—for once helped in holding the raging need at bay. This—she—was too important, this conquest above all others meant life and death to him.

Fingertips throbbing, acutely sensitive, he eased her thighs wider, parted her soft folds, traced, teased, tantalized, until she moved against his hand, deliberately, wantonly—with her usual decision demanding more.

Her fingers were lost in his hair, blindly clinging; he opened her and eased one finger into her scalding sheath. Her slickness burned him, seared through him, tempted beyond belief. He could barely breathe—couldn't think beyond the all but blinding surge of passion, the welling need to bury himself in the sweet feminine flesh his fingers so artfully teased.

Grimly, he held on, held the primitive urge back, ruthlessly contained. It didn't fade but simply hardened, solidified into a brutally painful reality that would not leave him.

It was enough to let him go on, to continue along the path he'd mapped unmindful of the price he would later pay.

Caught in the coils of passion, deeper than she'd imagined might be, Portia was only dimly aware of that fractional hiatus—the momentary shifting of his attention—before it returned, in full force, to her. To where he was touching her, caressing her, repetitively teasing in some way she didn't understand.

Her body seemed to know, to recognize some pattern that was beyond her conscious mind. She had to let it lead her, had to follow mentally behind, learning, seeing, realizing.

Feeling. She'd never imagined that physical sensation could be this acute, this consuming. His lips never left hers, his arm around her supported her, the hard wall of his chest was close, reassuring in the face of the whirlpool of sensations swirling through her, buffeting her mind, dragging at her senses.

The fact that his hand lay between her thighs, that he'd eased them apart and was stroking her there, her flesh slick and wet, swollen and hot, should have overwhelmed her, but did not. She could sense the heat, the furnace her own body had become, the deeper heat that flared within when he probed, then opened her and penetrated more deeply.

Her breath caught, her nerves, until then sensitized and alive, started to curl. Tight. Then tighter. Her muscles started to tense, but in some new and novel way.

Lungs locked, she gasped through their kiss, clung to him as between her thighs, deep inside her, sensation built.

He was stoking it deliberately; she knew that much. Knew this was what she'd asked for, what she needed to know, wanted to know.

She let go, let slide the last vestiges of inhibition,

and let the tide welling inside sweep her up. Sweep her on.

Into a landscape of sensation. Up to some pinnacle of cataclysmic feeling.

Her senses expanded until they filled her mind; her body felt aflame. He reached deeper within her; a rush of rapture flowed down her veins, under her skin, tightening her nerves, driving her senses . . .

Until they fractured. Shattered.

Sharp, almost biting delight gripped her, held her in a vise, poured radiant pleasure through her.

The wave swept on, past, through her, leaving in its wake a sense of earthly bliss. A sense of floating in tactile glory, lapped by waves of delight.

Gradually, the waves subsided; sensation diminished, the feelings ebbed. His hand left her.

To her surprise, she felt empty. Incomplete.

Unfulfilled.

As her wits returned fully, she made the connection. Realized this was a two-act play and he'd stopped at the intermission.

And had no intention of going any further.

She knew without asking; his decision was there, solid and real in his heavily locked muscles, in the brutual tension riding him.

In confirmation, like a curtain falling, he flipped down her skirts and locked his hand over her hip.

She had absolute confidence in his self-mastery. Drawing back from the kiss, she boldly reached between them, traced the hard line of his erection, the solid weight she could feel riding against her thigh.

Closed her hand as well as she could; felt him shift, heard the hiss of his indrawn breath.

Leaned close and whispered against his lips. "You want me."

The sound he made was guttural, a strangled laugh. "You can hardly doubt it."

She couldn't, not with the evidence burning her palm, yet the degree of that want, the sheer power of his desire was a surprise—a shock.

Even more a temptation.

Yet the realization—the physical fact, an ephemeral knowledge brought to life, translated to flesh and blood—sent a shiver of pure caution, an elemental sensing of danger coursing through her.

He drew in a tight breath; eyes closed, he pressed his hand between them, closed it over hers. Tightened her grip on him.

Then, slowly, drew her hand away.

He breathed out; she couldn't truly see his face in the darkness, but would have sworn the harsh planes had grown even more hard-edged.

Against his lips, she breathed, "Why?"

She didn't need to be more specific. He would know even better than she that he could have taken her if he'd wished.

His gaze touched her face, traveled it, then he lifted his hand and traced a finger across her lips. She scented, and tasted, her essence. Then he leaned close and kissed her, kissed it from her lips.

"Are you ready for that?"

His words drifted through her mind, not really a question.

She drew back, looked into his eyes, dark, shadowed, unreadable. Could still feel his desire, the powerful need that was riding him. Answered truthfully. "No. But—"

He kissed her; stopped her words. She hesitated for an instant, the understanding that he did not wish her to utter them, didn't wish to hear what she would have said—what he'd known she'd been about to say—sweeping through her. Then she returned the kiss. Gratefully.

Sensed the heat slowly dying between them. Let it fade. Ebb. Until . . .

Their lips parted, yet they remained close. Their gazes touched. Lifting one hand, she traced his chiseled cheek. Put their thoughts into words. "Next time."

He drew breath, chest swelling. Then he gripped her waist and eased her back. "If you wish it."

If you wish it.

The hardest words he'd ever had to say, yet he'd had to say them.

His hand locked about hers, they walked back to the house; a short discussion over whether or not he needed to escort her back to her room—a discussion he'd won—had helped get them back onto something resembling their normal footing.

Not that that was the same as it had been a week ago.

All well and good, but the desire now riding him had spurs a foot long. Never before had the need for a woman, let alone a particular woman, been so consuming; never before had he had to mask, to mute his natural inclinations to this extent.

Having to let her go tonight, to let her escape him, wasn't a script of which his inclinations, his warrior instincts, approved. Having to battle them, having to keep a cool head while his body went up in flames, did not please his temper at all.

A fact of which she was well aware; she'd been shooting quick glances at him ever since they'd left the summerhouse. His face, set and hard, bore witness to his feelings—feelings she knew him well enough to guess.

She knew, but he seriously doubted she understood. For all her talk of learning about sex and trust and marriage, he very much doubted that it had occurred to her yet just where they were— what the next stage encompassed, what destiny she was flirting with.

It would. Which was why he had to play a long game. To get what he wanted, to secure all he wanted, he needed her absolute, unqualified trust.

And the only way to get that was to earn it.

No shortcuts, no sleight of hand.

No pressure. Of any kind.

He felt like growling.

If you wish it.

When she stopped and thought about what that "it" encompassed, he was going to have problems enough. Their past wasn't going to make her smile fondly and forge ahead without long and earnest consideration; her temper, and his, weren't going to make her decision to embark on the final stage any easier.

As for her intelligence, her willfulness, and even worse, her independence . . . stacked against the panaply of his most fundamental characteristics, with which she was extremely familiar, convincing her to risk giving herself to him was going to be an uphill battle. He needed every advantage he could gain.

He trudged on through the balmy night. She kept pace with him easily, her stride long and free.

One consolation—she'd never been a chatterer. She spoke when she wished to; with him, she never seemed to feel the need, as so many other females did, to fill the silences. They lay between them, not awkward but comfortable, like well-worn shoes.

Familiarity, and her mind; two aspects from which, if he was cunning, he could wrest some advantage. She was, always had been, far more inclined to logical thinking than any other woman he'd known. He had some chance, therefore, of guessing her thoughts, predicting her tack, and by judicious prodding, herding her in the direction he wished.

Just as long as she didn't guess his ulterior motive.

If she did . . .

What pernicious fate had decreed he should set his sights on taking to wife the one woman he knew beyond all doubt he would never be able safely to manipulate?

Stifling a sigh, he looked up. Just as Portia stiffened.

He looked ahead, his hand tightening about hers, and saw the young gardener, once again watching the private wing of the house.

Portia tugged; he nodded, and they moved on, slipping through the shadows to the garden hall.

The house lay in darkness; no one else was about. They passed the candle left burning at the bottom of the stairs and he saw she was frowning.

"What?"

She blinked, then said, "Dennis—the gardener—was there when I came out."

He grimaced, and waved her up the stairs. When they stepped into the gallery, he murmured, "His fixation's unhealthy. I'll mention it to James."

Portia nodded. It was on the tip of her tongue to mention she'd seen Ambrose, too, but he hadn't been there when they'd returned. No reason for Simon to mention him, too.

They'd reached her room; she tugged and Simon stopped. She indicated the door with her head.

Simon glanced at it, then shifted his hold, twined his fingers with hers and lifted her hand to his lips. "Sleep well."

She met his hooded gaze, then stepped close,

stretched up, and touched her lips to his. "And you."

Sliding her hand from his, she opened the door and slipped through, closing it softly behind her.

A full minute passed before she heard him walk away.

Realizing just how real, how physical, Simon's desire for her was had definitely been something of a shock. A bigger, more eye-opening shock than all else she'd learned thus far.

It was also a temptation, a bigger temptation than all else put together, to go forward and learn what lay beyond, what, for them, was the emotion compelling them to intimacy. The emotion that, with every look, every shared moment, seemed to grow stronger, more definite.

More real.

That was somewhat shocking, too.

Portia halted on the terrace and looked about. After breakfasting with Lady O, she'd left her to dress and grasped the moment to herself—to stroll and think.

After what had transpired last night in the summerhouse, thinking ranked high on her list of things to do.

Traces of dew still remained on the grass, but wouldn't last long. The sun was already beaming down; it was going to be another warm day. The house party was decamping, taking a long drive through Cranborne Chase, then lunching at an inn before returning. Everyone was hoping a day away from the Hall would lift the atmosphere and bury the memories of yesterday.

The shrubbery was one area she'd yet to explore; stepping down from the terrace, she headed for the archway cut into the first hedge. Like all the regions of the Glossup Hall gardens, the shrubbery was extensive, yet she'd wandered only a little way when she heard voices.

She slowed.

"Don't you find the question of its paternity quite tantalizing?"

Paternity? Shock rooted Portia to the spot. It was Kitty who'd spoken.

"I really don't feel it's incumbent on me to guess. No doubt you'll reveal all when you're ready."

Winifred. The sisters were on the other side of the hedge from Portia. The green-walled path in which she stood turned farther along; presumably there was a courtyard of some sort, with a fountain or pool.

"Oh, I think you'll be interested in this. It touches so **close,** you see."

Kitty's tone was that of a vindictive child hugging a particularly obnoxious secret to her bosom, biding her time, keen to make most misery; it was plain who she wished Winifred to imagine was the father of her child.

There was a rustle and swish of skirts, then Winifred spoke again. "You know, my dear, there are times when I look at you and can only wonder if Mama played Papa for a fool."

The contempt in the words was all the more powerful because they were uttered in Winifred's soft voice. Worse, there was something else there, edging the contempt, that was even less pleasant.

"And now," Winifred said, "if you'll excuse me, I must get ready for the drive. Desmond's taking me up in his curricle."

Portia turned and walked quickly out of the shrubbery. She swung into the rose garden; sniffing the large blooms, she waited, one eye on the lawn, until she saw Winifred walk past and go into the house. When Kitty did not immediately appear, Portia started for the house herself.

Glancing back across the lawn at the shrubbery, she caught a glimpse of Dennis, weeding a bed at the foot of a hedge, one of the hedges that must enclose the shrubbery courtyard. He glanced her way; there were dark circles under his eyes.

Small wonder. Portia climbed to the terrace and entered the house.

She'd promised to return and help Lady O downstairs; when she reached her room, Lady O was ready, sitting waiting in the armchair by the hearth. One look at Portia's face and she waved the maid away. The instant the door shut, she demanded, "Right, then! Let's have your report."

She blinked. "Report?"

"Precisely—tell me what you've learned." Lady O waved with her cane. "And for goodness sake, sit down. You're almost as bad as a Cynster, towering over me."

Her lips not entirely straight, she sat, her mind whirling.

"Now, then!" Lady O leaned on her cane and fastened her black eyes, gimlet-fashion, on her. "Tell me all."

She looked into those eyes; she couldn't think of words in which to tell even half of it. "I've learned that things are . . . not as obvious as I'd supposed."

Lady O's brows rose. "Indeed. What things?"

"All sorts of things." She'd learned long ago not to let the old harridan unnerve her. "But never mind that. There's something else—something I've just learned that I think you should know."

"Oh?" Lady O was fly enough to know a distraction when she heard one, but curiosity, as Portia knew, was her besetting sin. "What?"

"I was just strolling in the shrubbery . . ."

She recounted as accurately as she could the exchange she'd overheard. When she finished, she studied Lady O's face. Quite how she managed it, Portia didn't know, but the old lady succeeded in conveying supreme disgust while her expression remained otherwise inscrutable.

"Do you think Kitty's really pregnant? Or was she making it up to hurt Winifred?"

Lady O snorted. "Is she stupid enough, immature enough, for that?"

Portia didn't answer. She watched Lady O

closely, glimpsed the possibilities being weighed behind her black eyes. "I've thought back—she hasn't been down to breakfast since we've been here. I didn't think anything of it before, but given her liking for male company and the fact the gentlemen gather in the breakfast parlor every morning, perhaps that, too, is a sign?"

Lady O humphed. "How did Kitty sound?"

"Kitty?" Portia replayed the exchange in her mind. "The second time she spoke, she was like a nasty child. But now you ask, the first time, she sounded a touch hysterical."

Lady O grimaced. "That doesn't sound promising." Thumping her cane on the floor, she heaved herself out of the chair.

Portia rose and went to take her arm. "So what do you think?"

"If I had to guess, I'd say the foolish gel really is increasing, but regardless of the truth of who the father is, she's unfortunately witless enough to use the question in her mad games." Lady O halted while Portia opened the door. Gripping Portia's arm again, she met her gaze. "Mark my words, that gel will come to a bad end."

She could hardly nod; she inclined her head a fraction, then steered Lady O to the stairs.

Cranborne Chase, with its towering oaks and beeches, provided a welcome respite both from the weather and the constraint that had gripped the party.

"If circumstances had been otherwise, I'm sure Lady Calvin would leave." On Simon's arm, Portia strolled beneath an avenue of beeches.

"She can't. Ambrose is here on business, so to speak. He's been busy sounding out Lord Glossup and Mr. Buckstead as well as Mr. Archer—"

"And Lady Calvin will always do right by her son. That's what I mean."

They were far enough from the rest of the party, all ambling in the cooler air beneath the thickly leaved trees, to speak frankly. As a group, dispersed in a handful of carriages, they'd spent the late morning driving slowly down the winding lanes threading through the ancient forest, before turning aside into a tiny hamlet that boasted an excellent inn for a prearranged meal. The inn was just down the lane up which they'd wandered, directed by the innkeeper to a small dell from which numerous walks radiated, a gentle landscape for a postprandial stroll.

Lord Netherfield and Lady O had declined the delights of the forest and remained at the inn; all the others were stretching their legs prior to piling into the carriages once more.

Halting, Portia swung about and looked back down the slope. They had chosen to walk up the steepest path; none of the others had followed. Everyone was still in view, spread out here and there below.

Locating Kitty, flanked by Lady Glossup and Mrs. Archer, she grimaced. "I don't think what they're trying to do with Kitty will serve."

Simon glanced down at the trio. "Sequestering her?"

"There's not much she can do about it here, but I'll wager she'll be even worse when we get back to the Hall."

Simon humphed. After a moment, he asked, "What's the matter?"

She glanced up, realized he'd been watching her face. She'd been watching Kitty, studying her sulky expression, her disaffected state. Trying to reconcile that with how she herself would feel if she'd learned she was carrying a child. She smiled briefly, shook her head, turned away from Kitty. "Nothing. Just woolgathering."

His eyes remained on her face; before he could press, she gripped his arm. "Come on—let's go up to that rise."

He acquiesced and they did, discovering an abbreviated view into a deeper, less accessible dell, where a family of deer grazed undisturbed.

A call summoned them back to the others and thence back to the inn. A slight altercation ensued over who would sit where for the return journey; everyone ignored Kitty's demands to go in James's curricle. Lucy and Annabelle squeezed onto the seat beside James and they left, following Desmond, who had Winifred beside him; Simon, with Portia alongside and Charlie hanging on behind, followed, leaving the rest to the heavier coaches.

The curricles reached the Hall well in advance of

the rest of the party. They drove straight to the stables. The gentlemen handed the ladies down; Winifred, rather pale, excused herself and walked quickly toward the house. The gentlemen became engrossed in a discussion of horseflesh. Portia would have joined them, but Lucy and Annabelle were clearly looking to her for a lead.

Inwardly sighing, resigning herself to a quiet hour indoors, she led them back to the house.

They were waiting in the morning room when the coaches finally lumbered up. Lucy and Annabelle, both dutifully embroidering, raised their heads and looked toward the front hall.

Portia could hear the raised voices even before people entered the hall. Suppressing a grimace, she rose.

The two girls glanced at her. Kitty's voice reached them, shrill and sharp; their eyes widened.

"Stay here," Portia told them. "There's no need for you to go out. I'll tell your mamas you're here."

They both bent grateful looks on her; with a reassuring smile, she headed for the door. In the hall, she paid no attention to anyone else, but mentioned their daughters' whereabouts to Mrs. Buckstead and Lady Hammond, then went straight to Lady O's side.

Lady O nodded in curt thanks and gripped her arm; the strength of her clawlike grip was a good indication of her temper, of how aggravated that was. Lord Netherfield, until then holding by Lady O's side, nodded his approval, cast one censorious look at his granddaughter-in-law and headed for the library.

Portia helped Lady O up the stairs and to her room. Once the door was closed, she braced herself for a diatribe; Lady O was nothing if not outspoken.

But this time, Lady O seemed too tired; Portia, concerned, helped her quickly onto her bed.

As she straightened, Lady O caught her eye. Answered the question in her mind. "Yes, it was bad. Worse than I'd anticipated."

Portia looked into her old eyes. "What did she say?"

Lady O humphed. "That's just it—it wasn't so much what she did say, as what she didn't."

After a long moment of staring across the room, Lady O closed her eyes and sighed. "Leave me, child, I'm tired."

Portia turned to the door.

Lady O continued, "And there's something very wrong going on."

Portia headed downstairs via the less-frequented stairs in the west wing. She didn't want to meet any of the others; she needed some time on her own.

A cloud had descended on Glossup Hall, both literally and figuratively. A storm was blowing up; the sun had disappeared behind leaden clouds, and the air had grown oppressive.

The atmosphere in the house was even heavier.

Brooding, tending toward dark. She was hardly a sensitive soul, yet she felt it. The effect on the Hammond girls, even on Lady Hammond, even on Mrs. Buckstead, was apparent.

Two more days—people would remain until then, as originally planned; leaving earlier would smack of an insult to Lady Glossup, one she had done nothing to deserve. Yet none of the guests would linger. She and Lady O had planned to return to London.

She wondered where Simon intended to go.

Reaching the ground floor, she heard the clink of billiard balls. She glanced down the west wing corridor; through the open door of the billiard room she could hear the low murmur of masculine voices, Simon's among them.

She went on, through the garden hall and out onto the lawns.

Looking up, she considered the clouds. Despite the closeness, there was no sign of any storm activity yet—no lightning, no thunder, no scent of rain. Just the heavy stillness.

Grimacing, she headed for the shrubbery. Surely the safest place in which to avoid overhearing any further revelations. Lightning, after all, did not strike twice in the same place.

Passing under the green archway, she strolled into the hedged walk; she'd reached the same spot as in her earlier foray when the old saw that theory frequently did not predict practice was proven.

"You witless child! **Of course** the babe's

Henry's. You **cannot** be so foolish as to suggest anything else."

Mrs. Archer, one step away from hysteria.

"It's not me who's foolish." Kitty's voice lashed. "And I won't have it, I tell you! But you needn't worry. I know who the father is. It's simply a matter of persuading him to see things my way, then all will be well."

Silence greeted that, then Mrs. Archer—Portia could almost hear her dragging in a deep breath—asked, her voice quavering, "Your way. Things always have to be **your** way. But what way is that?"

Portia wanted to turn and leave, but she understood precisely what Mrs. Archer was asking, what she feared. The matter lay too close to Portia's heart not to know . . .

"I told you before." Kitty's voice strengthened. "I want excitement. I want thrills! I won't simply sit by and have a baby—swell up and grow ugly—"

"You're a **fool**!" Mrs. Archer sounded distraught. "You married Henry—you wanted to—"

"Only because you told me I would be a lady and have everything I want—"

"But not this! Not like this. You can't—"

"I **can**!"

Portia swung on her heel and stalked away, her footfalls muffled by the thick grass. Her emotions were roiling, she couldn't think—didn't want to think about what Kitty intended. She walked fast, furiously, her skirts swishing, her gaze locked on the lawn before her.

She walked into Simon.

He caught her, steadied her, looked into her face, looked over her head toward the shrubbery. "What happened?"

One glance at his face, at the rocklike planes, the feel of the tensing muscles under his sleeve, had her gulping in a breath, quickly shaking her head. "I need to get out of here. At least for an hour or two."

He studied her face. "We can walk to the lookout."

"Yes." She hauled in another breath. "Let's."

CHAPTER 9

They walked side by side across the gardens, then on via the path through the woods. She didn't take Simon's arm, he didn't offer it, yet despite the lack of touch, she was very much aware he was with her. Beside her, not crowding her. Given the turmoil her temper was in, she appreciated the fact and was grateful.

He, of course, was the last person she'd actually wanted to meet, given the subject she wanted—**needed**—to think about. To dissect, examine, ultimately to understand. Given the nature of that subject, given he was so intimately involved, literally as well as figuratively, she'd expected to feel some degree of . . . not shyness, but uncertainty when alone with him. When close to him.

Instead, all she'd felt, still felt, was safe, both now and throughout the day. Not necessarily completely comfortable, but assuredly not trepidatious. She was absolutely certain he would always behave predictably, that he, all he was, would never change; he would never be, could never be, the source of any threat to her.

Not physically. Emotionally might be a different tale.

Mentally grimacing, she kept her eyes down and walked steadily on. Aware of him prowling beside her.

Aware she drew comfort from his presence.

It was Kitty and her doings that had once again distracted her, this time disturbing her in a more profound way. In response, it was doubtless only natural to draw close to those she understood and trusted. Like Lady O.

Like Simon.

They emerged onto the side of the ridge, a stretch of path where the wood fell back and the winds blew up from the distant sea. A breath of freshness reached them, the first stirrings of the storm still far away. The waft of cooler air lifted the curls from her nape, sent others dancing about her face.

She halted, tucking the wayward strands back, lifting her face to the faint breeze.

Simon stopped by her shoulder, raised his head, looked out over the fields to the black clouds roiling on the distant horizon. Then he let his gaze swing back to Portia's face.

He hadn't been surprised to find her in the gardens. Any other lady would have been resting, recuperating from the exertions of the day. Not Portia.

His lips twitched at a mental image of her listless and die-away, lethargic on her bed. She was

the most energetic woman he knew, full of restless, seemingly boundless energy, one facet of her
that had always attracted him in a flagrantly physical way.

He'd never known her to pretend to a delicacy
with which she wasn't afflicted. Her unflagging
zest had always been enough to keep up with him.

Quite possibly in any sphere.

He let his gaze sweep down, over her supple,
slender figure, down over the length of her long,
long legs. Poised as she was, she vibrated with
vitality, with vigorous life.

Definitely a point in her favor.

Currently, however, she was as distracted as he'd
ever seen her.

"What's the matter?"

She glanced at him, searched his face briefly,
confirming what she'd heard in his tone—that he
wasn't about to be fobbed off with anything short
of the truth.

Her lips twisted; she looked back at the view.
"Kitty's pregnant. This morning, I overheard her
telling Winifred—trying to get Winifred to think
the baby was Desmond's."

He made no effort to mask his distaste. "How
very unappealing."

"The baby isn't Henry's."

"So I would suppose."

She glanced at him, frowned. "Why?"

He met her gaze. Grimaced. "I gather she and
Henry have been estranged for some time." He
hesitated, then continued, "I suspect what we

overheard the other night between Henry and James was discussion of a possible divorce."

"Divorce?"

Portia stared at him. He didn't need to spell out the implications for her; a divorce would mean scandal, and in this case total ostracism for Kitty.

She looked away. "I wonder if Kitty knows?" She paused, then went on, "Just now, I heard Mrs. Archer and Kitty discussing the matter. What Kitty intends to do."

It wasn't his child, yet his gut chilled. "What was she proposing?"

"She doesn't want the child. She doesn't want to grow fat and . . . I think she simply doesn't want anything to get in the way of what she calls excitement—something she considers her due."

He was out of his depth. With a slew of sisters, older and younger, he'd thought he had at least a passing acquaintance with the female psyche, yet Kitty was beyond his comprehension. Portia turned and headed on; he followed, ambling beside her.

Knowing full well that whatever had been bothering her was still exercising her mind. He let her wrestle with it as they trailed along the crest, and through the next section of the wood. When they emerged onto the final open stretch along the ridge above Ashmore village, and the vertical crease between her brows was still there, he stopped. Waited until she realized and turned to look at him questioningly.

"What is it?"

Her eyes remained steady on his, then her lips twisted, and she looked away. He waited, silent; after a moment, she glanced at him. "You have to promise not to laugh."

He opened his eyes wide.

She frowned, looked away, started strolling, paused until he joined her, then walked on but slowly, brows drawn down. "I've been wondering . . . later . . . **after**, if . . . well, would I— **could I**—turn out like Kitty?"

"Like **Kitty**?" For one instant, he couldn't imagine what she meant.

She glanced at his face, frowned harder. "Like Kitty, with her addiction to **excitement**."

He stopped. She did, too.

He couldn't help it. He laughed.

Not even her thinning lips, not even the fury flaring in her eyes could stop him.

"You **promised**!" She swatted him.

That only made stopping all the harder.

"You—!" She biffed him again.

He caught her hands, held them down, locked in his. "No—stop." He dragged in a breath, his gaze on her face. The real worry and confusion in her eyes—clear now she'd lost her temper—hauled him back to sobriety with a thump. She couldn't believe . . . ?

He captured her gaze, held it. "There is no possibility in this world that you could ever be like Kitty. That you would ever convert to something like her." She didn't look convinced. "Believe me—none. No prospect at all."

Narrow-eyed, from behind the black screen of her lashes, she studied his face. "How do you know?"

Because he knew her.

"**You** are not Kitty." He heard the words, dragged in a breath and invested the next phrases with absolute conviction. "You could never—**would never**—behave like her."

She held his gaze, her expression still unsure.

He suddenly realized just what they were talking about—**all** they were talking about. His lungs contracted, his throat tightened as he realized she—they—stood teetering on a precipice. He'd known, expected, would have been shocked if she hadn't had reservations, if she hadn't thought long and hard before giving herself to him.

Knowing her so well, her curiosity, her willful need to know, he'd been confident of her ultimate decision. Never in his wildest dreams had he imagined Kitty would throw up a hurdle, let alone a hurdle like this.

He searched Portia's eyes as she searched his. Hers were so dark, the color of midnight, only strong emotions were easy to define. Now, they were simply less sharp, clouded by uncertainty—an uncertainty that was self-directed, not, as he'd anticipated, directed at him.

She blinked; he sensed her retreating. Instinctively reacted.

"Trust me." He gripped her hands tighter, captured her gaze anew, then he altered his grip and lifted her hands, first one, then the other, to his lips. "Just trust me."

Her eyes had widened. After a moment, she asked, "How can you be so sure?"

"Because it . . ." Lost in her eyes, aware he had to speak the absolute truth, he couldn't for the life of him think of words to describe all that they meant by that, the reality of what they were discussing. "**This**—all that's between us, all that could be—not even that would ever be strong enough to change **you**. To make you into a different person."

She frowned, but in thought, not rejection. He let her draw her hands from his; she turned and faced the fields, looking, perhaps, but not seeing.

After a moment, she swung around and walked on toward the lookout. He stirred, and followed on her heels. They reached the lookout and went inside. She stared out at the Solent. Two feet away, he shoved his hands in his pockets and waited.

He didn't dare touch her, didn't dare press her in any way.

She glanced at his face, then slowly ran her gaze down his frame, as if she could sense the tension investing every muscle. Returning her gaze to his eyes, she raised a brow. "I thought . . . expected you to be more persuasive."

Jaw locked, he shook his head. "The decision's yours. **You** have to make it."

She was going to ask why—he saw it in her eyes—but then she hesitated, looked away.

A minute later, she turned from the view. He followed her out, ducking under the wooden archway; they headed back to the Hall.

They walked in silence, their usual easy, oddly

connected silence. They were aware of each other, yet were content pursuing their own thoughts, knowing the other would not take umbrage, wouldn't expect attention.

His thoughts were all of her, of them. Of what was between them, that suddenly broadening, deepening connection. It was developing in ways he hadn't expected, yet now he saw them, far from reining back—something his rakish self was certain he should do—other instincts, deeper instincts, insisted he should press on, grab, seize, lay claim. That he should be pleased with the strength he sensed, with the emotional depth, with the strands that were being woven from elements unrelated to the physical, linking them in ways he doubted either had foreseen.

He'd recognized from the first that getting her to trust him enough to accept him as her husband would be a difficult task. Doing so against the backdrop of the disintegration of Henry and Kitty's marriage was creating unexpected scenarios, forcing him to consider things, to evaluate aspects, feelings, expectations he otherwise would have taken for granted.

Like the fact he trusted Portia completely, unequivocally—and why. Why the thought of her turning into another Kitty was so ludicrous, why he'd laughed.

She couldn't become another Kitty, and still be Portia.

Her strength of character—that backbone of steel he'd long known in his sisters and recognized long ago, even more intensely, in her—simply wouldn't permit it. In that, he knew her perhaps better than she knew herself.

He had unwavering confidence in her steel.

Never before had he considered that attribute at all necessary in a wife.

Now he realized how precious it was.

Recognized in it a guarantee sufficient to reassure that deeply buried part of him that, even now, even despite his decision and his own rigid will, shied from the mere thought of accepting the vulnerability of the Cynsters' Achilles' heel, from the emotional commitment that, for them, was an inherent part of marriage.

They'd reached the gardens and the wisteria-covered walk. The house loomed ahead.

Putting a hand on her sleeve, he slowed; she halted and turned to him. Sliding his fingers down to her hand, he interdigitated his fingers with hers, looked into her dark eyes.

"One thing I will promise." He raised her hand, placed a kiss in her palm, holding her gaze all the while. "I will never hurt you. Not in any way."

She didn't blink, didn't move; for a long moment, gazes locked, they simply stood. Then she drew breath, inclined her head.

Placing her hand on his arm, he turned to the house.

It was indeed her decision; she was relieved he saw and accepted that.

On the other hand, she wasn't at all certain how to interpret such uncharacteristic magnanimity on his part. Uncharacterisitic it certainly was; he wanted her, desired her—knowing him for the despot he truly was beneath the elegant glamor, Portia required some explanation for his restraint, his patience.

Later that evening, she stood before her window and considered what it might be. And how it might impinge on her decision.

During the half hour in the drawing room, Simon had found a moment to murmur, low enough so only she could hear, the precise location of the bedchamber he'd been given, just in case she needed to know. If she'd thought he was pressuring her she would have glared, but one look into his eyes had confirmed that he was, indeed, battling his own instincts not to do so, and to that point was still holding the line.

She'd inclined her head, then others had joined them, and their privacy was gone. Nevertheless, she remained highly conscious that he was waiting for some sign of her decision.

Throughout dinner, from across the table she'd watched him—covertly, yet if the other guests hadn't been so intent on managing the conversation, keeping it strictly within bounds, someone would have noticed.

Kitty had for once been useful; not, of course, intentionally. She'd reverted to her earlier role, but with greater dramatic flair; tonight, she was a lady grievously misjudged, determinedly, heroically, keeping her chin high despite the slings and arrows of those who should know better.

The ladies had repaired to the drawing room, leaving the gentlemen about the table. No one had had any wish for a lengthy evening; the atmosphere remained close, the emotions swirling between Kitty and various others fraught and tense. The tea trolley arrived early; after one cup, all the ladies had retired.

Which brought Portia to where she was now, staring out at the darkness considering her decision, the one she and only she could make.

For all that, her decision hinged on Simon.

Despite their previous history, indeed in part because of it, she hadn't been surprised when he'd stepped in and consented to act as her guide in her exploration of the physical interactions between a man and a woman. He hadn't approved, not at first, but he'd quickly capitulated once he'd seen she was set on her course; he'd known very well that if he'd refused, she would have gone ahead with some other man. From his insistently protective point of view, her going forward with him was, regardless of all else, better than her going forward with another.

None of which mitigated the facts that he was a Cynster, and she was an Ashford; they were both of the haut ton. If she'd been younger, a more innocent and gentle sort of lady, or one he didn't know well, she would have wagered her pearls any unintentional intimacy would have resulted in a "now I've seduced you, I'll have to marry you" decree.

Luckily, that wasn't the case between them. He did know her—very well. He wouldn't have aided her in her quest for knowledge if he'd believed that in so doing he was committing any dishonorable act; she felt ridiculously pleased that he'd accepted she had as much right to sexual exploration as he.

That right, she assumed, was enough to absolve him of any moral responsibility, any requirement to indulge in high-handed interference and paternalistic disapproval. He'd acted always at her behest, and subject to her active consent.

He wasn't seducing her in the customary sense; he was merely agreeable—available—should she wish to be seduced.

Presumably his steadfast reticence, his determination not to pressure her, was some reflection of that, some convoluted male dictate of what was honorable in such circumstances. Perhaps that was the way a willing seduction was played out.

All that had occurred between them thus far was as she'd wished, as she'd wanted. The decision facing her was whether she wanted more—whether she truly wanted to take the final step, draw aside the last veil, and learn all.

The scholar within her wanted to rush ahead; her more pragmatic side insisted she weigh the pros and cons.

To her mind—even to most other minds—her

age and status as an almost-confirmed apeleader freed her from missish considerations of virginity. If she didn't, at some point, stick her toe in the water and learn what she deemed necessary, then she might well never marry, so what would be the point? For her, virginity was an outdated concept.

The risk of pregnancy was real, but acceptable, one she didn't, in truth, mind running. Unlike Kitty, she wanted children of her own; given she had a strong and supportive family, given she cared little for the social world, there were ways such a circumstance could be managed. Provided she never admitted who the father was; her sense of self-preservation was far too strong to make such a mistake.

Otherwise, Simon's certainty had slain her worry that, if the emotion growing between them proved to be lust, she might become addicted to the physical excitement as Kitty seemed to be; his sincerity and conviction had been too strong to doubt, and his reputation guaranteed he'd had ample opportunity to form an expert opinion on such a question.

All in all, no insurmountable cons presented themselves, not from personal considerations.

As for the pros, she knew what she wanted, what she wished. She wanted to learn **everything** about marriage before she committed herself to the institution; she needed to understand the physical aspects of what she might be getting herself into. The mess Kitty had made of her marriage only underscored the necessity of gaining a proper understanding before approaching the altar; if after all she'd seen this week she allowed herself to make ill-considered choices, she'd never forgive herself.

Understanding marriage in all its aspects had been her initial goal . . . but now there was more. She also wanted to know what the emotional link that had developed between her and Simon truly was—the emotion that made it not just possible, but so very easy to imagine herself going to his bed.

Given Kitty's behavior, learning that, too, seemed wise.

As matters stood, the only risk she could see in going to Simon's bed was an emotional one. And that was hypothetical, something she could only guess at, given she did not yet know what the emotion that impelled her to intimacy with him was.

That emotion and its effect were quite real. Likewise, the risk, one to which she couldn't, with her extensive knowledge of him, close her eyes, nor yet pretend she couldn't see.

What if the emotion growing between them proved to be love?

She had no idea if it might be; along with men and marriage, love had not featured on her list of subjects to be studied.

She hadn't come looking for it; that wasn't why she'd availed herself of his offer to teach her what she wanted to know. Yet she wasn't fool enough, arrogant enough not to wonder, not to acknowledge that, strange though it seemed, the prospect, the possibility, might now be staring her in the face.

Once they'd indulged—once, twice, however many times it took for her to learn all she wished and to identify that emotion—if it wasn't love, then they would part, her experiment concluded, her discovery made. That outcome seemed certain and straightforward. The danger did not lie there.

The threat lay on the other side of the coin. If what lay between them proved to be love, what then?

She knew the answer; if it was love, either her for him or him for her, or both, **and he recognized it**, he would insist on marriage, and she would not easily be able to deny him.

He was a Cynster, after all. Yet if he prevailed, where would that leave her?

Married to a Cynster. Possibly bound by love **and** married to a Cynster—if anything, that was potentially worse. If love ruled them both, then the situation **might** be manageable—she really had no idea—but if love affected one but not the other, the outlook was inherently bleak.

Therein lay the risk.

The question facing her, now, tonight, was would she chance it? In essence, was she game?

She blew out a breath, focused on the silhouettes of the trees outside.

If she didn't pursue the question now—didn't accept his offer to be seduced—they would go their separate ways within days. She would return to Rutlandshire, curiosity aflame; who else would she find to satisfy her need to know? Who else could she trust?

The chances of their meeting again this summer, let alone in suitable surrounds, were slight, and she had no guarantee that he would remain agreeable to teaching her all she wished next month, let alone in three.

Could she bear to retreat, to turn aside, draw back and not know? Could she live without discovering what, for them, physical intimacy truly represented? What it was that drove them to it? Never learn if it was love, whether both of them were affected by it, and what such an outome would mean?

Her lips twisted, wryly self-deprecating. There was no question there. Reckless, often arrogantly heedless, willful to a fault, she didn't have the temperament to turn back. Regardless of the risk.

Yet as matters stood, going to Simon tonight might well be her safest, most sensible option. Others might label her reckless and wild, but that argument made perfect sense to her.

There was no sense wasting time.

In order to reach Simon's room, she had to circle the gallery around the top of the main stairs. Luckily, with all the ladies already in their rooms, there was no one around to see her as she glided from shadow to shadow, past the stairhead and into the corridor leading to the west wing.

At the junction of the west wing and the main house, she had to cross the foyer at the head of the west wing stairs. She'd just entered the open area when she heard heavy footsteps plodding up the stairs.

Quick as a flash, she whisked around, back into the shadows of the corridor she'd just left. The steps came steadily on, two sets, then she heard Ambrose's voice; Desmond replied. She sent up a quick prayer that their rooms were in the west wing and not in the main wing where she presently stood.

She listened; they reached the top of the stairs, discussing dogs, of all things. With barely a pause, they strolled on.

Down the west wing.

Hugely relieved, she hesitated, but knowing which rooms they were in would be useful. Easing from the concealing shadows, hugging the wall, she peeped around the corner.

Both Desmond and Ambrose were well down the corridor; they were nearly at the end when they parted, each entering a room, one to the left, the other to the right.

Letting out the breath she'd been holding, she straightened. Simon had said the third door from the stairs, so she wouldn't need to risk passing Ambrose's or Desmond's doors.

She set out across the foyer. As she passed the stairwell, the clink of billiard balls reached her.

She paused, glanced around, then went quickly to the stairhead. Straining her ears, she could just hear the murmur of voices rising from the billiard room.

Charlie's light voice, James's quick laugh—and Simon's deep drawl.

For one instant, she stood there, eyes narrowing, lips thinning, then she turned on her heel and continued to his room.

Opening the door, she swept in, recalled herself enough to shut the door quietly. Given the number of rooms available, it was unlikely any of the others would be quartered immediately next door, but there was no sense taking unnecessary risks.

She surveyed the room, cloaked in shadows, irritated that Simon wasn't there waiting to greet her. To distract her from thinking about what she was doing. Still, how long could a game of billiards take? She thought, then humphed. Presumably, he'd at least have the sense to come up and see if she'd made use of the information he'd oh-so-subtly imparted.

She moved into the room, ruthlessly quelling the nervous fluttering in her stomach. She'd made her decision; she certainly wasn't about to change her mind. Her courage was more than up to the challenge.

The west wing rooms were not as large as those in the east wing. This wing seemed older; the ceilings were just as high, but the rooms were narrower. There was no armchair by the hearth, no window seat, no dressing table and therefore no stool, just a tallboy. Two upright chairs flanked the shoulder-high chest of drawers, but they were narrow, hardly comfortable.

She looked at the bed. It was the only sensible place to sit and wait. Sweeping forward, she turned and sat. Bounced, approving the thickness and comfort of the mattress.

Wriggling back to lean against the pillows piled against the headboard, she crossed her arms and fixed her gaze on the door. There was, she supposed, another perspective on Simon's absence. He obviously hadn't expected her, hadn't taken her deciding in his favor for granted.

Given his Cynster arrogance, given his reputation, that definitely ranked as noteworthy.

The window was open; a cool breeze had sprung up. The storm that had threatened had blown past, leaving cooler air in its wake.

She shivered, shifted. She wasn't cold, yet . . .

She looked at the comforter on the bed, then lifted her gaze, and frowned at the door.

Parting from Charlie at his door, Simon opened it and walked in. Shutting the door, he glanced at the window, noted the moonlight streaming in, and decided not to bother lighting a candle.

Stifling a sigh, he shrugged out of his coat. Slipping the buttons on his waistcoat free, he walked to the chair beside the tallboy and tossed the coat across it. His waistcoat went the same way. Plucking the diamond pin from his cravat, he laid it on the tallboy, then set his fingers to the intricate folds, loosening them, untying the knot—studiously keeping his mind busy with mundane things rather than wondering for how many hours he'd toss and turn tonight.

Wondering how long it would take his obsession to make up her mind.

Wondering how much longer he could manage to play the role of nonchalant seducer. He'd never previously attempted a role so totally foreign to his nature—but he'd never before seduced Portia.

Flicking the ends of the cravat free, he drew it from his throat, went to drop it on the other chair—

A silk gown of some pale shade lay draped neatly across the chair. Apple green silk—his memory supplied the color of the gown Portia had worn that evening. The shade had made her skin appear even whiter, thrown her black hair into sharp contrast, made her dark blue eyes even more startling.

He reached down, trailed his fingertips across the folds—in truth, to convince himself he wasn't hallucinating. His touch disturbed a pair of diaphanous silk stockings, laid over two lace-trimmed, ruched silk garters.

His mind leapt—to a vision of Portia clad in nothing more than her silk chemise.

Slowly, hardly daring to believe what his rational mind was telling him, he turned.

She was asleep in his bed, her hair a black wave breaking over the pillows.

Soft-footed, he moved closer. She lay on her side, facing him, one hand beneath her cheek. Her lips were fractionally parted. Her lashes lay, ebony crescents against her fair skin.

He could smell the scent she wore; a light, flowery fragrance it rose from her warmth, wreathed through his brain, sank sensual claws into him and tugged.

All he could sense, all he could see, left him giddy.

Triumph soared—immediately he grabbed hold and reined it in. Set his jaw, waited a moment, feeling the blood pound beneath his skin. He'd spent all evening warning himself not to expect this— that with Portia, nothing was ever straightforward and simple.

Yet here she was.

He couldn't quite grasp it—he felt almost winded. Sucking in a breath, he blew it out softly, reminded himself he shouldn't overinterpret, read too much into her presence. This was definitely not the moment to let his instincts loose and simply seize.

Yet it had to have taken courage to come to his bed.

She knew him—no other lady he'd bedded knew him as she did. She knew his character, his personality—knew what he'd be like as a husband. Or could make a very well-educated guess.

He'd agreed to teach her all she wanted to know; they'd never spoken of anything more. Anything more binding. Regardless, she would have recognized that in coming to him—in accepting his offer to introduce her to intimacy—she was risking, trusting him with, a great deal more than her maidenhead.

Her independence was a vital part of her, of who she was; to toss something so fundamental on the scales took precisely the kind of reckless courage with which she was so well-endowed. But she wouldn't have taken the decision lightly, not Portia.

She wouldn't have missed seeing the danger, even though he'd disguised it as much as he was able.

He had no idea how they—he and she—would make a marriage work; by no stretch of the imagination would it be easy. But it was what he wanted.

All he had to do now was lead her to convince herself that it was what she wanted, too.

Without revealing that marrying her had been his aim all along.

No matter that he trusted her, that was one piece of information she did not need, one vulnerability he had no intention of revealing.

He stood looking down at her as the minutes ticked by, plotting, planning, far too wise to rush in. Once he had the best approach clear in his mind, he girded his loins, stepped to the bed, and sat on the edge beside her.

She didn't stir. He raised a hand, twined his fingers in her hair, let the silky strands slide. He studied her face, innocent in sleep, then bent and kissed her awake.

She roused slowly, warm and sweetly feminine, then she murmured something unintelligible, shifted onto her back, slid her fingers into his hair and kissed him back.

Invitingly.

He drew back, looked into her eyes, darker than night behind the screen of her lashes. Looked at her lips. "Why are you here?"

Full, sensuous, her lips slowly curved. She drew him back down. "You know perfectly well. I want you to teach me—all."

On the last word, she kissed him, her tongue sliding between his lips to find his and stroke, caress, taunt. Passion rose, spread like wildfire beneath his skin.

His reins started to slide—he caught them. Pulled back, met her gaze.

"You're sure? Absolutely sure?" When she raised her brows, faintly mocking, he growled, "You're sure you won't change your mind come morning?"

Even as the words left his lips, he realized their idiocy; this was Portia—she never changed her mind.

And, God above, he didn't want her to.

"Never mind—forget that." He held her gaze. "Just tell me one thing—does this mean you trust me?"

She didn't answer immediately—she actually thought. Then she nodded. "In this, yes."

He let out the breath he'd been holding. "Thank God for that."

Pulling out of her arms, he stood, yanked his shirt from his breeches, then hauled it off over his head.

CHAPTER 10

Portia stared at the muscled expanse of bare chest suddenly on display. Her mouth dried; her logical mind was fighting to pay attention to what he'd asked—**why** he'd asked . . . the rest of her mind didn't care.

This, after all, was what she'd wanted to know. To learn.

The rush of uncertainty, of mild panic when his hands fell to his waistband and he flipped the buttons free, was, she lectured herself, only to be expected. Yet it seemed wise to focus on other things—she was warm and cozy, comfortable . . . she shifted, acutely conscious of the caress of her chemise against her skin, of the rougher texture of the sheets.

He turned and sat on the bed; it bowed beneath his weight as he wrenched off his boots and let them fall. His face seemed a study in single-minded determination, set in concentration.

A concentration shortly to be focused on . . .

A shiver slithered down her spine. Her senses leapt when he stood, stripped off his trousers, then turned.

Her eyes locked—not on his. She was conscious of her lips parting, of her eyes growing wider, rounder.

She'd touched, but hadn't before seen.

The visual was even more impressive than the tactile—at least to her mind. In fact, her mind wasn't at all sure—

"For God's sake, stop thinking!"

She blinked; he grabbed the covers and slid beneath. She refocused on his face in the instant he reached for her. Drew her to him.

"Si—"

He kissed her—hard. Arrogantly commanding. Domineering. Instinctively she responded with her own brand of aggression; he immediately gentled—gentled her as she stiffened, shocked by the sheer heat of his skin against hers, of the reality of the heavy, muscled body, tense, naked, and intent, suddenly surrounding her, more than capable of overpowering her.

Despite all, it was a shock—a real, in some ways frightening, shock. In this arena, too, theory was one thing, reality another.

He kept his lips on hers; she couldn't breathe but through him. She tried to break away, to free her mind enough to think—he wouldn't allow it. And then, quite abruptly, she was drowning, being dragged inexorably down into a sensual sea.

Above her, angled over her, his legs tangled with hers, his hands spread over her skin, fingers flexing, he held her senses captive, ruthlessly submerged them, held them down until all thought of resistance faded.

Until her mind was filled, not with pleasure, but with anticipation, with yearning. He didn't let her resurface, but kissed her even more deeply, ravaging her mouth with not even the thinnest veil to screen his intent, his possession. On a gasp, she yielded, not just her mouth, but to the welling need to assuage, to give, to surrender. To appease by offering her body, her self.

And he took. She hadn't before realized how much he had wanted—quite what he wanted of her. As she glimpsed the reality, a long shudder shook her.

His possession of her mouth eased, but didn't cease.

He turned his mind to other conquests.

To her breasts. Heated and aching, they swelled beneath his hand. Artful as ever, his fingers teased, kneaded, stroked, caressed. Squeezed.

Heat lanced through her, spread beneath her skin. She moaned, the sound trapped in their kiss; he didn't stop, didn't cease his excruciating play.

Only when she arched beneath him and cried out did he release her lips. His hand left her breast; he tugged up her chemise.

"Raise your arms."

She did, dragging in a huge breath as he drew the chemise up and off. Before she could lower her arms, he caught first one wrist, then the other, shackling them in one fist, anchoring them in the pillows behind her head, lightly bowing her spine.

His chest met her sensitized breasts; she gasped. Fiery delight sliced through her. He bent and took her mouth again, ravenously, then slowly moved his shoulders, back and forth across her, the raspy crinkly hair abrading her breasts, teasing the tight peaks, creating a pleasure that was close to pain.

She was beyond gasping when he finally released her lips to trail hot, openmouthed kisses down the curve of her throat, over the thudding pulse at its base, possessively tracing one collarbone before bending his head and feasting. Trapped as she was, hands above her head, her body bowed, displayed for his delectation, she couldn't avoid, couldn't duck the towering wave of awareness that crashed through her—that he ruthlessly sent rushing through her.

It caught her, lifted her up, opened her senses wide. So the reality poured in—the hot wetness of his mouth as he suckled her, the hard heaviness of muscle and bone holding her down, the rampant ridge of his erection pressed to her hip, ready to claim her.

The promise—the certainty—of what was to come overwhelmed her—and she let it.

Stopped fighting. Let him teach her. Show her.

Simon knew when she acquiesced, when she stopped trying to judge—to think. To manage. Her body, nowhere near as strong as his yet with its own supple strength, eased beneath him. A sign he was too much a conqueror not to recognize and relish; he lifted his head, took her lips, her mouth—now his to savor as he wished—and shifted over her.

Let her feel his weight, let her know and learn, as

she assuredly needed to. When she tugged, he released her hands, lowered his to her breasts, then slid them lower, tracing her curves, pushing between the sheets and her silken skin to close his hands over the globes of her bottom and angle her hips against him.

She murmured, deep in her throat; inwardly gloating, he caught her senses, dragged them deeper yet into the kiss.

When he released her lips and trailed his down her body, licking, laving, kissing his way to her breasts, she didn't try to stop him. Her hands lay on his shoulders, fingers clenching then easing as he sampled her bounty; her breathing was ragged, her eyes, when he glanced at her face, were closed. A fine line of concentration lay between her brows.

He licked one tight nipple, curled his tongue about it and drew it into his mouth, then suckled, deep, deeper—until her concentration fractured and she gasped.

Shifting lower, he let his reins slide—knew better than to imagine he could control his baser instincts, not tonight, not with her. He'd wanted her—not just, he could now admit, for the days they'd spent here, but for much, much longer. Her body was a prize his rakish soul had long coveted, even if he hadn't admitted it.

Tonight she would be his. More—tonight, she would give herself to him completely, without reservation. If they were to have a future, there was no point pretending he was not what he was, that he wouldn't demand, and command that of her.

How she would react—that was something else, but he'd never known her courage to falter.

Deep in his heart, he knew he could ask of her everything, and she would—knowing and knowingly—give. It was, ultimately, impossible for him to hurt her. She knew that as well as he.

He sent his lips cruising the taut skin of her stomach, and she caught her breath, restlessly shifted. His hands closed, locking about her hips; he shifted lower, spreading her thighs, with his shoulders wedging them wide.

She guessed. Her fingers clenched in his hair. He felt her haul in a breath as he bent his head, and set his lips to her softness.

"Simon!"

She uttered his name on a fractured scream; the sound seared him to his very soul. He licked, probed, then settled to savor her, sucking lightly, then more explicitly tracing the swollen folds. Her slick honey flowed as he feasted; she tasted of pippins, tart yet sweet. He found the tight nubbin erect and swollen beneath its hood, and lightly sucked, his every sense locked on her, on her reactions.

Step by step, he pushed her on, until her fingers curled to claws, until her head pressed back and her hips tilted, wordlessly surrendering. He opened her, tauntingly probed her entrance, then slowly, deliberately, penetrated her with his tongue.

She fractured, broke apart; he gloried in her soft cry, savored her contractions, but the instant they eased, he rose over her. Spread her thighs even wider, sank his hands into the bed on either side of her, set his erection to her slick, swollen folds.

Found her entrance. Nudged in.

Then drove home.

She cried out, arching wildly beneath him. He didn't stop, but drove deeper yet, fighting to absorb the sensations—of her heated sheath yielding, then encasing him, so tightly, of the firmness of her body, the cushioning feminine flesh, the succulent heat clamping about him. Battling desperately to savor all that, yet not let the moment sweep him away, not let his most primitive instincts have their way. He could—and would—plunder later, once she'd agreed, once she understood.

Trapped beneath him, she'd stilled. Head bowed, he could feel her panting breath close by his ear. Could feel, where they joined, where she'd clamped tight about him, the thudding tempo of her racing heart. Every muscle locked against the almost overpowering urge to ride her, he lifted his head and looked into her face.

From beneath heavy lids, from behind the black lace of her lashes, her eyes glinted—glittered—into his. Her lips, swollen, slightly parted, seemed to firm. He felt her draw breath.

"I thought you promised never to hurt me."

Not quite an accusation—her lips twisted briefly in the lightest grimace; to his immense relief, her body was already easing beneath his, the defensive tension slowly seeping away.

He bent his head, brushed her lips with his, made them cling for an instant. "I think," he murmured, shifting very slightly within her, "that you'll find it's not a lasting hurt."

He lifted over her again; eyes locked with hers, he withdrew a fraction, then slid home once more.

She blinked. "Do that again."

He would have grinned, but couldn't; his features were locked, passion set. He did as she asked, letting out a little of the air locked in his lungs when neither her expression nor her body retensed.

Looking into his face, Portia struggled to assimilate the feeling of fullness, of being so full of him. Not in her wildest dreams . . . the sensations of intimacy, of having given herself to him, of having taken him into her body, were not only more powerful than she'd foreseen, but powerful in a different way.

A more fundamental, earth-shattering, soul-shaking way.

But she couldn't stop and examine that now— neither her body nor his would permit it. Both were primed, coiled, ready. For what, she had only the vaguest idea.

Her hands had dropped from his shoulders to close, viselike, on his upper arms; releasing one, she raised her hand to his cheek, brushed back the fall of his silken hair. Drew his face, slowly, down to hers.

Opened her mouth beneath his, urged him on, invited him to take her—teach her more—in the only way she knew.

His lips closed over hers, his tongue filled her mouth, tangled with hers, thrust deep—withdrew as his body did, then echoed the surge as he filled her anew.

A surge repeated again and again until it caught her, drew her up, had her riding the wave of sensation again, with him, this time, as he rode her. Her body, no longer hers to command, following instinct, following him, rose to his until flames flared, until fire danced under her skin, until her bones were molten, her body a furnace into which his plunged, like a burning brand, deeper, harder, rhythmically, repeatedly stoking the flames.

Her senses were caught, locked in the moment; never had she felt so alive. So aware of herself, and of him. Of their bodies merging, giving and taking, of their skins, slick and hot, rubbing and sliding, touching, brushing, caressing. Of their breaths mingling, their hearts thundering in unison, their bodies striving, their wills as one.

Diving into the flames, bathing in the passion, in the hot furnace of mutual desire. Clinging, gasping, then stoking the flames to new heights.

Until they erupted in a towering wall of heat that fell on them and consumed them, that cindered all remnants of rational thought, poured in molten sensation down every nerve as wildfire flashed across their skins.

Desperate, they danced on, breaths fractured, hearts racing, fingers sinking deep.

He lifted his head, dragged in a gigantic breath—as did she. Their gazes met.

"Do something for me."

She could barely make out the words. "What?"

"Wrap your legs about my hips."

She wanted to ask why but didn't, instead simply did as he asked—and learned the answer.

He drove into her—deeper, harder, faster—drove, it seemed, straight to her heart. She arched beneath him, gripped tight with her thighs, heard herself cry as her senses fractured—not as before but infinitely more intensely, shattering into shards, bright, sharp, gilded with glory.

She felt him hold still, buried deep within her, then he was with her, caught, trapped, swept up and away in the pure energy swirling around them, through them, that battered them, buoyed them. Ultimately fused them.

Fused their bodies, heated and damp—then imploded in a sunburst powerful enough to fuse their very souls.

She'd wondered what would happen after; no amount of wondering had prepared her for this.

For the sheer weight of him, slumped on top of her, for the thundering of their hearts, for the glory still coursing through their veins, the heat still pulsing under their skins.

Over. The raging storm had swept past and left them washed up, exhausted, tossed up by the waves on some deserted island.

Only they were real. In that moment, the rest of the world did not exist.

Boneless, she lay beneath him, stunned, yet at peace. He turned his head. Their breaths mingled, then, blindly, their lips met. Clung. Held.

"Thank you."

His words feathered her cheek. Lifting a hand, she brushed back his hair, then stroked down, over the powerful lines of his torso, the long muscles of his back.

"No—thank you."

For teaching her, for letting her see . . . possibly more than he'd intended.

She'd been right; there was something special between them, something worth fighting for. But there was also so much she'd yet to learn . . .

His lips cruised over hers, then he drew in a breath, and eased from her. The change was dramatic—the difference in sensations, in how her body felt when he was there, joined with her, and when he was not.

He lifted from her, then slumped on the bed beside her. One heavy arm reached across, settling her against his side, locking her there.

"Go to sleep. We'll have to get you back to your room before dawn—I'll wake you before then."

She smiled. Refrained from telling him she was looking forward to it—to having him wake her up.

Turning onto her side, she snuggled down, snuggled her back against him.

She'd never slept with a man before, but sleeping with him seemed perfectly natural. Perfectly normal.

Perfectly meant to be.

Dawn came too soon.

She was dimly, dreamily aware when Simon left her side, when his weight left the bed. She grumbled, turned over, grabbing the tangled sheets and comforter to her to hold in his warmth, and slid back into bliss-filled slumber.

She was floating, boneless and content on some warm and gentle sea when a hard hand closed on her shoulder and shook.

"Come on—wake up. It's getting light."

Cracking open an eye took serious effort; squinting up, she saw Simon, fully dressed, leaning over her. It was light enough to see that his eyes were blue, his expression concerned.

She smiled, closed her eye, reached up and curled her fingers in his lapel. "No one else will be up for hours." She tugged. "Come back in here." Her lips curved as the memories washed over her. "I want to learn more."

He sighed. Heavily. Then the hand that had risen to close about hers locked about her hand and wrist—and he straightened, yanking her unceremoniously from her warm cocoon.

Her eyes snapped open. "**Wha**—?"

He caught both her arms and half lifted, half wrestled her to her knees. "We have to get you dressed and back in your room **before** the servants are everywhere."

Before she could say a word, he dropped her chemise over her head. She struggled to get her arms up through the delicate armholes, then tugged the fabric down. Scowling came easily; she fixed him with a narrow-eyed glare. "This is not what I expected."

He stood looking down at her; he was having trouble keeping his lips straight. "So I'd gathered." Then his jaw firmed. "However, we're only here for another two days, and we are not going to cause a scandal in that time." He tossed her dress at her.

She caught it, tilted her head, and considered him. "As we do have only two more days, wouldn't it be wiser to—"

"No." He hesitated, studying her, then added, "We can continue your lessons tonight." Turning, he sat on the bed and reached for his boots. "Don't think to learn anything more before then."

Mulling that over, she struggled into her gown, then wriggled around to sit and pull on her stockings. "Why," she eventually asked, "do we have to wait until tonight?"

Her tone reflected honest curiosity, but also an underlying uncertainty; Simon heard both. He glanced at her, watched, his body slowly tensing as, one long, long leg extended, she—with transparently guileless grace—drew on her stocking. He blinked, struggled to remember her question.

He managed it; he lifted his gaze to her face, met her eyes. His instinct was to slide around the topic, avoid it.

She raised her brows, waiting. Jaw setting, he stood, gave her his hand and helped her from the bed. She looked down, sliding her feet into her evening slippers.

"Your body . . ." He spoke to the top of her head. "You'll need a little time to recover."

She looked up, blinked—was about to argue—

"Trust me, you will." He shepherded her to the door.

To his immense relief, she went—still thinking. She halted before the door; he reached around her for the knob. Shifting, she leaned her shoulder against his chest, traced his cheek with one fingertip.

Met his eyes. "I'm not exactly a fragile flower. I won't break."

He held her gaze. "I'm neither small nor gentle." He bent his head and brushed her lips. "Trust me—tonight, but not before."

Her lips clung; he felt her sigh.

"All right."

Gripping the knob, he opened the door.

He insisted on seeing her back to her room. In order to reach it, they had to traverse the length of the main wing. The oldest part of the house, it contained numerous reception rooms, many open-ing one into the other; he used that route to avoid the tweenies scurrying about the main corridors.

They were close to the east wing, slipping along a rarely used gallery when Portia glanced out of the mullioned windows, and stopped. Tugged back when he tried to tug her on, then stepped closer to the window.

He looked over her head, and saw what she had.

Kitty, in a peignoir that did nothing to hide her charms, standing on the lawn in full sight, remon-strating with Arturo and Dennis. She was talking, gesticulating.

He drew Portia back; Kitty was facing away from them, but Arturo or Dennis might see them if they glanced up.

Portia met his gaze, shook her head as if to say it was all completely beyond her, then let him hurry her along.

They reached her room. Brushing a quick kiss on her fingertips, he urged her inside. The minute the door closed, he headed back to his room.

A pair of giggling maids forced him down the east wing stairs; safe enough—he could cut through the ground floor of the main wing and reach the west wing that way. Swinging down off the stairs, he stepped out—

"Well, well—what have we here?"

He halted, swung around—to face Kitty.

Clutching her peignoir about her, she locked her eyes, widening as full realization struck, on his face, then her gaze traveled slowly down, narrowing.

Simon inwardly cursed; he'd thrown on the same clothes he'd worn last night.

Kitty looked up, her expression brittlely arch. "A trifle late to be leaving Miss Ashford's bed, but then no doubt you were entertained to the point of distraction."

The fury of a woman scorned rang in her tone; he'd turned her down any number of times—the malicious gleam in her eyes suggested she remembered every instance.

"Not so distracted as to imagine the local gypsies normally call at dawn to consult with the lady of the house."

She paled, then flushed, with temper as much as guilt. She opened her lips, met his eyes—and thought better of whatever she'd been about to say. With an icy glare, she gathered her draperies about her, turned, and swept up the stairs.

Simon watched her go, his own eyes narrowing, a sense of danger tickling his spine. Her footsteps died; he swung on his heel and strode for the west wing.

"Can we go riding this morning, do you think?" Cecily Hammond looked around the breakfast table, her blue eyes hopeful.

All those present knew exactly what she hoped—that by organizing such an impromptu event now, in Kitty's absence, they could avoid her presence for the morning at least.

James looked at Simon. "I can't see why not."

"A sensible idea," Charlie pronounced. He looked at the others—at Portia, Lucy, Annabelle, Desmond, Winifred, Oswald, and Swanston. "Where should we go?"

Numerous suggestions were made; while discussion raged, Portia looked down at her plate. At the mound of food she was steadily consuming. She normally had an excellent appetite; this morning, however, she felt hungry enough to eat a horse.

She didn't, however, think she could sit one. Not for any length of time.

Quite aside from the discomfort—the twinges and aches she'd ignored at first but which had progressively made themselves felt—if going riding were to worsen her condition such that her recovery was postponed beyond tonight . . . she'd rather not ride than forgo tonight's lesson.

Tonight's opportunity to investigate further—something she was determined to do.

The others settled on riding south down the old Roman road to the Badbury Rings, to view the ancient Iron Age fort. Chasing a forkful of kedgeree around her plate, she wondered what excuse she could give.

"I want to give my pair another run." Simon spoke to James. "They're eating their heads off, and after the last months, idleness doesn't suit their temperaments." He looked across the table at

Portia, caught her eye. "I could take you up with me if you'd prefer?"

She blinked at him, then realized—as he already had—that no one there, bar Lady O who wasn't about to hear, knew of her love of riding. No one would think it odd if she elected to be driven instead.

"Thank you." She shifted slightly on her chair, realized he must have some inkling of her state . . . looked down before she blushed. "I would rather sit and watch the scenery."

She didn't look up to see if his lips quirked. A moment later, she felt his gaze leave her, and he spoke to James.

Fifteen minutes later, they all gathered in the garden hall, then set out for the stables. Sorting out horses and saddles took some time; Portia consoled the little chestnut mare while Simon's bays were harnessed.

He came to fetch her, one brow rising as he walked down the aisle to her side. "Ready?"

She met his gaze, read the watchful concern in his eyes, smiled lightly and gave him her hand. "Yes."

He led her out, handed her up, then climbed up beside her.

"We'll see you along the road," he called to James, still supervising the ladies' mounts. James waved. The groom holding the bays' heads leapt back. With a flourish of his whip, Simon sent the pair sweeping out into the drive.

They didn't talk, didn't need to. She looked around eagerly, keen to see a part of the country she hadn't before explored. After they left the tall trees of Cranborne Chase behind, stands of beeches occasionally lined the road as it crossed the gently undulating heathland. Simon let the bays stretch their legs, then reined them in to a gentle trot. The others, riding cross-country, caught up with them close to their destination; they rode in convoy about the curricle, chatting, exchanging quips and stories.

About them, the morning waxed glorious—blue skies above, sunshine streaming down, and a breeze fresh enough to clear the stuffiest head. The party enjoyed themselves in innocent exploration, clambering up and about the three rings of defensive earthworks surrounding the old fort. Everyone was so relieved by the respite from the snarled tensions at the Hall, each and every one went out of their way to be gracious and charming—even Oswald and Swanston.

Throughout, Portia was aware of Simon watching her—watching over her. She was used to such attention from him; previously, it had invariably pricked her temper. Today . . . while she strolled beside Winifred and Lucy, lifting her face to the breeze blowing from the distant sea, even though he wasn't near, she still felt his gaze, and, to her surprise, felt . . . cared for. Cherished.

There was something quite different in how he watched her now.

Intrigued, she stopped walking, let the others go ahead, then turned and looked across to where he stood, idly listening to Charlie and James arguing. Across the green dip between two of the rings, he met her gaze, then, taking his hands from his pockets, he left the others and walked to join her.

As he neared, he searched her face. He stopped beside her, holding her gaze, screening her from the others. "Are you all right?"

For one instant, she didn't answer, too busy reading—savoring—the expression in his eyes. Not his face, that was set in its usual arrogantly austere lines, but his eyes were softer, his concern quite different—of a different nature—to what it had been in years past.

The sight warmed her. From her heart outward, like a sudden upwelling of joy.

She smiled, inclined her head. "Yes. Perfectly."

A cry reached them—they looked across to where Oswald and Swanston had engaged in mock-battle for the entertainment of the Hammond sisters. Her smile deepening, she put her hand on Simon's arm. "Come—walk with me."

He did, keeping by her side as they ambled. Words were superfluous; not even glances were needed to maintain the connection.

Her gaze on the horizon, Portia sensed that connection's shimmering touch, felt her heart swell as if to accommodate it. Was this what happened? That somehow a link grew between two people—a channel of understanding independent of all things physical?

Whatever it was, it felt special, precious. She glanced at him briefly, too wise to imagine he didn't sense it, too. He didn't seem to be fighting it, or denying it; she wondered what he truly thought.

After an hour of simple pleasures, in complete and relaxed accord, they reluctantly returned to the horses and curricle and headed back to the Hall.

They returned just in time for luncheon, just in time to be treated to another petulant performance by Kitty. The lighter mood the morning had engendered rapidly dissipated.

The seating was not specified at luncheon; Simon claimed the chair beside Portia, sat, ate, and watched. Most of the company did the same; if Kitty had possessed the slightest sensibility, she would have noticed the distancing, the guardedness, and muted her behavior accordingly.

Instead, she seemed in the oddest mood, pouting, threatening to sulk over the news of their morning's outing on the one hand, on the other brittlely excited, eyes alight with almost frenetic anticipation—an expectation of something desperately significant no one else knew of.

"Why, we've been to the Rings many times before, dear," Mrs. Archer reminded Kitty. "I declare it would be quite fatiguing to have to see them again."

"Indeed," Kitty averred, "but I—"

"Naturally," Mrs. Buckstead joined in, smiling benignly down the table at her daughter and the Hammond girls, "the younger ones need to get out in the fresh air."

Kitty glared at her. "Winifred—"

"And, of course, once one's married, gadding about on morning adventures does lose its appeal." Unperturbed, Mrs. Buckstead helped herself to more iced asparagus.

For one instant, Kitty was dumbfounded, then her gaze swung down the table. To Portia. Unaware, Portia continued eating, her gaze lowered, a faint but definite smile—a gentle, abstracted, in many ways revealing smile—curving her lips.

Eyes narrowing, Kitty opened her mouth—

Simon reached out, picked up his glass. Kitty glanced at him—he caught her gaze. Held it as he sipped, then slowly lowered his glass to rest it on the table.

Let Kitty read in his eyes what he would do if she dared vent her jealousy on Portia—if she made the slightest allusion to the morning adventures she suspected he and Portia had enjoyed.

For an instant, Kitty teetered on the brink, then sanity seemed to reassert itself; she drew breath and looked down at her plate.

Elsewhere about the table, Mr. Archer, to all appearances oblivious of his younger daughter's shortcomings, continued a discussion with Mr. Buckstead; Lord Glossup was talking to Ambrose, while Lady O chatted to Lady Glossup with superb disregard for all else about her.

Gradually, with Kitty sunk in silence, other conversations commenced, Lady Calvin claiming James's and Charlie's attention, Desmond and Winifred trying to draw out Drusilla.

Simon exchanged light comments with Annabelle Hammond, on his other side; inwardly, his mind raced. Kitty's discretion was nonexistent; who knew when, provoked, she would blurt something out? If she did . . .

The meal drew to a close; he bided his time. The instant Portia set down her fork, he reached out and stroked a finger over her wrist.

She glanced at him, raised a brow.

"Let's go for a walk."

Her brows rose higher; he could see the thoughts—the speculation—whirling through her mind. Lips twisting, he clarified, "I want to talk to you."

On the subject that, courtesy of Kitty, could no longer safely be left unbroached.

She studied his eyes, saw he was serious; curious, she inclined her head. Lifting her napkin to her lips, she murmured, "Slipping away from the others might not be that easy."

In that, she was correct; although the table broke up and in the main the guests scattered to spend the afternoon in various ways, Annabelle, Cecily, and Lucy clung to Portia, clearly expecting to follow her lead. Excusing himself from a billiard match with

James and Charlie, Simon followed the four females out to the terrace, wondering how to lose three.

He paused in the doorway from the morning room, considering and discarding various options, then he heard stumping behind him. He turned as Lady O came up; she grasped his arm as he instinctively offered it.

She looked out at the four young ladies standing in a group by the balustrade. Shook her head. "You'll never manage it."

Before he could think of any suitable rejoinder, she shook his arm. "Come on—I want to go and sit in the shrubbery courtyard." A distinctly evil grin curved her lips. "Seems like a place where one hears all sorts of things."

Assuming she had some scheme in mind, Simon led her out. They crossed the terrace, and he helped her down the steps. When they reached the lawn, she abruptly stopped.

And turned back. Waved to the young ladies. "Portia—fetch my parasol, if you would, my dear."

Portia had been watching them. "Yes. Of course."

Excusing herself to the other girls, she went indoors.

Lady O turned and stumped on.

He was settling her in the shrubbery courtyard, on a wrought-iron garden seat set beneath the spreading branches of a magnolia, when Portia joined them.

She looked at the tree. "You won't need this after all."

"Never mind. It's served its purpose." Lady O took the parasol, then settled her many layers and leaned back, closing her eyes. "You may go, the pair of you."

Simon looked at Portia; she opened her eyes wide, shrugged.

They turned.

"Incidentally," Lady O said, "there's another exit from this place." They turned back. Barely opening her eyes, she pointed with her cane. "That path. From memory, it leads through the back of the rose garden to the lake."

She closed her eyes again.

Simon looked at Portia.

Smiling, she returned to the seat, bent and kissed Lady O's cheek. "Thank you. We'll come back—"

"I'm perfectly able to get myself back to the house if I wish." Cracking open both lids, she fixed them with her best basilisk stare. "You two take yourselves off—no need in the world to hurry back."

When they didn't immediately move, she lifted both cane and parasol and shooed them. "Go! Go!"

Smothering grins, they went.

"She's incorrigible."

Gazes touching, they ducked through the archway into the rose garden.

"I don't think she's ever been anything else."

He reached for Portia's hand, twined his fingers with hers. They walked on, swiftly leaving the rose garden for the less structured gardens above the lake.

Ten minutes later, they paused where the path they'd followed crested the rise above the lake. He looked out over the water; not another soul was in sight. "Come on." He led Portia down the narrow path and onto the wider path circling the lake.

She fell into step beside him. He kept hold of her hand; he was reasonably sure none of the others was likely to wander this way, not in the next hour.

When he led her past the front of the summer-house, she glanced at him. He could sense her thoughts, but instead of asking where they were going, she went straight to the heart of things. "What did you want to talk about?"

Now the moment was upon him—them—although he knew what he needed to say, he wasn't sure how to proceed. Thanks to Kitty, he hadn't had time to plan what was, in truth, a most crucial engagement in his campaign to win Portia to wife. "I ran into Kitty after I left you this morning." He glanced at her, met her widening eyes. "She's guessed, more or less correctly."

She grimaced, then turned thoughtful. Frowned. "So she may cause problems."

"That depends. She's so caught up in her own games, she'll only lash out and mention us if provoked."

"Perhaps I should speak with her."

He stopped. "No! That's not what—"

She halted, looked at him questioningly.

He glanced about the lake path, heard a high-pitched girlish voice float down from the gardens above. They'd reached the pinetum; a path led on, winding beneath the specimen trees. Tightening his hold on Portia's hand, he drew her on.

Stopped only when they were surrounded by tall trees, cloaked in dappled shade—totally private.

He released her, turned, faced her.

She watched, waited, mildly curious . . .

Ignoring the constriction about his lungs, he drew breath, met her midnight blue eyes.

"I want to marry you."

CHAPTER 11

She blinked, then stared. "What did you say?"

Her voice was oddly weak.

He set his jaw. "You heard me." When she continued to stare, dumbfounded, he repeated, "I want to marry you."

Her eyes only grew rounder. "When did you decide this? And **why**, for heaven's sake?"

He hesitated, trying to see ahead. "Kitty. She almost said something over the luncheon table. At some point, she will—she won't be able to resist. I was already thinking of marriage and didn't want you imagining, if I waited to speak until **after** she caused a ruckus, that I was offering because of that."

With any other lady, letting Kitty create a scandal and then offering ostensibly because of it might have been a reasonable way forward, but not with Portia. She'd never accept an offer made out of social necessity.

"You were **already** thinking of marriage? To **me**?" The stunned look in her eyes hadn't faded. "Why?"

He frowned at her. "I would have thought that was obvious."

"Not to me. What, precisely, are you talking about?"

"I'm sure you haven't forgotten you spent last night in my bed."

"You're perfectly right—I haven't. I also haven't forgotten that I specifically explained that my interest in such proceedings was academic."

He held her gaze. "That was then. This is now. Things have changed." An instant passed. Eyes locked on hers, he asked, "Can you deny it?"

Portia couldn't, but his sudden talk of marriage—as if the subject had always been there, an unstated element between them—left her feeling like a deer suddenly facing a hunter. Paralyzed, unsure which way to turn, shocked, astonished, her wits literally reeling.

When she didn't immediately reply, he went on, "Aside from all else, your involvement in last night's proceedings was anything but academic."

She blushed, lifted her head. Why on earth was he taking this tack? She tried to harry her whirling wits into order. "Regardless, that's no reason to imagine we should wed."

It was his turn to stare. **"What?"**

He uttered the word with such force, she jumped. He took a prowling, menacing step closer.

"You came to my bed—gave yourself to me— and you **didn't** expect we would wed?"

Their faces were no more than six inches apart;

he really was stunned. Eyes wide, she held his gaze. "No. I didn't." She hadn't got that far in her deliberations.

He didn't immediately answer, but something changed behind his mask. Then his eyes grew darker, his features harder; a muscle flexed along his jaw.

"You didn't . . . just what sort of man do you think I am?"

His voice was a low growl—a very angry growl. He shifted fractionally nearer; she nearly took a step back, only just stopped herself. Spine rigid, she held his gaze, struggled to understand why he was suddenly so furious . . . wondered if he was pretending . . . felt her own temper rise.

"You're a rake." She said the word clearly, distinctly. "You seduce ladies—it's the primary characteristic in the occupational description. If you'd married every lady you'd seduced, you'd have to go and live in Arabia because you'd have a harem." Her voice had gained strength; her belligerence rose to meet his. "As you're still living here, in this sceptered isle, I feel confident in concluding you **don't** marry every lady you seduce."

He smiled, a feral gesture. "You're right, I don't. But you need to revise your occupational description because, like most rakes, I **never** seduce unmarried, virginal, gently bred ladies." He stepped closer; this time she backed. "Like you."

She fought to keep her eyes on his, aware her breathing had accelerated. "But you did seduce me."

He nodded, and closed the gap between them again. "I did, indeed, seduce you—because I intend to marry you."

Her jaw dropped; she nearly gasped. Then she dug in her heels, tipped her chin high and locked her eyes, narrowing to shards, on his. "You seduced me **because** you intended to marry me?"

He blinked. Halted.

She saw red. "**What** aren't you telling me?" She jabbed a finger into his chest; he eased fractionally back. "You **intended** to marry me? Since when?" She flung her arms wide. "**When** did you decide?"

Even she could hear the almost hysterical, certainly horrified note welling in her voice. She'd evaluated the threat, accepted the risk in going to his bed, but she hadn't seen, hadn't **known** the real threat, the real risk.

Because he'd hidden it from her.

"**You—!**" She went to box his ear but he caught her fist. "You deceived me!"

"I didn't! You deceived yourself."

"**Hah!** Anyway"—she twisted her hand; he let her go—"you didn't seduce me—I seduced myself! I was **willing**. That's different."

"Maybe, but it doesn't change the fact. We were intimate, whatever led to it."

"Rubbish! I'm not going to marry you because of it. I'm twenty-four. The fact I was a gently bred virgin doesn't matter."

He caught her gaze. "It did—it does."

That he considered the fact gave him some claim

over her didn't need to be stated; it hovered, very real, a tangible truth between them.

She set her chin. "I always knew you were a throwback to medieval times. Regardless, I won't marry you because of it."

"I don't care why you marry me, just as long as you do."

"**Why?**" She'd asked before; he still hadn't answered. "And **when** did you decide you wanted to marry me? Tell me the truth, all of the truth, now."

His eyes hadn't left hers; he drew in a deep breath, then exhaled. Other than that, not a single line in his face or muscle in his body eased. "I decided after the picnic in the ruins. I'd thought of it after we first kissed on the terrace."

She wished he wasn't standing so close she couldn't fold her arms defensively before her. "You must have kissed millions of women."

His lips twisted. "Thousands."

"And I'm supposed to believe that because of one kiss—no, two—you decided to marry me?"

Simon very nearly told her he didn't care what she believed, but behind her anger, he sensed growing fright, the welling of a deep-seated fear, one he understood and had tried hard not to trigger.

He was very close to seriously queering his pitch with her; he might take months, even years, to win her back.

"It wasn't only that."

Her jaw set; she tipped her face higher. "What, then?"

Her eyes had clouded; he couldn't read them. He eased back a little, wasn't surprised when she shifted back and folded her arms across her chest.

"I'd already decided I wanted a wife and family before leaving London. When I met you here, I realized we would suit."

She blinked. "**Suit?** Are you mad? We're—" She gestured, searching for words. Lowering her arms.

"Too alike?"

"Yes!" Her eyes snapped. "You can hardly claim we're compatible."

"Think of the last days. Think of last night. In what matters in marriage, we're perfectly compatible." He caught her gaze. "In every conceivable way."

Portia refused to blush again—he was doing it on purpose. "One night—that's hardly a reasonable basis on which to make such a decision. How can you tell the next time won't be"—she gestured wildly—"**boring?**"

His eyes, burning blue, pinned her. "Trust me. It won't."

There was something in his face, a hardness, a ruthlessness, that was quite different from anything she'd seen in him before. She kept her eyes on his, tried to ignore the aggression flowing from him. "You . . . really are serious." She was having great trouble taking that in. One moment, she'd been logically following her step-by-step investigation into the physical attractions of matrimony—next thing, here they were, discussing a marriage between them.

He looked up, exhaled through his teeth. "Why is it so hard to imagine I'd want to marry you?" He'd addressed the question to the heavens; he looked down at her. Growled, "And what's wrong with the idea of marrying me?"

"What's wrong with the idea of **me** marrying you?" She heard her voice rise, tried to rein it in. "We'd make our lives a living hell, that's what! You"—she landed a backhanded slap on his chest—"you're a despot, a tyrant. A **Cynster**! You decree and expect to be obeyed—no, not even that! You **assume** you'll be obeyed. And you know what I'm like." She met his gaze, defiant and direct. "I won't meekly agree with what you dictate—I won't meekly agree with anything you say!"

His lips had thinned, his eyes had narrowed. He waited a heartbeat. "So?"

She stared at him. "Simon—this is not going to work."

"It is. It will."

That was her cue to appeal to the skies. **"See?"**

"That's not what's worrying you."

She lowered her gaze, looked at him. Blinked. Into soft blue eyes she'd long known to be deceptive—there was nothing soft behind them, nothing but invincible, steely determination, inflexible resolution, rocklike, conqueror-like will . . . "What . . . do you mean?"

"I've always known what worries you about me."

Something inside her physically shook. Rocked.

She held his gaze for a long moment, finally found the courage to ask, "What?"

He hesitated; she knew he was deciding how much to reveal, how much to confess he'd seen. When he spoke, his voice was even, low, yet still hard. "You're frightened I'll try to control you, to curtail your independence, to turn you into the sort of lady you're not. And that I'll be strong enough to succeed."

Her mouth was dry. "And you won't? Try, or succeed?"

"I'll almost certainly try, at least to curtail your wilder starts, at times, but **not** because I want to change you. Because I want to **preserve** you. I want you for what you **are,** not for what you're not."

The emotional risk she faced with him had just intensified and increased, well-nigh beyond bearing. Her heart had swollen and blocked her throat; it was difficult to draw breath.

"You're not just saying that?"

He was quite capable of it; he'd just proved he saw far more than she'd ever guessed, that he understood her far better than any other ever had. And he was ruthless, relentless in getting what he wanted.

He wanted her.

She had to believe it—there was no longer any option.

He exhaled, looked down, then met her gaze again. She could see his temper, still very real, in the locked lines of his face. Could sense, even more clearly, his desire to seize, to capture, to simply take.

A conqueror looked at her from behind his eyes.

Slowly, he raised a hand, held it out palm up between them. "Take a chance. Try me."

She looked at his hand, then raised her gaze to his face. "What are you suggesting?"

"Be my lover until you're sure enough to be my wife. For the few days we've left here, at least."

She breathed in deeply; her wits were whirling—she couldn't think. Instinct warned her she hadn't yet heard all—hadn't heard why he so amazingly thought they would suit—and perhaps never would. There were other ways to deal with that, to learn what he would not say.

But if she wished to . . . she'd have to take a chance.

Take a risk far bigger than any she'd imagined.

She'd thought to approach marriage one step at a time, standing on firm ground all the way. Who knew?—she might, at some point, have reached the stage of contemplating marrying him. If she'd followed her logical, cautious route, she would have known what to do. Felt sure what she wanted.

Instead, he'd leapt ahead to a stage she hadn't until now envisaged, leaving her no time to catch up. Her mind was still reeling, but he was waiting for an answer—would insist on one—indeed, deserved one; she had to rely on instinct alone in deciding what to do.

Her heart quaked; she stiffened her spine.

Lifting her hand, she placed her fingers in his.

They closed strongly, firmly about hers.

The possessive touch jolted her. She lifted her chin, met his eyes. "This doesn't mean I'm agreeing to marry you."

He held her gaze, then shifted his hold, lifted her hand to his lips. "You're agreeing to give me a chance to persuade you."

Quelling the shiver the brush of his lips and the intent in his eyes evoked, she inclined her head.

Simon silently let out the breath he'd been holding, felt the vise locked about his lungs ease. Never had he imagined dealing with his intended would mean dealing with Portia; she tied him in knots in ways no other ever had.

But he'd got over the worst of it, eased her past the hurdle of his recent shortcomings and refocused them both on what mattered—what was to come. He wasn't going to dwell on the fact she'd imagined he would seduce her, then let her go; there was no point arguing about her error.

She glanced at him, then turned to continue along the path. He consented but kept hold of her hand, striding slowly beside her.

Knowing she was thinking, analyzing, dissecting. There was no way he could prevent it.

The air beneath the trees was silent, still. Somewhere in the distance a bird called. The path wound through the trees; they could see the forecourt ahead when she stopped. Turned to him.

"If I don't agree to marry you, what then?"

Lying would make life so much easier. But this was Portia. He met her gaze. "I'll speak to Luc."

She stiffened; her eyes flashed. "If you do, I'll **never** marry you."

He let the moment stretch. "I know."

After a moment, he grimaced. "If it comes to that, we'll be at stalemate. But it won't, so there's no sense worrying about it."

She narrowed her eyes at him, but then grimaced, too, and turned to walk beside him once more. "You're very sure."

They emerged into the forecourt; he looked up at the house. "Of what should be, yes." Of what was to come—that was another matter.

Reaching the front steps, they went up and through the front door, presently set wide.

In the hall, Portia halted. "I need to think."

An understatment. She still felt as if she were walking in a dream, that none of what had happened had been real. She wasn't at all sure what she'd got herself into, what she was now facing.

Where they, he and she, now were.

She drew her hand from his; he released it, but reluctantly. One glance at his face told her he'd much rather she didn't think, that he was considering distracting her, but then he caught her eye, realized what she'd seen.

He inclined his head. "I'll be in the billiard room."

She nodded, turned away, opened the library door, and walked in. The long room was empty.

Relieved, she shut the door behind her, leaned back against it. An instant later, she heard his footsteps heading down the hall.

Her back against the panels, she waited for her whirling wits to subside, for her emotions to settle.

Was he right? Could a marriage between them work?

There seemed little point examining the past; now she knew he'd been thinking of marriage all along, his behavior made perfect sense. Even the fact he'd not mentioned marriage until Kitty had made it unavoidable; given all he knew of her, in his shoes, she'd have done the same.

She'd never been one to cut off her nose to spite her face; their past was behind them—it was the future she now had to deal with. The future he'd set so forcefully before her.

Yet she felt as if her horses had bolted and her life was running away with her—out of her control. She'd been so focused on the emotional connection between them, she hadn't spared much thought for the state that connection might lead them to—eventually, perhaps. He'd obviously been thinking of the state, but had he considered the emotion?

While she'd been investigating that connection step by logical step, he'd impulsively leapt far ahead to one possible conclusion—and was convinced that conclusion was right. Meant to be.

She was usually the impulsive one; he was the stoic male. Yet in this, he was convinced while she was still uncertain, searching for proof, for reassurance.

Grimacing, she pushed away from the door. Doubtless, her caution was a reflection of the fact that she had most at stake; it was **she** who would take the risk in giving him her hand. Giving him all rights over her—whichever rights he chose to exercise.

He said it would work; he understood her fears—said he wanted her as she was. Again, her decision hinged on trust. Did she trust him to live by that creed, day by day for the rest of their lives?

That was the question to which she would need to find the answer.

One thing, however, was clear. Their connectedness—the emotional link she'd been working to understand—born of their past, immeasurably strengthened by their recent interactions, was very real, all but tangible now between them.

It was still growing, still strengthening.

And he knew it, felt it, recognized it as she did; he was now capitalizing on it, using it. Adding his will to it—something she'd never expected—deliberately pushing it in the direction he, apparently, now wished.

Which led her to the most pertinent question. Was what she sensed between them real or, given his expertise combined with his ruthless will, was it a fabrication to beguile her into marrying him?

The way she'd reacted to his concern that morning replayed in her mind; was he ruthless enough to have fabricated that? She knew the answer: yes.

But had he?

She could sense the emotions—the passions, the

desires—he kept reined, held back but insufficiently disguised. Still felt in response an instinctive skittering, an impulse to draw back, from him, from them, from their power and the inherent threat they posed to her, yet that impulse was countered by curiosity, by a potent fascination with what evoked those same desires—with what lay between them, and the promise of all that could.

He could read her thoughts and feelings well—in general, she'd never bothered to conceal either from him. That he should have guessed the single truth she'd always thought she'd kept well hidden simply confirmed that he'd been more attuned to her than she'd guessed. More aware of her than she'd been of him.

Until now, her thoughts of marriage had been abstract, although definitely not with him or any like him. Circumstances had conspired to entrap her, through her curiosity to draw her into his web; he'd now made the prospect of marriage to a tyrant very real.

If she had any sense, she'd refuse him—and run. Fast. Far away.

Yet the notion of running from what might be, what might exist between them, evoked such a strong reaction she knew she'd never do it, turn her back and blithely let it die. If she did, she'd never be able to live with herself; the possibilities along the road he was proposing they follow were endless, exciting—recklessly enticing. Different, unique. Challenging.

All the things she wanted her life to be.

The prospect of marriage to a Cynster without love to ease the way, no longer distant theory but now very real, was like a sword hanging over her head, threatening all she was. Yet despite that, she still did not feel, did not react to **him,** the man, as if he threatened her at all. He'd been her unwanted and reluctant protector for years; some stubborn part of her adamantly refused to rescript his role.

She sighed. Contraditions assailed her every way she turned; confusion still clouded her mind. The only thing she felt totally confident about was that he, amazingly, was committed to marrying her, while she'd yet to make up her mind.

The magnitude of the change in her life in the past hour left her giddy.

She looked around, forced herself to take slow, steadying breaths. She needed to calm her mind, find her usual even mood in which her intellect normally functioned so incisively.

Her gaze drifted along row upon regimented row of leather-bound spines; she started to circle the room. Forcing herself actually to focus, to note familiar volumes, to think of other things. To connect again with the world she normally inhabited.

She walked around one end of the rectangular room, passing the huge fireplace. The French doors facing the garden stood open; she paced along, admiring the busts set on pedestals between each set of doors, trying not to think of anything else, eventually once again reaching walls covered with shelves.

A desk stood at that end of the room, facing down its length to the main hearth. A smaller fireplace was set in the wall behind it. She glanced at it, her attention caught by the intricate detail of the mantelpiece—

Saw, just visible from where she stood, a small foot clad in a lady's slipper, lying on the floor behind the desk.

The foot, of course, was attached to a leg.

"Good gracious!" She hurried to the desk and rounded it—

Halted, quivering. Stared.

Grabbed the edge of the desk. Slowly raised her hand to her throat.

She couldn't drag her gaze from Kitty's face, suffused, blotched, darkened tongue protruding, blue eyes blankly staring . . . or the silken cord wound tight about her neck, digging deep into the soft flesh . . .

"Simon?"

Her voice was far too weak. It took effort to force her lungs to work, to haul in huge breath. **"Simon!"**

A moment passed; she could hear the clock on the mantelpiece ticking. She felt too faint to let go of the desk, wondered if she'd have to go and look for help . . .

Footsteps pounded down the corridor, nearing.

The door burst open.

A heartbeat later, Simon was there, hands locking on her arms, eyes searching her face. He followed her gaze, looked, swore—then hauled her to him, away from the dreadful sight, interposing his body between her and the desk.

She locked her fingers in his coat and clung, shaking, buried her face in his shoulder.

"What is it?" Charlie stood in the doorway.

With his head, Simon indicated the area behind the desk. "Kitty . . ."

Simon held Portia close, aware of her trembling, of the shivers coursing her spine. Propriety be damned; he tightened his arms about her, locked her against him, against his warmth, lowered his head, brushed her temple with his jaw. "It's all right."

She gulped, clung even tighter; he felt her battle her reaction, and the shock. Eventually felt her spine stiffen even more. She lifted her head, but didn't step back. Glanced toward the desk.

At Charlie, who'd looked behind the desk and now sat slumped against the front edge, white-faced, tugging at his cravat. He swore, then looked at Simon. "She's dead, isn't she?"

Portia answered, her voice wavering. "Her eyes . . ."

Simon looked at the door. No one else had arrived. He glanced at Charlie. "Go and find Blenkinsop. Shut the door on your way out. After you've sent Blenkinsop here, you'd better find Henry."

Charlie blinked, then nodded. He got to his feet, drew in a huge breath, tugged his waistcoat down, then headed for the door.

Portia's shivering was growing worse. The

instant the door shut, Simon bent and swung her into his arms. She clutched his coat, but didn't protest. He carried her to the chairs grouped before the main hearth, set her down in one.

"Wait here." Visually quartering the room, he located the tantalus, crossed to it, poured a large measure of brandy into a crystal glass. Returning to Portia, he hunkered down beside the chair. Searched her pale face. "Here. Drink this."

She tried to take the glass from him, in the end had to use both hands. He helped her guide the tumbler to her lips, steadied it so she could sip.

He sat there and helped her drink; eventually, a trace of color returned to her cheeks, a hint of her customary strength returned to her dark eyes.

Easing back, he met them. "Wait here. I'm going to look around before chaos descends."

She swallowed, but nodded.

He rose, swiftly crossed the room, stood and looked down at Kitty's crumpled form. She lay on her back, hands high, level with her shoulders—as if she'd struggled to the very last with her murderer.

For the first time, he felt real pity for her; she might have been a social disaster, but that didn't give anyone the right to end her life. There was anger, too, not far beneath his surface, but that was more complex, not solely on Kitty's account; he reined it in, mentally cataloging all he could see.

The murderer had stood behind Kitty and strangled her with—he turned and checked—a curtain cord taken from the nearest French doors. Kitty had been the smallest woman present, only a little over five feet tall; it wouldn't have been all that hard. He looked around the body, looked at her hands, but saw nothing unusual, except that her gown was not the one she'd worn to lunch. That had been a morning gown, relatively plain; this was prettier, a tea gown cut to showcase her voluptuous curves, yet still perfectly acceptable for a married lady.

He looked at the desk, but there was nothing out of place, no half-finished letter, no scratches on the blotter; the pens lay neatly in their tray, the inkstand closed.

Not that he imagined Kitty had repaired to the library to write letters.

Returning to Portia, he shook his head in answer to her questioning look. "No clues."

He took the glass she held out to him. It was still half-full. He drained it in one gulp, grateful for the warmth the brandy sent spreading through him. He'd been on edge before, thinking of the possible ramifications of his and Portia's discussion. Now this.

He dragged in a breath and looked down at her.

She looked up, met his eyes.

A moment passed, then she raised a hand, held it up.

He closed his hand about it, felt her fingers lock tight.

She looked toward the door; it burst open—

Henry and Blenkinsop rushed in, Ambrose and a footman on their heels.

The following hours ranked among the most ghastly Simon could recall. Shock was far too mild a word to describe how Kitty's death struck them all. Everyone was stunned, unable to take it in. Despite all that had been going on under their noses throughout the past days, no one had dreamed it would end like this.

"I might at times have thought of strangling her," James said. "I never dreamed anyone would."

But someone had.

Of the ladies, most were distraught. Even Lady O; she forgot to lean heavily on her cane, and forgot entirely to thump it on the floor. Drusilla was the most composed, yet even she shook, paled, and sank into a chair when she heard. In death, Kitty garnered far more sympathy than she ever had in life.

Among the men, once the first shock wore off, confusion was the most prevalent emotion. That, and increasing concern over what was to come, how the situation would develop.

Simon's attention, his awareness, remained fixed on Portia. Hours later, she was still in shock, racked by occasional shivers. Her eyes were huge, her hands still clammy. He wanted to sweep her up, take her away, far away, but that simply wasn't possible.

Lord Willoughby, the local magistrate, had been sent for; he arrived and, after saying the right things and viewing the body, still sprawled behind the library desk, he repaired to Lord Glossup's study. After talking to each of the gentlemen in turn, he summoned Portia to tell him her tale.

Simon accompanied her as if by right. She didn't ask him, he didn't ask her, but since taking his hand in the library, she'd released it only when absolutely necessary. Ensconced in an armchair by a hastily lit fire in the study, with him sitting beside her on the chair's arm, she haltingly recounted the details of her gruesome discovery.

Lord Willoughby, pince-nez perched on his nose, took notes. "So you weren't in the library for more than, shall we say five minutes, before you found Mrs. Glossup?"

Portia thought, then nodded.

"And you didn't see, or hear, anyone leaving the room, either when you entered the front hall or when you entered the library—is that right?"

She nodded again.

"No one at all?"

Simon stirred, but Willoughby was only doing his job, and as gently as he could. He was an elderly, fatherly sort, but his gaze was sharp; he seemed to realize Portia's lack of response wasn't because she was hiding something.

She cleared her throat. "No one."

"I understand the terrace doors were open. Did you look out?"

"No. I didn't even go up to the doors—just walked past."

Willoughby smiled encouragingly. "And then you saw her, and called for Mr. Cynster. You didn't touch anything?"

Portia shook her head. Willoughby turned to Simon.

"I didn't see anything—I did look, but there seemed to be nothing unusual in any way, nothing out of place."

Willoughby nodded and made another note. "Well, then. I believe I needn't trouble you further." He smiled gently and rose.

Portia, her hand still in Simon's, rose, too. "What will happen now?"

Willoughby glanced at Simon, then back at her. "I'm afraid I must summon one of the gentlemen from Bow Street. I'll send my report off tonight. With luck, an officer will be here by tomorrow afternoon." He smiled again, this time reassuringly. "They are a great deal better than they used to be, my dear, and in such a case . . ." He shrugged.

"What do you mean—such a case?"

Again Willoughby glanced at Simon, then grimaced. "Unfortunately, it appears that other than Mr. Cynster here, and Mr. Hastings, none of the gentlemen can account for the time during which Mrs. Glossup was killed. Of course, there are gypsies in the neighborhood, but these days, it's best to follow proper procedures."

Portia stared at him; Simon could read her thoughts with ease. She wanted the murderer caught, **whoever** he was.

Simon turned to Willoughby, and with a nod, he led Portia out.

Willoughby spoke to Lord Glossup, then took his leave.

Dinner, a cold collation, was served early. Everyone retired to their rooms before the sun set.

Sitting on the window seat, arms folded on the sill, chin propped upon them, Portia watched the golden light of the sun slowly fade from the sky.

And thought of Kitty. The Kitty—the many Kittys—she'd glimpsed in recent days. She'd been beautiful, capable of vivacity, of being pleasant and charming, but she'd also been vindictive, shallow, knowingly hurtful to others. Demanding— that, perhaps, had been her greatest crime, perhaps her ultimate folly. She'd demanded that life, all life around her, center on her and her alone.

In all the time Portia had watched, she'd never seen Kitty truly think of anyone else.

A shiver racked her. One point she couldn't get out of her head. Kitty had trusted someone— she'd gone to meet someone in the library, a place to which she never would have gone for any other purpose. She'd changed her gown; the expectation that had fired her through lunch returned to Portia's mind.

Kitty had trusted unwisely. And fatally.

But there was more than one way in which to lose your life.

She paused, mentally halted, testing to see if she was yet ready to set Kitty's death aside and move on to the questions facing her. The evolving, emotionally escalating questions affecting her future, her life, and Simon's—the lives they had to live regardless of Kitty's demise.

She'd always known there were deaths that, if a lady wasn't careful, she might find herself living. How long she'd known the notion applied to her . . . she honestly couldn't remember. Perhaps, at base, deep down inside, that had been the reason she'd so determinedly eschewed men—and marriage—for so long.

Marriage, for her, was always going to be a risk, hence her search for the **right** husband, one who would provide all she required, and allow her to manage him, dictate their interaction, and otherwise go her own way. Her temper would never let her live within a relationship that sought to confine her; she would either break it, or it would break her.

And now here she was, facing the prospect of marriage to a man more than strong enough to bend her to his will. A man she didn't have it in her to break, but who, if she gave him her hand, could break her if he wished.

She'd always known what Simon was; never, not even at fourteen, had she mistaken his caliber, not seen him for the tyrant he was. But never had she dreamed he would take it into his head to marry her—certainly not before she had thought of marrying him. Yet he had, and she, with her curiosity about marriage born of her wish for a husband—something, thankfully, he still didn't know—had, quite literally, played into his hands.

And he'd let her.

Hardly surprising; that rang so very true to his nature.

Staring out at the darkening gardens, she thought again of him, of all they'd shared. All she still did not know.

All she still wished to learn.

Was it love that was growing between them? Or something he'd concocted to draw her to him?

Separate from that, was he truly capable of allowing her free rein within reason, allowing her to be as she was? Or was his offer simply a tactic to gain her agreement to their marriage?

Two questions—both were now clear in her mind.

There was only one way to learn the answers.

Try me.

She would have to put him to the test.

She sat by the window and watched the shadows lengthen, darken. Watched night descend, wrapping the gardens in silence.

Thought again of Kitty lying dead in the icehouse.

Felt the blood still coursing her own veins.

She still had her life to live, and that meant making of it what she could. She'd never lacked for courage; never in her life had she walked away from a challenge.

Never had she faced a challenge like this.

To take the situation he had wrought and shape from it the life she wanted, to claim from him—him of all men—the answers, the guarantees she needed to feel safe.

The truth was there was no going back. No pretending that what had happened between them hadn't, or that what had grown between them, still was growing between them, didn't exist.

Or that she could simply walk away, from it, from him—that he would let her.

No point pretending at all.

In waistcoat and shirtsleeves, Simon stood by the window in his room watching the waters of the lake turn to ink.

Feeling his mood turn equally black.

He wanted to go to Portia—now, tonight. Wanted to wrap her in his arms and know she was safe. Wanted, with a desire that was new and novel and so unlike passion he couldn't believe its strength, to make her feel safe.

That was his governing impulse, one he couldn't indulge.

The fact only fed his deepening disquiet.

She was in her room, alone. Thinking.

There was nothing he could do about it—nothing he could do to influence her conclusions.

He couldn't recall being so totally uncertain of any other woman in his life; he'd certainly never been so hobbled in his ability to turn a woman to his will.

There was nothing he could do. Unless or until she came to him, he was powerless to persuade her further. To convince her to go forward with him and explore making a marriage work—something to which he was now fully committed. He'd been perfectly serious in promising to find ways to accommodate her as far as he was able.

He would do whatever it took to get her to marry him; the alternative was not something he was prepared to face.

Yet presently, he was helpless. He was accustomed to being in control of his life, to being able to do something about anything that mattered. But in this—something that mattered more than anything else—until she came to him and gave him the chance, there was no action he could take.

His life, his future, were in her hands.

If she gave him few chances to persuade her, then decided against him, he would lose her, no matter that he was stronger than she in all ways that mattered. He could bring all society down on her head, and yet she would not bend. She would not yield. None knew that better than he.

Why he had fixed on a woman of indomitable will he didn't know, but it was too late to change things.

Chest swelling, he drew in a breath. He'd laughed at his brothers-in-law, hoist years ago with their own petards. He wasn't laughing now. He was in equally dire straits.

The latch clicked; he turned as the door opened.

Portia entered, turning to close the door behind her. He heard the lock snib before she turned and surveyed him, then, head rising, crossed the room to him.

He held perfectly still. Barely breathed.

Felt every inch the predator watching his prey innocently waltzing his way.

The faint moonlight reached her as she neared; he saw her expression, her level gaze, the determination in her face.

She walked directly to him, reached a hand to his nape, and drew his lips down to hers.

Kissed him.

The fire was still there, between them; it sprang to life as she parted her lips beneath his, as he instinctively responded.

Moving slowly, giving her plenty of time to break away if she would, he slid his hands about her waist, then, when she didn't complain, slid them further, ultimately closing his arms about her and drawing her close.

She sank against him; something in him unlocked, unfroze, melted away. He kissed her back, wanting more, and she gave it. Unhesitatingly, unstintingly.

He didn't know what she'd decided, what tack

she was now on, knew only the inexplicable relief of having her in his arms. Of having her want him.

She did; she made that abundantly clear, stretching against him, pressing close. Her tongue tangled with his, sensuously sliding, taking the kiss deeper, step by step. Wanting more, taking more, giving more. Kissing him with her usual one hundred percent focus, her customary devotion to the moment.

He knew it was deliberate—that she'd made up her mind to go this way.

Equally deliberate, he set aside his arguments, his persuasions, and simply followed.

Wound his arms about her upper thighs and lifted her against him. She responded with an ardent murmur, twined her arms about his neck and, head bent to his, feasted on his mouth. He paused, distracted, momentarily lost as he fought to appease her demands, then he ravaged her mouth, took command again, and carried her to the bed.

He tumbled them onto it, across it, instinctively rolling to trap her beneath him. She gasped, then grabbed his hair, his shoulders, clung to the kiss and wriggled, wrestled, until he rolled back and let her have her way, let her sprawl atop him, unencumbered by his weight.

Remembered he was the supplicant now, knew she wouldn't forget. Set himself to appease her, to enthrall and entice her all over again.

Devoted his mind, and his hands, lips, mouth,

and tongue, to the task. To giving himself, body and soul, to her.

Felt, in the moment the thought registered, the moment he accepted it and let it stand, a welling rightness, the rising swell of some deeper sea. It infused his touch, flowed through his fingers as he caressed her nape, eased through his body as he settled beneath her.

Openly prepared to let her have her way.

She hesitated, suspicious, but then accepted the unvoiced invitation, rising above him to better savor his mouth. Spreading her hands, she grasped the sides of his face and held him captive as she let out a satisfied sigh, released his lips, and, dark eyes glinting beneath heavy lids, ran her fingers back, into his hair.

Taking that as a sign, he sent his hands stroking over her back, smoothing her gown, then set his fingers to the buttons down her back.

She made a sound of protest; bracing her hands on his chest she pushed up, wriggled until she was straddling his waist, then looked down into his face.

He had no idea what she could see, but he lay still, his hands passive at her sides, watched her study him, waited for her lead.

Portia looked down at him, at his face, lit by the strengthening moonlight pouring through the window. She could read his acquiescence, his will-ingness to, at least tonight, at least here, be what-ever she wanted. Behave in whatever way she decreed.

She wanted—needed—more.

"You suggested a trial. Did you mean it?"

With her above him, he couldn't see her eyes well enough to read them. He searched her face, hesitated, then said, "I meant we should behave as if we were married so you can see—convince yourself—that it's possible. That being married to me won't be the disaster you fear."

"So you won't dictate, decree?" She gestured with one hand. "Simply take charge, take control?"

"I'll **try** not to." His jaw firmed. "I'm willing to bend as much as I'm able, to accommodate you within reason, but I can't—"

When he didn't go on, she supplied, "Change your stripes?"

She felt him exhale.

"I can't be someone I'm not, any more than you can accept being forced to be someone you're not." He held her eyes with his. "All we can do is try, and make of it what we can."

The sincerity in his tone slid beneath her guard and touched her. It was enough for now—assurance enough, invitation enough to test him and see.

"Very well. Let's try it, and see how far we get."

His hands, large, powerful, strong, remained passive at her sides, not pushing, not pressing . . . waiting.

She smiled, bent and set her lips to his. Taunted, then, as she felt his hands tense, draw back. Froze him with a glance.

And set her fingers to his cravat. Drew the diamond pin free and slid it into his waistcoat's edge, then settled to untie the knot, eventually dragging the long strip free. She paused with it dangling from her hand, the possibilities winging through her mind, then she smiled.

Took the long strip between both hands, flipped it to form a blindfold.

Caught his eyes over it. "Your turn."

The look on his face was priceless, yet he couldn't refuse to ease up from the bed, propped on his elbows, head bent forward while she secured the white band in place.

"I hope you know what you're doing," he muttered.

"I believe I'll manage."

With him blind, she could forget all need for guarding her expression, could focus completely on him, on securing what she wished from him.

Fingers on his shoulders, she pressed him back; he lay down again, stretched beneath her across the bed. The headboard and its pile of pillows lay to her right; from behind her left shoulder, the moon shone in, casting faint but sufficient light over him.

She set about creating the scene she had in mind, the stage on which tonight she would test him.

CHAPTER 12

The idea was too intriguing to deny. Pushing the halves of his waistcoat wide, she eased it off his shoulders, then tugged him up enough to yank it away; she sent it flying to the floor.

He eased back to the bed; she pounced on the line of buttons closing his shirt. Fingers busy, she watched his face; blindfolded, he couldn't see her watching, so was less vigilant in guarding his expression. From what she could see, he'd guessed at least some of her intention, and wasn't entirely sure how he felt.

Her smile turned determined as she freed the last button, yanked the tails from his waistband, then wrenched his shirt open. He'd have to grin and bear it.

"Think of England," she said. And spread her hands over him.

Greedily, fingers splayed, she filled her senses with the sculpted beauty of his chest, enthralled by the tactile bounty of firm, smooth skin over-layed by raspy, crinkly hair, feasted on the resilient muscles beneath, worshipped the width and inherent strength, gloried in its promise.

He shifted. "I'll survive."

Her smile turned wicked. She wrestled the shirt free and flung it away, then leaned low and touched the tip of her tongue to his collarbone. Surreptitiously, he sucked in a breath; the muscles of his abdomen tensed as he held it. Intent, she settled on his bare chest—settled to tease, to taunt, to torture.

To lick, lave, and rasp the tight buds of his nipples. With her teeth nip, here, there, then suck.

Until he shifted, until his hands, until then passive on her hips, started to tighten, until the muscles in his upper arms tensed.

With one last, long lick, she sat up.

Rose up on her knees, shifted back, pulling her skirts from under her, then sat straddling his hard thighs.

Leaning forward, she placed her hands again on his chest, then slowly, gradually, slid them down.

Over the corrugated muscles of his stomach. Down to his waist.

Beneath her palms, muscles shifted. Locked.

Satisfied, she sat back, waited. Watched as his anticipation eased. He drew in a breath.

She reached for his waistband.

Flicked the buttons free, laid open the flap, and closed her hands, both her hands, about him.

He went rigid, all of him, every muscle in his body seized; for the first minute, as she eased her hold, then tightened her grip again, then caressed, explored, fondled, he didn't breathe.

Then he did, shallowly. "If I can make a suggestion?"

She considered, then invited in her sultriest tone, "Suggest away."

He lifted his hands from where they'd fallen to the coverlet and closed them about hers.

Taught her exactly what she wished to know. How to touch him, how to pleasure him, how to press delight on him until his breath strangled in his throat.

Until he dragged in a huge breath, pulled her hands away and shifted beneath her, struggling to remove his trousers.

She rose and helped, wriggled back down his legs and stripped him.

Naked.

Flat on his back, with only the white band of his cravat over his eyes, with not a stitch to conceal him, he was a sight that took her breath away.

All this was hers.

If she dared claim it.

She licked her lips, then on her knees moved back up over his legs. Lifting and flicking out her skirts so they pooled around her, to the side and behind her, so that he could feel them against his bare skin—and feel the heat of her, of the place that ached and throbbed between her thighs, tantalizingly close as she again sat across his thighs, watching his face carefully all the while.

Gauging his state as she settled, hitching up her chemise so her bare skin met his—in the instant she closed her hands once more about his rigid erection.

The rush of impulses through him was strong as a tide; it broke against the wall of his will, straining under the pressure, but it refused to break. He clung on, his breathing increasingly harried.

She smiled; she wasn't finished with him yet.

Looking down, she admired the prize locked between her hands, then bent her head and set her lips to the hot, baby-soft skin.

He jerked; caught his breath.

Lovingly, she traced the head with her lips, then licked, around, down the long shaft . . . watched his face, watched his jaw lock, clenched tighter than she'd ever seen it . . .

Brazenly bold, she opened her lips and took him in.

He uttered a strangled sound. Reached for her, his fingers tangling in her long hair.

"No. Don't."

The words were barely understandable.

She released him, looked more closely at his face. "Why? You like it."

From all she could see, taking him between her lips had been the most exquisite torture she'd yet devised.

"That's not the point." He drew in a shattered breath. "At least, not at the moment."

"Hmm." She liked the taste of him, liked the sensation of having him so much in thrall.

"For God's sake, take pity." His hands had fallen

to her arms; he urged her forward. "Later—some other time."

She grinned. "Promise?"

"Word of a Cynster."

She laughed. Rising up on her knees, she came forward until she was straddling his hips, with nothing between his skin and hers, nothing bar inches of air separating his erection and the aching softness between her thighs.

He'd stopped tugging as soon as she'd moved; he seemed to be holding his breath.

She considered, then leaned down, and kissed him lovingly—unsurprised when he grabbed her head and ravaged her mouth, drank from her ravenously.

Coiling tension rose in the hard body rigidly supine beneath hers.

She drew back. He let her . . . waited, chest laboring . . .

When she didn't move, he ground out, "You do know what you're doing . . . ?"

She wasn't that innocent, not when it came to this. There were a number of books in the library at Calverton Chase that her brother, Luc, had always insisted be placed on the top shelf. He'd refused to lift them down. Consequently, she and Penelope had, at the first opportunity, climbed up and fetched the restricted volumes down. Many had proved to be picture books—with quite eye-opening pictures. She had never completely forgotten what she'd seen.

"In a manner of speaking." She edged back a fraction more. "I know it's possible, but tell me." Leaning forward from the hips, she drew her tongue slowly across one tight nipple, tasting the salt on his skin. Purred, "How exactly does this work?"

The laugh that racked him was harsh, abrupt—as if he were in pain. His chest swelled. "Simple." He grasped her hips. "Like this."

Even though he couldn't see, he guided her expertly back and down, until his rigid staff prodded her entrance; he tilted his hips, nudged in, then obediently stopped before she ordered him to.

She smiled. "Now I assume I sit up . . ." Bracing her hands on his chest, she eased upright. "Like this . . ."

She needed no answer. The slow slide of his body into hers fractured her breathing, sent a long, sensual shudder down her spine. Her eyes closed as her body gave, sheathing the rigid strength of his, gradually taking him in, accepting him. Inch by inch, all under her control, she pressed down, shifting and taking him deeper, then deeper still. The sensations were mind-numbing, all consuming—the heat, the pressure, the rock-solid reality. Exhaling, she spread her knees wider the better to sink lower yet, to take all of him, press him as high inside her as she could.

Then hold him tight.

"God!" His fingers sank into her hips; he held her down. "For pity's sake, hold still for a minute."

His voice was beyond strained, almost breaking.

She looked down at his face, at the blankness passion had wrought in his expression, and gave him his minute, used it herself to absorb the feeling of him high inside her, of how he filled her, completed her, of how her body welcomed him in. Her senses were thrumming, heated and alive, ready and waiting for all that was to come.

Beneath her, Simon clung to sanity by his fingernails. He'd told her he'd survive . . . he was no longer so sure. To be sheathed in such a way in scalding feminine flesh, slicker than silk, while unable to see, knowing she was fully dressed, feeling the air cool against his naked skin, feeling her stockinged thighs gripping his flanks—knowing she intended to ride him to oblivion, but with no idea what she intended after that . . . if he hadn't been lying down she would have brought him to his knees.

His time was apparently up; she grasped his wrists, eased his restraining hands from her hips— turned his hands, locked her fingers with his and leaned on his arms as slowly, muscles clinging and caressing him, she eased up.

Up.

Just before she lost him, she reversed direction.

And sank even more slowly, clingingly, down.

His jaw locked; his teeth clenched. She was still so damned tight it was a wonder he didn't spontaneously combust simply from the friction. As it was, his hips involuntarily jerked as she sank the last inch down.

"Uh-huh. You are to lie still. Completely still."

He bit back a caustic inquiry as to which army she planned to use to hold him down. Told himself he'd brought this on his own head and would simply have to endure it.

She experimented again, rising, then sinking down. Then her fingers, interdigitated with his, tightened; she started to ride him in earnest.

Her training had been exemplary, albeit in a different field. She'd ridden since she could walk, spent years riding wild across the Rutlandshire wolds. There was no chance she would tire soon.

His body rose to her challenge; he fought to remain as still as he could, to defer to her stated wishes. She held him, clasped him tightly, continued to ride steadily, transparently savoring him, only gradually moving faster and faster.

His breathing became labored, as was hers. She held tighter to his hands but didn't break her stride. He could feel her tightening about him, feel the tension coiling through her, feel it start to coalesce, condense.

On a gasp, she released his hands, grabbed his wrists, and guided his fingers to her breasts. Breath hitching, he cupped the firm mounds, then kneaded evocatively, searched and found the tight peaks, closed his fingers and squeezed . . . until she gasped anew, clamped hard about him, swayed, then braced her hands on his chest, caught her rhythm again, and rode on.

Rode him. Harder, faster, sliding her knees wider

still to take him ever deeper. The fight to remain passive nearly ruptured his heart. His pulse thundered, galloping with her, caught in the escalating heat, trapped in the relentless driving rhythm. Running with her. Urging her on.

Her breasts filled his hands, swollen and tight; she moaned when he kneaded, gasped when he squeezed.

She leaned forward, pressing her breasts into his palms. Hoarsely instructed, "Touch me."

He didn't need to ask where. Releasing her breasts, pushing aside her frothing skirts, he reached beneath, closed his hands about her flexing thighs, then followed them up. Slid one hand around to grip her hip. With the other stroked her damp curls once, heard her breath hitch, felt her body constrict almost painfully about him.

Set one fingertip to her pearl.

Knowingly caressed.

Paused. Heard her earnest, breathless entreaty.

Pressed.

And she imploded.

With a soft cry, she climaxed about him, her body contracting powerfully, her hands clenching tight on his chest.

His body reacted.

The surge of primitive need, of fueled lust, desire, and so much more, nearly shattered his control. Head back, he gasped, dragging air into his locked lungs; fingers gripping her hips, sinking in, he held her down, impaled to the hilt, held her still, fought to hold on to the reins of his demons, aroused, teased, taunted, and now slavering, fully expecting, now, to be released—to be allowed to feast on her soft, feminine, satiated body.

Jaw locked, teeth clenched, breath bated, he waited . . .

She slumped on his chest. Then reached up, guided his lips to hers, and kissed him.

Invitingly—or so he hoped. Prayed.

The tension thrumming just beneath his skin, the rigidity of his body, reached her. He felt her hesitate, then she reached up again—and tugged the blindfold from his eyes.

Watched him blink, then met his gaze. Held it as she stretched luxuriously against him—smiled as his hands locked on her hips, keeping her precisely where she was, fully sheathing him.

Her expression that of a cat who'd had her fill of cream, she held his gaze, and tossed the blindfold away. Lowered her arm and traced his cheek.

Whispered softly, "Take me, then."

His senses leapt; reflexively, so did the rest of him, before he slammed his control back into place and locked every muscle again. Her eyes widened, but the tenor of the smile curving her lips—knowingly wanton—didn't fade.

He met her eyes, dark, dreamy with spent passion, yet very much awake. Watching, waiting, for what he would do . . .

Their breaths mingled, his still tense and labored, hers softer in the aftermath of climax.

Yet another spur he did not need.

She'd issued an open invitation, hadn't specified. He wondered if she could even conceive of the primitive urge riding him, evoked by her game.

He wanted to take her from behind, to position her on her knees before him, her skirts flipped up over her shoulders, a surrended captive, to drive into her and feel her open for him, yield to him.

His.

He licked his lips. Easing his hands from her hips, he reached up and around, and set his fingers to the buttons closing her gown.

Held her gaze as he undid them.

Told himself he'd have her as he wished—one day.

But not yet. Later, if he played tonight's hand wisely, kept his head through the following days— even weeks—then one day he'd be able to let fall the reins and show her precisely what she was to him.

Precisely how she made him feel.

Shifting within her as little as possible, he drew her gown off, over her head. She helped, lifting her arms, wriggling free of the folds, aiding him in removing her chemise as well.

Leaving her naked but for her stockings.

He rolled her beneath him.

Nearly lost his mind when she pressed his shoulder back. "Wait."

His control shivered, fractured, started to fall away . . .

She shifted beneath him. He sucked in a breath, opened his lips to tell her he **couldn't** wait—

Instead, blinked, watched, amazed as, lifting one of her long legs high, she rolled her stocking down—or rather up and off. She caught his gaze as she flung it away. "I like to feel my skin against yours."

He wasn't about to argue; he allowed her to shift enough to perform the same feat with her other leg, noting with increasing fascination the ease with which she accomplished the deed.

New vistas blossomed in his mind.

But then she flung the second stocking away, twined both arms about his neck and drew his head down.

"There. Now you may—"

He stopped her words with a searing kiss.

Took her breath from her, ravaged her mouth, and sent her senses spinning—faster, harder, faster yet—until she arched beneath him, inchoately pleading . . . until he anchored her hips and drove into her.

Again, and again, and again.

He felt the reins slide and couldn't grab them back, could only surrender to the storm. To the blinding urgency that drove his body to plunder hers.

Far from complaining, she arched beneath him, fingernails raking his back. Flagrantly demanding, commanding, wanting . . . as desperate as he in needing more.

He wedged her thighs wider; she went one step further, lifting her long legs, wrapping them about his hips, opening herself to him, giving him all he wished.

Heart pounding, he took, took her, gave himself.

Head back, braced above her, he let go, closed his eyes—and let the swirling power have him. Infuse him, drive him.

Felt it close in, sweep him up.

Shatter him.

Felt her cling as he shuddered, knew when she joined him.

Felt ecstasy flow through them, melding their bodies.

Felt it thunder through their veins and fuse their hearts.

Portia lay back, high on the pillows where Simon had lifted her once the tumult had passed.

Passed, but it hadn't yet died. The aftermath still held them, heat slowly dissipating, languor weighting their limbs.

She could grow used to this; this sense of intimate closeness, the sharing, the fury. The bliss.

One arm draped over the pillows behind her head, with the other, she idly sifted his hair, the fine texture a sensual delight. He lay slumped half beside her, half over her, one arm beneath her, his head pillowed against her breast, his other hand splayed possessively over her stomach.

He was heavy, hot, and oh so real. He'd withdrawn from her only moments before; her body was slowly returning to itself, to being hers, not his, not filled with him. She felt curiously alive, senses still bright with the lingering glory, her flesh still swollen, hot, still throbbing, her pulse still racing.

In the icehouse, Kitty lay cold, beyond all such feeling.

For long moments, Portia thought of all she and Simon had already shared, and of all they might yet find between them.

And silently vowed not to make Kitty's mistakes.

She would value trust and devotion, see love for what it was, accept whence it sprang, and with whom.

And make sure—absolutely sure—he did, too.

If what lay between them was love, she wasn't fool enough to fight it. On the contrary; if it was love, it was worth fighting for.

She glanced down, feathered her fingers through his soft, burnished brown locks, silkier than many a woman's.

He lifted his head, met her gaze.

She held his, then said, "I'm not going to marry you unless I want to."

"I know."

She wondered, wished she could see his eyes more clearly, but the moonlight had faded, cloaking them in shadows.

He exhaled, lifted from her, shifted higher in the bed and settled on his back, drawing her into his arms. The bonelessness of satiation still infusing her, she rested her head on his chest, in the hollow below his shoulder. "I want to learn more, **need** to learn more, **but** don't read it as any degree of agreement."

After a moment, he lifted his head and pressed a kiss to her hair. Lay back. "Go to sleep."

The words were gentle enough; his thoughts, she suspected, were anything but. He wasn't an intrinsically gentle man; he wasn't the sort to resign from a fight, to ride away from the field at the first reverse. He would rally—and drive relentlessly, ruthlessly on toward his goal.

Much good would it do him; she wasn't going to bend.

But she'd warned him—and he'd warned her. A truce of sorts, complex and conditional but enough to allow them to go on. Not just in exploring what lay between them, but in facing what the next days would bring. The "gentleman from Bow Street" and the inevitable unmasking of Kitty's murderer. Whatever came, they would face it shoulder to shoulder, bound by an understanding so fundamental it didn't require stating.

The day had been long; its events had wrought untold upheaval.

Minutes ticked by; the heavy thud of Simon's heart just beneath her ear soothed and comforted.

Closing her eyes, she surrendered to the night.

Simon woke her as she'd wished to be woken the morning before.

She was a sound sleeper; her body responded to his practiced ministrations even while she slumbered. Spreading her thighs, he settled between and eased into her.

Felt her arch, felt her breath catch, then she sighed, and opened brilliant blue eyes. Eyes so dark they mesmerized; as he moved within her, he felt like he was drowning in their depths.

She rose with him, clinging, clutching, lids falling at the last as she fractured with a soft cry.

A cry that ripped through him, sank talons through striving muscle and bone, wrapped about his gut, his heart, his soul, and hauled him into the void, over the edge of the world and into sweet oblivion.

Cocooned in the covers, he lay fully atop her, acutely conscious of how well they fitted, how perfectly she matched him. She turned her head and their lips met, clinging, caressing. She held him easily in her arms, cradled between her slim thighs.

Dawn was near. He couldn't let her sleep. He roused her further, rousted her out of bed and into her clothes.

Grumbling, she gave him to understand that early morning was not her favorite time to be sneaking around country houses.

He got her back to her room unobserved, opened her door, kissed her fingers, then bundled her in and shut the door.

Portia heard his retreating footsteps, frowned at

the closed panel. She would much rather have remained, safe and warm in his arms, for at least the next hour. Long enough to recoup her energies—energies he'd very efficiently drained. Keeping pace with him through the corridors had required concentration—to keep her muscles moving, ignoring the odd twinges and aches.

She had a strong suspicion he had no real idea how . . . vigorous he was.

Stifling a sigh, she turned and surveyed the room.

It was as she'd left it last night, the bedcovers turned invitingly down, the window still open, curtains undrawn.

She considered the bed, surely the most sensible option given her state. But if she lay down, she'd fall asleep—she'd have to take off her gown and don her nightdress, or how would she explain to the maid?

The problem was insoluble, at least in her present state; she had insufficient energy to undo the buttons down her back that Simon had just done up.

That left the chair by the hearth or the window seat. The breeze wafting through the window carried a dawn chill; she headed for the armchair. The cold hearth was an uninspiring sight; tugging the chair about to face the window, she dropped into its cushioned comfort with a deep sigh.

And let her mind roam. Looked into her own heart, wondered about his. Revisited her goals, reassessed her aspirations. Recalled with a grimace her earlier thought that of all the gentlemen present, Simon, Cynster as he was, epitomized the most marriageable qualities—what she'd meant, could now see clearly enough to admit, was that the qualities he possessed were those most likely to persuade her to marriage.

His less attractive aspects she also knew well. His overprotectiveness had always irked, yet it was his dictatorial possessiveness that most frightened her. Once she was his, there would be no escape; that was simply the way he was.

She shivered, wrapped her arms around herself—wished she'd thought of fetching her shawl but couldn't raise enough energy to get up and do so now.

The only way she could accept Simon's suit— give him her hand and accept all that that meant— was if she trusted him always to consider her feelings, to deal with her, treat with her, not arbitrarily to dictate.

Not a small thing to demand of a tyrant.

Last night, she'd gone to him knowing she'd have the whip hand, trusting that he would allow her to wield it. He could have filched the reins from her whenever he'd wished—yet he hadn't, even though that restraint had, from all the evidence, cost him dearly.

He'd abided by the conditions she'd set. She'd spent the night safe, reassured of her own vitality, her ability to live and even love. Her ability to trust and gain trust's reward.

Previously, he'd never have let her dictate terms

as he had last night, regardless of the situation. It simply wasn't in his nature . . . hadn't been, but now was, at least with her.

A willingness to share the reins, to try to accommodate her as he'd promised. She'd felt it in his touch, read it in his eyes . . . events confirmed it truly had been there, and wasn't just a figment of her wishful imagination.

Which left them going forward, examining the possible.

Beyond the window, the sky turned rosy, then faded into the pale, washed-out blue of a hot summer's day.

The click of the latch jerked her from her thoughts. Swiveling in the chair, she watched, mentally scrambling, as the cheery little maid who tended her room came bustling in.

The maid saw her; her eyes turned round, her face filled with sympathy. "Oh, miss—did you spend all night there?"

"Ah . . ." She rarely lied, but . . . "Yes." She looked back at the window, gestured. "I couldn't sleep . . ."

"Well, that's hardly to be wondered at, is it?" Bright and breezy, the maid produced a cloth and set to wiping and polishing the mantelpiece. "We heard tell as how it was you found the body— stumbled right over it."

Portia inclined her head. "Indeed."

"We was all talking in the servants' hall, frightened it might be one of the gentlemen, but Mrs.

Fletcher, she's the housekeeper, told us it was the gypsies, sure as anything."

"The gypsies?"

"That Arturo—he's always hanging about, putting on airs. 'Andsome devil, he is, and quick with the ladies, if you take my meaning."

Portia inwardly frowned. She wrestled with her conscience for all of two seconds. "Did any of you have any reason to think it might have been one of the gentlemen?"

"Nah—that was just us, imagining-like."

"Did the staff like Mrs. Glossup?"

"Mrs. G?" Picking up a pewter vase, the maid rubbed hard, concentration in her face. "She was all right—had a temper on her, o'course, and I suppose some might call her flighty, but then all young married ladies are, aren't they?"

Portia bit her tongue.

The maid set down the vase, tucked her cloth into her pocket. "Ah well, wouldn't you know it—it's the day for the sheets." She strode across the room to the bed; Portia watched her, envying her her energy.

"Blenkinsop says as how there'll be a man coming down from Lunnon." Gripping the turned-down corner, the maid glanced at Portia. "To ask about what happened."

Portia nodded. "Apparently it's required."

The maid's lips formed an O; she yanked back the sheet—

Furious hissing filled the air.

The maid leapt back, her gaze locked on the bed. She paled. **"Oh my Gawd!"** The last word rose in a shriek.

Portia leapt up and rushed to the girl's side.

The hissing escalated.

"Oh my heavens!" Portia stared at the adder, angry and irritated, coiling in the middle of her bed.

She tugged the maid's sleeve.

The maid squealed.

As one, they turned and fled across the room, yanking open the door, then slamming it shut behind them.

The maid collapsed against the nearby stair rail, gasping for breath.

Portia checked that the bottom of the door fitted flush to the floor—no space for an angry adder to slide through—then slumped against the wall.

An hour later, she sat in Lady O's room, her hands wrapped about a steaming mug of cocoa. Not even the scalding brew could stop her shivering.

Her bedchamber was at the end of the wing; Blenkinsop, doing his morning rounds opening up the great house, had been at the bottom of the stairs when she and the maid had come flying out of her room. He'd heard the commotion and come hurrying up, just in time to quell the maid before she launched into hysterics.

Portia had explained. Blenkinsop had paled, then quickly taken charge. He'd ushered her downstairs to a small parlor, summoning footmen to assist him, and the housekeeper, into whose charge he assigned the sobbing maid.

In an unsteady voice, she'd asked for Simon to be summoned. Didn't stop to consider the proprieties, only knew she wanted him, and he would come.

He had; he'd taken one look at her, and insisted on sweeping her upstairs again—to Lady O's room, into Lady O's keeping.

Propped high on her pillows, Lady O had listened to Simon's abbreviated explanation, then fixed him with a black stare. "Fetch Granny."

When Simon blinked, she'd snorted. "Granville—Lord Netherfield. He may be a trifle feeble these days, but he was always a good man in a crisis. His room's in the middle of the main wing—closest to the main stairs."

Simon had nodded; Lady O had transferred her gaze to Portia. "As for you, gel—you'd better sit down before you fall down."

She'd complied, sinking into the chair by the hearth; Simon had left.

Sliding from the bed, tugging her wrap about her shoulders, Lady O had picked up her cane and clomped over to take the other armchair. Easing down into it, she'd fixed her with a sapient eye. "Right then. Tell me what happened and don't leave anything out."

By the time she'd satisfied Lady O—allowing the fiction that she'd fallen asleep in the armchair in her room to stand—Blenkinsop had appeared.

"We've removed the viper, miss. The footmen have searched the room—there's no danger there now."

She'd murmured her thanks, inwardly struggling to believe that such a thing had actually happened, that this wasn't some disordered dream. Lady O had summoned maids to help her dress and sent another to fetch Portia fresh clothes. And the cocoa.

When a tap on the door heralded Lord Netherfield and Simon, she was sitting, primly neat in a gown of magenta twill, sipping the cocoa and trying to assimilate the fact that someone had tried to kill her. At the very least, to scare her witless.

Lord Netherfield was concerned yet practical; after she'd recounted her story, catching Simon's eye when she explained why she'd not slept in her bed, his lordship, perched on a stool between the armchairs, sat back and regarded them all.

"This is all most distressing. I've asked Blenkinsop to keep the matter quiet. None of the other ladies heard the commotion, it seems, and the staff are all trustworthy—they'll keep mum."

One arm braced against the mantelpiece, Simon frowned. "Why?"

Lord Netherfield looked up at him. "Starve the enemy of information, what?" He looked again at Portia. "It might not be much, but we have to face the fact that that adder could not have got under your covers by itself. Someone's expecting you to be dead, or if not that, then at least hysterical enough to leave immediately."

"Before the gentleman from Bow Street arrives?" Simon glanced at his lordship, who grimly nodded.

"That's the way I see it." Again, he looked at Portia. "How do you feel, my dear?"

She thought, admitted, "Shaken, but not shaken enough to flee."

"That's my girl. So"—his lordship slapped his palms on his thighs—"what can we learn from this? Why did Kitty's murderer—in the circumstances, I think we must assume it was he or she—want you gone, one way or t'other?"

Portia looked blankly back at him.

"Because," Simon answered, "the murderer believes you saw something that identifies him."

"Or heard something, or in some other way know something." Lady O nodded. "Yes, that has to be it." She skewered Portia with her black gaze. "So—what is it you know?"

She looked back at them. "Nothing."

They questioned her—took her back over all she'd done, all she'd seen since entering the front hall the previous afternoon. She knew what they were doing, and why, so kept her temper. In the end, she put down her empty cup, and simply said, "I can't tell you something I don't know."

With a humph, a sigh, and a concerned frown, they finally accepted that.

"Well, then!" Lord Netherfield rose. "Next thing is to see this fellow Bow Street sends down. When you speak with him, tell him everything you know—about Kitty and everyone else here, too.

Not just from yesterday, but ever since you arrived . . . no, more than that. Anything you know about those presently here from farther afield, too." He met Portia's gaze. "We can't tell what little piece of information you may have that points a finger at the blackguard."

She blinked, then nodded. "Yes, of course." She started mentally cataloging those of the guests she'd known before.

Lady O snorted. "What is this business of persons from Bow Street? Why are they involved?"

"It's the way things are done now. Not comfortable, but in the interests of justice, it seems to have its merits. Heard about a most peculiar case at my club not long ago. Gentleman done to death with a poker in his own library. They were all set to blame the butler, but then the investigating chappie proved it was the man's brother. Huge scandal, of course. The family were devastated . . ."

His lordship's words trailed away. They all remained silent, all thinking the same thing.

Whoever had killed Kitty, there was a good chance it was one of the guests or one of the Glossups, either Henry or James, his lordship's grandsons. If the murderer was unmasked, there would be a scandal. Potentially a very damaging one. For someone, for some family.

Lord Netherfield eventually sighed. "You know, I can't say I liked Kitty. Didn't approve of her, of how she played fast and loose with Henry. She was a supremely silly and brazen chit, yet"—his lips twisted—"for all that, she didn't deserve to be done in like that."

He focused on them all. "I wouldn't want her murderer to escape retribution. The poor woman deserves at least that."

They all nodded. A pact had been made. They knew each other well enough to recognize all they held in common, a belief in justice, an instinctive reaction against those who flouted it. Together, they would work to unmask the murderer regardless of who it was.

"Well, then!" Lord Netherfield clapped his hands together, looked first at Portia, then Lady O. "Let's head down to breakfast—and see who's surprised to see Miss Ashford in the pink."

They rose, shook out skirts, settled coats and cuffs, then headed downstairs to do battle.

CHAPTER 13

Much good did it do them; there was so much nervousness about the breakfast table, some starting at every little thing, others sunk in abstraction, that it was impossible to point to any one response to Portia's appearance as especially indicative.

Everyone was already pale; many looked wan, as if they'd slept poorly.

"If we were to judge by looks alone, at least half the party would qualify as suspects," Simon muttered, as he and Portia, having quit the breakfast parlor, stepped off the terrace onto the lawn.

"I think there's a certain amount of guilt doing the rounds." Many of the older ladies had broken their habit of breakfasting in their rooms and joined the rest of the company in the parlor. "If instead of trying to ignore her, and when they couldn't do that, trying to rein her in, if they'd talked to Kitty, tried to understand . . . she didn't seem to have a friend, a confidante, or anyone to advise her. If she had, maybe someone would know why she was killed. Or maybe she wouldn't have been killed at all."

He raised his brows, but forebore to comment. In his family and Portia's all the females from their earliest years were surrounded by strong women. He had difficulty imagining any other existence.

By unvoiced consent, he and Portia headed for the lake path—cool, soothing. Quiet. Calming.

"The ladies seem to think it's someone from outside, by which I infer they mean the gypsies." He glanced at her. "Do you know if any of them have reason to think it really might have been Arturo or Dennis?"

She shook her head. "It's simply the most unthreatening possibility. To imagine the murderer is someone they know, someone in whose company they've spent the last days . . . that's quite frightening."

It was on the tip of his tongue to ask if she was frightened, then he glanced at her face, and swallowed the words. She was too intelligent not to be. While he'd much rather protect her from all such feelings, he couldn't stop her from seeing, thinking, understanding.

Reluctantly, he accepted that between them it would always be so; if he was to deal with her as she was, that was something that wouldn't change. She might adjust a little to please him, but it was he who would have to change most—adjust his thinking and modify his reactions—to have any chance of meeting her at the altar.

"This is senseless!" They'd reached the spot before the summerhouse; leaving the path, Portia stalked to the summerhouse steps, swung her skirts around, and sat.

The sunshine washed over her; looking down at her, he wondered if she was still chilled, then he turned and sat beside her, close enough that she could, if she wished, lean against him.

Elbows on her knees, she cupped her chin in her palms and frowned out at the lake. "Which of the men could have killed Kitty?"

"You heard Willoughby—other than Charlie, who was with Lady O, and me, any of them." After a moment, he added, "As far as I know, that also applies to most of the ladies."

She turned her head and stared at him. "Winifred?"

"Drusilla?"

She grimaced. "Kitty was so short, it could have been either."

"Or even one of the others—how can we say?" Setting an elbow on the step behind, he leaned back, a little to the side so he could see her face. "Perhaps Kitty did something in London last Season to make one of them her sworn enemy?"

Portia frowned, then shook her head. "I didn't get any sense of that—of old and hidden emnity."

After a moment, he suggested, "Let's decide who it couldn't have been. Not the Hammond sisters—they're too short and I can't believe it of them. And I think Lucy Buckstead's in the same class."

"But not Mrs. Buckstead—she's large enough,

and perhaps Kitty was planning on doing something that would damage Lucy's chances—she's the Bucksteads' only child, after all, and she has set her heart on James."

He inclined his head. "Mrs. Buckstead remains possible. Not probable, perhaps, but we can't cross her off our list."

"And for the same reason, Mr. Buckstead stays a suspect, too."

He glanced at Portia. "As far as I'm concerned, they're all suspects. Except me and Charlie."

She blinked at him. "What about Lord Netherfield?"

He held her gaze. Eventually said, "Until we know who it really is, I'm assuming it could be anyone—anyone still on our list."

Her lips thinned, then she opened them to argue—

"No." She blinked at his tone; when she continued to stare, he felt forced to explain, "The murderer tried to kill you. Given it's **you** he now has his eye on, I'm not willing to take any chances." He felt his face harden as he added, in case she'd missed the point, "None. Not one."

She searched his eyes. He could almost see her thoughts whizzing behind her dark eyes, almost see the balance as she weighed his arguments against what she knew of his character, and all that flowed from it.

In the end, she inclined her head. "All right."

She looked back at the lake; he quietly exhaled.

"Not Lady O, and not Lady Hammond, either."

He considered, then acquiesced. "Agreed. Similarly, I think we can eliminate Mrs. Archer."

"But not Mr. Archer."

"He's something of a dark horse. I agree—we can't ignore him."

"If we follow your line, theoretically at least any of the Glossup men could be responsible."

He hesitated. "What do you think of Oswald?"

She frowned, then grimaced. "I honestly felt he avoided Kitty—I think because she saw him and treated him as a child."

"Hardly comfortable for his ego, but . . . unless there's something that would account for him being transformed into a murderous rage—and I honestly haven't seen any propensity for that in him—then he seems unlikely."

"Granted. What about Swanston—do we cross him off for the same reason?"

He frowned. "I don't think we can. He's Kitty's brother—there might have been some bone of contention in their past we know nothing of, and he's neither as easygoing nor as soft as Oswald. If Kitty had prodded too hard, Swanston could physically have done the deed. Whether he did . . . ?"

"Which brings us to Winifred." She paused, considering. Eventually said, "Do you really think she might have been angry enough over Kitty's poaching her suitors—even Desmond, even now— that she might have . . . ."

He watched her face. "You know Winifred better than I—do you think she could have?"

For a long minute, she stared out at the dark waters of the lake, then glanced at him, grimaced. "Winifred will have to remain on the list."

"And Desmond is certainly on it, which, in fact, gives Winifred an even stronger motive."

Portia pulled a face, but didn't argue. "Ambrose is on the list, too, which means Lady Calvin and Drusilla must stay on as well."

After a moment, he asked, "Why Drusilla? I can understand Lady Calvin—she has a great deal invested in Ambrose's future, and although she's so reserved, he's very much the apple of her eye. But as I read things, Drusilla and Ambrose don't share even the weakest brother-sister bond."

"True. Nevertheless, Drusilla's reasons are twofold. One, of us all, she was the **angriest** at Kitty—Kitty had all the attributes Drusilla lacked, and still she wasn't content. I'm sure that rankled—Drusilla hadn't met Kitty before coming down here, so that's the only explanation I can see for her reaction."

"And her second reason?"

"Lady Calvin, of course. Not Ambrose, but the pain Lady Calvin would be forced to bear if Ambrose became involved in any scandal." She met his gaze. "Drusilla is utterly devoted to her mother."

He raised his brows, but now that she'd pointed it out . . . "That leaves us with the gypsies, or one of the servants."

Portia frowned. "I might not approve of Arturo slipping through the shrubbery at all hours, but I can't see any reason why he would **bother** to kill Kitty. If it was his child she was carrying . . ." She stopped. "Oh."

She looked at him. "Is that a motive do you think? That Kitty told him she was planning on getting rid of the baby . . . don't gypsies have a code or something about that?"

He held her gaze. "Most men have a code or something about that."

She colored. "Yes, of course—but you know what I mean."

"Indeed, but I think you're forgetting one thing."

She raised her brows.

"The timing. Kitty must have conceived in London, not down here. Arturo wasn't in London."

"Ah." Her face cleared. "Of course. So there's really no reason Arturo would have killed her."

"Not that I can see. And as for Dennis, even imagining an unrequited love, given he knew Arturo was consorting with Kitty, I can't see Dennis imagining himself in the running. Again, why kill her?"

"I talked to the maid about how the staff saw Kitty. The girl's a local and has lived here on the estate all her life. She knows everyone, and is old enough to scent any scandal between stairs. There wasn't even a hint she considered such a thing vaguely possible—in fact, she told me the maids were frightened the murderer was one of the gentlemen, and they'd been reassured by the housekeeper that it was sure to be the gypsies."

He snorted. "The gypsies. Always the most convenient scapegoats."

"Especially if they up stakes and leave." She paused, mused, "I wonder if the murderer, whoever he is, has thought of that?"

"I'd say he might be counting on it—the gypsies decamping in the dead of night would be his salvation."

They both sat staring out at the lake, watching the breeze send ripples across the glassy surface. Minutes passed, then Portia sighed.

"The Glossups. We've left all of them except Oswald, even Lady Glossup, on our list. Why do you think one of them would have killed Kitty? They'd put up with her for three or more years, and the Archers were staying. Why kill her—and especially why now? There would have to be a very good reason."

"Two reasons," he replied, his tone flat and even. "One, divorce—a topic Henry's only recently been forced to consider. Two, the baby she was carrying that wasn't any of theirs, but which, if she'd borne it, would have been the next Glossup heir. They might not rank as high as either the Cynsters or the Ashfords, but the Glossups have been around almost as long—they're an old and, in their way, distinguished house."

"But she wasn't going to bear it—she was quite definite about that."

"You overheard her telling her mother that—how many others knew?"

Portia spread her hands. "How many others knew she was having a baby at all?"

"Only you, those she told, and those they might in turn have told."

Portia wrinkled her nose. "I told Lady O. And you."

"Precisely. And there's always the servants—they overhear more than we think."

"And the household must have known Kitty and Henry were estranged."

"Which means it would have been obvious to all that any child Kitty was carrying was not—"

When he stopped, Portia looked at him, then grimaced horrendously. "If the baby wasn't a Glossup—and it most likely wasn't—then that would have been bad enough, but what if it was indeed a Glossup?"

"Worse, what if it wasn't, but Kitty claimed it was?"

"No—you forget. She didn't want to carry the child."

"I hadn't forgotten." There was ice in his tone. "If she wanted to persuade the father—or someone who might have been the father, or even someone who could not possibly be the father—that it would be wise to help her abort the child . . ." He met Portia's gaze. "What better way to persuade James, or Harold, or even Lord Netherfield to aid her than by claiming the baby was a Glossup, just not Henry's."

Portia stared at him, her eyes growing round.

"You mean . . . she'd tell James it was Harold's, or Harold it was James's, or Lord Netherfield either . . ."

She put her hand to her chest and swallowed. "Good God!"

"Exactly. And what if Henry found out?"

She held his gaze, then looked away.

After a moment, he went on, "And that's not even considering the looming likelihood of divorce. For Harold and Catherine, and Lord Netherfield, too, the very concept is shocking, more than it is for us. For their generation, it's an unthinkable scandal reflecting on all the family.

"We know what Kitty was like, how she delighted in irritating people. We know that she went to the library to meet someone, but we don't know whom or why. We don't know what they discussed—what topic drove the murderer to silence her."

Portia said nothing, her understanding and agreement implicit. After a few minutes, she slipped her hand into his, leaned against his shoulder. Flicking free of her fingers, he lifted his arm and she wriggled closer as he gathered her in.

She sighed. "Kitty was playing with fire on so many fronts, it's hardly surprising she got burned."

Luncheon was a subdued affair. Lord Willoughby had informed them they would need to remain until the investigator from Bow Street arrived. Since that individual was expected later in the afternoon, many spent the hours after lunch making discreet arrangements to leave that evening.

Aside from all else, most felt the Glossups should be left to deal with their loss in peace, without the distraction of houseguests; anything else was quite shockingly unthinkable.

The investigator duly arrived—and promptly informed them that they would need to think again.

A large man, heavily built but with an air of determined energy, Inspector Stokes had first spoken with Lord Glossup and Lord Netherfield in the study before being conducted into the drawing room and introduced to the guests en masse.

He inclined his head politely. Portia noticed his eyes, a steady slate grey, moving over each face as their names were said. When her turn came, she regally inclined her head, watched Stokes duly note Simon sitting on the arm of her chair, his arm on its back; then his gaze rose to Simon's face, he acknowledged his name with a nod, and moved on.

Despite all, her interest was piqued—not in Stokes the man, but Stokes the investigator. How was he going to unmask the murderer?

"I take it, Mr. Stokes, that now you have met us, you have no objections to our departing?" Lady Calvin asked the question, the full weight of her status as an earl's daughter echoing in her tone.

Stokes didn't blink. "I regret, ma'am, that until

the murderer's identified, or until I've investigated as far as I'm able, that I must request that you all"—his gaze swept the company—"remain at Glossup Hall."

Lady Calvin colored. "But that's preposterous!"

"Indeed, sir." Lady Hammond fluffed her shawl. "I'm sure you mean well, but it's quite out of the question—"

"Unfortunately, ma'am, it's the law."

There was not an ounce of anything anyone could take exception to in Stokes's tone, nor yet any comfort they could draw from it.

He inclined his head in something resembling a bow. "I regret, ma'am, but it's quite essential."

Lord Glossup huffed. "Standard procedures and all that, I understand. No point quibbling—and really, there's no reason the party can't continue, except for . . . well, yes, except for that."

Portia was sitting across from the Archers. Mrs. Archer appeared still in shock; it was questionable whether she'd taken anything in since being told her younger daughter had been strangled. Mr. Archer, however, was pale but determined; he sat at his wife's side, a hand on her arm. At Stokes's words, a glimmer of pain had crossed his features; now he cleared his throat, and said, "I would take it kindly if we could all assist Mr. Stokes in whatever way we can. The sooner he finds Kitty's murderer, the better it will be for us all."

There was nothing to be heard in his voice beyond a father's grief, controlled yet unflaggingly genuine. Naturally, his appeal was met by quiet murmurs and assurances that yes, of course, put like that . . .

Stokes hid it well, but he was relieved. He waited until the murmurs died, then said, "I understand Miss Ashford, Mr. Cynster, and Mr. Hastings were the first to see the body." His gaze swung to Portia and Simon; she nodded slightly. "If I could speak with you three first . . . ?"

No real question, of course; the three of them rose and followed Stokes and Lord Glossup to the door.

"You can use the estate office—I told them to clear the rubbish."

"Actually." Stokes halted by the door. "I would much prefer to use the library. I believe that's where the body was found?"

Lord Glossup frowned, but nodded. "Aye."

"Then it's unlikely your guests will be keen to spend time there. It would expedite my questioning if I can establish specific points at the scene, so to speak."

Lord Glossup had to agree. Portia went through the door Stokes held open and led the way to the library; she exchanged a glance with Simon as he opened the library door, was sure he, too, felt Stokes's request had rather more reason than that.

Whatever it was, it felt undeniably strange to reenter the room where she'd discovered Kitty's body. Had it only been just over twenty-four hours ago? It felt more like days.

They all paused just inside the door; Stokes closed it, then waved them to the armchairs gathered before the fireplace, at the opposite end of the room from the desk.

Portia sat on the chaise, Simon sat beside her. Charlie took one armchair. Stokes considered them, then sat in the other armchair, facing them. Portia wondered if he was sensitive enough to read the arrangement; it was indeed him against the three of them, at least until they decided if they would trust him.

He drew a notebook from his coat pocket and flipped it open. "Miss Ashford, if you could start by describing exactly what happened from the point where you entered the front hall yesterday afternoon." He looked up at her. "You were with Mr. Cynster, I understand?"

Portia inclined her head. "We'd been walking in the pinetum."

He glanced at a sheet he'd unfolded and laid on his knee. "So you'd gone out together through the front door?"

"No. We'd left from the terrace after lunch, and circled around via the lake path, and so on to the pinetum."

He followed the route on what was clearly a sketch of the house and grounds. "I see. So you entered the front hall from the forecourt. What happened then?"

Step by step, he led her through the moments, leading her to describe her movements remarkably accurately.

"Why did you wander around the room like that? Were you looking for a book?"

"No." Portia hesitated, then, with a fleeting glance at Simon, explained, "After my discussion with Mr. Cynster I was somewhat overset. I came in here to think and circled the room to calm down."

Stokes blinked. His gaze shifted to Simon; faint puzzlement showed in his eyes. Neither of them exhibited the slightest sign of any tension between them—quite the opposite.

She took pity on him. "Mr. Cynster and I have known each other since childhood—we frequently upset each other."

Stokes looked back at her. "Ah." He met her gaze; she saw a glimmer of respect—he'd realized she'd followed his thoughts well enough to answer the question he hadn't yet posed. He looked down at his notebook. "Very well. So you continued on around the room . . ."

She continued her story. When she came to the point of Simon's rushing in, Stokes stopped her, and switched his interrogation to Simon.

It was easier to appreciate Stokes's art when it wasn't directed at her. She watched and listened as he drew a highly detailed and factual account from Simon, then turned his attention to Charlie; Stokes was really very good. All three of them had come prepared to tell him all, yet there remained a reticence, a barrier over which they would speak, but not cross; Stokes was not of their class, not of their world.

They'd all entered the room reserving judgment. She exchanged a glance with Simon, noted Charlie's more relaxed pose; both of them were revising their opinions of "the gentleman from Bow Street."

He'd be fighting an uphill battle if they didn't reach over that barrier and help him understand what had truly been going on, what concerns drove the various members of the house party, what tangled webs Kitty had been weaving before she'd come to grief.

Stokes himself was intelligent enough to know it. Clever enough, now he had their measure, to openly acknowledge it. He'd taken them to the point where others had rushed in and Kitty's death had become more widely known. Setting aside his map, he looked up, let his gaze linger, then gravely asked, "Is there anything you can tell me—any fact you know, any reason at all you can even imagine—that might have led one of the guests here, or the staff, or even one of the gypsies, to kill Mrs. Glossup?"

When they didn't immediately react, he straightened in the chair. "Is there anyone at all you suspect?"

Portia glanced at Simon; so did Charlie. Simon met her gaze, read her decision, checked with Charlie, who almost imperceptibly nodded, then looked at Stokes. "Do you have a list of the guests?"

At the end of an hour, Stokes ran his fingers through his hair, and stared at the network of notes he'd made around Kitty's name. "Was the damned woman **looking** to get herself strangled?"

"If you'd known her, you'd understand." Meeting Portia's gaze, Simon continued, "She seemed incapable of seeing how her actions were affecting others—she didn't think of others' reactions at all."

"This is not going to be easy." Stokes sighed, waved his notebook. "I'm usually searching for motive, but here we've motives aplenty, opportunity for all the household to have done the deed, and precious little to tell us which of them actually did."

He searched their faces again. "And you're sure no one has given the slightest sign since—"

The library door opened; Stokes swung around, a frown gathering, then he saw who it was; his expression blanked as he rose to his feet.

As did the others as Lady Osbaldestone and Lord Netherfield, looking like a pair of aged conspirators, carefully shut the door, then—as silently as two largish people using canes could—swept across the room to join them.

Stokes tried to assert his authority. "My lord, ma'am—if you don't mind, I really need to—"

"Oh, posh!" Lady O declared. "They're not going to play mum just because we're here."

"Yes, but—"

"We came to make sure they told you all." Leaning on her cane, Lady O fixed Stokes with her best basilisk stare. "Have they told you about the serpent?"

"Serpent?" Stokes's face was a study in impassivity; he shot a glance at Simon and Portia, clearly hoping they'd rescue him . . .

When they didn't immediately respond, his eyes narrowed; he looked back at Lady O. "What serpent?"

Simon sighed. "We hadn't got that far yet."

Naturally, there was no getting rid of Lady O after that. They all sat again, Simon relinquishing his seat on the chaise to Lady O and Lord Netherfield and taking up a stance by the hearth.

They related to Stokes the tale of the adder found in Portia's bed which, by sheer luck, she'd not attempted to lie in having fallen asleep in a chair instead. Stokes accepted the explanation without a blink; Portia exchanged a glance with Simon, relieved.

"Good God! The blackguard!" It was the first Charlie had heard of the adder. He looked at Portia. "I can't believe you didn't retire with a fit of the vapors."

"Yes, well," Lord Netherfield said. "That's what the blackguard wants, don't you see?"

"Indeed." Stokes's eyes gleamed. "It means there's something—something that will give the murderer away." He looked at Portia, frowned. "Something he thinks you know."

Portia shook her head. "I've thought and thought, and there's nothing I've forgotten, I swear."

Deep in the house, the dinner gong clanged. It was the second summons, calling them to the table; they'd already ignored the earlier warning that it was time to go and dress. Tonight, they weren't standing on ceremony; filling Stokes in had seemed far more important than donning silks and retying cravats.

Stokes shut his notebook. "Clearly, the villain, whoever he is, doesn't realize that."

"Didn't realize, maybe, but now I've spoken to you and yet still you don't know his identity, presumably he'll let be." Portia spread her hands. "I've told you all I know."

They all rose.

"That's as may be." Stokes exchanged a meaningful glance with Simon as they headed for the door. "But the villain might well think you'll remember the vital point later. If it was important enough for him to try to kill you once, there's no reason he won't try again."

"I say!" Charlie stared at Stokes, then looked at Portia. "We'll need to guard you."

Portia halted. "That's hardly nec—"

"Day and night." Stokes nodded gravely; he was quite patently sincere.

Lady O thumped the floor. "She can sleep on a trestle in my room." She grimaced at Portia. "Daresay even you would think twice before getting between the sheets where once you'd seen a serpent."

Portia managed not to shudder. Glanced instead—pointedly—at Simon; if she was sleeping in Lady O's room . . .

He met her gaze directly; his face was set. "Day

and night." He glanced at Charlie. "You and I should be able to handle the days."

Stunned—not a little irritated by being thus disposed of, like an item to be handed one to the other—Portia opened her lips to protest . . . realized every face was turned her way, all set, all determined. Realized she'd never win.

"Oh, all right!" Flinging her hands in the air, she stepped to the door. Lord Netherfield opened it for her and offered her his arm.

She took it, heard him chuckle as he led her out.

He patted her hand. "Very wise, m'dear. That was one battle you couldn't hope to win."

She managed not to humph. Head high, she swept down the corridor and into the dining room.

Simon followed more slowly, Lady O on his arm. Stokes and Charlie came behind. At the door to the dining room, Stokes took his leave of them, charging Simon with telling the company he'd resume his questions on the morrow before retiring to the servants' hall.

Charlie headed in to find his seat. Simon steered Lady O through the door.

Pausing on the threshold, ostensibly to rearrange her shawl, she chuckled evilly. "Don't look so glum. I can't see across the room—how will I know if she's there or not?"

Under cover of retaking his arm, she poked him in the ribs. "And I'm a horribly heavy sleeper . . . no use at all in the guardian stakes, now I think on it."

Simon managed not to gape—he'd long known she was an incorrigible matchmaker, just plain incorrigible most of the time, yet the idea that she might actually **aid** him, actively support his pursuit of Portia . . .

She allowed him to help her into her seat, then dismissed him with a wave. As he headed down the table to the empty place beside Portia, pulled out the chair, paused to look down on her dark head, presently set at an angle that from experience he could interpret quite well, then sat, he reflected that having Lady O as an ally was not a bad thing.

Especially now. Aside from all else, Lady O was pragmatic to a fault; she could be counted on to insist Portia behave sensibly. Safely.

Shaking out his napkin, he glanced briefly at Portia's haughty face, then allowed the footman to serve him. He—they—might not be out of the woods yet, but he felt more positive than at any time since Portia had learned of his true goal.

By consensus, the tone of the house party was consciously and deliberately altered. As Portia sat sipping tea in the drawing room, she couldn't help but note that Kitty wouldn't have approved. The atmosphere was akin to that of a large family gathering, but without any attendant gaiety; those present were comfortable with each other and seemed to have dropped their masks, as if deeming themselves excused by the circumstances from maintaining the usual social facades.

The ladies had retired there; no one expected the gentlemen to join them. The company sat in groups about the long room, talking quietly, no laughter, no drama, just gentle conversation.

Conversation designed to soothe, to settle, to let the horror of Kitty's murder and the very concept of the investigation now upon them slide into the background.

The Hammond sisters remained pale, but had started to cope; Lucy Buckstead was little better. Winifred, in dark navy, a color that didn't suit her, looked pallid and wan. Mrs. Archer had not come down for dinner.

As soon as their tea had been drunk, everyone rose and retired. There seemed an unstated sentiment that they would all need their rest to face what the morrow and Stokes's questions might bring. Only Drusilla had thought to ask Portia what Stokes was like, whether she thought him competent. Portia had answered that she rather thought he was, but there seemed so little evidence that the matter may well remain unresolved.

Drusilla had grimaced, nodded, and moved away.

On helping Lady O to her room, Portia noted the threatened trestle bed had indeed been set up by the empty hearth, on the other side of the room from the main bed. Lady O's maid was there to help her mistress undress; Portia retreated to the window seat, only then noticing that her own clothes had been fetched from her room. Her gowns hung on a string stretched across the room's corner; her linens and stockings were neatly laid in her chest, sitting open in the corner. Lifting her head, she saw her brushes and hairpins, her perfume flask and combs all neatly arrayed on the mantelpiece.

Sinking onto the cushioned window seat, she looked out at the darkening gardens, and put her mind to devising an excuse to go wandering that Lady O would accept.

Nothing useful had occurred to her when the maid came to ask if she desired any help getting out of her gown. She shook her head, bade the maid good night, then rose and crossed to the bed.

The candle on the nightstand had already been blown out; Lady O lay propped high on her pillows, eyes closed.

Portia leaned close and kissed her papery cheek. "Sleep well."

Lady O chuckled. "Oh, I will. Don't know how you'll fare, mind you, but you'd better get along and find out." Eyes still closed, she lifted a hand and made shooing motions toward the door. "Go on, now—off with you."

Portia simply stared. Then decided she had to ask, "Get along where?"

One old eye cracked open; one black eye transfixed her. "Where do you think?"

When she stood staring, mind swinging wildly, Lady O snorted and closed her eye again. "I'm rather more than seven—gracious heavens, I'm more than seventy-seven! I know enough to recognize what's going on under my nose."

"You do?"

"Indeed. Mind you, I'm not sure that you do, and he certainly doesn't, but that's as may be." She settled deeper into her pillows. "Now off you go—no sense wasting time. You're twenty-four—and he's what? Thirty? You've both wasted time enough as it is."

Portia couldn't think how to respond, in the end decided not responding was wisest. "Good night, then." Turning, she headed for the door.

"Wait a minute!"

At the irritated command, Portia turned.

"Where are you going?"

She pointed to the door. "You just said—"

"Great heavens, gel—do I have to teach you everything? You should change your gown first."

Portia looked down at her magenta twill. She seriously doubted Simon would care what she wore; knowing him, she wouldn't be wearing it for long. Lifting her head, she opened her lips to ask why it mattered—

Lady O sighed. "Change into the day gown you intend wearing tomorrow. That way, if any one sees you coming back in the morning, they'll simply assume you got up early and went for a walk. If they see you in the corridors tonight, they'll assume you got ready for bed, then remembered something you needed to do, or I've sent you to fetch something." She let out an exasperated snort and fell back on her pillows. "You young things—the things I could teach you . . . but then again"—she closed her eyes; a wicked smile curled her lips—"as I recall, learning them was half the fun."

Portia grinned; what else could she do? Obediently, she stripped off the magenta twill and wriggled into a day gown of blue poplin. As she struggled to do up the tiny buttons closing the bodice, she thought of Simon—shortly struggling to undo them again. Still, Lady O's suggested practice made eminent sense . . .

She stopped, lifted her head, struck by a wayward thought, a sudden suspicion . . .

When the last button slipped into place, she walked, not to the door, but back to the bed. Pausing by the bedpost, she looked at Lady O, wondered if she was sleeping . . .

"Still here?"

"I'm just going, but I wondered . . . did you know Simon would be here, attending the house party?"

Silence, then, "I knew he and James were close friends from their Eton days. Seemed likely he'd drop by."

Portia thought of the arguments that had raged at Calverton Chase with Luc, Amelia, her mother, and herself insisting Lady O take someone with her on her journey, thought of Lady O resisting . . . then finally giving way, agreeing, grudgingly, to take her with her . . .

Eyes narrowing on the old lady feigning sleep in the bed, Portia wondered how much her and Simon's present situation owed to the oh-so-subtle manipulations of the ton's most dangerous harridan.

Decided she didn't care. Lady O was right—they'd wasted enough time. Straightening, she turned to the door. "Good night. I'll see you in the morning."

And it would be morning. One excellent aspect of Lady O's scheme, now she was in her morning gown, she wouldn't need to leave Simon before dawn.

Simon was in his room, waiting, wondering if Portia would find a way to come to him—or whether she'd grasp the chance to stay away, to think, to consider, to revisit all the reasons she didn't want to marry him, and set up barriers against him.

Halting by the window, acutely aware of the tension holding him, he sipped from the glass of brandy he'd been nursing for the past half hour, and looked out at the darkening scene.

He didn't want her to think too hard about what he would be like as a husband. At the same time, he knew if he tried, no matter how subtly, to steer her away from that path, he'd only dig himself deeper, only confirm he was not to be trusted to let her come to her own decisions.

Hamstrung. That's what he was. And there was not a damned thing he could do.

She would go her own road, regardless; she was too clear-sighted, too forthright, not to face the facts—his character, hers, and the inherent difficulties—head-on. The only solace he could draw from that was that if—**when**—she finally decided in his favor, he would know she was committed, eyes open, heart true.

He hesitated, then drained the glass. That was almost worth the torment.

The latch clicked; he turned as she entered, slim, elegant, in a fresh gown. He noted it as she neared, a gentle, confident smile on her lips. He set the glass on the windowsill, freeing his hands to slide about her waist as she came to him—straight into his arms.

He bent his head and their lips met, clung. The embers that, these days, glowed just beneath their cool surfaces ignited, glowed, sent flames licking, teasing.

Realizing the gown closed down the front, he eased his hands around between them. But the buttons were tiny, secure in their loops; he had to release her lips and look to manage them.

"Why did you change?" He could have had her out of her other gown in a minute.

"Lady O."

He looked up; Portia smiled. "She pointed out that in a day gown, I wouldn't appear suspicious coming back in the morning."

His fingers stilled. "She knows you're here?" Support was one thing; he hadn't expected such blatant encouragement.

"She virtually pushed me out of the door and suggested we stop wasting time."

Gaze on the buttons, he caught the laughing note in Portia's voice, glanced up at her face—and cursed the shadows; he couldn't see her eyes well enough to read them. "What?"

He knew there was something . . . something she knew, or had thought of that he hadn't. That was confirmed when she studied his face, then smiled anew, and shook her head. "Just Lady O— she's a shocking old lady. I think I'm going to grow up to be like her."

He humphed derisively. The last button finally slid free.

Reaching up, she drew his lips back to hers. "Now if you've finished, I really think we should pay attention to her instructions."

They didn't waste time, yet neither did he allow her to rush. This time—for the first time—they were meeting as equals. Both knowing where they were heading, and why; both knowingly going forward, stepping into the furnace hand in hand, side by side.

It was a time to be savored. Remembered. Each touch a reverence, a moment of distilled passion.

He didn't know what she wanted from the night, what more she was seeking from him, what more he could give. He could only give her all he was, and hope it was enough.

They didn't move from the window, but shed clothes where they stood, piece by piece. Each earlier discovery revisited, each curve, each hollow, each indentation worshipped anew.

Until they stood naked, until their bodies met skin to skin.

Fire licked over them, hungry, greedy, growing.

Their mouths melded, feeding the conflagration, stoking the flames. Their tongues taunted, teased, tormented.

Hands feasted, fingers spreading, caressing, kneading, probing.

Their urgency grew.

He lifted her. She wrapped her arms about his neck and kissed him voraciously. Wrapped her long legs about his waist, sighed when he entered her, sheathed him lovingly as he pulled her hips down.

Impaled, she held him, speared her fingers through his hair, clenched them, drew his lips back to hers. Feasted as he savored her, filled her, withdrew, then filled her again.

She gave herself unstintingly, holding nothing back, asking for no reassurance.

And he took, claimed her body, yet wanted, yearned for, more.

Portia knew it, could sense in the locked muscles that held her, that flexed and gripped and moved her upon him, that there was a great deal more she had yet to learn, a great deal more he could give her.

If she would.

If she dared.

If she trusted enough . . .

Her skin was on fire, her body liquid flame, yet he was filling her only so far . . . not enough. She wanted to feel him deeper, harder, wanted to glory in the solid weight of him holding her down as he filled her.

She dragged her lips from his, realized she was panting. "Take me to the bed."

Kissed him again as he did; when he bent to set her down on the pillows, she held on, tugged, and toppled him down with her. He swore, went to pull away, thinking he'd hurt her; she wrapped her hands over his buttocks, and hauled him nearer.

"More."

She sank her nails in and he reacted as she wished, driving farther into her. He shifted, then lifted over her, arms braced, looking down as he thrust deeper, then deeper yet. Until he was there, full and hard and heavy inside her.

Simon looked down at her, and struggled to breathe. Struggled to cling to some semblance of sophistication, to hold back the powerful tide of need that threatened to consume him. And her.

She seemed to sense it, reached up, trailed her fingertips down his cheeks, over his shoulders, down his chest, then pressed her palms to his sides, and urged him down to her.

He bent his head and kissed her, gave her that much, but she wanted more—demanded more. He surrendered and let himself down atop her, degree by degree. Until his weight held her pinned beneath him. He expected her to panic, to wriggle; instead, her tongue thrusting against his, she lifted her legs a touch higher and locked them about his waist.

Eased beneath him, tilted her hips. Opened herself fully to his penetration.

Caught his lower lip between her teeth. Tugged, let go. "Now," she breathed, her breath flame on his lips. "Show me."

He met her gaze, eyes glittering under heavy lids. And did.

Locked his eyes on hers as he drove into her, as she'd wished—harder, deeper. He wanted more than anything to see the color of her eyes, to watch them change, certain they'd be black when she climaxed.

Even as the flames dragged him down, even as he lost touch with reality as his world became only her, his senses caught in the wonder, the glory, the splendor of her body sheathing him, holding him, accepting him, as urgent as his in reaching for the peak, yet still he wanted.

Vowed he would have.

That he'd make love to her in daylight, so he could see her as he took her.

See her eyes, and more.

See her skin. So white and flawless it gleamed like purest pearl; in the shadows, the flush of desire was barely discernible. He wanted to see it, needed to see what he brought her.

Wanted to see the color of her ruched nipples, of her softly bruised lips, of the slick swollen folds between her thighs.

He was aware of every pore of her body moving

with his, of the complementarity, the deep and abiding link that seemed to fuse them.

That, at the last, locked them together as they reached the bright peak, senses exploding in a starburst of pleasure before tumbling headlong into bliss.

Satiation, sensual satisfaction—what he experienced with her was so much more than that. Withdrawing from her, slumping by her side, glory singing in his veins, he drew her close, locked her to him, close by his heart.

Where he needed her to be.

Inexpressible comfort flowed through him; he sank into sated dreams.

CHAPTER 14

The next morning, Kitty, more accurately Catherine Glossup née Archer, was laid to rest in the Glossup family plot beside the tiny church in Ashmore village.

Everyone from the house attended, bar only the handful of servants left to prepare the wake.

As for the county, the surrounding families were represented by the patriarchs; none of their ladies attended.

Therein lay a message Portia, Simon, and Charlie could read with ease. Standing back, ready to lend an arm should Lady O or Lord Netherfield require one, they watched as the usually jocular neighbors, many of whom they'd met at Kitty's luncheon, somberly came forward to speak with the family, to murmur condolences, then, clearly uncomfortable, walk away.

"That doesn't look good," Charlie murmured.

"They're reserving judgment," Portia replied.

"Which means they believe there's a reasonable chance one of the Glossups . . ." Simon let his words trail away; none of them needed to hear the truth stated.

The service had been the usual sober affair,

somewhat abbreviated given the circumstances and of a darker tone. As if a cloud now hovered over them all, or at least over Glossup Hall. A cloud that would only be dissipated by the unmasking of Kitty's murderer.

When the right words had been said, all condolences offered and received, the gathering broke up. After seeing Lady O and Lord Netherfield into the carriage they were sharing, Simon handed Portia up into his curricle, followed, and took up the reins as Charlie clambered up behind; with a flick of his wrist, he set his bays in motion, stepping smartly down the lane.

Minutes went by, then Charlie swore.

Portia turned to look at him.

"Sorry." He grimaced. "I was just recalling James's face. And Henry's."

"Let alone Lord and Lady Glossup's." Simon's tone was tight. "They're all trying to put a brave face on it, yet they can see what's coming, and there's precious little they can do to avoid it."

Portia frowned. "It's not fair. They're not the only ones who might have murdered Kitty."

"Given Kitty's performance at the luncheon party, doubtless repeated, embroidered, and spread far and wide, **polite** society will see no reason to look further."

Charlie swore again, this time with more feeling. "That's just what I meant. No matter that they were the victims of Kitty's antics in the first place, dashed if now they aren't the victims of her murderer."

Portia felt forced to point out, "It **could** be one of them."

Charlie snorted. "And pigs might fly."

She glanced at Simon; he kept his eyes on the road, but from the grim set of his mouth, she assumed he agreed with Charlie. Understandable, she supposed; they were such close friends of James's, and of the family, too.

Facing forward, she thought about what she felt, not with her head but with her heart. When the gates of the Hall loomed ahead, she said, "Actually, everyone here, excepting you both and me, and the younger girls, Lady O, Lady Hammond, and Mrs. Archer, are in similar straits, even if they haven't understood that yet."

Charlie humphed. "If the silence over the breakfast table this morning was anything to judge by, most have realized—they're just avoiding thinking about it." After a moment, he added, "Not every day one attends a house party and finds oneself embroiled in murder."

Simon drew up in the forecourt; a groom came running. Simon handed over the reins, then helped her down. The first of the other carriages was coming slowly up the drive; Simon exchanged a glance with her, then caught Charlie's eye—the three of them moved off, taking the path into the pinetum.

Reversing the route she and Simon had walked prior to her stumbling on poor Kitty's body . . . Portia caught herself up. **Poor** Kitty?

After a moment, she linked her arm in Simon's;

he glanced at her face, but said nothing. They walked slowly under the trees, Charlie trailing, equally pensive, behind them.

In their indignation over their friends' being tarred with unwarranted suspicions, they, and very likely all others, had forgotten that Kitty was indeed poor Kitty; Kitty was dead. No longer able to walk under trees with a man by her side, to wake in his arms, filled with a soft urgency that blossomed into bliss.

She had it all, and Kitty had nothing.

Poor Kitty, indeed.

"We have to find out who the murderer is." She looked up, looking ahead. "Surely we must be able to do **something** to help Stokes."

"Can we?" Charlie asked. "I mean . . . will he let us, do you think?"

"He was at the funeral." Simon paced by Portia's side. "He was watching everyone, but he's guessing where we know enough to be sure." He caught Portia's eye. "Perhaps we should offer our services?"

She nodded, determined. "We should."

"But before we do that"—they'd reached the lake path; Charlie came up beside them—"we'd better head back to the house and put in an appearance at the wake."

They did. The gathering was held in the drawing room, curtains half-drawn. With a meaningful nod to them both, Charlie went to talk to James, standing a little apart, a glass in his hand.

Simon and Portia circulated; few of the local gentlemen had come back to the house—the company was primarily composed of the houseguests. Portia stopped to chat to the Hammond sisters, subdued and somewhat crushed. Simon left her and moved on, eventually coming up beside Stokes.

The "gentleman from Bow Street" was hanging back by the wall, consuming a pastry. He caught Simon's eye. "Lord Netherfield suggested I attend." He took another bite, looked away. "Seems a nice old codger."

"Very. And no, I don't think he did it."

Stokes grinned, and met Simon's gaze. "Any particular reason for thinking so?"

Thrusting his hands into his pockets, Simon looked across the room. "He's of a type and a generation where stooping to murder someone as essentially powerless as Kitty—Mrs. Glossup— would be seen as very bad form."

Stokes munched on the pastry, then quietly asked, "Does 'very bad form' still matter?"

"Not to all by any means, but to those of his ilk, yes." Simon met Stokes's questioning look. "To him, it would be a matter of personal honor, and that, I assure you, matters to him very much."

After a moment, Stokes nodded, then pulled out a handkerchief and dusted his fingers. He didn't look up as he said, "Do I take it you're willing to . . . assist me in my inquiries?"

Simon hesitated, then replied, "Perhaps in interpreting any facts you might find, attaching the correct weight to anything you might hear."

"Ah, I see." Stokes's lips curved. "You're a very old friend of Mr. James Glossup, I hear."

Simon inclined his head. "Which is why I, and Miss Ashford and Mr. Hastings, are all eager the murderer—the real murderer, whoever he is—be unmasked." He met Stokes's gaze. "You'll need us to get anywhere. We need you to get a result. A fair enough bargain, to my mind."

Stokes mulled it over, then stuffed his handkerchief back in his pocket. "I'll be conducting interviews all afternoon—I haven't yet spoken to all who were here. Then I'm going down to the gypsy encampment. I doubt I'll be back before dinner, but perhaps we can talk when I return?"

Simon nodded. "The summerhouse—it's down by the lake. You can't miss it. It's private, and no one else is likely to wander that far at dusk. We'll wait for you there."

"Agreed."

With an inclination of his head, Simon moved away.

He, Portia, and Charlie decamped to the summerhouse the instant tea, served as soon as the gentlemen returned to the drawing room, had been dispensed with. Normal custom having been observed, most guests retired to their rooms, although a light still burned in the billiard room; with the library inhabited by Bow Street's best, it had become the gentlemen's retreat.

Stokes had spent all afternoon interrogating the rest of the houseguests, then disappeared. There'd already been a curious tension in the air, as if the desperate fiction that the murderer was, of course, one of the gypsies was already wearing thin; Stokes's unexplained absence only ratcheted that tension one notch tighter.

Beside Simon, Portia walked down the lawns and onto the path around the lake, puzzling, as she had since quitting his bed that morning in great measure restored to her customary spirits, over why Kitty's murder had come about.

"You have to admit Stokes was mightily brave to specifically interview Lady O." Charlie followed in their wake, frowning as he ambled.

"He seems very thorough," Simon replied.

"And determined."

"That, too."

"Do you think he'll succeed?"

Simon glanced at Charlie. "For the Glossups' sakes—for everyone's sakes—I hope so." He seemed to catch something of Charlie's concern. "Why do you ask? What is it?"

They paused, as one turning to confront Charlie.

Halting, he grimaced. "I spoke to James at the wake, and again this afternoon. He's . . . not his usual self."

Portia raised her brows. "I wouldn't be my usual

self either if I knew I was a prime suspect for murder."

"Yes, well, it's rather more than that." Charlie looked at Simon. "You know how close James and Henry really are. This business, if anything, has drawn them closer . . ." Charlie ran a hand through his hair. "Point is, James feels guilty over Kitty—not because he harmed her, but over her preferring him to Henry. Even though he never encouraged it . . . well, it was pretty clear how it was. Deuced awkward enough while she was living—hell now she's not."

Simon had stilled; Portia sensed the change in him.

"What exactly are you saying?"

Charlie sighed. "I'm worried that James will do something foolish—especially if things look to be going badly for Henry, and heaven knows, it already looks bad enough. I think he might confess to spare Henry."

Simon exhaled. "Damn!"

Portia looked from one to the other. "Would he really do that?"

Simon nodded. "Oh, yes. If you knew their past, you'd understand. James will do anything to protect Henry, because Henry spent half his life shielding James."

"So what can we do?" Charlie asked. "That's what I want to know."

"The only thing we can do," Simon replied. "Help unmask the real murderer with all speed."

It was late when Stokes, clearly weary, joined them.

"Dealing with gypsies is never easy." He sank into one of the armchairs. "They always assume we're about to haul them off." He grimaced. "Can't say I blame them, given how things used to be."

"Given you haven't hauled anyone off," Simon said, "I take it you don't think Arturo is guilty?"

"I can't see it, myself." Stokes looked across at him. "Can you?"

"No," Simon acknowledged. "But everyone will suggest it, I'm sure."

"Aye, they have, but it's drawing a very long bow. I've no reason to suspect he—or that other one, the younger one . . . Dennis, that was it—did the deed."

Portia leaned forward. "Have you any theories on who did?"

"Not as such." Stokes relaxed back in the chair. "But I have some thoughts."

He shared them; they, for their part, told him all they knew—all Kitty's little snipes, all her recent barbs. While waiting for Stokes, they'd agreed to hold nothing back, trusting that the truth in Stokes's hands would not harm the innocent. There was too much at stake to toe the line of polite reticence.

So they told him of all Portia had overheard, all they individually and collectively surmised of Kitty's propensities for meddling in others' lives.

Stokes was impressed—and impressive; he questioned them, truly listened, and tried to follow their explanations.

Eventually they reached a point where he had no more questions, but they'd yet to see even a glimmer of a conclusion. They all rose and walked back to the house, silently mulling all they'd touched on, as with a jigsaw trying to see a pattern prior to aligning the pieces.

Portia was still mulling, still deep in thought, when she slipped into Simon's room an hour later.

Standing beside the bed, he looked up, then continued lighting the six candles in the candelabra he'd borrowed from one of the unused parlors.

He heard the door lock snib, heard Portia's footsteps cross the floor.

Knew the instant she noticed.

She stopped, staring at the candelabra, now with all candles burning. Then she looked around—at the window, the heavy winter curtains normally tied back through the warmer months fully drawn, then at the bed, bathed in the golden glow thrown by two six-armed candelabra perched on the angled bedside tables, a seven-armed cousin on the tallboy against the corridor wall, and a five-armed one standing on the chest against the opposite wall.

"What . . . ?" She looked at him across the warmly lit expanse.

He shook out the taper, adjusted the second six-armed candelabrum so its light fell on the massed pillows. Then he lifted his head. Met her gaze. "I want to see you, this time."

She blushed. Not fierily but the wash of color was readily discernible under her alabaster skin.

He hid a wholly predatory smile. His gaze on her, gauging her reaction, he rounded the bed, walked to her side.

She was staring at the counterpane, a silky soft crimson sheening in the candlelight.

He reached for her, slid his hands around her slender form, and drew her into his arms. She came easily, but when she lifted her eyes to his, she was frowning.

"I'm not at all sure this is one of your better ideas."

He ducked his head and kissed her, gently, persuasively.

"You'll be able to see me, too." He whispered the temptation across her lips, then took them again, made them—and her—cling.

Her body sank into his arms, his unreservedly, yet she drew back from the kiss, her hesitation clear in her eyes. He gathered her closer, molded her hips to his. "Trust me. You'll enjoy it."

He shifted suggestively against her.

Portia inwardly humphed, decided not to tell him that that was what she feared, that she would enjoy the wanton adventure, enjoy being drawn deeper and deeper into his web—one she knew he was deliberately weaving.

But she'd already accepted the challenge, decided on her path.

Holding his gaze, she slid her hands, until then braced between them, up, over his shoulders, twined her arms about his neck. Stretched up against him. "All right." Just before their lips met, she hesitated. Long enough to feel the tension he reined back. Feel it build . . .

Her gaze on his lips, she murmured, deliberately sultry, "Show me, then."

And offered her mouth.

He took—ravenously. Captured her senses, feasted on her, ripped her wits away.

Plunged them both straight into passion's furnace, into the roaring flames of desire.

A desire they both let rage—his hands roved her body, powerfully possessive, every touch flagrantly evocative; she speared her fingers through his hair and clung, urging him on—then he reined the fire in. Held it back, seething, simmering, waiting to erupt. Shifted, and trapped her against the bed, his legs outside hers.

Broke from the kiss, waited, head bowed to hers until she lifted her heavy lids.

He trapped her gaze. "Tonight, we are not going to rush."

The words were deep, gravelly—dictatorial. Fearless, she held his gaze, arched a brow. "I wasn't aware we had previously."

Consideration flashed behind his eyes, then he murmured, "I've a proposition. Let's see how slow we can go."

She had no idea what she was letting herself in for. Nevertheless she lightly shrugged. "If you wish."

He bent his head. "I wish."

He took her mouth again in a long, slow, achingly pleasurable, disturbingly arousing kiss. She was long past resisting in even a token way, long past trying to hold on to her wits, or her will. She let both slide as he drew her ever deeper into mesmerizing delight.

Didn't even think of the revealing light as he unbuttoned her gown, eased it off her shoulders, then, when she obligingly freed her arms, peeled it down until it fell slack about her waist. With his lips on hers, his tongue dueling with hers, artfully promising, she barely registered the tugs as he unraveled the ribbon ties of her chemise.

But then he drew back from the kiss, looked down, and drew the fine silk down, exposing her breasts.

To him, to his sight, to the burning blue of his eyes.

The look on his face made her lungs lock; he raised a hand, ran the backs of his fingers from her collarbone down over the upper swell of one breast, then turned his hand and cupped the firm weight, a conqueror assessing an offered prize. Then he closed his hand. And sanity rocked.

She couldn't breathe, could only watch, caught, trapped, ruthlessly held by a sensual spell as he visually feasted, examining, caressing, fondling—unhurriedly, almost languidly.

Then he flicked her a glance from under his lashes, caught her gaze, then shifted before her and slowly bent his head. Set his lips to one tightly puckered nipple, sucked lightly. At her indrawn breath, he released her, traced and kissed, licked, savored . . . eventually moved to her other breast while his fingers closed over the heated peak and continued its torture.

Until he returned, opened his mouth and drew it in. Suckled fiercely. Fingers spasming on his skull, clenching tight, she cried out, let her head arch back as she held him to her, spine lightly bowed.

Tried to focus on the pattern of the tapestry lining the bed's canopy. Couldn't.

Closed her eyes as he suckled again, wondered how long her legs would hold her.

As if he'd heard the thought, his hands slid down, around, and gripped her bottom, hard, possessively.

On a gasp, she forced her lids up, looked down, watched him feast. He caught her gaze, watched her watching as he rolled one aching nipple over his tongue, then rasped it.

She shuddered and closed her eyes again.

Felt him straighten—let her hands slide down to his chest as his fingers slowly unclenched and released her; she opened her eyes regardless of the effort.

She had to see this—his face as he eased her gown and chemise down, as he pushed the fabric over the swell of her hips, then down until, with a soft swoosh, both garments fell to pool on the floor.

He stepped back a fraction, but his eyes didn't follow the material; they stopped, locked, on the dark curls at the apex of her thighs.

She tried to imagine what he was thinking; couldn't. Wasn't even sure, looking at the hard-edged planes of his face, that he was thinking at all.

Then his hands, which had risen to her waist, feathered down, thumbs tracing the slight curve of her stomach, down to the crease between thigh and torso. Head rising, he stepped closer—something she glimpsed in his face made her breath catch. She braced her hands on his chest; held him back.

"No—your clothes." Their gazes locked; she licked her lips. "I get to see you, too."

"Oh, you will." His hands closed about her waist and he bent his head to kiss her. "But not yet. We're not rushing, tonight. We've time to savor it all—each step, each experience."

He invested the last word with enough promise to distract her, to let him capture her lips, her mouth, then her wits, and send them spinning.

He drew her against him and her breathing fractured. He was still fully dressed; her skin came alive, prickling with awareness as the fabric of his coat and trousers brushed, then pressed against her, increasingly as he gathered her closer, blatantly molding her soft curves to his hard frame, to the rigid column of his erection, emphasizing the fact she was naked and he still clothed.

That she was in his power. His to do with as he pleased.

At least as far as she permitted it.

That last was still clear in her mind, a point so much a given she didn't hesitate, didn't think to protest when he lifted her and set her on her knees on the bed before him, facing him. Hands on his shoulders for balance, fingers sinking, gripping as he ravaged her mouth, he kept her trapped in the kiss as his hands roamed. Over her breasts, over her sides, her back, sweeping down to close, then evocatively knead her bottom, finally sliding down, caressing the backs of her thighs, slipping around, fingers trailing upward, following the taut muscles, then sliding inward to trace the quivering inner faces.

All the way up to where she was hot and wet and swollen.

Her lungs slowly locked as he traced, teased, circled the tight bud of her desire, then parted her folds, fingers sliding easily as her slickness welcomed him. He found her entrance, probed until she stopped breathing, until her fingers sank into his shoulders, then he slid inside, first one finger, languidly stroking, then two, making her shudder.

Simon let her break from the kiss, let her lift her head high. One hand on her hip, he held her steady before him, slowly, rhythmically, rigidly controlled, working his hand between her thighs, feeling her scalding sheath close tight about his fingers.

Watched her as he slowly, deliberately pushed her onward.

Watched the blush of desire color her fine skin, changing it from alabaster to the faintest rose. Her face was soft, passion blank, the determination that was usually so much a part of her expression in abeyance as she gave herself up, to his touch, to him, to what he wished to do, to her, with her. Her lips parted, her breathing increasingly ragged as she tried to follow his lead, tried to stay with him, tried not to rush ahead.

Beneath her lashes, her dark eyes glinted, the deep sapphire so intense it was almost black.

As she watched him watching her. Visually savoring her as he brought her slowly, steadily, inexorably to climax.

Her nipples, rosy and tight, beckoned, the most succulent fruit.

As step by step passion claimed her, as her body undulated to the rhythm he set, as the blush of desire intensified and her lids fell, he bent his head and took one nipple into his mouth.

Tasted her, teased, waited, feeling her urgency well, feeling the tide rushing through her veins.

Then he suckled fiercely, heard her cry, felt her hands clench tight on his skull as release claimed her.

He held her and feasted as the contractions faded, as all tension flowed from her. Withdrawing his hand from between her thighs, he swept her up; kneeling on the bed, he laid her down.

Her eyes opened, and she watched him. Displayed naked and delectable on the red silk coverlet, she followed his every move as, languidly, unhurriedly, he undressed.

There was no reason to rush, as he'd said; he intended tonight's performance to be a play of multiple acts—she would need at least a few minutes to recover, the longer the better. The better for the next time; the better for him.

He was a past master at thinking of other things, of ignoring the driving beat in his blood, yet it was only that experience, the knowing what was possible if he stuck to the script, and his iron will, that kept him from falling on her and ravishing her.

Her skin was incredibly fine; although the flush of desire was fading, it was so pale and translucent it took the golden glow from the candlelight, sheened with a sensual gilding. Her raven black hair, thick, falling in large wavy locks, lay spread beneath her shoulders, a frame for her face.

The face of a very English madonna, softened even more by passion's stamp and lit by a sensual glow.

And slowly dawning expectation.

Fascinated anticipation.

He moved about the bed, divesting himself of coat, waistcoat, shirt—all in the usual manner of a gentleman preparing for bed with the intention of sleeping rather than indulging himself to the hilt with a delectable houri he'd already rendered boneless.

She followed his every move.

They said not a word, but the tension rising between them, around them, intensifying about the bed, was a palpable thing.

It kept his heart racing, pulse thudding; when he finally stripped off his trousers, it was with intense relief.

Laying them neatly aside, he straightened, then came to the side of the bed.

From under the black screen of her lashes, she lay back and watched, blatantly let her gaze run down from his face, over his chest, down over his ridged stomach to feast lovingly on his erection.

Hers.

He could almost hear the word in her mind, saw her fingers curl.

Crawling onto the bed, he sat back on his ankles, just out of her reach.

Lifted one hand, beckoned. "Come here."

At his tone, harsh, gravelly, very much a command, her gaze flicked up to his face. Then she shifted, came up on her elbow. He was reaching for her arm to help her to her knees when instead she bent toward him.

Her hair swept his groin; before he could react, he felt her breath caress his aching flesh, then she licked. Long. Lingeringly.

And he was lost.

Forgot his script entirely as she shifted and settled to her task, leaning on his thighs, one hand caressing, gliding up and down, fondling as her tongue licked, laved, winding him tighter, then she drew back, considered all she could see, then bent her head and took him into her mouth.

His fingers speared through her thick hair, spasmed on her skull when she sucked. He had to cling for dear life to his control as she tormented him, had to fight to summon enough will to, the moment she paused to draw breath, grab her shoulders and lift her up. Away.

She met his gaze. "I haven't finished yet."

"Enough," he ground out. "Later."

"You said that last time."

"For good reason."

"You promised."

"That you could look. Not taste."

She narrowed her eyes as she complied with his wishes and, now on her knees, straddled his lap. Their faces again close, she frowned into his eyes. "Methinks you protest too much. You like it. A lot."

He clamped his hands about her hips. "I like it too damned much."

She opened her lips; he stopped her words in the most effective way he knew.

He slid into her, slowly, working his way steadily into her soft sheath, drawing her down, down, until she lost the last of her breath on a gasp, closed her hands about his face, framing it, holding it so she could kiss him.

As evocatively as any houri ever birthed.

He didn't need any encouraging; he moved beneath her, into her, moving her on him to the same rhythm. She caught it, grabbed it, danced with him. On him. Clamping tight about him, then easing as he lifted her. He didn't lift her far; she liked him deep, it seemed, and he was quite content to humor her, at least in that regard.

There was, to his mind, nothing more sensually satisfying than being sheathed to the hilt in hot, slick, voluptuous feminine flesh.

Especially hers.

With her, the satisfaction went much deeper than mere sex. Far deeper than sensual gratification. It went to the heart of him; like some heavenly elixir, it soothed, fed, eased, then became an addiction and incited.

He changed tempo, let the urgency build; she wrapped her arms about his shoulders and clung tight. To him, to their kiss.

To the building, growing, swelling need that rose through them, more primitive than lust, more powerful than passion.

Like a tide rushing in, it filled them; they rode it, faster, higher, deeper, harder.

Until she shattered. Her body tightened unforgivingly around him, then her tension imploded. She cried out, the sound smothered between them. He held her down, brutally forceful, keeping her immobile while her contractions rippled through her, about him, and faded.

All strength went from her, and she slumped against him.

Only then did he dare draw back from the kiss, draw breath, think. Of his next move.

Portia finally managed to drag in a shuddering breath. Realized he'd stopped, that he was still iron-hard, rigid inside her. His hands ran soothingly down her back, but his body was tense, locked—waiting.

Lifting her head, she looked into his eyes. Saw the beast prowling behind the bright blue.

"What now?"

He took a moment to answer; when he did, his voice was a bass growl. "Next act."

He lifted her from him, gently pushed her toward the pillows piled at the bed's head.

On her knees, she slumped that way.

Landed on her stomach. Waited for him to turn her over. When he didn't, she came up on one elbow and looked back at him.

He was still sitting on his haunches, flagrantly erect; as she watched, his gaze rose from her bottom.

"What?" She glanced back, around.

He hesitated, then shook his head. "Nothing." He reached for her legs. "Lie back."

He flipped her over, spread her thighs wide, came over her and wedged his hips between, and entered her. With one powerful thrust that had her arching wildly, that nearly made her forget.

But not quite.

He withdrew and thrust again, seating himself fully, then, obedient to her tugging, let his body down atop hers.

She caught his eye. "What aren't you telling me?"

"Nothing you need to know." He pressed a hand

beneath her hip, tilted her up to meet his next thrust.

"I won't pay attention until you tell me."

He laughed. "Don't tempt me."

She tried to glare, but his next thrust, deeper, harder, wiped the impulse from her mind.

He shifted, rising slightly over her, moving more deeply than ever into her. "If you learn everything at once, there'll be nothing left to teach you. I wouldn't want you to grow bored."

"I don't think . . ." **There's any likelihood of that, not ever. Not in this lifetime.** She left the words unsaid, closed her eyes. Tried to hold back the tide of urgent need that rose so powerfully, stoked by every deep penetration, by every rocking thrust of his body into hers.

Couldn't. Let it sweep through her, catch her, buoy her, carry her.

On.

Into the sea in which they'd bathed often enough for her to relish the moments, to value them, savor them, appreciate all they were.

Intimate. Those precious moments were assuredly that, but also a great deal more, far more than the merely physical.

She felt it in her bones, wondered, in the distant part of her mind that still functioned, if he felt it, too.

Felt the power of what was growing between them. Felt how it linked them as their bodies relentlessly fused. Harder, faster, reaching for the pinnacle of ultimate bliss. Sure that they would reach it.

As inevitably they did, cresting, rising high on a wave of ecstasy, before tumbling, locked together, into a sea of pleasured satiation.

It had been easy. So very easy she wasn't sure she could trust her intuition. Surely nothing so important could be this straightforward.

Was it really love? How could she tell?

It was certainly more than lust that bound them; inexperienced though she was, she was sure about that.

Quitting the breakfast table the next morning, praying no one had noticed her amazing appetite, Portia headed for the morning room and the terrace beyond. She needed to think, to reevaluate, to reassess where they now were, and where, together, it was possible they might go. She'd always thought best while walking, rambling, preferably outdoors.

But she couldn't think at all with him prowling beside her.

Halting on the terrace, she faced him. "I want to think—I'm going for a walk."

Hands in his pockets, he looked down at her. Inclined his head. "All right."

"Alone."

The change in his face was not due to her imagination; the planes really did harden, his jaw firmed, his eyes sharpened, narrowed.

"You can't go wandering anywhere alone. Someone tried to murder you, remember?"

"That was days ago—they must have realized by now that I don't know anything to the point." She spread her hands. "I'm harmless."

"You're witless." He scowled. "If he thinks you'll remember whatever it is he imagines you know but have forgotten, he won't stop—you heard Stokes. Until the murderer's caught, you go nowhere without protection."

She narrowed her eyes. "If you think I'm going to—"

"I don't think—I know."

Looking into his eyes, she felt her temper rise, like a volcano filling her, seething, building, preparing to erupt . . .

Her earlier thought echoed in her mind. Easy? Had she really thought it would be, with him?

She glared; others would cringe and slink away—he, his resolve, didn't so much as flicker. Suppressing a growl—she really didn't want to return to their previous sniping ways—she shackled her temper, then, seeing no other way forward, nodded curtly.

"Very well. You can follow." She sensed his surprise, realized he'd tensed for a battle royal. Defiantly held his gaze. "At a distance."

He blinked; some of his tension drained. "Why at a distance?"

She didn't want to admit it, but he wouldn't oblige if she didn't. "I can't think—not clearly, not so I trust what I'm thinking—if you're on my heels. Or anywhere close." She didn't wait to see his reaction—her imagination was quite bad enough; turning, she headed for the steps. "Stay back at least twenty yards."

She thought she heard a laugh, abruptly smothered, didn't look back. Head up, she set off, striding across the main lawn in the direction of the lake.

Halfway across, she glanced back. Saw him leisurely descending the steps. Didn't look to see if his lips were curved or straight. Facing forward, she walked on.

And turned her mind determinedly to her topic.

Him. And her. Together.

An almost unbelievable development. She recalled her original aim, the one that had landed her in his arms. She'd wanted to learn about the attraction that flared between a man and a woman, the attraction that led a woman to consider marriage.

She'd learned the answer. Quite possibly too well.

Frowning, she looked down. Hands clasped behind her back, she ambled on.

Was she truly considering marrying Simon, latent, ofttimes not-so-latent tyrant?

Yes.

Why?

Not because she enjoyed sharing his bed. While that aspect was all very nice, it wasn't of itself compelling enough. Out of ignorance, she'd assumed the physical aspects weighed heavily in the scale; now, while she would admit they had some weight, indeed, were pleasantly addictive, at least with a gentleman like him, she couldn't imagine—even now, even with him—that that alone had tipped the scales.

It was that elusive something that had grown between them that had added definitive weight and influenced her so strongly.

She might as well call it by its real name; love was what it had to be—there was no longer any point doubting that. It was there, between them, almost tangible, never truly absent.

Was it really new to them? Was there something different he was offering that he hadn't before? Or had age and perhaps circumstances shifted their perspectives, opened their eyes, made them appreciate things about each other they hadn't until now?

The latter seemed most likely. Looking back, she could admit that the potential might, indeed, always have been there but masked and hidden by the natural clash of their personalities.

Their personalities hadn't changed, yet she and apparently he . . . perhaps they'd both reached an age when they could accept each other as they were, willing to adjust and cope in pursuit of a greater prize.

The lawn narrowed into the path leading toward the lake. She looked up as she turned the corner—

Nearly tripped, stumbled—grabbed up her skirts and leapt over some obstacle. Regaining her balance, she looked back.

Saw . . .

Was suddenly conscious of the soft breeze lifting tendrils of her hair, conscious of the thud of her heart, the rush of blood through her veins.

Of the icy chill washing over her skin.

"Simon?"

Too weak. He was close, but momentarily out of sight.

"Simon!"

She heard the immediate pounding as he rushed to her. Put out her hands to stop him as he, as she had, tripped, then stumbled.

He caught his balance, glanced down, swore, and grabbed her, held her tight.

Swore again, and wrapped his arms around her, holding her close, swinging her away, shielding her from the sight.

Of the young gypsy gardener, Dennis, lying sprawled on his back, strangled . . . like Kitty.

Like Kitty, quite dead.

CHAPTER 15

No." Stokes answered the question put to him by Lord Netherfield; they—Stokes, Simon, Portia, Charlie, Lady O, and his lordship—were gathered in the library, taking stock. "So early in the morning, no one had any real alibi. Everyone was in their rooms, alone."

"That early, heh?"

"Apparently Dennis often started soon after first light. Today, the head gardener passed him and spoke with him—the exact time's uncertain, but it was long before the household was up and about. One thing, however, we can say." Stokes stood in the middle of the room and faced them, gathered on the chaise and armchairs before the main hearth. "Whoever killed Dennis was a man in his prime. The lad put up quite a struggle—that much was clear."

Perched on the arm of the chair in which Portia sat, Simon glanced at her face. She was still white with shock, and far too quiet, even though half a day had passed since her gruesome discovery. Second gruesome discovery. Lips thinning, he looked back at Stokes; remembering the gouges in the grass, the twisted body, he nodded. "Kitty could have been murdered by anyone; Dennis is another matter."

"Aye. We can forget all thought of any woman being the murderer."

Lady O blinked. "I didn't know we were considering the ladies."

"We were considering everyone. We can't afford to guess."

"Humph! I suppose not." She fluffed her shawl. Her customary air of invincible certainty was wavering; the second murder had shocked everyone, not just anew, but to a deeper level. The murderer was unquestionably still there, among them; some had, perhaps, started to push the matter aside in their minds, but Dennis's death had forced all to realize the horror couldn't be so easily buried.

Lounging against the mantelpiece, Charlie asked, "What did the blackguard use to strangle the poor blighter?"

"Another curtain cord. This time from the morning room."

Charlie grimaced. "So it could have been anyone."

Stokes nodded. "However, if we assume the same person's responsible for both murders, we can reduce the list of suspects considerably."

"Only men," Lady O said.

Stokes inclined his head. "And only those strong

enough to be sure of subduing Dennis—I think the being sure is important. Our murderer couldn't risk trying but not succeeding, and he had to get the deed done quickly—he would have known there'd be others about."

He hesitated, then went on, "I'm inclined to say the murderer must be Henry Glossup, James Glossup, Desmond Winfield, or Ambrose Calvin." He paused; when no one argued, he continued, "All have strong motives for killing Mrs. Glossup, all could physically have done the deeds, all had the opportunity, and none has an alibi."

Simon heard Portia sigh; he glanced down in time to see her shiver, then she looked up. "His shoes. The grass must have been wet that early. Perhaps if we check . . ."

Grim-faced, Stokes shook his head. "I already did. Whoever our man is, he's clever and careful. All their shoes were clean and dry." He glanced at Lord Netherfield. "I have to thank you, sir— Blenkinsop and the staff have been most helpful."

Lord Netherfield waved the remark aside. "I want this murderer caught. I won't have my grandsons—or the family—tainted by this sort of thing, and they will be unless we catch the blackguard." He met Stokes's gaze. "I've lived too long to shrink from reality. Not exposing the villain will only ensure the innocent are shunned along with him. We need the blackguard caught, now, before things get any worse."

Stokes hesitated, then said, "If you'll pardon the

observation, my lord, you seem very confident neither of your grandsons is our villain."

His old hands folded on the top of his cane, Lord Netherfield nodded. "I am. I've known them from babes, and neither of them has it in him. But you can't be expected to know that, and I'm not going to waste breath trying to convince you. You must look at all four, but mark my words, it'll be one of the other two."

The respect with which Stokes inclined his head was transparently genuine. "Thank you. And now"—his gaze swept them all—"I must ask you to excuse me. There are details to check, although I confess I'm not expecting to find any useful clue."

With a small bow, he left them.

As the door closed, Simon noticed Lady O trying to catch his eye, directing his attention to Portia.

Not that it needed directing. He glanced at her, then reached for her hand. "Come on—let's go for a ride."

Charlie came, too. They found James and asked him if he wanted to join them, but he uncharacteristically demurred. The awkwardness he felt, knowing he was suspect, was patently clear; he was uncomfortable, which meant so were they. Reluctantly, they left him in the billiard room, idly potting balls.

They found the other ladies sitting silently in the

back parlor. Lucy Buckstead and the Hammond girls jumped at the invitation; their mothers encouraged them, looking relieved.

Once they'd all changed, crossed to the stables, and found mounts, the afternoon was well advanced. Once again atop the frisky chestnut mare, Portia led the way out; Simon followed close behind.

He watched her; she seemed distant. However, she managed the mare with her usual assured ease; it wasn't long before they'd left the others behind. Reaching the leafy rides of Cranborne Chase, in unspoken accord they let their mounts stretch their legs . . . until they were galloping, thundering down the rides, hard, fast, side by side.

Suddenly, so suddenly he shot straight past her, Portia wrenched the mare aside. Startled, he reined in, wheeled and came about—saw her fling herself from the saddle, leaving the chestnut quivering, reins dangling. She rushed up a small rise, her boots shushing through the old fallen leaves; at the top, she halted, spine rigid, head erect, looking out through the trees.

Mystified, he halted his gelding beside the mare, tied both sets of reins to a nearby branch, then strode after Portia.

Seriously concerned. To have wrenched her horse about like that, then dropped the reins . . . it was so unlike her.

He slowed as he neared. Halted a few feet away. "What is it?"

She didn't look at him, just shook her head. "Nothing. It's—" She broke off, waved one hand, her voice choked with tears, the gesture helpless.

He closed the distance, reached for her, drew her close; ignoring her token resistance, he wrapped her in his arms.

Held her while she cried.

"It's so **awful!**" She sobbed. "They're both dead. Gone! And he—he was so **young**. Younger than us."

He said nothing, just touched his lips to her hair, then rested his cheek against the black silk. Let all he felt for her well within him, rise up and surround them.

Let it soothe her.

Her hand clenched tighter in his coat, then, very slowly, relaxed.

Eventually her sobs eased; the tension drained from her.

"I've wet your coat."

"Don't worry about it."

She sniffed. "Do you have a handkerchief?"

He eased his hold on her, found it, handed it over.

She patted his coat with the linen, then mopped her eyes and blew her nose. Stuffed the crumpled item into her pocket and glanced up at him.

Her lashes were still wet, her dark blue eyes still glistening. The expression in them . . .

He bent his head and kissed her, gently at first, but gradually drawing her to him, gradually deepening the caress until she was caught.

Until she stopped thinking.

Thinking that crying in his arms was infinitely more revealing—between them perhaps an even greater intimacy than lying naked together. Emotionally, for her, it was, but he didn't want her dwelling on that.

Or dwelling on how he might feel about it, how he might exult that she would allow him that close, to see her with her defenses completely down. See her as she really was, behind her shields, a woman with a kind and inherently soft heart.

One she habitually guarded very well.

A heart he wanted.

More than anything else in life.

Evening came, and with it an uneasy, watchful tension. As he had foreseen, Stokes had uncovered nothing of any value; a sense of foreboding hung over the house.

There was no laughter or smiles left to lighten the mood. No one suggested music. The ladies conversed quietly in somber tones, talking of inconsequential things—faraway things, things that didn't matter.

When, with Lord Netherfield and Lord Glossup, he rejoined the ladies, Simon sought out Portia, and led her out onto the terrace. Out of the heavy, brooding atmosphere, outside where they could breathe a little easier and talk freely.

Not that outside was all that much better; the air

was heavy and sultry, just beginning to stir as another storm blew in.

Releasing his arm, Portia walked to the balustrade; leaning both hands on it, she looked out over the lawn. "Why kill Dennis?"

He'd halted in the middle of the flags; he stayed where he was, giving her some space. "Presumably for the same reason he had a try at you. Dennis wasn't so lucky."

"But if Dennis had known anything, why didn't he say something? Stokes questioned him, didn't he?"

"Yes. And he might have said something, only to the wrong person."

She turned, frowning. "What do you mean?"

He grimaced. "When Stokes went to tell the gypsies, one of the women said Dennis had been brooding over something. He wouldn't say what— the woman thought it was something he'd seen on his way back from the house after he'd learned of Kitty's death."

She turned away, facing the deepening shadows. "I've thought and thought, but I still can't re-member . . ."

He waited. When she said nothing more, he shifted back; hands in his pockets, he leaned his shoulders against the wall. And watched the night slowly wash over the trees and lawns, wash over them as the last of the light faded.

Watched her, and quelled the welling urge to corral her, to somehow claim her, seal her off in some tower away from the world and all possible harm. The feeling was familiar, yet so much stronger than it had been before. Before he had realized all she truly was.

The wind rose, bringing with it the scent of rain. She seemed content, as was he, simply to stand and let the peace of the night restore their own.

He'd followed her that morning, stepping off the terrace obediently twenty yards in her wake, wondering what she intended to think about. He'd thought himself—had wished for the ability, at any time, to stop her thinking about them at all.

When she did . . . it worried him, bothered him. The prospect that she would think too much about their relationship, and convince herself it was too dangerous, too threatening to pursue, frightened him.

A telling fear, a revealing vulnerability.

He knew that, too.

Finally, perhaps, was close to understanding it.

She'd always been "the one"—the only female who effortlessly impinged on his consciousness, and on his senses, simply by existing. He'd always known she was in some way special to him, but being acquainted from the first with her attitude to men, men like him in particular, he'd hidden the truth away, refused to acknowledge what it was. What it might grow—had grown—to be.

He no longer had the option of denying it. The past days had stripped away all the veils, all his careful screens. Leaving what he felt for her starkly revealed, at least to him.

She hadn't seen it yet, but she would.

And what she would do then, what she would decide then . . .

He focused on her, standing slender and straight by the balustrade. Felt the welling urge to simply seize her and be damned, to give up all pretense of letting her come to her own decision, to come to him of her own accord, rise up and flow through him, fed and strengthened by the latest dangers . . . yet he knew the first step he took in that direction would be like a slap in the face to her.

She'd stop trusting him, step back.

And he'd lose her.

The rising wind set the ends of her hair dancing. It felt fresh, cooler; the rain was not far away.

He pushed away from the wall, stepped toward her—

Heard a grating sound high above. Looked up.

Saw a shadow detach from the roof high above.

He flung himself at Portia, caught her, threw them both along the terrace, cushioning her fall, shielding her.

An urn from the roof crashed to the flags precisely where she'd been. With a sound like a cannon shot, it shattered.

One flying fragment struck his arm, raised to shelter her; pain stabbed, then was gone.

Silence—absolute—descended, shocking in contrast.

He looked up, realized the danger, quickly urged Portia to her feet.

Inside, someone screamed. Pandemonium followed; Lord Glossup and Lord Netherfield appeared at the terrace doors.

One glance was enough to tell them what must have happened.

"Good Lord!" Lord Glossup strode out. "Are you all right, m'dear?"

Her fingers clenched tight in Simon's coat, Portia managed a nod. Lord Glossup awkwardly patted her shoulder, then hurried on and down the steps. Striding onto the lawn, he turned and looked up at the roof.

"Can't see anyone up there, but my eyes aren't what they used to be."

From the drawing room door, Lord Netherfield beckoned. "Come inside."

Simon glanced down at Portia, felt her straighten, stiffen her spine, then she stepped out of his arms and let him guide her to the door.

Inside, alarmed, her color high, Lady O scowled and thumped the rug with her cane. "What **is** the world coming to, I'd like to know?"

Blenkinsop opened the door and looked in. "Yes, my lord?"

Lord Netherfield waved. "Get Stokes. There's been an attack on Miss Ashford."

"Oh, dear." Lady Calvin went deathly pale.

Mrs. Buckstead shifted to sit beside her and chafed her hands. "Now, now—Miss Ashford is here, and unharmed."

Seated beside their mother on the chaise, the Hammond sisters burst into tears. Lady Hammond and Lucy Buckstead, both not much better, tried to comfort them. Mrs. Archer and Lady Glossup looked stunned and distressed.

Lord Netherfield looked at Blenkinsop as Lord Glossup returned. "On second thought, tell Stokes to come to the library. We'll wait for him there."

They did, but try though they might, there was nothing—no useful information—to be gained from the incident.

With Blenkinsop's help, the staff pooled their knowledge and fixed the whereabouts of the four principal suspects. James and Desmond had left the drawing room, presumably for their rooms, Henry had been in the estate office, and Ambrose in the study writing letters. All had been alone; all could have done the deed.

Stokes and Lord Glossup went onto the roof; when they returned, Stokes confirmed that it was a simple enough matter to gain access, and any able-bodied man could have pushed the stone urn from its plinth.

"They're heavy, but not fixed in place." He looked at Simon; his frown grew blacker. "You're bleeding."

Simon glanced at his upper arm. The shard had torn his coat; the jagged edges were bloodstained. "Flesh wound. It's stopped."

Portia, in the chair beside him, leaned forward, grabbed his arm, and tugged him around so she

could see. Stifling a sigh, he obliged, knowing if he
didn't she'd stand and come to look; she was so
pale, he didn't want her on her feet.

Sighting the wound, minor to his eyes, she paled
even more. She looked at Stokes. "If there's nothing more you need of us, I should like to retire."

"Of course." Stokes bowed. "If anything comes
up, I can speak with you tomorrow."

He caught Simon's eye as both he and Portia
stood.

Guessing Stokes was considering reiterating the
obvious—that Portia should not be left alone at any
time—Simon shook his head. She wasn't going to
be left alone; she didn't need to be reminded why.

Cupping her elbow, he guided her out of the
room, and on through the hall to the stairs. Drawing in a breath, she picked up her skirts and
ascended without his assistance.

Reaching the top, she let her skirts fall. "We'll
need to tend that cut." Turning, she headed for
his room.

He frowned, and followed. "It's nothing. I can't
even feel it."

"Cuts people can't feel have been known to turn
gangrenous." Reaching his room, she turned to
look at him. "You can't possibly be worried about
washing and salving it. If you can't feel it, it isn't
going to hurt."

He halted before her, looked down into her
face—determined, stubborn—and still ghostly
pale. It was going to hurt, just not in the way she

meant. Setting his jaw, he reached past her and pushed the door wide. "If you insist."

She did, of course, and he had to surrender. Had to sit bare-chested on the end of the bed and let her fuss and fret.

From his earliest years, he'd hated having any female fuss over him—passionately hated having his hurts tended. He had more than his share of scars because of it, but the scars didn't bother him—feminine fussing, especially the focused, tender care, always had.

Still did; he gritted his teeth, swallowed his pride, and let her get on with it.

He still felt like a conqueror reduced to a helpless six-year-old—helpless in the face of the feminine need to care. In some indefinable way trapped by it, held by it.

He focused on her face, watched, outwardly stoic as she gently bathed, anointed, and bound the cut—which was deeper than he'd supposed. She smoothed gauze about his arm; he looked down at her fingers, long, supple, slender, just like her.

Felt the emotions he had until then held at bay rush in. Fill him.

He lifted his head as those minutes on the terrace replayed in his mind; his muscles hardened in inevitable reaction.

She'd been within his sight, yet he'd come so very close to losing her.

The instant she straightened, he rose and walked to the window. Away from her. Away from the temptation to end the game and seize, claim, decree, and take her from here, out of all danger.

Fought to remember there was more than one way of losing her.

Portia watched him walk away, noticed the stiffness, the way his fists had clenched. Letting him go, she tidied away the basin and cloths. That done, she paused by the bed and studied him.

He stood by the window, looking out, so tensed for action yet so restrained, his will was like a living thing, binding him, constraining him. That suppressed inner tension—was it fear or the reaction to fear, to danger, to her being in danger?—was palpable, thrumming through him, emanating from him, affecting him, and her.

It was all the murderer's fault. The urn had been the last straw. She'd been frightened, upset, more than she'd realized, but now she was getting angry.

Bad enough that the fiend had murdered, not once but twice, but what he was doing to her now—even worse, what the situation was doing to Simon, to what they were trying to come to grips with between them . . . she'd never been one to let anyone tamper with her life.

Irritation edging through annoyance into outright anger rode her; her temper had always outweighed her fear. She walked to lean against the other side of the window frame. Looked at him across it. "What is it?"

He glanced at her, considered, for once didn't attempt to evade the question. "I want you safe."

She considered what she could see in his face, in his eyes. Hear in the harsh tones of his voice. "Why is my safety so important? Why have you always needed to protect me?"

"Because I do." He looked away, out over the garden. "I always have."

"I know. But why?"

His jaw set; for one long moment, she thought he wouldn't answer. Then he said, his voice low, "Because you're important to me. Because . . . in protecting you, I'm protecting myself. Some part of me." The words, ones of discovery, hadn't come easily. He turned his head, met her gaze, considered, but left the admission unchanged, unmodified.

She crossed her arms, looked into his eyes. "So what's really worrying you? You know I'll let you hover, that I'll let you protet me, that I'm unlikely to do anything rash, so it's not that."

His resistance was a tangible thing, a shimmering wall he slowly, gradually, deliberately, let fall. "I want you **mine**." His jaw clenched. "And I don't want this getting in the way." He drew a deep breath, looked out again. "I want you to promise you won't hold whatever happens here—whatever happens between us because of this—against me." Again he met her gaze. "That you won't put it in your scales. Let it affect your decision."

She read his eyes, saw both the turmoil, and the lurking predator. The power, the raw force, the primitive need he held back. The masculine need to dominate, reined in only by his iron will; it took courage to see it, recognize it, know she was its object, and not flee.

Equally, its very strength bore witness to his commitment to adjusting as much as he was able, to be her champion against his own instincts.

She held his gaze. "I can't promise that. I'll never close my eyes and not see you for what you are, or myself for what I am."

A tense moment passed, then he said, voice sinking low, "Trust me. That's all I ask. Just trust me."

She didn't answer; it was still too soon. And his "all" encompassed a lifetime.

When she remained mute, he reached for her, turned and drew her fully to him. Bent his head. "When you make your decision, remember this."

She lifted her arms, wound them about his neck, offered her lips, and her mouth—his, as he wished. In this arena, she was already that, every bit as much as his conqueror's soul might crave.

He took, accepted, wrapped his arms around her and sank into her mouth, then flagrantly molded her body to his, explicitly foreshadowing all that was to come.

She didn't draw back, held nothing back—in this sphere, between them, all the barriers had come down.

At least, all hers.

Even as she let him sweep her into his arms and carry her to the bed, let him strip away her gown and chemise, stockings and slippers, and lay her naked on his sheets, even as she watched him strip and, naked, join her, set his hands and his lips, his mouth and his tongue to her skin, her body, pressing pleasure and delight on her, even as he parted her thighs and she cradled him as he joined with her, as they rode through the now familiar landscape of passion, through the valley of sensual desire and on, deeper into intimacy, until their skins were slick and heated, their breaths were ragged gasps and their bodies plunged desperately toward ultimate bliss, even then she knew, with an intuition she didn't question, that he yet held something back, kept some small part of him, some deeper need, screened from her.

He'd asked her to trust him; in this sphere she did. But he didn't yet fully trust her—not enough to reveal that last little part of him.

Someday, he would.

In the moment that, locked together, they reached the bright peak and tumbled headlong into the void, she realized she'd reached her decision, already committed herself to learning that last fact, gaining that last piece of the jigsaw that was him.

To do it, she would have to become his in all the ways he wished, in all the ways he wanted, and, perhaps, needed.

That was the price of knowing, of being made privy to every last corner of his soul.

As she eased beneath him and they slumped together in the bed, she spread her hands on his back and held him to her, marveling at his weight, at the solid muscle and bone that pressed her into the mattress, yet at the same time protected her, left her feeling safe, cherished, guarded like some treasure.

Running her hands upward, she slid them into his hair, ruffling the silky locks, then smoothing them. She glanced at his face, shadowed in the gloom. Wished he'd lit the candles again, for she loved to see him like this, sated, deeply satisfied, having found his release in her.

There was power, a delicious power, in knowing she had brought him to this.

Shifting her head, she brushed her lips to his temple. "I haven't thanked you for saving me."

He humphed. After a moment added, "Later."

She smiled, lay back, knew that while they lay there together, neither fear nor the murderer could impinge on her world. That the only currency there was what lay between them.

The emotional connection, the shared physical joy—the ephemeral bliss.

The love.

It had been there all the time, waiting for them to see it, understand it, and claim it.

She glanced at him. Realized he was watching her.

Realized she didn't need to tell him—he knew.

She rolled toward him, let their lips meet in a kiss that said it all. His hand was cradling her head when it ended.

Again their gazes met, locked, then he ran his hand down, over her shoulder, down her back, gathered her against him, let his hand rest on her hip. Closed his eyes. Settled to sleep.

An utterly simple gesture of acceptance.

She closed her eyes and accepted, too.

"We have a problem." Stokes stood in the middle of the summerhouse, facing Portia, Simon, and Charlie. They'd just quit the breakfast table, this morning all but deserted, when he'd met them in the hall and requested a meeting. "Mr. Archer and Mr. Buckstead have asked to take their families and leave. I can delay them for a day or so, but not more. That, however, isn't the real problem."

He paused, as if debating with himself, then said, "The truth is, we've no evidence, and very little likelihood of catching this murderer." He held up a hand when Charlie would have spoken. "Yes, I know that's going to be black for the Glossups, but it's actually worse than that."

Stokes looked at Simon. Portia did, too, and realized that whatever Stokes meant, Simon understood.

He glanced at her as Stokes went on, "Miss Ashford appears to be the murderer's only remaining mistake. After last night, we know that, no matter she doesn't know anything that would identify him, he's still convinced she does. The adder— that might have been an attempt to frighten her off, but the attempt last night was intended to kill. To silence, as he's silenced Dennis."

Simon looked at Stokes. "You're saying he won't stop. That he'll feel compelled to keep on, to dog Portia beyond the boundaries of Glossup Hall, through her life, wherever she goes, until he can make sure she's no longer a threat to him?"

Curtly, Stokes nodded. "Whoever he is, he clearly feels he has too much to lose to risk letting her go. He must fear she'll remember at some point, and that what she'll remember will point too definitely to him."

Portia grimaced. "I've racked my brains, but I really **don't** know whatever it is. I just don't."

"That I accept," Stokes said. "It doesn't matter. He believes you do, and that's all that counts."

Charlie, unusually grim, said, "It's actually very hard to protect someone who's going about in society. Plenty of ways accidents can happen."

All three men looked at her. Portia expected to feel fear; somewhat to her relief, all she felt was irritation. "I am not going to be"—she waved— "'cribb'd, cabin'd, and confin'd' for the rest of my days."

Stokes grimaced. "Yes, well—**that's** the problem."

Simon looked at Stokes. "You didn't bring us here to tell us that. You've thought of some plan to put paid to this villain. What?"

Stokes nodded. "Yes, I've thought of a plan, but it's not going to be something you"—his gaze swept the three of them—"any of you, are going to like."

A momentary pause ensued.

"Will it work?" Simon asked.

Stokes didn't hesitate. "I wouldn't bother suggesting such a thing if I didn't think it had a real chance of succeeding."

Charlie leaned forward, his forearms on his thighs. "Just what are we aiming for here—the murderer unmasked?"

"Yes."

"So not only will Portia be safe, but the Glossups, and whoever of Winfield and Calvin it isn't, will be free of suspicion?"

Stokes nodded. "All will be revealed, the murderer apprehended, and justice done. Better yet, justice seen and publicly acknowledged as being done."

"What's this plan of yours?" Portia asked.

Stokes hesitated, then said, "It revolves around the fact that you, Miss Ashford, are the only means we have of drawing the murderer into the open."

Deliberately, Stokes looked at Simon.

For a long minute, Simon held his gaze, his face unreadable, then he leaned back in his chair, waved one long-fingered hand. "Tell us your plan."

CHAPTER 16

None of them liked it.

All three agreed to it.

They could think of nothing better, and clearly they had to do **something**. They felt compelled to at least try, to do their best and make it work, horrible though the entire performance was certain to be.

Portia wasn't sure who looked forward to it least—she, Simon, or Charlie. The charade required them to trample on virtues they all held dear, that were fundamental to who they were.

She glanced at Charlie, pacing the lawn beside her. "I warn you—I know nothing about flirting."

"Just pretend I'm Simon—behave as you would with him."

"We used to snipe constantly. Now we simply don't."

"I remember . . . what made you stop?" He seemed genuinely puzzled.

"I don't know." She considered, added, "I don't think he does either."

Charlie looked at her; when she merely looked

back, he frowned. "We're going to have to think of something . . . we don't have time to coach you. You don't think you could, well, copy Kitty? Poetic justice and all that—using her wiles to trap her killer."

The notion definitely held appeal. "I could try—like charades. I could pretend to be her."

"Yes. Like that."

She looked at Charlie, and smiled. Delightedly. As if he were a sought-after edition of some esoteric text she'd been searching for for years and had at last found—something she had every expectation of thoroughly enjoying.

The sudden wariness that flared in his eyes had her laughing.

"Oh, stop! You know it's all a sham." Her smile even more real, she linked her arm in his and leaned close, then cast a glance back, over her shoulder—to Simon, lounging on the terrace, frowning if not scowling at them.

Her smile started to slip; she quickly reinforced it and, determinedly brazen, returned her attention to Charlie. Unintentionally, she'd done just the right thing—played the right Kitty move. She could imagine how it had looked to the others seated or strolling, taking the early-afternoon air on the terrace.

Charlie drew breath, patted her hand. "Right, then—did I tell you about Lord Carnegie and his greys?"

He did his part, told her ridiculous tale after tale, making it easier for her to laugh, giggle, and lean heavily on his arm, to paint herself as, if not quite of Kitty's ilk, certainly as a flirt determined to make Simon jealous.

Creating a rift between them.

Stokes had done his part, too, exercised his authority as far as he was able and gained them two days—today and tomorrow—in which to lure the murderer forth. Told they could depart on the day after tomorrow, the house party had started to relax; the matter of the falling urn had been, with Lord Netherfield's and Lord Glossup's connivance, passed off as an accident.

Their lordships, however, were not privy to their desperate plan; other than the three of them and Stokes, no one was. As Stokes had rightly said, the fewer who knew, the more realistic it would seem. "It" being their attempt to lead the murderer to believe that, by tomorrow evening, Simon would have stopped watching over Portia.

"The murderer will prefer to deal with you now, here, if he can," Stokes had said. "What we have to do is create an opportunity that will seem believable, and too good to pass up."

They'd agreed, and so here she was, flirting—attempting to flirt—with Charlie.

"Come on." Still smiling, she tugged him toward the path to the temple. "I'm sure Kitty would have inveigled you away if she could."

"Probably." Charlie allowed himself to be persuaded.

As they neared the path's entrance, Portia glanced back at the tall figure on the terrace. Turning back to Charlie, she met a surprisingly sharp glance.

"Just as well they're all at a distance—you drop your mask the instant you look at him. You're going to have to do better if we're to have any hope of convincing this blighter you and Simon have fallen out."

She went to freeze him with a glance, caught his eye, and dissolved into spurious giggles, hanging heavily on his arm. "You are so **droll**!"

Charlie sniffed. "Yes, well, no need to overdo things either. We're supposed to be believable."

Portia grinned, fleetingly genuine; head rising, she swept down the path, walking close—as close as she would with Simon, her arm locked with Charlie's.

Once they were out of sight of the terrace, he grasped the moments to instruct her in how to openly encourage gentlemen such as he.

"A good trick is to hang on our every word— keep your eyes wide. As if every word we say ranks with . . ." He gestured.

"Ovid?"

He blinked. "I was thinking along the lines of Byron or Shelley, but if you've a penchant for Ovid . . ." He frowned. "Does Simon know what strange tastes you have?"

She laughed, playfully tapped his arm as if they were teasing. But her eyes flashed. They'd reached the temple; grabbing his hand, she towed him up the steps. "Come and look at the view."

They crossed the marble floor to the far side, and stood looking out over the distant valley.

Charlie stood close, just behind her shoulder. After a moment, he bent his head and murmured, "You know, I've never been able to understand it—God knows, you're quite attractive enough, but . . . now for pity's sake don't rip up at me— the notion of taking liberties with you scares me witless."

She did laugh then, genuinely amused. Glancing back, she met Charlie's mock-chagrined gaze. "Never mind. Doubtless it's Ovid's fault."

They heard footsteps on the path. Turned, stepped apart—appearing as subtly guilty as they wished.

Simon led Lucy Buckstead up the steps.

Portia felt herself react—as if her very senses were reaching out to him, focusing on him, locking exclusively on him now he was near. Charlie had been much nearer, yet had affected her not at all; just by appearing in her vicinity, Simon made her pulse thrum.

Remembering Charlie's earlier comment, she summoned up her most disinterested mask and fixed it firmly in place.

Lucy saw it; her smile faltered. "Oh! We didn't mean to interrupt."

"Indeed," Simon drawled. "Although the discussion seemed quite fascinating. What was the subject?"

His tone was coldly censorious.

Portia looked at him with chilly disdain. "Ovid."

His lip curled. "I might have known."

She'd fed him the opportunity, knowing what he would do; she knew it was all a charade, yet that sneer still hurt. It was much easier than she'd expected to give him her shoulder, to reach for Charlie's arm. "We've had our fill of the view. We'll leave you to enjoy it."

Poor Lucy was obviously uncomfortable; Charlie had maintained an easy, socially confident if watchful mien, but as they headed back to the lawn, still walking close, he blew out a long breath. Looked ahead. "I don't know if I can do this."

She squeezed his arm. "We have to—the alternative is worse."

They returned to the lawn, to the terrace, to the rest of the company. Worked at, kept up, further developed their charade through the rest of the day.

After taking that first step, Portia girded her loins and forced herself to treat Simon, not just as she used to, but with even greater dismissiveness, even deeper disdain. It wasn't easy; she couldn't meet his eyes, kept her gaze locked on his lips, thin, hard, set in something very close to contempt.

His attitude, his coldness, his overt disapproval, helped on the one hand, and hurt, scored deeply, on the other.

Even knowing it was all pretense, the illusory world was the one they now inhabited. And in it, their behavior threatened not just her, not just him, but all that lay between them.

She reacted to that threat, perceived if not real; her heart still contracted until it ached. By the time night fell, and the household had retired, her composure, the inner shield between herself and the rest of the world, felt bruised and dented.

But all members of the company had seen and, if their expressions and hints of disapproval were any guide, had believed.

That, she assured herself, as she tossed and turned on the trestle before the hearth in Lady O's room, was what mattered.

Even Lady O had bent a cold eye on her, but, as if she knew too much to be so easily led, had made no direct comment. Just watched, eagle-eyed.

Now, across the room, she was quietly snoring.

The clocks in the house started to chime—twelve o'clock. Midnight. All others in the house were doubtless snug in their beds, sleeping soundly . . . settling on her back, she closed her eyes, and willed herself to do the same.

Couldn't. Could not still the turmoil inside her.

It was irrational, emotional, but it felt so very real.

She dragged in a breath, felt it catch, sensed the tightness about her chest that hadn't eased since that moment in the temple.

Stifling a curse, she tossed back the covers and rose. She'd left out her gown for the morning; she wriggled into it, laced it up well enough to pass muster, slipped on her shoes, stuffed her stockings in her pocket, cast one last glance at Lady O in the big bed, then stole to the door, eased it open, and slipped out.

Standing by the window, coatless, waistcoatless, a glass of brandy in his hand, Simon looked down into the garden, and tried not to think. Tried to still his mind. Tried to ignore the growling predator within, and all its fears. They were groundless, he knew, yet . . .

The door opened; he looked across—turned as Portia whisked in and quietly shut it.

Then she straightened, saw him; through the shadows, she studied him, then she crossed the room. Halted a yard away, trying to read his face.

"I didn't expect you to still be up."

He looked into her face, sensed more than saw her sudden uncertainty. "I wasn't expecting you— I didn't think you'd come."

He hesitated only an instant more, then set the glass on the sill and reached for her—as she walked into his arms.

They closed around her; her arms went around his neck and locked as their lips met, then their mouths melded, their aching bodies pressing close. For one long minute, they both clung to the kiss— salvation in a world suddenly dangerous.

She sighed when it ended and he lifted his head; she laid hers on his shoulder. "It's **awful**—dreadful. How could Kitty have done it? Even acting . . ." She shuddered, lifted her head and looked into his eyes. "It makes me feel literally ill."

His laugh, harsh, abrupt, shook. "The script's not doing anything for my stomach, either."

The feel of her, long, slender, vibrantly warm and alive between his hands, the mounds of her breasts firm against his chest, her hips flush to his thighs, her stomach cradling his erection—her simple physical closeness soothed him as nothing else could. The promise that she was his was so inherent in her stance, the predator in him lay down and purred.

He stroked her back, felt her instant response. Smiled. "We'd better go to bed."

"Hmm . . ." She smiled back, stretched up and touched her lips to his. "We'd better—it's the only way either of us is going to get any sleep."

He laughed, and it felt so good; the shackles of the day melted away, left him free to breathe, to live, to love again.

Free to love her.

He let her take his hand and lead him to the bed, let her script their play as she wished. Gave her all she wanted, and more, even though he had no notion if she'd yet realized.

If she'd guessed or seen or deduced that he loved her.

It didn't, anymore, seem to matter if she had; what he felt was simply there, too real, too strong, too much a part of him to deny.

As for her . . . she wouldn't be here, tonight, sharing herself and the moment with him as she was, if she didn't, in her heart, feel the same. Again, he had no idea if she'd realized her state, let alone if she would readily, easily, acknowledge it.

He was prepared to be patient.

Lying on his back, sprawled naked on the bed, he watched as she rode him, as she used her body to caress him, and flagrantly, blatantly enjoyed every second. He filled his hands, drew her down and feasted, then eased back to watch as she climaxed, perfectly sure he'd never seen any sight so wondrous in his life.

The only thing that felt better was what followed, when she slumped, replete, and he rolled her beneath him, and sheathed himself fully in her warmth. In the slick, scalding haven of her body, and felt her hold him, then stir and rise to him as he filled her, deeper, more powerfully, with every stroke.

And then they were there, where they'd wanted to be, the pinnacle they'd set out to reach.

Bliss filled them, ecstasy overwhelmed them, taking their wits, leaving nothing behind but the fused beat of their lovers' hearts.

The warmth closed around them, drawing them down.

They slumped together, limbs tangled, and slept.

Parting was hard. They both felt it. Both struggled to slip from the bonds that now linked them, more deeply than either had ever expected, more precious than either had ever imagined such things might be.

When just after dawn, Portia slipped from his room—alone after a hissed argument that she'd won—Simon remained sitting up in bed, consciously dwelling on the past hours, on all they'd meant, to him and to her.

The clock on the mantelpiece ticked on; when it struck seven, he sighed. Deliberately, reluctantly, set aside what was—tucked it all away in his mind, safe, real, not to be affected, besmirched, by anything they were forced to say or do today. By any act they were forced to play.

Throwing back the covers, he rose and dressed.

Charlie was already in the breakfast parlor when Simon entered. So were James, Henry, and their father. Simon exchanged the usual morning greetings, let his gaze touch Charlie's as he took the seat opposite James.

Lucy Buckstead arrived, then Portia breezed in. Bright, cheery, her smiles were directed predominantly at Charlie.

Simon she ignored.

She took the seat beside Charlie, and instantly engaged him in a laughing conversation centering on shared acquaintances in town.

Simon sat back, watched, his expression hard, unforgiving.

James glanced at him, then followed his gaze to

Charlie and Portia. After a moment, he cleared his throat and asked Simon about his horses.

The day was theirs, but it would definitely be the last—they had to make the most of it. Throughout the morning, their barbs became progressively more pointed, the brittleness between them escalating step by deliberate step.

James tried to intervene, to draw Charlie off; they all understood, appreciated the gesture—couldn't afford to humor it.

Realizing the difficulty both Simon and Charlie faced in rejecting James's help, Portia put her nose in the air and haughtily snubbed him—inwardly apologizing, praying their ruse worked and she'd be able, later, to explain.

She might as well have slapped him. His face like stone, James inclined his head and left them.

Their eyes met, briefly, then they drew in a collective breath, and carried on.

It was increasingly hurtful. By the time she went in to luncheon, Portia felt physically unwell. A headache threatened, but she refused to let the others down.

Stokes was playing least-in-sight; in all ways, the day was perfect for their purpose. With a death in the house, no one was expecting to be entertained, or even to ride or play cards. The entire company was a captive audience for their little drama; if they played it well, there was no reason their plan wouldn't work.

Again, she sat beside Charlie; blithely gay, she

openly courted his attention, repaying him with her best smile.

From across the table, Simon, unusually silent, watched with a burgeoning, brooding, increasingly malevolent air.

More than anything else, that air of suppressed reaction, of reined unhappy passion, infused the atmosphere and sank into everyone. Once, when Portia laughed at a quip of Charlie's, Lady O opened her mouth—then shut it. Looked down at her plate and poked at her peas. Shot a sharp black glance up the table, but in the end said nothing.

Letting out the breath she'd held, Portia met Charlie's eye, gave an infinitesimal nod, and they continued.

When they rose from the table, Portia's temples were throbbing. Lord Netherfield stumped up, fixed Charlie with a straight glance, and asked to have a private word.

Charlie looked at her, panic in his eyes. They hadn't expected direct interference, had no contingency plan.

She forced her smile to grow even brighter. "Oh, dear—Mr. Hastings was going to accompany me for a walk in the gardens." She clung to Charlie's arm, inwardly hating her role.

Lord Netherfield glanced at her; his gaze was condemnatory. "I daresay you could find someone else to guide you—one of the other young ladies, perhaps?"

Charlie tightened his hold on her arm.

Her smile felt sickly as she replied, "Well, they are rather **young**, if you take my meaning?"

Lord Netherfield blinked. Before he could respond, Lady O stumped up and poked him in the ribs. "Leave them be." Her tone was curt, and unchartertistically low. "Use the brains you were born with, Granny. They're up to something." Her black eyes narrowed, but there was a hint of approval in the darkness. "They're playing a very close hand, but if that's what's needed, then the least we can do is stand aside and let them try."

"Oh." Lord Netherfield's expression underwent a series of changes—as if, as his brain digested Lady O's news, he had to shuffle to find the most appropriate face. He blinked. "I see."

"Indeed." Lady O rapped his arm. "You may give me your arm and lead me onto the terrace. The lame leading the lame, perhaps, but let's leave the field to these youngsters"—something of her usual evil gleam shone through—"and watch to see what they make of it."

Both Portia and Charlie stood back; relief flooding them, they let their elders precede them onto the terrace, then followed, aware Simon had seen the exchange from the other side of the room. Even from that distance, something of his tension reached them; exchanging glances, they went down the terrace steps and out onto the lawn.

They ambled, but it quickly became apparent Charlie was seriously flagging. When he countered one of her teasing sallies completely at random,

Portia looped her arm in his and pressed even more brazenly near, conscious that, despite the physical closeness, there was nothing at all between them, except, perhaps, a burgeoning friendship and the trust of a shared endeavor. Luckily, that was enough to allow them to behave sufficiently intimately to carry off their charade. Providing neither of them stumbled.

Leaning close, she murmured, "Let's go down by the lake—if there's no one about, we can duck into the pinetum and rest for a while. After all our hard work, if we fall at the last hurdle and give ourselves away, we'll never forgive ourselves."

Charlie straightened. "Good idea." He redirected their footsteps toward the lake path. Surreptitiously wriggled his shoulders. "Simon's watching—I can feel it."

She glanced at him; she wouldn't have marked him as a particularly sensitive soul. "I'm assuming he'll follow."

"I think we can count on it."

Charlie's grim pronouncement had her studying his face. Realizing . . . "You're not enjoying this any more than we are."

The look he shot her, safe enough with all the others far behind, was ascerbic. "I think I can confidently state that I'm enjoying this considerably **less** than you both, and that's despite knowing both of you hate it."

She frowned as they followed the narrowing lawn path on toward the lake. "Can't you just think of me in the same vein as one of the married matrons I assume you occasionally consort with?"

"That's just the problem. I **do** think of you like that, only you're **his** wife. Makes a rather big difference, you know. I don't relish the prospect of being rent limb from limb—I avoid jealous husbands on principle."

"But he's not my husband."

"Oh, ain't he, though?" Charlie's brows rose high. "You couldn't prove it by his behavior—or yours, come to that. And I think I can lay claim to some expertise in that sphere."

He looked down as they walked on, didn't see her smile.

"In fact, I think," he continued, grimacing as he lifted his head, "that that's the reason our plan just might work."

Given the distance from the house, and the clear area around them, it seemed safe to talk freely. "Do you think it truly is working?"

He grinned at her, lifted a hand and flicked back a lock of black hair that the wind had sent sneaking across her cheek; they still had to keep up appearances. "Henry looked as sick as a horse—all because of us. After this morning, James has retreated, but he's watching us, too. Desmond . . . he's a quiet one, but now Winifred's drawn back, he has plenty of time on his hands, and he's definitely been frowning our way."

"Frowning? Not just watching?"

"Frowning," Charlie averred. "But in what sense I couldn't say—I don't know him well enough."

"What about Ambrose?"

Charlie grimaced. "Oh, he's noticed, but I can't say I've seen him paying much attention. He's the only one of us who's got anything from the last days; he's been using the time to bend Mr. Buckstead to his cause. Mr. Archer, too, although the poor man isn't really taking much in."

They'd reached the lake path; they started to amble around it. When the path leading into the pinetum lay just ahead, Portia tugged Charlie's arm. "Look back—can you see anyone?"

Charlie twisted around and scanned the lawn paths rising toward the house. "No one—not even Simon."

"Good—come on." Portia caught up her skirts and whisked onto the smaller path; Charlie followed close behind. "He'll find us."

He did, but not before weathering a moment of sheer panic. He'd assumed they'd go to the summerhouse; when he reached it and found it empty . . .

Tramping through the pinetum, Simon caught a glimpse of Portia's blue gown through the trees ahead. The vise locked about his chest finally loosened; drawing a freer breath, he trudged on, the thick carpet of dried pine needles crunching with every step.

What he'd felt in that moment when he'd stood and stared around at the empty chairs and sofa in the summerhouse . . . clenching his jaw, he pushed the memory away. He'd never before been conscious of jealousy, but the corrosive emotion that had seared him—it couldn't be termed anything else.

No, he wasn't going to be an easy husband to live with; he had to admit Portia was right to consider very carefully before accepting him. He had a sneaking suspicion that when it came to the more emotional aspects of their potential, soon-to-be union, she saw him more clearly than he saw himself.

They'd stopped in a small clearing; Charlie was leaning against the bole of one tall tree, Portia was leaning against another, opposite, her spine supported by the bole, her head back, eyes closed.

He marched into the clearing, halted, and fixed both with a very straight glance. "What the devil are you doing?"

He kept his voice low, even.

Portia opened one eye, looked at him. "Resting."

She closed her eye again, straightened her head against the tree. "Charlie was getting worn out and slipshod. So was I. We needed a respite from the fray."

He frowned. "Why here?"

She sighed, turned her head, opened both eyes. Ran her gaze down to his feet. "The pine needles. We heard you coming from a long way off. No one can sneak up on us here."

Charlie straightened away from his tree. "Now that you're awake, can you please sit down?" With an exaggerated bow, he waved her to the low bank edging the clearing. When she stared at him, he pointedly added, "So we can?"

Simon glanced at Portia, saw the look on her face, smiled for the first time since she'd left him that morning. He reached for her hand, tugged, and towed her to the bank. "She's not accustomed to having her sensibilities treated with such care. In fact," he met her gaze as he swung her about. "I'm not sure she approves."

Her eyes flashed, the Portia of old appearing briefly. Tipping her nose in the air, she humphed, but consented to sit.

They did, too, one on either side of her, lounging on the grassy bank.

The minutes ticked by and they sat in relaxed silence, looking out through the trees, letting the peace enfold them. Drinking it in, like a potion to give them strength through what they knew was yet to come.

The westering sun was slanting through the trees when Simon at last stirred. The other two looked at him.

He read the lack of enthusiasm in their faces, also their resolve. Grimaced. "We'd better rehearse our last act."

The curtain went up in the drawing room before dinner. Portia arrived late, after everyone else. She swept in, magnificent in her deep green silk gown;

pausing on the threshold, head high, she scanned the company.

Her gaze stopped on Simon; the look she bent on him was cold, chilly, with an underlying fury. Something close to dismissive contempt. Then she shifted her gaze to Charlie—all her ice melted as she smiled.

Ignoring Simon and all the others, she crossed to Charlie's side.

He returned her smile, but his gaze flicked to Simon. Whether it was the way he shifted as she joined him, offering his arm—which she was clearly intending to take—but stepping a little aside, as if to step away from the company, to withdraw to a more seemly privacy, whether it was the slight awkwardness he managed to infuse into his actions, his reception conveyed the impression he was suddenly having second thoughts as to his role in her transparent scheme.

Her scheme to strike at Simon—whether to make him jealous, or to punish him for some transgression or omission, no one could guess.

Whatever the cause, everyone by now recognized her intention.

She laughed, cajoled, held Charlie captive, mesmerized him with her eyes. Flirted to the top of her bent. Simon and Charlie had spent an hour lecturing her, teaching her how; bowing to their expertise, she followed their instructions to the letter.

It felt so wrong, yet . . . they had both been earnest in insisting she carry the charade through.

As she gaily chattered, freely dispensing her smiles on Desmond, who wandered up, and Ambrose, who joined them later, she nevertheless kept her sights set firmly on Charlie, her hand on his sleeve.

Simon stood across the room with Lucy, Drusilla, and James, yet his eyes rarely left them. His gaze could only be described as black.

He had a temper, something everyone instinctively recognized on meeting him; he didn't have to show it for all to know. Now he was deliberately giving it rein, it was like a living force, growing, swelling, ballooning as he watched them.

Winifred came up. "Tell me, Miss Ashford, will you be returning to your brother's house tomorrow?"

It was undoubtedly the most pointed comment on her unseemly behavior Winifred could bring herself to make. Portia inwardly apologized as she let her smile brighten. "Actually . . ."—she cast a glance at Charlie, fractionally raised one brow, then looked back at Winifred—"I might go up to London for a few days. Look in on the town house for my brother, tend to a few matters. Of course," she went on, her transparent expectations giving her words the lie, "there's so little real entertainment to be found in town in July, I daresay I'll be quite moped."

She glanced again at Charlie. "You'll be heading back to town, won't you?"

Her implication was blatant. Winifred was so shocked she gasped, then looked thoroughly unhappy. Desmond raised a brow, subtly disapproving. Ambrose looked coldly bored.

"Ma'am—dinner is served."

Portia had never in her life been so thankful to hear those words. Quite what the others would have said if the moment had lengthened, how Charlie might have replied, what riposte she might have been forced to make . . . thank heaven for butlers.

Desmond offered Winifred his arm; she glanced at it, then met his eyes, then, as if making a decision, laid her hand on his sleeve and let him steer her to the dining room. Portia followed on Charlie's arm. He pinched her fingers when, her gaze fixing on Winifred and Desmond—her mind praying the murderer would not prove to be he—she failed to play her part.

She turned her lapse to advantage; as they passed into the dining room, she slanted him a playfully knowing glance. "You're altogether too demanding."

The smile that went with the words clearly invited him to demand as much as he wished; taking their seats about the dinner table, many of the company noticed.

The Hammond sisters had regained something of their youthful exuberance; with the prospect of escape nearing, and the incident with the urn reduced to mere accident, they were sufficiently restored to laugh and chatter gaily with Oswald and Swanston—thoroughly innocent play that cast

Portia's endeavor in an even stronger, more contrasting light.

She was grateful to Lady Glossup, who had clearly attempted to separate the warring parties, thereby reducing the opportunity for further conflict. Portia was seated close to one end of the table, Simon in the middle on the opposite side, and Charlie at the far end, on the same side as she so they couldn't even exchange glances.

With perfect equanimity, ignoring Simon's unrelievedly dark looks, she set herself to entertain her neighbors, Mr. Archer and Mr. Buckstead, the two of the company least aware of the drama being enacted under their noses.

When the ladies rose, she joined them, her expression easy and content. But as she drew level with Simon on the other side of the table, on his feet as were all the gentlemen as the ladies filed out, she deliberately, coldly, challengingly, met his gaze. Held it. Equally deliberately, as she came to Charlie, she raised a hand and ran her fingers along the back of his shoulders, briefly ruffling the hair at his nape, before smiling into Simon's furious eyes. Letting her hand fall, she turned and, head high, glided out of the dining room.

Most had caught the moment.

Lady O's black eyes narrowed to shards, but she said nothing. Just watched.

The other matrons were more openly censorious, but in the circumstances, could do little to interfere. Flirting, even of the type she was indulging in, had never been a crime within the ton; it was only the memory of Kitty that now made it seem so dangerous in their eyes.

Nevertheless, she gave them no other opening to reproach her actively; she behaved as she normally would, with perfect grace, while they waited for the gentlemen to join them. Tonight, the last night of the house party, it would be viewed as odd if any gentleman excused himself, for whatever reason. They would all come, and relatively soon; they would all be present to witness the penultimate scene.

As the minutes ticked by, Portia felt her nerves tighten. She tried not to think of what was to come, yet, notch by notch, a vise closed about her lungs.

Finally, the doors opened and the gentlemen walked in. Lord Glossup led the way, Henry beside him. Simon followed, strolling beside James; his eyes searched the company and found her.

As they'd arranged, Charlie ambled in a few feet behind Simon.

Portia fixed her gaze on Charlie, let her face light with anticipation and more. Smiling delightedly, she left her position beside the chaise and crossed the room toward him.

Simon stepped sideways, blocking her path. His fingers closed about her elbow; he swung her to him. "If you could spare me a few minutes of your time."

No question, no request.

Portia reacted, let her face set. She tried to twist her elbow free—winced when his grasp tightened and his fingers bit. Head rising, she met his gaze squarely—as belligerent, as challenging as she needed to be. "I think not."

She felt it then—felt his anger rise like a wave and crash down on her.

"Indeed?" His tone was controlled; his fury swirled around them. "I believe you'll find you're mistaken."

Even knowing the script they'd agreed to, knowing what he would do next, she still felt shocked when he bodily swung her to the windows and, her arm locked in an unforgiving grip, walked to the terrace doors.

Taking her with him.

She had to go—it was that or be openly dragged. Or lose her footing and fall. She'd never been physically compelled in her life; the sensation— her helplessness—was enough to send her temper into orbit. She could feel her cheeks flame.

He opened the doors and propelled her outside, marched her ruthlessly along until they were beyond the drawing room windows.

Not, quite, out of earshot.

They'd agreed that once they'd set the stage, they couldn't afford not to play out the scene, not perform according to the script.

She finally succeeded in dragging in a breath. "How **dare** you?" Out of sight of the others, she halted, struggled.

He released her, but she sensed the momentary hesitation—the fractional pause while he forced his fingers to let her go.

She faced him, glared, searched his eyes—saw he was as close to truly losing his temper as she was to losing hers.

"Don't you dare upbraid me." She took a step back—remembered their rehearsed script. Lifted her chin. "I'm not yours to dictate to—I don't belong to you."

She hadn't thought his expression could get harder, but it did.

He stepped toward her, closing the distance. His eyes were shards of blue flint, his gaze sharp enough to slice. "And what of **me**?" The suppressed fury in his voice vibrated through her. "Am I some toy you enjoy and then blithely toss away? Some lapdog you tease with your favors, then kick aside when you grow bored?"

Staring into his eyes, she abruptly wavered her resolve. Her heart wrenched as she realized he was voicing real fears—that the pretense, for him, echoed a reality he was supremely vulnerable to . . .

The urge—the need—to reassure him nearly flattened her. She had to call on every ounce of her will to hold his gaze, lift her head until her spine ached, and lash back at him. "It's not **my** fault you misread things—that your never-faltering masculine ego couldn't believe I wasn't fascinated to blindness with you." Her voice rose, contemptuous and defiant. "I never promised you **anything**."

"Hah!" His laugh was harsh and hollow. "You and your promises."

Simon looked at her, deliberately let his gaze travel down, then insolently back up to her face. His lip curled. "You're nothing but a high-bred cocktease."

Her eyes blazed. She slapped him.

Even though he'd intended to goad her into it, it still shocked. Stung.

"**You're** nothing but an insensitive clod." Her voice wavered with genuine passion; her breasts swelled as she drew breath. "Why I bothered with you . . . I can't believe I wasted my time! I never want to see you or speak to—"

"If we never exchange another word in this lifetime, it will still be too soon for me."

She held his gaze. Between them, around them, temper—both his and hers—swirled, touching but not investing, coloring but not truly driving. They were still acting, but . . .

Dragging in a shaky breath, she drew herself up and looked down her nose at him. "I have nothing more to say to you. I don't wish to set eyes on you again—**not ever!**"

He felt his jaw clench. "That's one thing I'll be happy to promise." He ground out the words, capped them with, "If you'll do the same?"

"**That** will be a pleasure. Good-bye!"

She spun on her heel and stormed off down the terrace. The tempo of her steps echoed, a clear indication of her state.

He hauled in a breath, held it—desperately

fought the urge to follow her. Knew the moon cast his shadow back along the terrace, that anyone watching from the drawing room would know she'd gone off alone—that he wasn't following her.

She reached the lawns and headed straight for the lake path.

Swinging around, he strode back up the terrace, past the drawing room doors, ajar as he'd left them; without a glance to left or right, he headed for the stables.

Prayed he'd have time to circle around and join her before the murderer did.

CHAPTER 17

Portia strode rapidly across the lawn and on toward the lake. She'd imagined doing so eagerly if anxiously; the tumult of emotions roiling inside her made it easy to appear overset.

Cocktease? That hadn't been in the script they'd rehearsed. Nor had her slapping him. He'd done it deliberately; she could, perhaps, understand why, but she wasn't going to forgive him easily. In the heat of the moment, the accusation had hurt.

She could feel her cheeks still flaming; as she walked, she put her hands to her face, trying to cool the burning.

Tried, desperately, to get her mind back on track—to focus on why she was here, why they'd had to stage that horrible fight.

Stokes had pointed out that the murderer would only approach her if he thought she was alone— alone in a suitable environment in which he could murder her and escape undetected. No one would readily believe she'd be witless enough to go wandering in the gardens alone in the gathering twilight—not unless she had a damned good reason.

Even more, no one would believe Simon would allow her to do so—not unless he had a damned good reason. Not unless, as Charlie had remarked, something cataclysmic had happened to stop him watching over her.

Apparently his habit, one admittedly he'd never concealed, had been widely noted.

Until Charlie had mentioned it, she'd never really thought of how Simon's behavior must have, over all the years, appeared to others . . .

Wondered how, knowing what she now did, she'd managed to be so blind.

Remembered with a start that she should keep her eyes peeled for the murderer. If they'd succeeded, he'd be on his way down to find her.

Her liking for the lake path was, so Stokes and Charlie had averred, also well-known, but they'd chosen that venue for other reasons; the path was completely visible all the way around—easy for Stokes and Charlie to hide here and there and watch over her. Simon would join them, of course, but to avoid scuppering their plan, he had to go all the way to the stables before circling back.

Blenkinsop was also on watch, the only other person in their confidence. Simon had wished to seed the gardens with footmen, standing like statues in the shadows; only the argument that the murderer was bound to come across one while following Portia, and thus get the wind up and after all their hard work not appear, had changed his mind.

But Blenkinsop was trustworthy and, like all

good servants, next to invisible. He'd keep watch from the house and follow whichever gentleman set out for the lake.

She reached the edge of the main lawn and headed down the first slope toward the lake. Raising her head, she scanned the skies, drew in a breath.

The weather was the only thing that, thus far, had not gone their way. Clouds had blown up, ragged and dark, not quite preempting the sunset but deepening the twilight.

She strode along as if furiously angry, not inwardly calmly expectant as she'd expected to be, but with her nerves jumping, twitching at every sound. The emotions stirred by their argument had yet to settle; roused, uncertain, they left her uneasy.

They'd presumed that, walking quickly, she'd easily reach the lake before the murderer . . . she hoped they hadn't overlooked some minor detail— like the murderer's having already been out, strolling the gardens and thus being much closer—

The bushes just ahead of her rustled. She stopped, quivering . . .

A man stepped out.

She was so surprised she didn't scream.

A hand rising to her lips, she squeaked. Then dragged in a breath—

Recognized the man. Saw the startled expression on his face.

Arturo held up both hands placatingly and

backed away two steps. "My apologies, miss. I didn't mean to frighten you."

Portia exhaled through her teeth. Frowned. "What are you doing here?" She kept her voice low. "Mrs. Glossup's dead—you know that."

He wasn't intimidated; he frowned back. "I came to see Rosie."

"Rosie?"

"The maid. We are . . . good friends."

She blinked. "You . . . before . . . you weren't coming up here to see Mrs. Glossup?"

His lip curled. "That **putain**? What would I want with her?"

"Oh." She shuffled her thoughts, reorganized her conclusions.

Noticed Arturo was still frowning at her.

She straightened her shoulders, lifted her head. "You'd better be off." She waved him away.

He frowned harder. "You shouldn't be out here alone. There's a murderer here—**you** should know **that**."

The last thing she needed, another overprotective male.

He took a step toward her.

She lifted her head higher, narrowed her eyes. "Go!" She pointed imperiously down the narrow path he'd been following. "If you don't, I'll scream and tell everyone **you're** the murderer."

He debated whether to call her bluff, then grudgingly stepped away. "You are a very aggressive female."

"It comes from dealing with very aggressive males!"

The acid response settled the matter; with a last frown, Arturo went, melting into the bushes, his footsteps cushioned by the grassed path.

Silence closed in, like a cloak falling about her. With a quick breath, she headed on, as fast as she could. The shadows seemed to have grown darker, denser. She jumped, her heart in her mouth, at one—only to realize it truly was just a shadow.

Pulse pounding, she finally reached the crest beyond which the path ran down to the lake. Pausing to catch her breath, she looked down at the water, ink black, silent, and still.

She listened, strained her ears, but all she could hear was the faint murmuring of leaves. The breeze wasn't strong enough to disturb the lake; the surface lay like obsidian glass, smooth but not reflective.

There was no true light left; as she went down the slope, she wished she'd worn a brighter color— yellow or bright blue. Her dark green silk would blend into the shadows; only her face, her bare arms and shoulders, her upper chest, would show.

Glancing down, she let the fine Norwich silk shawl she'd draped about her shoulders slide down to her elbows. No need to conceal more of her than necessary. Reaching the lake, she turned away from the summerhouse and followed the circling path.

Her nerves were tensed, tight, poised to react to an attack. Both Stokes and Charlie were concealed nearby; given the minutes she'd spent with Arturo, Simon would be close, too.

Simply thinking it was comforting. She walked along, still brisk, but gradually slackening her pace, as she naturally would as the supposed fury that had propelled her this far slowly dissipated.

She'd passed the path to the pinetum but was still some way from the summerhouse when the bushes lining the path rustled.

Her heart leapt. She halted, scanned the dark, waited . . .

"It's only me. Sorry."

Charlie. She let out her breath in an exasperated hiss, looked down, fussing with her shawl as if the fringe had caught and she'd stopped to untangle it. "You nearly scared me into hysterics!"

She'd whispered; he did, too.

"I'm keeping watch along this side, but it's hell to get along here. I'm going to edge back toward the pinetum."

She frowned. "Don't forget the pine needles."

"I won't. Simon should be somewhere just past the summerhouse, and Stokes is near the path to the house, on the way to the pinetum."

"Thank you." Flicking out her fringe, she lifted her head and walked on.

Breathed deeply to calm her skittering nerves.

The breeze had dropped; the night itself seemed to have stilled, silent yet expectant, as if it, too, was waiting.

Reaching the space before the summerhouse, she

paused, pretended to consider, but had no intention of going in. Inside, her faithful watchers couldn't see her. Turning away, she continued on.

Pacing, as if thinking. She kept her head down, but watched her surrounds from under her lashes. Let her senses reach, search. They'd assumed the villain would try to strangle her—a gun was too noisy, too easy to trace, a knife would be far too messy.

She hadn't really thought about who it was—which of the four suspects she expected to meet; as she walked and waited, she had time and reason enough to consider it. She didn't want it to be Henry or James, yet . . . if, from all she knew, she'd had to make a choice and pick one of the four, she would have picked James.

It was, in her mind, James she was expecting to meet.

He had the inner strength. The resolve. It was something she recognized both in him and in Simon.

James was, to her, the most likely possibility.

Desmond . . . he'd put up with Kitty's interference for so long, had used avoidance of her as his tactic for literally years. She had difficulty seeing him suddenly in the grips of a murderous rage, murderous enough to kill.

As for Ambrose, she honestly couldn't see him doing anything so rash. Tight-lipped—she'd heard Charlie mumble something about him being tight-arsed and couldn't find it in her to disagree—he was so careful of his behavior, so calculating, so cold-bloodedly focused on his career, the idea of him falling into a murderous rage just because Kitty propositioned him in public . . . it was simply too much to believe.

James, then. Regardless of their feelings for him, she knew that, if it indeed proved to be so, Simon and Charlie would not try to shield him. They would find it incredibly painful, but they would hand him over to Stokes themselves. Their code of honor would demand it.

She understood that—indeed, better than most gentlemen. Her brother, Edward, a few years younger than Luc, was no longer spoken of. Many families had a rotten apple; they'd weeded theirs out; despite all, she could find it in her to hope the Glossups wouldn't have to weather such a scandal.

The path up to the house lay just ahead. She'd nearly completed a circuit of the lake . . . and no one had arrived. Had she walked too fast? Or was the murderer lying in wait for her back up the path, in the shadows lining the route to the house?

Drawing level with the path, she looked up, scanning the shadows bordering the upward rise— and saw a man. He stood just below the lip of the rise, to one side, in the shadow of a large rhododendron. It was the dark foliage behind him that allowed her to see him well enough to be sure.

It was Henry.

She was shocked, surprised . . . looked down and kept walking as if she hadn't seen him, while her mind raced.

Had it been he? Had he learned about Kitty's pressuring James over her baby, as they'd surmised might have happened? Had that been the last straw?

She felt chilled, but kept walking. If it was Henry, she had to draw him down here—where she was safe. She kept walking, her skirts swaying about her as she steadily paced on, heading once more toward the pinetum, her nerves strained, her senses even more so, waiting, aching to hear the soft thud of a footstep behind her . . .

Ten feet ahead of her, a figure stepped smoothly out from one of the myriad minor paths between the bushes and waited, elegantly at ease, for her to join him.

Portia stared at Ambrose. **Damn!** He was going to ruin everything! He smiled as she approached; mind reeling, wits in a whirl, she struggled to find some means, some excuse, to send him packing.

"I heard your altercation with Cynster. While I can appreciate your need for solitude, you really shouldn't be out walking alone."

What was it about her that made every last gentleman think he needed to protect her?

Thrusting her irritation aside, she stopped beside him, inclined her head. "Thank you for your concern, but I really do wish to be left quite alone."

His smile turned distinctly patronizing. "I'm afraid, my dear, that we really can't allow that." He didn't move to take her arm, but turned to pace beside her.

Frowning, she found herself walking on while she debated her next move. She had to get rid of him—did she dare tell him that this was a planned trap, that she was the bait and he was interfering . . . that the murderer may very well, even now, be watching, closing in from behind?

The darkness of the pinetum rose on their right. The lake, black and still, lay to her left. Ambrose was on her right, between her and the gloom beneath the soaring trees. According to Charlie, they must have just passed Stokes. The temptation to glance back, to see if Henry was taking the bait and coming down the slope, pricked, but she resisted.

The path into the pinetum lay ahead; she racked her brains to think of a reason to send Ambrose back to the house that way . . .

"I have to admit, my dear, that I never thought you'd be as stupid as Kitty."

The words, calm, perfectly even, jerked her back to the moment. She glanced at Ambrose. "What do you mean—as stupid as Kitty?"

"Why, that I hadn't believed you to be one of those silly women who delights in playing one man against another. In treating men as if they're puppets and you're in control of their strings."

He continued walking, looking down, not at her; his expression, what she could see of it, seemed pensive.

"That was," he went on, in the same even, considered tone, "poor Kitty's style to the last. She thought she had power." His lips twisted wryly. "Who knows—she might have had some, but she never learned how to wield it properly."

He finally glanced at Portia. "I'd thought you were different—certainly more intelligent." He met her gaze, smiled. "Not that I'm complaining, of course."

It was the smile that did it—that sent a wave of ice washing over her. Convinced her she was walking beside Kitty's murderer, that it wasn't Henry, or James . . .

"Aren't you?" She halted. Managed a frown. She wasn't walking another step closer to the path through the pinetum—leading into the darkness where no one could see. "If you didn't come here to comment—impertinently—on my behavior, what, then, is your point?"

She swung around as she said it, planting herself before him—facing back along the path so she'd be able to see Stokes, but Ambrose, facing her, wouldn't.

His smile remained. "That's simple, my dear. My point is to silence you and leave Cynster to take the blame. He's out walking, so are you. After that scene on the terrace . . ." His chilling smile deepened. "I couldn't have scripted it better myself."

He lifted his hands, until then clasped behind his back. She saw a curtain cord dangling from one, then he caught the swinging tassel, wound the cord between his hands—

She grabbed it. Locked both fists around the cord between his hands and hung on.

He swore. Tried to shake her loose, but couldn't—couldn't break her grip without letting go himself.

Behind him, she saw the burly shadow that was Stokes burst from the bushes and rush toward them.

Snarling, Ambrose released the curtain cord—throwing her off-balance. She staggered; he grabbed the trailing end of her silk shawl.

Swung about her, whipping it around her neck.

She didn't think—didn't have time. She got a hand inside the folds; in the instant before he wrenched them tight, she leaned back toward him, pushing the shawl simultaneously away, and slid down.

Out of the noose.

She ended crouched at Ambrose's feet, hard by the lake's edge. Stokes was thundering up. Ambrose was too close, standing, snarling over her, looping the shawl between his hands.

She flung herself sideways, into the lake.

The black waters closed over her—the banks were precipitous, there was nothing beneath her feet. But the water was cool, not icy; the long summer had warmed it. There was neither current nor waves to fight; it was easy to rise to the surface and swim.

As she did, she caught a fleeting glimpse of Ambrose's stunned face—then he heard Stokes. Saw him. Realized . . .

Ambrose's face contorted with fury—

She swam. Behind her, she heard a thud and an "oomph!" as Stokes collided with Ambrose. Kicking as well as her skirts allowed, she stroked away from the bank, then, at a safe distance, turned.

Charlie was rushing up to assist. Henry was lumbering down the path. Simon had been on his way to help the others but had stopped on the lake circuit at the point closest to her. He now stood at the lake's edge. Watching. Poised to react . . .

Reaching the fray, Charlie joined in, grappling to help Stokes hold his prey. Ambrose fought like a madman—wrenched free—

And jumped into the lake.

Her heart leaping again, Portia turned to swim away—saw Simon tense on the bank—

But he didn't dive in.

Hearing splashing—too much splashing, surely?—she glanced back.

And realized, as all the others had, that Ambrose had assumed the lake was ornamental—not fathoms deep.

He couldn't swim. Certainly not well enough.

Within a few strokes he was foundering.

She drifted, watching . . .

Stokes and Charlie stood on the bank, hands on hips, chests heaving, and watched as Ambrose, now panicked and thrashing wildly, sank.

He came up spluttering. "Help! I'm drowning, you bastards! **Help me!**"

It was Stokes who answered. "Why should we?"

"Because I'm drowning—I'll **die!**"

"The way I see it, that might be best all around. Save us all a lot of bother."

Startled, Portia looked at Stokes. It wouldn't do—they had to have Ambrose known as the murderer—

But Stokes knew his man.

Ambrose went down again, and came up screeching, "All right. All **right**! I did it. I strangled the little bitch!"

"That would be Mrs. Glossup, I take it?"

"Yes, dammit!" Ambrose was yelling at the top of his lungs. "Now get me out of here!"

Stokes looked at Charlie, then at Henry, who, stunned, had slowly come to join them. "You heard?"

Charlie nodded; when Henry realized Stokes had included him, he nodded, too.

"Right, then." Stokes looked down at Ambrose. "I can't swim either. How do we fetch him out?"

From the water, Portia raised her voice. "Use my shawl." It was lying on the ground where Ambrose had dropped it. "Wind it and knot the fringes as well—it should reach him. It's silk—if it's not torn, it'll hold."

She waited, watching while they followed her instructions. Heard, from the bank a little way behind her the growled words, "Don't you dare even **think** of going to his aid."

For the first time in too many hours, she smiled.

Luckily, with rescue assured, Ambrose calmed enough to, very clumsily, keep his head above water until they flung the shawl out to him.

He lunged, grabbed the knotted fringe, and clung. The dunking and his resulting panic had drained all the fight from him. As they drew him, shaking, from the water, she turned and stroked to the nearer shore.

Where Simon stood waiting.

She couldn't read his expression as he stood looking down at her. Relief and something more poured through her. Smiling—simply glad to be alive—she held up both hands. He grasped them, waited until she'd brought her feet against the rocky wall of the lake, then pulled her smoothly out, onto the bank.

Released her hands and caught her in his arms.

Yanked her close, locked her to him.

Ignoring her dripping state, he kissed her— hard, ruthless, ravishing, and desperate—kissed her witless.

Much better than being shaken witless.

When he finally consented to lift his head, she looked into his face, didn't need her intellect to correctly interpret the tension holding him, to know that he had come very close to the edge of his control.

"I'm perfectly all right." She spoke directly to what she knew to be his fear, the vulnerability he possessed, all because of her.

He humphed. The telltale tension eased only slightly. "As I remember it, the plan did not call for you to jump into the lake."

His arms loosened; she pushed back. Stepped out of his arms as he reluctantly let her go. Lifted her hands to her shoulders and pressed down on her gown, following the line of her body to her hips and thighs, squeezing the water out and down, then grasping her skirts and wringing them.

"It seemed the most sensible way to go." She kept her tone determinedly mild, as if they were discussing a hunt meet rather than her flight from a murderer.

"What if he'd been able to swim?" The aggravated growl was still tense and accusatory. "You didn't know he couldn't."

She straightened, looked him in the eye. "I didn't know about Ambrose, but I swim quite well." She raised her brows fractionally, let a smile touch her lips. "And you swim even better."

He held her gaze. She could feel him weighing what she'd said . . .

Suddenly realized. "You did know I could swim, didn't you?"

His lips, until then a tight line, twisted, then he exhaled. "No." His gaze locked with hers; he hesitated, then grudgingly added, "But I assumed you could or you wouldn't have jumped in."

She read his face, his eyes, then smiled delightedly as sudden joy infused her, rushed up through her. Left her feeling slightly giddy. She looked down, still smiling. "Precisely." Linking her arm with his, she turned to see what the others were doing.

He continued to study her face. "What?"

She glanced back, met his eyes. Smiled gently.

"Later." Once she'd fully savored the moment, and found the words to tell him how much she appreciated his restraint. He'd stood at the lake's edge, ready to step in and protect her, but, given she'd been able to do so, he'd held back and let her save herself. He hadn't treated her as a helpless female; he hadn't smothered her in his protectiveness. He'd behaved as if she were a partner, one with skills and talents somewhat different from his own yet perfectly capable of dealing with the moment.

He'd have stepped in the instant she needed him—but he'd resisted the temptation to step in before.

A future together really would work—with time, with familiarity, his overprotectiveness would become a more rational, considered response. One that considered her and her wishes, not just his.

Hope filled her, buoyed her with a joy totally divorced from their recent activities.

But those activities were still unfolding. Blenkinsop had joined the group in the shadow of the pinetum. Now he and Stokes turned, Ambrose supported between them. They marched him along the path, passing Simon and Portia at the bottom of the upward slope. His hands bound with her sodden shawl, Ambrose was still shaking; he didn't even glance their way.

Charlie and Henry followed close behind, Charlie explaining all they'd been doing.

Henry halted beside her and took her hands in

his. "Charlie hasn't yet told me all, but I understand, my dear, that we owe you a great deal."

She colored. "Nonsense—we all had a hand."

"Not nonsense at all—without you and your bravery, they couldn't have pulled it off." Henry's eyes had shifted to Simon's face. A glance passed between them, deep with masculine meaning. "And you, Simon." Henry reached out and clapped his shoulder.

Then glanced at her gown, suddenly became aware that she was clad in only two layers of silk, both drenched.

He coughed, looked away—up at the house. "Charlie and I will go on ahead, but you should hurry inside and change. Not wise to stand around in wet clothes, even in summer."

Charlie grinned at Portia, nodded to Simon. "We got him!" His transparent happiness that all was now well, that they'd succeeded in rescuing James, Henry, and Desmond, too, was infectious.

They both smiled. Henry and Charlie walked on; they fell in behind, walking slowly up the rise.

As they crested it, the breeze sprang up, and sent cool fingers sliding down her skin. She shivered.

Simon halted. He shrugged out of his coat and swirled it around her, draping it over her shoulders. She smiled, grateful, even in the balminess of the night, for the caress of heat—his heat—lingering in the silk lining. Holding the coat closed, she met his eyes. "Thank you."

He humphed. "It'll do for the moment."

He retook her hand. She went to walk on but he didn't move, held her back. The others were well ahead.

She glanced at him, brows rising.

Looking at the others, he drew in a breath. "What happened on the terrace—what I said. I apologize. I didn't mean . . ." He waved, as if to wipe the scene from their minds, glanced fleetingly at her, then away.

She stepped across him, raised her free hand to his face, and turned it to hers.

Reluctantly, he let her.

Until, in the fading light, she could read his eyes, until she could sense, as if it were stated, the vulnerability he sought, as always, to hide. To excuse.

She understood that much at least. At last. And was touched beyond measure.

"It won't ever happen. Believe me." She would never take from him, then turn from him, never love, then leave him.

His face, hard, set, didn't soften. "Is it possible to promise such a thing?"

She held his gaze. "Between you and me—yes."

He read her eyes in turn, saw her sincerity; his chest swelled. She felt the change in the tension holding him, the swift return of his possessiveness, the sinking of his protectiveness.

His arm locked around her; he drew her close.

"Wait." She pressed a hand to his chest. "Don't rush."

His brows rose—she could hear the incredulous **"Rush?"** in his mind.

She eased back in his arms. "We need to end what we've started—we need to hear what truly happened and put Ambrose and the murders behind us. Then we can talk about"—she drew breath, finally said the crucial word—**"us."**

He held her gaze, then grimaced and released her. "Very well. Let's get this over with."

He took her hand; together, they climbed the lawns to the house.

It was as grim a scene as he'd foreseen; there was relief but no triumph. In rescuing the Glossups, and to some extent the Archers in that Desmond had been invited at their behest, they'd shifted the weight of opprobrium to the Calvins. To the continuing distress of everyone.

Simon ushered Portia into the library through the terrace doors. The scene that met their eyes was, very likely, Stokes's worst nightmare; they exchanged glances, but knew it was beyond their ability to remedy.

The ladies had rebelled. They'd realized something was going on and had come sweeping into the library; now they'd been told the bare facts—that it was Ambrose who had killed Kitty—they'd all slumped into chairs and sofas, and refused to depart.

Literally everyone was there, even two footmen.

The only one with any connection to the drama not present was Arturo; studying the shocked and, in some instances, disbelieving faces, imagining the angst to come, Simon suspected the gypsy would be eternally grateful to have been spared the ordeal.

So would he. He glanced at Portia, from the set of her features accepted that she would not consent to go upstairs and change before she'd learned the answers she didn't yet know. Fetching the admiral's chair from behind the big desk, he wheeled it down the room, set it beside the end of the chaise where Lady O sat, and handed Portia into it.

Lady O cast a glance at her sodden attire. "No doubt that, too, will be explained?"

There was a note in her old voice, a flicker in her black eyes, that told them both she'd been seriously alarmed.

Portia put out a hand and gripped one ancient claw. "I was never in any danger."

"Humph!" Lady O cast a warning glance up at him, as if to put him on notice that she would disapprove mightily if he fell short of her expectations in any way.

Apropos of which . . . glancing at Stokes, absorbed calming Lady Calvin, assuring her he would explain if she would permit it, Simon stepped back and beckoned one of the footmen; when he came, he rattled off a string of orders. The footman bowed and departed, very likely glad of an opportunity to carry the latest news back to the servants' hall.

"Ladies and gentlemen!" Stokes stepped to the middle of the room, his tone harassed. "As you've insisted on remaining, I must ask you all to remain mute while I question Mr. Calvin. If I wish to know anything from any of you, I will ask."

He waited; when the ladies merely composed themselves as if settling to listen, he exhaled, and turned to Ambrose, slumped in a straight-backed chair under the central chandelier, facing the congregation before the hearth.

Blenkinsop and a sturdy footman, both standing to attention, flanked him.

"Now, Mr. Calvin—you've already admitted before a number of witnesses that you strangled Kitty, Mrs. Glossup. Will you please confirm how you killed her?"

Ambrose didn't look up; his forearms on his thighs, he spoke to his bound hands. "I strangled her with the curtain cord from the window over there." With his head, he indicated the long window closest to the desk.

"Why?"

"Because the stupid woman wouldn't let be."

"In what way?"

As if realizing there would be no way out, that speaking quickly and truthfully would get the ordeal over with that much faster—he couldn't but be aware of his mother, sitting on the chaise deathly pale, a woman who'd been dealt a deadly blow, one hand gripping Lady Glossup's, the other clutching Drusilla's, her eyes fixed in a type of pleading horror on him—Ambrose drew in a huge breath, and rushed on, "She and I—earlier in the year, in London—we had an affair. She wasn't my type, but she was always offering, and I needed Mr. Archer's support. It seemed a wise move at the time—she promised to speak to Mr. Archer for me. When summer came, and we left town, we parted." He shrugged. "Amicably enough. We'd arranged that I would attend this party, but other than that, she let go. Or so I thought."

He paused only to draw breath. "When I got down here, she was up to her worst tricks, but she seemed to be after James. I didn't worry, until she caught me one evening and told me she was pregnant.

"I didn't see the problem at first, but she quickly fixed that. I was appalled!" Even now, the emotion rang in his voice. "It never entered my head that she and Henry weren't . . . well, I never dreamed a married lady would behave as she did knowing she no longer had the protection of her marriage."

He halted, as if stunned anew. Stokes, frowning, asked, "How did that contribute to your reasons for killing her?"

Ambrose looked up at him, then shook his head. "There are any number of tonnish ladies who bear children who are not their husband's get. I didn't foresee any problem until Kitty roundly informed me that under no circumstances could she, or would she, bear the child, and if I didn't want it known it was mine—if I didn't want her to make a fuss and tell her father—I'd have to make arrangements for her to get rid of it. That was the ultimatum she gave me that night."

He studied his hands. "I had no idea what to do. My career—being selected for a sound seat and being elected—all I needed was Mr. Archer's support, and while here I'd found Lord Glossup and Mr. Buckstead well-disposed as well—it was all going so swimmingly . . . except for Kitty." His voice hardened; he kept his gaze on his hands. "I didn't know how to help her—I honestly don't know if I would have if I'd known. It's not the sort of thing ladies should ask of their lovers—most women would know how to deal with it themselves. I thought all she needed to do was ask around. She's here in the country, there's surely plenty of maids who get in the family way . . . I was sure she could manage. Either that, or engineer a reconciliation with Henry."

Clasping his hands tight, he went on, "I made the mistake of telling her so." A shudder ran through him. "God—how she took on! You'd have thought I'd recommended she drink hemlock— she ranted, railed—her voice rose and rose. I tried to shut her up and she slapped me. She started to screech—

"I grabbed the curtain cord and wound it about her neck . . . and pulled." He fell silent; the room was still—a pin dropping would have echoed.

Then he tilted his head, his gaze far away, remembering . . . "It was surprisingly easy—she wasn't at all strong. She struggled a bit, tried to reach back and scratch me, grab me, but I held her until she stopped struggling . . . when I let her go, she just crumpled to the floor."

His voice changed. "I realized I'd killed her. I rushed out—upstairs. Away. I went to my room and poured myself a brandy—I was gulping it down when I saw my coat sleeve had been torn. The flap was gone. Then I remembered that was where Kitty had grabbed. I realized . . . then I remembered seeing the flap in Kitty's hand when I'd looked at her lying on the floor. It was plaid—only I wore a plaid coat that day.

"I raced out of my room. I was at the top of the stairs when Portia screamed. Simon came running, then Charlie—there was nothing I could do. I stood there, waiting to be accused, but . . . nothing happened."

Ambrose drew in a breath. "Charlie came out and closed the library door. He looked up and saw me. I could see in his face he didn't think I was the murderer. Instead, he asked where Henry and Blenkinsop were.

"When he left, I realized there was hope—no one had noticed the flap yet. If I could get to it and retrieve it, I'd be safe." He paused. "I had nothing to lose. I went down the stairs. Henry and Blenkinsop came rushing up and entered the library. I followed.

"Portia and Simon were at the other end of the room, Portia deeply shaken, Simon focused on her. Both saw me, but neither reacted. I was still wearing the plaid coat—they couldn't have seen the flap.

"I followed Henry and Blenkinsop to the desk. They were shocked, stunned—they just stared. I looked at Kitty—at her right hand." Ambrose lifted his head. "It was empty.

"I couldn't believe it. The fingers were open, the hand lax. Then I realized both her hands and arms had been moved, her head shifted. I immediately thought of Portia coming in, finding Kitty, rushing to her, then touching her, chafing her hands—doing all those useless little things women do. The flap was narrow, only a few inches long. If it had fallen from Kitty's hand . . ."

He looked down at the Turkish rugs spread over the library floor. "Brown, green, and red. The plaid was the same colors as the rugs. The flap could easily have caught in Portia's skirts or petticoats, or even a man's trouser hem. Once out of Kitty's grasp, it could have ended anywhere, and in this room, it would have been difficult to see. I looked about the body, but it wasn't there. I couldn't risk openly searching. Henry and Blenkinsop were still stunned, so I seized the moment. I walked around the desk and bent as if to look closer, and snagged my sleeve on a handle of one of the desk drawers. I straightened, and it ripped. I swore, then apologized. Both Blenkinsop and Henry were dazed, but they did notice. If the flap was found later, I could say I'd lost it then."

Ambrose's gaze remained distant. "I felt safe. I left the library, and then it struck me—what if someone else had found Kitty before Portia, recognized the flap and taken it away? But I couldn't imagine any of those here doing such a thing. They'd have raised the alarm, denounced me . . . all except Mama. She'd told me she was going to spend the afternoon writing letters, keeping in touch with people whose support I needed. I went up to her room. She was there, writing. She didn't know anything about the murder. I told her, then left."

He paused, head slightly tilted, as if looking back on a strange time. "I returned to my room and finished the brandy. I thought about the servants. No reason any should have gone to the library at that hour, but one can never be sure what an enterprising footman or maid might think to do.

"I decided to burn the coat. No one would be surprised that I'd got rid of it after ripping it. If anyone later tried to blackmail me, with the coat destroyed, I could say the plaid of the flap was like mine but not the same. No one can ever be sure about plaids."

He shifted on the chair. "I took the coat into the woods and burned it. The gypsy undergardener saw me, but I didn't worry about him then. I felt sure I'd successfully covered all eventualities . . . except for the possibility that, as I'd first supposed, the flap had been in Kitty's hand when Portia found her, but the shock had driven it from Portia's mind."

He looked down, lifting his bound hands to rub his forehead. "I could see the flap in Kitty's hand—the image was so vivid in my mind. The more I thought of it the more I felt certain that Portia **had** to have seen it. Even with both flap and coat gone . . . she's usually calm and collected, and very well-connected. Any suggestion from her that I was the murderer would make people step back. An accusation from her could easily ruin my career. I realized I had no guarantee that when she recovered from the shock, she wouldn't remember."

Stokes stirred. "So you tried to scare her witless by putting an adder in her bed."

Gasps and a ripple of consternation broke the spell holding the gathering; for most, it was the first they'd heard of the adder.

Staring down at his hands, Ambrose nodded. "I came across the adder on my way back to the house—I still had the sack I'd used to carry the coat. I thought another shock would keep her from remembering, even make her leave . . . but she didn't. And then you arrived, and I had to be careful. But as the days passed, and no one came to tell me they'd found the flap, I realized that it was as I'd thought—no one else had taken the flap. It was there when Portia found Kitty."

Raising his head, he looked directly at Portia. "Do you remember now? You must have seen it. She had it clutched in her right hand."

Portia met his gaze, then shook her head. "It wasn't there when I found her."

Ambrose pulled a patronizing face. "It **had** to be—"

"You **fool**!"

The exclamation startled everyone. Drew all eyes to Drusilla, sitting bolt upright beside Lady Calvin. Her face was white, her eyes huge, her whole body in the grip of some powerful emotion.

Her gaze remained locked on her brother. "You . . . you . . . **idiot**! Portia said nothing—she would have if she'd seen it. She might have been shocked but she hadn't lost her wits."

As stunned as anyone, Ambrose simply stared at her.

Stokes recovered first. "What do you know of this missing flap, Miss Calvin?"

Drusilla looked up at him, and paled even more. "I . . ." The emotions flitting across her face were visible for all to see. She'd only just realized . . .

Lady Calvin lifted a hand to her lips as if to suppress a cry. Lady Glossup put an arm about her.

Mrs. Buckstead, seated beside Drusilla, leaned forward. "You must tell us all, my dear. There really is no choice."

Drusilla looked at her, then dragged in a breath, and glanced at Stokes. "I was walking in the gardens that afternoon. I came back into the house by the library doors. I saw Kitty lying there and saw the flap in her hand. I recognized it, of course. I realized Ambrose had finally had enough and . . ." She paused, moistened her lips, then went on, "For whatever reason, he'd killed her. If he was caught . . . the scandal, the shame . . . it would kill Mama. So I prised the flap from Kitty's fingers, and took it with me. I heard voices in the front hall—Simon's and Portia's—so I went out by the terrace doors."

Stokes regarded her gravely. "Even when the attempts to silence Miss Ashford commenced, you didn't think to tell anyone?"

Drusilla's gaze flew to his face. She swayed; her skin turned grey. "What attempts?" Her tone was weak, horrified. "I didn't know about the adder." She looked at Ambrose, then at Stokes. "The urn . . . that was an accident—wasn't it?"

Stokes looked down at Ambrose. "You may as well tell us."

Ambrose fixed his gaze on his hands. "I'd taken to pacing on the roof—I couldn't let anyone see how worried I was. I saw Portia on the terrace. She looked to be alone—I couldn't see Cynster by the wall. I was there—it was easy to do . . ." He suddenly drew a huge breath. Lifted his head but didn't meet anyone's eyes. "You have to remember I had **no choice**—not if I wanted to win a seat and become a Member. I'd set my heart on it, and . . . ."

He stopped, looked down. Clasped his hands tightly. Stokes shifted his gaze to Drusilla.

She was staring at Ambrose. Her face was ashen.

When she lifted her gaze to Stokes, he asked, "Why didn't you tell your brother you'd taken the flap?"

For a long moment, she stared at Stokes; he was

about to repeat the question when Drusilla lowered her gaze to Ambrose.

Drew breath, and said, "I hate him, you know. No—how could you? But in our house, it was always Ambrose. He got everything, I was given nothing. Only Ambrose mattered. Even now. I love Mama, I've cared for her dutifully, I remain by her side—I even took the flap to protect her—**her**, not Ambrose, never Ambrose." Her voice was rising, more strident and strong. "Yet even now, all Mama thinks about is Ambrose."

She kept her gaze fixed on her brother's bowed head. "He inherited everything from Papa—I was left nothing. Even Mama's estate will all go to him. I'm his pensioner—he can throw me out whenever he wishes, and don't think he doesn't know it. He's always been quick to make sure I understand my position."

Her face contorted. Vitriol had infused her; jealousy, suppressed and now loosed, poured from her. "The flap—taking it, keeping it, was my chance to pay him back. I didn't tell him—I wanted him to feel fear, to squirm—more, to know someone had it in their hands to ruin him."

Suddenly she looked at Stokes. "Of course I would have told him eventually. When next he thought to tell me how useless I was, how unflattering an ornament I was to a man of his future position."

She stopped, then added, "I honestly didn't think he wouldn't realize . . . he only had to think to know only Mama or I would protect him by concealing the flap. And Mama would have told him straightaway. When he didn't say anything, I thought he'd guessed I had it, but was too careful to broach the subject while we were here." She met Stokes's gaze. "It never occurred to me that he would think Portia had seen it and was witless enough not to remember."

Silence filled the room. The ticking of the clock on the mantelpiece was clearly audible.

Drusilla dropped her gaze to the floor. Ambrose sat with head bowed. Lady Calvin looked from one to the other, as if she no longer recognized them—her own children—then she buried her face in her hands and softly wept.

The sound released others from the grip of the revelations; they stirred, shifted. Charlie stood as if he could no longer remain seated, as if he longed to leave, to get away.

Lord Netherfield cleared his throat. He glanced at Stokes. "If I may . . . ?"

Stokes nodded.

His lordship looked at Ambrose. "You haven't mentioned Dennis, the gypsy. Why did you kill the lad?"

Ambrose didn't look up. "He saw me burning the coat. Then Stokes came and started questioning everyone." He twisted his hands, then went on, "I didn't mean to kill Kitty—I didn't intend to. She drove me to it . . . it didn't seem fair that killing her should ruin me. There was only Portia and the gypsy who could . . ." He stopped, then rushed on, a spoiled child excusing himself, "It was them or me—it was my **life**!"

Lord Glossup rose, his well-bred features reflecting patent disgust. "Mr. Stokes, if you've heard all you need?"

Stokes straightened. "Indeed, sir. I'm sure we can . . ."

He and Lord Glossup discussed arrangements for holding Ambrose. The rest of the company dispersed.

All the ladies hesitated, then Lady O heaved herself to her feet. "Catherine, my dear, I think we should retire to the drawing room—tea would be most welcome. I daresay Drusilla will wish to retire immediately, but I believe the rest of us could do with a restorative."

Portia rose; Simon laid a restraining hand on her arm. Lady O glanced back at them, saw, nodded. "Indeed—**you** should go up and take a bath, and get out of those wet clothes. Unhealthy to do otherwise—your brother won't forgive me if I send you home with a chill."

There was just enough emphasis in her words, just enough gleam in her old black eyes to tell them she was determined to send Portia home with something else.

Simon merely inclined his head, acknowledging her message. Lady O humphed and stumped off, the other ladies in her train, Lady Calvin supported by Lady Glossup and Mrs. Buckstead.

"Come on." Taking Portia's arm, he steered her toward the far doors, those closer to the main stairs.

Stokes intercepted them. "One last thing—I have to consider whether or not to lay charges against Miss Calvin."

Both Simon and Portia looked back at Drusilla, sitting alone on the chaise now that the others had all departed. She was staring at her brother; he was leaning forward, forearms on his thighs, his gaze fixed on his bound hands.

Portia shivered, and looked at Stokes. "What a dreadful thing jealousy can be."

Stokes nodded, met her gaze. "She didn't mean to harm anyone else. I accept she had no idea Ambrose was so murderously inclined."

"I don't think charges are necessary." Portia lifted her head. "She's brought censure enough down on her head—her life will not be easier because of what she's done."

Stokes nodded, looked to Simon.

He was far less inclined to be lenient, but was aware much of his reaction was because Portia had been the one most threatened. When he didn't immediately speak, she glanced at him . . . he realized he had no choice. She would read him like a book if he gave rein to his impulses. He nodded curtly. "No charges. No point."

She smiled slightly, then looked at Stokes.

The three of them exchanged glances, relieved, satisfied. Little needed to be put into words. Stokes was not of their class, yet they'd formed a friendship; they all recognized that.

Stokes cleared his throat, looked away. "I'll be off at first light with Mr. Calvin. It's best—lets people get back to their lives that much sooner." He looked back at them. Put out his hand. "Thank you. I'd never have nabbed him if you and Mr. Hastings hadn't helped." They shook hands. "I hope . . ." Stokes colored slightly, but forced himself to go on, "the necessary charade didn't do any real violence to your feelings."

Simon glanced at Portia. She smiled at Stokes. "The revelations were quite interesting—I believe we'll survive."

She slanted a glance at him; feeling exposed, he fought to suppress a growl. Retook her arm. "There's a bath awaiting you upstairs."

With last smiles and farewells, they left Stokes.

James was waiting with Charlie in the hall.

"Thank you—both of you." James beamed; he took Portia's hands. "I haven't heard it all yet, but even so—how very brave you've been."

This time Simon didn't suppress his growl. "For God's sake!—the last thing I need is for **that** to go to her head."

James laughed; Simon nudged him aside and he stood back, letting Simon steer Portia up the stairs.

"We'll catch up with you later," James called as they ascended.

Simon flicked him a look. "Tomorrow."

Jaw set, he drew Portia on.

CHAPTER 18

A footman was waiting at the top of the stairs to conduct them to the room that, on his orders, had been prepared. Not her original room, because of the adder, not Lady O's room, which had the trestle in it and therefore was too crowded to hold a bath as well. One of the suites that was not often used—a large bedchamber with a large bed, and an adjacent private parlor.

Simon ushered Portia into the bedchamber; two maids were tipping buckets of steaming water into the bath. More buckets stood waiting on the hearth.

He caught Portia's eye. "Get rid of the maids."

She raised a mock-haughty brow; her lips were gently curved. She shrugged his coat from her shoulders and handed it to him. One of the maids hurried up to help her out of her gown. Taking the coat, he crossed to the connecting door and went into the parlor to wait.

The coat was damp; he dropped it on a chair and went to stand before the window. Stared out at the silhouettes of the trees and tried not to think, not to dwell on the emotions the day had stirred.

Tried, vainly, to rein in the most powerful—the emotion she and only she had always aroused in him, the emotion he'd always been careful to hide, even from her. Even now.

The past days had seen it grow even more strong, even more insistent.

He heard the main door of the bedchamber open, then shut. Heard the patter of light footsteps, two pairs, die away down the corridor.

Drew in a deep breath, shackled his demons, then crossed to the connecting door.

He eased it open and confirmed Portia was alone.

In the bath. Shampooing her hair.

Girding his loins, he entered and shut the door. Crossed to the main door and snibbed the lock. A straight-backed, spindle-legged chair stood before an escritoire; he picked it up as he passed, carried it to the area before the hearth and set it down, its back to her, and straddled it.

She glanced at him. "As you were so insistent that I dispense with the maids, I presume you're willing to perform in their place?"

He forced himself to shrug, not to react to the speculation in her dark eyes; the bath was too small. "Whatever you need . . ."

Crossing his arms on the chair's back, he let the words trail away, met her gaze, and settled to watch.

Left himself open to a calculated torture.

She made the most of it—lovingly soaping her graceful arms, seductively stroking her long, long legs. When she rose on her knees, the water fell to lap around the very tops of her thighs. The globes of her bottom gleamed invitingly; he had to close his eyes—had to think of something else.

Then she called him to pour water to rinse off her hair. He stood, stiffly, grabbed up a bucket—

She caught his eye. "Slowly. I need to get all this lather out."

Obediently, he stood beside the tub and poured the water over her while she squeezed and rinsed out her hair. He hadn't realized how long it was; wet, it reached to her hips, drawing his eyes down . . .

He had to close them briefly again; jaw clenched, focusing on her head, he continued to tip, the bucket held in a desperately tight grip.

The water ran out.

She slicked back her hair, then grasped the sides of the tub and stood. Water cascaded down, over her shoulders, her breasts, her hips, down her thighs.

His mind blank, his mouth dry, he set the bucket aside, blindly reached for the towels left stacked on a stool. Flicked one out and held it for her, stepping back as, smiling, she stepped out of the tub toward him.

She took the towel, held it to her breasts—considered him.

He met her gaze as stoically as he could,

grabbed another towel, opened it, and dropped it on her head.

Heard a smothered giggle.

He proceeded to dry her hair; it held enough water to soak a bed. She let him, ducked and turned as she used the first towel to mop her curves, dry her long limbs.

Then she dropped the towel, wrestled the other from him, and dropped that, too. Nearly stopped his heart by stepping into his arms, arms he was helpless to stop closing about her.

She draped hers about his neck and lifted her face for a kiss.

He obliged without thought, took her lips and her mouth as she offered them, felt his control quake when she blatantly pressed nearer, setting her body to his.

She met his eyes when he lifted his head, determination clear in her gaze. "I want to celebrate." Her gaze dropped to his lips; stretching up, she brushed them lingeringly with hers. "Now."

"On the bed." She was going to be the death of him—he was increasingly sure of that.

As if hearing something of his thoughts in his tone, she tilted her head, studied him. Then smiled. A smile that held too much knowledge, far too much resolution for his liking.

"On one condition." Her tone had descended to that sultry purr that sent heat shooting straight to his loins. "This time, I want it all."

He felt something inside him quake. "All?"

"Hmm-mmm." Her eyes remained locked on his. "All—including whatever it is you hold back."

For the first time in his life he felt dizzy from sheer lust. He gritted his teeth, spoke gratingly through them. "You don't know what you're asking for."

One dark brow arched, haughty—deliberately challenging. "Don't I?"

Her tone was beyond teasing.

Before he could respond, smooth as any houri, she turned in his arms, fitted herself back against him, looked over her shoulder, capturing his stunned gaze as she provocatively shifted her bare bottom against his aching erection. Waited for a heartbeat before asking, "Are you sure?"

She did know—it was there in her eyes, a blue so intense it was almost black. He wanted to ask how the devil she knew, but couldn't think enough to form the sentence.

Couldn't think beyond the fact she somehow did know his deepest, most primitive desire. And was willing to grant it. Accede to it.

That last was clear as she reached one hand up and, leaning her head back, drew his lips to hers. Took him in, drew him in, took his tongue, caressed it with hers. Urged him to feast. When he did, her hand drifted away; she found both his hands with hers, lifted them to her breasts.

Caught her breath on a soft gasp when he captured the firm mounds.

The sound, half-smothered by their kiss, shot

fire through him. He released her lips, his hands full of her bounty, breathed, "Are you sure?"

Her lids flickered as he kneaded, blatantly possessive, then she lifted them. Her eyes were brilliant as she looked into his.

"I'm yours." The words were certain, assured. "Take me as you wish, however you wish." She held his gaze steadily. "I want to know **all** of you—all your wants, all your needs. All your desires."

The last shackle fell, shattered. Passion roared through him, immeasurely stronger than anything he'd felt before. He released her, turned her, caught her in his arms, locked her to him as he bent his head, captured her mouth—and devoured.

What rode him was not lust, not desire, not even passion, but something that grew from all three, yet was fueled by something more. By a desperate, primitive need—something buried so deep beneath his civilized exterior that few women would ever guess it was there.

Let alone tempt it.

Invite it.

Without breaking the kiss, he lifted her; she clung to him, as greedily desperate as he, as wantonly hungry.

His legs hit the end of the four-poster bed. Gathering his strength, he eased her from him, broke the kiss, juggled her and tossed her onto the brilliant crimson coverlet.

"Wait."

Portia lay as she'd fallen, on one hip, half over on her stomach, knew she wouldn't have long to wait. She watched as he stripped off his clothes, let her gaze rest on his face, drank in the austere lines as he flung his waistcoat aside. His features looked harder, more set and angular, than she'd ever seen them. The strength in his body, that invested every movement, was somehow clearer, more intense. Less veiled.

His shirt followed the waistcoat; she twisted back a little to get a better view of the wide expanse of his chest, the hard ridges across his abdomen rippling as he shifted, then bunching as he bent to pull off his boots.

Trousers and stockings went in seconds. And then he stood naked, flagrantly aroused. His gaze locked on her, traveled slowly up her body as he walked to the bed.

He reached out. Traced his palm up the back of her leg, curved his hand about her bottom as he set one knee on the crimson silk.

Lifted his eyes to hers. "You can call a halt at any time."

She met his gaze, dark and burning—couldn't quite smile. "You know I won't."

He searched her eyes one last time, then he closed his hand and shifted her.

Onto her stomach.

She felt the bed bow as he knelt on either side of her legs. Felt the heat of his body run like fire over the backs of her thighs, over the dewed skin of her bottom as he leaned down, close—and pressed his lips to the base of her spine, just above the cleft of her bottom.

Closed his hands about her hips, held her steady as he worked his way upward, following her spine, planting hot, openmouthed kisses as he went, as if he in truth meant to devour her.

The rough hair of his chest brushed her skin; the heat of him poured over her yet he didn't lean on her, hovered just an inch above her, taking his weight on his hands as he moved steadily higher, over her, surrounding her—a potent masculine animal who had captured her and was now intent on possessing her.

She couldn't stop a reactive shiver; closed her eyes for a moment, savoring the wave of heat rising over her, steadily engulfing her, glanced over her shoulder as, pushing her hair aside, he neared her nape.

He lifted his head; for one instant, his blue eyes locked on hers, then he drew back a fraction, straddling her thighs, set his hands to her hips, swept both hard palms slowly up her body, tracing the indentation of her waist, rising up her sides, fingers boldly caressing the sensitive sides of her breasts before sliding down the backs of her arms to grip her elbows.

"Stretch your arms up, above your head."

He pushed them up and she let him; without their support, she slumped onto the bed, her breasts, nipples already tight, pressing into the crimson silk.

Placing her wrists among the pillows, he released them. "Leave them there—don't draw your arms down again."

A command, gravelly and absolute. Her heart thudded, her senses leapt as he reversed the direction of his slow, possessive stroking. She could feel him close, but other than the occasional brush of raspy hair across her skin, he'd touched her only with his hands and lips.

And his gaze. She could feel that, another sort of flame, following his hands as he traced the long lines of her back, down, past her waist, until his thumbs caressed the shallow indentations below her hips.

Her skin prickled; anticipation welled and rushed through her.

To her surprise, he shifted back, shuffling down the bed, his knees on either side of her legs . . . then his hands closed about her hips; smoothly, he lifted them and drew them back.

Until she was curled on her knees before him.

She started to lift her shoulders from the bed—

"Leave your arms as I told you."

The tenor of the words sent a flash of expectation sheering through her, wound her nerves even tighter. She'd obeyed before she'd thought—without the use of her arms, she slumped over her knees. Helpless.

Even before she'd fully assimilated the total submission inherent in the pose, one hand settled heavily on her back, just above her waist.

Holding her down.

In the instant she realized, his other hand spread over her bottom, boldly caressed until her skin was damp, then reached farther, to the slick, swollen flesh between her thighs, in this position readily accessible to his probing fingers.

He held her down, ruthlessly touched, stroked, teased—caressed but never penetrated, never gave her greedy, wanting senses the slightest succor, instead stoked her fire until her skin was aflame, until her breaths came in ragged pants.

Until she moaned.

The wanton, abandoned sound shocked her, but it was quickly followed by more. Held immobile, she could gain no surcease from the unrelenting stimulation, from the need that was flaring inside her—burgeoning, building, rising high.

Eyes closed, her hair fanning about her with the restless motion of her head—the only part of her free to move—she bit her lip, tried to hold back the sound welling in her throat.

Couldn't.

She sobbed. Sobbed again as he raised her hips, turned the sensual rack one notch tighter . . .

In the instant before she broke and told him precisely what she wanted him to do, he shifted. Opened her with his fingers, guided the broad head of his erection to her entrance—and thrust deliberately and heavily home.

Filled her with one long, sure stroke that pushed all the air from her lungs.

That left her feeling more full of him that she ever had before.

His thighs outside hers, his groin to her bottom, he gripped her hip, withdrew a little way, then surged within her.

Still holding her down, a supplicant before him, her body offered for the enjoyment of his.

An offering he took, accepted, savored—with every hard, deep, too-knowing thrust.

She'd told him she was all his; he'd taken her at her word. As he held her before him and possessed her, deeper, harder, faster, she finally fully understood what that meant.

Couldn't find it in her to complain.

The fire, the flames, and the love were there, around them, about them, within them. She gave herself up to it all, lost herself in the inferno.

Willingly surrendered.

Simon gasped as he felt her body tighten. Closed his eyes, savored the exquisite sensation of the firm curves of her bottom riding against him as he buried himself in her scalding heat. Again and again and again.

Taking his hand from her back, he clamped both palms about her hips and held her still as, all restraint long gone, he took all he wished—all she'd offered him.

The most potent invitation a woman could issue—to have her however he wished. To possess her, all she was, all the delights her body could offer, without reservation.

His heart thundered, filled to bursting as he filled his senses with her. As, step by step, her body responded, as did his, wanting more, reaching further.

Releasing her hips, he leaned over her, ran his hands up and around, filling them with her breasts, hot, swollen, finding and squeezing her nipples until she cried out, until she sobbed anew.

She'd come alive beneath him, riding his thrusts, meeting them. He bent his head, nuzzled her hair aside, set his teeth to the tendon running along the curve of her neck, and nipped.

Laved as she reacted, as on a wild gasp her body rose beneath his and clenched tight, then imploded, fractured, pulsing as he drove relentlessly into her, deep into the heart of her fire.

Closed his arms around her, holding her immobile as his body reacted to the rippling contractions of hers, as he plunged deeper yet, filling her, following her, over the peak of sensual glory, over the edge of worldly delight and into earthly bliss.

Into a deep void of unutterable satisfaction. The deepest satiation he'd ever known. Her celebration had created a new dimension, taken them to a different plane.

How many minutes passed before he could summon the strength and the wit to lift from her, wrestle the covers from beneath them and, curling her body against his, slump, all but exhausted, into the bed, he had no idea.

He lay there and let the moment wash over him. Let the peace, the knowledge, the absolute certainty sink into him.

They both fell asleep.

When he woke, he found he'd turned on his side, one arm slung over her hip, his body curved spoon-fashion about hers.

She, too, was awake. He knew it from the tension in her body; she was lying on her side facing away from him—he couldn't see her face.

Coming up on his elbow, he leaned over her.

She turned her head, looked at him, and smiled.

Even in the moonlight, the gesture was glorious.

Raising one hand, Portia touched his cheek, then, still smiling, settled back on her side, feeling him hard, strong, and hot behind her.

He lay passive, yet . . .

Her smile deepened. Reaching back, she wrapped her fingers around his length. Caressed as she remembered. "You called me a cocktease—did you mean it?"

He grunted. "I wasn't even sure you'd know what it meant."

She grinned as, slowly, she ran her thumb over the blunt head of his erection. "Admittedly it's not something one comes across much in Ovid, but I do know my modern derivations."

"Derivations?"

The reply was meaningless; he wasn't thinking about words.

She closed her hand more firmly. "You haven't answered my question."

He sucked in a breath; there was a pause before he said, "Not in general, but in specific."

She thought about that for a moment, fondled not quite absentmindedly as she did. "You mean I tease you?"

It was her turn to catch her breath as he nudged her upper thigh higher, and his artful fingers slid into the softness between her legs.

His fingers played. "You tease my cock simply by existing."

Her smile threatened to split her face. "How?"

The word was breathless; she angled her hips farther, felt him shift behind her.

"I see you, and all I can think about is sinking it into you." He fitted the object under discussion to her. "Like this."

Her eyes fell closed as he slowly, oh-so-slowly slid home. Withdrew, then gave her time to savor every inch of his return.

Her lungs locked; her whole body came alive. Determined, she managed enough breath to say, "I think I rather like being a cocktease—at least in the specific."

He leaned over her, around her, set his lips to the curve of her ear, pushed his hand beneath her arm, and closed it about her breast—and gave her to understand that, far from disapproving, he liked it, too.

Later, much later, they lay slumped in the bed; he'd settled her, sprawled comfortably over him, her head pillowed on his chest. Idly, Simon played with her hair, sifting the long strands.

Eventually, drew a deep breath.

"I love you. You know that, don't you?"

Her reply was only a moment in coming. "Yes." Raising her head, she smiled at him, then crossed her arms, rested her chin on her wrists, and studied his face.

Her eyes were dark and brilliant; he looked into them, waited.

Her smile, that of a woman smugly well satisfied, eased. "I love you, too." A frown invaded her expression. "I still don't understand it."

He hesitated, then offered, "I don't think love is something one necessarily understands." God knew he didn't.

She frowned openly. "Perhaps. But I still can't stop thinking. . . ."

He stroked his hands lovingly down the long planes of her back. "Has anyone ever told you you think too much?"

"Yes. You."

"So stop thinking." He reached farther, suggestively caressed.

She met his eyes, arched a brow. "Make me."

He held her gaze, confirmed the words were the invitation he'd thought, then smiled—wolfishly. "My pleasure."

He rolled, taking her with him, trapped her beneath him, and obliged.

Her next coherent thought did not surface until well past dawn.

She might not have been thinking, but he certainly had been. He'd been plotting, planning, but just what she didn't know.

By the time she reached the breakfast table, he'd convinced Lady O that it was imperative he drive her, Portia, somewhere. She arrived too late to hear where.

"You'll know when we get there," was all he would say. Jaw setting in a way she knew well, he gave his attention to a plateful of ham.

She turned to Lady O.

Who waved aside her question before she could ask it.

"Take my word for it—best you let him drive you up to town. You won't like rocking along slowly with me in the coach—not if you've a better option." She grinned; the old evil light was back in her eyes. "If I were you, I wouldn't hesitate."

Which left Portia little option but to go along for the ride.

Helping herself to tea and toast, she looked around the table. The transformation was marked;

a lighter atmosphere had taken hold once again. There were still lingering shadows in most people's eyes, but the relief was immense, and showed in their smiles.

Lady Calvin, of course, had not come down, but neither had the other older ladies, except for Lady O and Lady Hammond.

"She's taking it hard, poor thing," Lady Hammond confided. "It was always her dream to see Ambrose in Parliament, and now . . . to have to face this, and with all it's revealed of Drusilla as well, she's quite overset. Catherine's asked her to stay on for a day or so, at least until she's well enough to travel."

Drusilla, unsurprisingly, had not joined the company.

Later, everyone gathered in the front hall for farewells. The coaches were at the door; the Hammonds left first, then the Bucksteads.

Portia noted that, despite his earlier stance, James stood a little apart with Lucy, then walked her to the carriage and handed her up. A plan to invite Lucy to another house party sometime, and James as well, sprang into her wind, fully formed.

To which house was the only point in question.

Then Lady O completed her good-byes and, on Lord Netherfield's arm, led the way onto the front steps. She and Simon followed in time to hear Lady O tell his lordship, "Quite a lively break, but next time, Granny, leave out the murders. They're a bit much for my aging constitution to take."

Lord Netherfield snorted. "Yours and mine both, m'dear. But at least these youngsters acquitted themselves well." He bent a beaming smile on Simon and Portia, and Charlie and James who'd followed them out. "Seems there's hope yet for the younger generation."

Lady O's snort was infinitely dismissive. "Bite your tongue—don't want to swell their heads."

Struggling to hide his smile, Charlie bravely came forward and offered to assist Lady O into the carriage. She accepted with aplomb; once settled, she looked out at Simon and Portia. "I'll see you two in London." She met their eyes. "Don't disappoint me."

It sounded like a warning to behave; they both read it for what it was—an exhortation of quite a different character.

Lord Netherfield smiled and waved; they did, too, waiting only until the carriage lumbered off before walking to Simon's curricle, waiting, horses prancing, across the forecourt.

James and Charlie followed them. While Simon ran a careful eye over his bays, James took her hands. "I won't embarrass you by thanking you again, but I hope we'll meet in London later in the year." He hesitated, then glanced at Simon. "You know, Kitty had driven all thoughts of marriage firmly out of my head. Now . . ." He raised one brow, teasing yet quizzical, "Perhaps there really is hope, and I should revisit the notion."

Portia smiled. "Indeed, I think you should." She stretched up and kissed his lean cheek. Then turned to Charlie, raised her brows.

Smiling, too, he met her gaze—then blinked. Glanced at James. "Oh, no—not me. Devotedly fancy-free, that's me—far too shallow for any discerning lady."

"Nonsense." She kissed his cheek, too. "One of these days some **highly** discerning lady is going to see straight through your facade. And what then?"

"I'll emigrate."

They all laughed.

James helped her into the curricle. "And what of you?" he asked Simon as he came up.

Simon looked at her, a long, considering glance, then gave James his hand. "Ask for my opinion in three months."

James laughed, shook his hand. "I suspect I'll know your opinion somewhat earlier than that."

Simon shook Charlie's hand, then climbed up beside her. He flicked the reins the instant they were settled; with smiles and waves, they were off.

She sat back, and wondered. Her box and bandbox were strapped behind and Wilks had been dispatched with Lady O. There was, of course, nothing the least noteworthy in Simon driving her up to town, nothing the least scandalous in driving in an open carriage alone. They were following Lady O, in whose care she was. All perfectly aboveboard.

Except that he and she were not heading directly

to London, but by way of somewhere else. Where she couldn't imagine, let alone why.

Even though she'd expected not to head for town, she was nevertheless surprised when, on reaching the main gate and the lane, Simon turned his horses west, away from Ashmore.

"The west country?" She racked her brains. "Gabriel and Alathea? Or Lucifer and Phyllida?"

Simon grinned, shook his head. "You don't know the place—you've never been there. I haven't been there in years."

"Will we reach there tonight?"

"In a few hours."

She sat back and watched the hedgerows slide by. Realized the feeling enfolding her was contentment. Even though she didn't have a clue where he was taking her.

A smile threatened; she suppressed it. Knew if he saw it he'd ask for an explanation; although she could make a good attempt, now was neither the time nor place.

The simple truth was, with no other man could she imagine being in such a situation and simply accepting it with such inner serenity.

She let her gaze drift to his face, watched for a while, then looked forward before he felt her gaze. She trusted him. Absolutely. Not just physically, although between them, in that arena, the truth was now clear—she was his, but he was also hers, and, it seemed, always had been—she also trusted him in all other spheres.

She trusted his strength—that he would never use it against her, but that it would be there, always, whenever she needed its protection. She trusted his loyalty, his will—most importantly, she trusted his heart.

Knew, in her own, that in the vulnerability he'd embraced, faced, and let her see, accepted that she had to see, lay a guarantee to last a lifetime.

Love. The wellspring of trust, the ultimate cornerstone for marriage.

Trust, strength, security—and love.

She, and he, had it all.

All they needed to go on with.

Wherever he was taking her.

Settling back, she faced forward, willing to follow the road before them wherever it led.

It led to the town of Queen Charlton in Somerset, and ultimately to a house called Risby Grange. Simon stopped in the village and took a large room at the inn. Portia made sure she kept her gloves on all the time, but detected no hint that the innwife suspected they were not man and wife.

Perhaps Charlie was right, and the underlying truth showed, regardless of the existence of formalities.

Leaving their bags at the inn, they followed a winding lane, and in midafternoon drove in through the arched gatehouse of Risby Grange.

Simon halted the horses just inside the gate-house. Before them, sprawled across the crest of the gently rising lawns, the house lay basking in the sunshine, its pale grey stone half-covered with creeper, mullioned windows winking below crenellated battlements.

The house was old, solid, well-kept, but appeared to be deserted.

"Who lives here?" she asked.

"At present, no one other than a caretaker." Simon set the bays trotting up the drive. "I doubt he'll be around. I've got a key."

She looked at him, waiting, but he said no more. Reaching the court before the shallow steps leading up to the front door, he turned the horses onto the adjacent lawn. They both jumped down; after tying the reins to a tree and checking the curricle's brake, he took her hand and they crossed the graveled court, climbed the steps.

He rang the bell; they could hear it jangling deep in the house. They waited, but no one came to let them in.

"The caretaker's also the gamekeeper—he's probably out." Drawing a large key from his pocket, Simon slid it into the lock, turned, then pushed the door wide.

He went in first, looking around; she followed on his heels.

Immediately forgot all her questions over why they were there as curiosity took flight. From the wood-paneled hall with its stained-glass windows, she went from room to room, not waiting for him but leading the way.

From outside, the house had appeared sprawling; inside, it was even more so. Rooms opened from flagged corridors, more corridors sprang from halls, leading hither and yon. Yet every room was gracious, warm, filled with excellent furniture lovingly cared for, with rich fabrics and pretty things, with antiques, and some pieces she recognized as more than that. They were heirlooms.

A fine patina of dust lay over everything, but the house did not exude the musty chill of a place long deserted. Instead, it felt like it was waiting—as if one owner had recently departed, but another was expected at any time. It was a house built for laughter, for warmth and happiness, for a large family to fill its sprawling vastness. That atmosphere pervaded, so definite it was tangible; this was a house that had seen generations grow, that lived and breathed and remained confident of its future, indeed, was eagerly awaiting it.

She knew the Cynster motto, **To have and to hold,** well enough, recognized it and their coat of arms in various forms—on cushions, on a carved panel, in a pane of stained glass.

Eventually, in the big room on the first floor at the top of the main stairs, standing before the magnificent bay window that overlooked the forecourt, she turned to Simon; he stood leaning against the doorframe, watching her. "Whose house is this?"

He studied her, replied, "Mine."

She raised her brows, waited.

He grinned. "It was Great-aunt Clara's. All the others were already married and had their own homes, so she willed this place to me."

She tilted her head, studied him in return. "Why did we come here?"

Simon pushed away from the doorjamb, walked toward her. "I was on my way here all along—I stopped at the house party on the way."

Halting beside her, he took her hand, drew her around to face the long view over the lawns to the gatehouse. "I told you—I hadn't been here for years. My memories of it . . . I didn't know how accurate they were. I wanted to confirm it was as I remembered—a house that calls for a wife and family."

He glanced at her as she glanced at him. "I was right. It does. It's a house that's supposed to be a home."

She held his gaze. "Indeed. And what were you planning to do once you'd confirmed your recollection?"

His lips lifted. "Why, find myself a wife"—he raised her hand to his lips, kept his eyes on hers—"and start a family."

She blinked. "Oh." Blinked again, looked out over the lawns.

He closed his hand about hers. "What is it?"

A moment passed, then she said, "You remember when you found me at the lookout, and I vowed I would consider every eligible gentleman . . . the reason I'd decided to do so was that I'd realized I wanted to have children of my own—a family of my own. To do that, I needed a husband."

Her lips twisted; she looked at him. "Of course, by that I meant a suitable gentleman who would fall in with my wishes and allow me to rule our joint lives."

"No doubt." His tone was acerbic. When she said nothing more but continued to watch him, as if studying him, assessing him anew, he softly asked, "Is that why you're marrying me?"

She hadn't said she would, yet both knew it, a given—an understanding already acknowledged, albeit not in words. Her dark eyes sparked, registering his tack, then they softened. Her lips curved.

"Lady O is really quite amazing."

He'd lost the thread. "How so?"

"She informed me that wanting children, while a perfectly acceptable reason to bring one to consider marriage, was not of itself a sufficiently good reason to marry. However, she assured me that if I kept looking—considering gentlemen to marry—the right reason would eventually present itself."

He twined his fingers with hers. "And has it?"

She met his eyes, her smile serene. "Yes. I love you, and you love me. Lady O is, as always, right—no other reason will do."

He drew her into his arms, felt their bodies react the instant they touched, not just sexually but with a deeper, more comforting familiarity. He gloried in the feeling, gloried in her as she draped her arms over his shoulders, as between his hands, he felt her supple strength, in her dark eyes saw an intellect every bit the equal of his. "It won't be easy."

"Assuredly not—I refuse to promise to be a comfortable wife."

His lips twitched. "You're quite comfortable enough—'obedient' is the word you want, or 'acquiescent'—you've never been either."

"Nonsense—I am when it suits me."

"Therein lies the rub."

"I'm not going to change."

He looked into her eyes. "I don't want you to. If you can accept that I'm similarly unlikely to change, we can go on from there."

Portia smiled. Theirs would not be the marriage she'd wanted; it would be the marriage she needed. "Despite all prior experience, we've managed remarkably well so far. If we try, do you think we could make this last a lifetime?"

"With both of us trying, it'll last." He paused, then added, "We have the right reasons, after all."

"Indubitably." She drew his lips to hers. "I'm starting to believe that love can indeed conqueror all."

He paused, their lips separated by a breath. "Even us?"

She made a frustrated sound. "You, me—**us**. Now kiss me."

Simon smiled. And did.

He'd reached the end of his journey and found all he'd been seeking; in her arms, he'd found his true goal.

Announcement of
THE BASTION CLUB novels,
the exciting new series from
Stephanie Laurens,
the first to be released
later in 2003.

PROLOGUE

His Royal Highness's straits must be dire indeed if he needs must summon His Britannic Majesty's best simply to bask in the reflected glory."

The drawled comment contained more than a little cynicism; Tristan Wemyss, fourth Earl of Trentham, glanced across the stuffy music room, packed with guests, sycophants, and all manner of toadies, at its subject.

Prinny stood in the center of a circle of admirers. Decked out in gold braid and crimson, with epaulets high and fully fringed, their Regent was in genial and expansive good humor, retelling heroic tales of derring-do drawn from the dispatches of recent engagements, most notably that of Waterloo.

Both Tristan and the gentleman standing beside him, Christian Allardyce, Marquess of Dearne, knew the real stories; they had been there. Easing free of the throng, they'd retreated to the side of the opulent chamber to avoid hearing the artful lies.

It was Tristan who'd spoken.

"Actually," Tristan murmured, "I'd viewed tonight more in the nature of a distraction—a feint, if you will."

Christian raised heavy brows. "Listen to my stories of England's greatness—don't worry that the Exchequer's empty and the people are starving?"

Tristan's lips quirked downward. "Something like that."

Dismissing Prinny and his court, Christian surveyed the others crowding the circular room. It was an all-male company primarily composed of representatives from every major regiment and arm of the services recently active; the chamber was a sea of colorful dress uniforms, of braid, polished leather, fur, and even feathers. "Telling that he chose to stage what amounts to a victory reception in Brighton rather than London, don't you think? I wonder if Dalziel had any say in that?"

"From all I've gathered, our Prince is no favorite in London, but it seems our erstwhile commander has taken no chances with whose names he volunteered for the guest list tonight."

"Oh?"

They were talking quietly, out of habit disguising their communication as nothing more than a social exchange between acquaintances. Habit died hard, especially since, until recently, such practices had been vital to staying alive.

Tristan smiled vaguely, distantly, indeed **through** a gentleman who glanced their way; the man decided against intruding. "I saw Deverell at the table—he was seated not far from me. He mentioned that Warnefleet and St. Austell were here, too."

"You can add Tregarth and Blake—I saw them as I was arriving—" Christian broke off. "Ah, I see. Dalziel has only allowed those of us who have sold out to appear?"

Tristan caught his eye; the smile that was never far from his mobile lips deepened. "Can you imagine Dalziel allowing even Prinny to identify his most secret of secret operatives?"

Christian hid a smile, raised his glass to his lips, and sipped. Dalziel—he went by no other name or honorific—was the Foreign Office taskmaster who, from his office buried in the depths of Whitehall, managed His British Majesty's foreign spy network, a network that had been deeply involved in handing victory to England and her allies, both in the Peninsula campaign and more recently at Waterloo. Together with a certain Lord Whitley, his opposite number in the Home Office, Dalziel was responsible for all covert operations both within England and beyond its borders. "I didn't realize Tregarth or Blake were in the same boat as we two, and I know of the others only by repute." He glanced at Tristan. "Are you sure the others are leaving?"

"I know Warnefleet and Blake are, for much the same reasons as we. As for the others, it's purely conjecture, but I can't see Dalziel compromising an operative of St. Austell's caliber, or Tregarth's or Deverell's for that matter, just to pander to Prinny's latest whim."

"True." Christian again looked out over the sea of heads.

Both he and Tristan were tall, broad-shouldered, and lean, with the honed strength of men used to action, a strength imperfectly concealed by the elegant cut of their evening clothes. Beneath those clothes, both bore the scars of years of active service; although their nails were perfectly manicured, it would be some months yet before the telltale signs of their unusual, often ungentlemanly erstwhile occupation faded from their hands—the calluses, the roughness, the leatherlike palms.

They and their five colleagues known to be present had all served Dalziel and their country for at least a decade, Christian for nearly fifteen years. They'd served in whatever guise had been required, from nobleman to streetsweeper, from clerk to navvy. There had, for them, been only one measure of success—discovering the information they'd been sent behind enemy lines to acquire and surviving long enough to get it back to Dalziel.

Christian sighed, drained his glass. "I'm going to miss it."

Tristan's laugh was short. "Aren't we all?"

"Be that as it may, given that we're no longer on His Majesty's payroll"—Christian set his empty glass down on a nearby sideboard—"I fail to see why we need stand here talking, when we could be

much more comfortable doing the same elsewhere . . ." His grey gaze met the eyes of a
gentleman clearly considering approaching; the
gentleman considered again and turned away.
"And without running the risk of having to do the
pretty for whichever toady captures us and
demands to hear our story."

Glancing at Tristan, Christian raised a brow.
"What say you—shall we adjourn to pleasanter
surrounds?"

"By all means." Tristan handed his empty glass
to a passing footman. "Do you have any particular
venue in mind?"

"I've always been partial to the Ship and Anchor.
It has a very cosy snug."

Tristan inclined his head. "The Ship and Anchor,
then. Dare we leave together, do you think?"

Christian's lips curved. "Heads together, talking
earnestly in hushed and urgent tones—if we make
for the door unobtrusively but determinedly, I can
see no reason we shouldn't walk straight through."

They did. Everyone who saw them assumed one
had been sent to summon the other for some secret
but highly significant purpose; the footmen rushed
to get their coats, and then they strode out, into
the crisp night.

Both paused, drew in a deep breath, clearing the
stultifying stuffiness of the overheated Pavilion
from their lungs, then, exchanging faint smiles,
they stepped out.

Leaving the Pavilion's brightly lit entrance, they emerged onto North Street. Turning right, they walked with the relaxed gait of men who knew where they were going, toward Brighton Square and the Lanes beyond. Reaching the narrow, cobbled ways lined with fishermen's cottages, they dropped into single file, at every crossroads changing place, eyes always watching, searching the shadows . . . if either realized, realized they were now at home, at peace, no longer fugitives, no longer at war, neither commented nor tried to suppress the behavior that had over the years become second nature to them both.

They headed steadily south, toward the sound of the sea, soughing in the darkness beyond the shore. Finally, they turned into Black Lion Street. At the other end of the street lay the Channel, the border beyond which they'd lived most of the past decade. Halting beneath the swinging sign of the Ship and Anchor, they both paused, eyes on the darkness framed by the houses at the end of the street. The smell of the sea, the brine on the wind, the familiar tang of seaweed, reached them.

For an instant, memory held them both, then, as one, they turned. Christian pushed open the door, and they went inside.

Warmth enveloped them, the sounds of English voices, the hop-infused scent of good English ale. Both relaxed, an all but indefinable tension falling from them. Christian walked up to the bar. "Two pots of your best."

The landlord nodded a greeting and quickly pulled the pints.

Christian glanced at the half-closed door behind the bar. "We'll sit in your snug."

The landlord glanced at him, then set the frothing tankards on the bar, shooting a quick glance at the snug door as he did. "As to the snug, sir, you're welcome, I'm sure, but there's a group o' gen'lemen in there already, and they might not welcome strangers, like."

Christian raised his brows. He reached for the flap in the counter and lifted it, stepping past as he picked up one tankard. "We'll risk it."

Tristan hid a grin, tossed coins on the counter for the ale, hoisted the second tankard, and followed on Christian's heels.

He was standing at Christian's shoulder when Christian sent the snug door swinging wide.

The group gathered around two tables pushed together looked around; five pairs of eyes locked on them.

Five grins dawned.

Charles St. Austell sat back in the chair at the far end of the table and magnanimously waved them in. "You are better men than we. We were about to take bets on how long you'd stand it."

The others stood so the tables and chairs could be rearranged. Tristan shut the door, set down his tankard, then joined in the round of introductions.

Although they'd all served under Dalziel, they'd never met all seven together. Each knew some of the others; none of them had previously met all.

Christian Allardyce, the eldest and longest serving, had operated in the east of France, often in Switzerland, Germany, and the other smaller states and principalities; with his fairish coloring and facility for languages, he'd been a natural in that sphere.

Tristan himself had served more generally, often in the heart of things, in Paris and the major industrial cities; his fluency in French as well as German and Italian, his brown hair, brown eyes, and easy charm, had served him and his country well.

He'd never crossed paths with Charles St. Austell, the most outwardly flamboyant of the group. With his tumbling black locks and flashing dark blue eyes, Charles was a magnet for ladies young and old. Half-French, he possessed both the tongue and the wit to make the most of his physical attributes; he'd been Dalziel's principal operative in the south of France, in Carcasonne and Toulouse.

Gervase Tregarth, a Cornishman with curling brown hair and sharp hazel eyes, had, so Tristan learned, spent much of the last decade in Britanny and Normandy. He knew St. Austell from the past, but in the field they'd never met.

Tony Blake was another scion of an English house who was also half-French. Black-haired, black-eyed, he was the most elegant of the group, yet there was an underlying sharpness beneath the smooth veneer; he was the operative Dalziel had most often used to intercept and interfere with the French spymasters' networks, a hideously dangerous undertaking centered on the northern French ports. That Tony was alive was a testament to his mettle.

Jack Warnefleet was outwardly a conundrum; he appeared so overtly English, startlingly handsome, with fairish brown hair and hazel eyes, that it was hard to imagine he'd been consistently successful in infiltrating all levels of French shipping and many business deals as well. He was a chameleon even more than the rest of them, with a cheery, hail-fellow-well-met geniality few saw beyond.

Deverell was the last man Tristan shook hands with, a personable man with an easy smile, dark brown hair, and greenish eyes. Despite being uncommonly handsome, he possessed the knack of blending in with any group. He had served almost exclusively in Paris, and had never been detected.

The introductions complete, they sat. The snug was now comfortably full; a fire burned cheerily in one corner as in the flickering light they settled about the table, almost shoulder to shoulder.

They were all large men; they had all at some point been guardsmen in one regiment or another, until Dalziel had found them and lured them into serving through his office.

Not that he'd had to persuade all that hard.

Savoring his first sip of ale, Tristan ran his eye

around the table. Outwardly, they were all different, yet they were, very definitely, brothers beneath the skin. Each was a gentleman born of some aristocratic lineage, each possessed similar attributes, abilities, and talents, although the relative balance differed. Most important, however, each was a man capable of dicing with danger, one who could and would accept the challenge of a life-and-death engagement without a flicker—more, with an inbred confidence and a certain devil-may-care arrogance.

There was more than a touch of the wild adventurer in each of them. And they were loyal to the bone.

Deverell set down his tankard. "Is it true we've all sold out?" There were nods and glances all around; Deverell grinned. "Is it polite to inquire why?" He looked at Christian. "In your case, I assume Allardyce must now become Dearne?"

Wryly, Christian inclined his head. "Indeed. Once my father died and I came into the title, any choice evaporated. If it hadn't been for Waterloo, I would already be deeply mired in issues pertaining to sheep and cattle, and no doubt leg-shackled to boot."

His tone, faintly disgusted, brought commiserating smiles to the others' faces.

"That sounds all too familiar." Charles St. Austell looked down the table. "I hadn't expected to inherit, but while I was away, both my elder brothers failed me." He grimaced. "So now I'm the Earl of Lostwithiel and, so my sisters, sisters-in-law, and dear mother constantly remind me, long overdue at the altar."

Jack Warnefleet laughed, not entirely humorously. "Entirely unexpectedly, I've joined the club, too. The title was expected—it was the pater's—but the houses and the blunt came via a great-aunt I barely knew existed, so now, I've been told, I rank high on the list of eligibles and can expect to be hunted until I succumb and take a wife."

"**Moi, aussi.**" Gervase Tregarth nodded to Jack. "In my case it was a cousin who succumbed to consumption and died ridiculously young, so now I'm the Earl of Crowhurst, with a house in London I haven't even seen and a need, so I've been informed, to get myself a wife and heir, given I'm now the last of the line."

Tony Blake made a dismissive sound. "At least you don't have a French mother—believe me, when it comes to hounding one to the altar, they take the cake."

"I'll drink to that." Charles raised his tankard to Tony. "But does that mean you, too, have returned to these shores to discover yourself encumbered?"

Tony wrinkled his nose. "Courtesy of my father, I've become Viscount Torrington—I'd hoped it would be years yet, but . . ." He shrugged. "What I didn't know was that over the past decade the pater had taken an interest in various investments. I'd expected to inherit a decent livelihood—I hadn't expected to succeed to great wealth. And then discover the entire ton knows it. I stopped briefly in town on my way down here to call on my godmother." He shuddered. "I was nearly mobbed. It was horrendous."

"It's because we lost so many at Waterloo." Deverell gazed into his tankard; they were all silent for a moment, remembering lost comrades, then all lifted their mugs and drank.

"I have to confess I'm in much the same straits." Deverell set down his tankard. "I'd no expectations when I left England, only to discover on my return that some distant cousin twice removed had turned up his toes, and I'm now Viscount Paignton, with the houses, the income—and just like you all, the dire need of a wife. I can manage the land and funds, but the houses, let alone the social obligations—they're a web far worse than any French plot."

"And the consequences of failing could drive you to your grave," St. Austell put in.

There were dark murmurs of assent all around. All eyes turned to Tristan.

He smiled. "That's quite a litany, but I fear I can trump all your tales." He looked down, turning his tankard between his hands. "I, too, returned to find myself encumbered—with a title, two houses and a hunting box, and considerable wealth. However, both houses are home to an assortment of females, various great-aunts, cousins, and other more distant connections. I inherited from my great-uncle, the recently departed third Earl of

Trentham, who positively loathed his brother—my grandfather—and also my late father, and me.

"His argument was we were wastrel ne'er-do-wells who came and went as we pleased, traveled the world, and so on. In all fairness, I must say that now I've met my great-aunts and their female army, I can see the old boy's point. He must have felt trapped by his position, sentenced to live his life surrounded by doting, meddling females."

A frisson ran around the table.

Tristan's face grew grim. "Consequently, when his own son's son died, and then his son as well, and he realized I would inherit, he devised a devilish clause to his will. I've inherited title, land, and houses, and wealth for a year—but if I fail to marry within that year, I'll be left with the title, the land, and the houses—all that's entailed—but the bulk of the wealth, the funds needed to run the houses, will be given to various charities."

There was silence, then Jack Warnefleet asked, "What would happen to the horde of old ladies?"

Tristan looked up, eyes narrow, lips curled. "That's the devilish heart of it—they'd remain my pensioners, in my houses—there's nowhere else for them to go, and I could hardly turf them into the streets."

All the others stared at him, appreciation of his predicament dawning in their faces.

"That's a dastardly thing to do." Gervase paused, then asked, "When's your year up?"

"Next July."

"So you've got the next Season to make your choice." Charles set his tankard down and pushed it away. "We're all in large measure in the same boat. If I don't find a wife by then, my sisters, sisters-in-law, and dear mother will drive me demented."

"It's not going to be plain sailing, I warn you." Tony Blake glanced around the table. "After escaping from my godmother's, I sought refuge in Boodles." He shook his head. "Bad mistake. Within an hour, not one, but **two** gentlemen I'd never before met approached and asked me to dinner!"

"Set on **in your club**?" Jack Warnefleet voiced their communal shock.

Grimly, Tony nodded. "And there was worse. I called in at the house and discovered a pile of invitations, literally a foot high. The butler said they'd started arriving the day after I'd sent word I'd be down—I'd warned my godmother I might drop in."

Silence fell as they all digested that, extrapolated, considered . . .

Christian leaned forward. "Who else has been up to town?"

All the others shook their heads. They'd only recently returned to England and had gone straight to their estates.

"Very well," Christian continued. "Does this mean that when next we each show our faces in town, we'll be hounded like Tony?"

They all imagined it . . .

"Actually," Deverell said, "it's likely to be much worse. A lot of families are in mourning at the moment—even if they're in town, they won't be going about. The numbers calling should be down."

They all looked at Tony, who shook his head. "Don't know—I didn't wait to find out."

"But as Deverell says, it must be so." Gervase's face hardened. "But such mourning will end in good time for next Season, then the harpies will be out and about, looking for victims, more intense and even more determined."

"Hell!" Charles spoke for them all. "We're going to be"—he gestured—"precisely the sort of targets we've spent the last decade **not being**."

Christian nodded, serious and sober. "In a different theater, maybe, but it's still a form of war—at least it is the way the ladies of the ton play the game."

"It's a sad day when, having survived everything the French could throw at us, we, England's heroes, return home—only to face an even greater threat." Shaking his head, Tristan sat back in his chair.

"A threat to our futures like none other, and one we haven't, thanks to our devotion to king and country, as much experience in facing as many a younger man." Jack Warnefleet sounded somber, echoing their feelings.

Silence fell . . .

"You know . . ." With one long finger, Charles

St. Austell poked his tankard in circles. "We've faced worse before, and won." He looked up, glanced around at their faces. "We're all much of an age—there's what, five years between us?— we're all facing a similar threat, and all have a similar goal in mind, for similar reasons. Why not band together—help each other?"

"One for all and all for one?" Gervase asked.

"Why not?" Charles glanced around again. "We're experienced enough in strategy—surely we can, and should, approach this like any other engagement."

Jack sat up. "It's not as if we'd be in competition with each other." He, too, glanced around, meeting everyone's eyes. "We're all alike to some degree, but we're all different, too, all from different families, different counties, and there's not too **few** ladies but too **many** vying for our attentions— that's our problem."

"I think it's an excellent idea." Leaning his forearms on the table, Christian looked at Charles, then glanced at the others. "We all have to wed—I don't know about you, but I'll fight to the last gasp to retain control of my destiny—**I** will chose my wife—I will not have her foisted, by whatever means, upon me. We now know, thanks to Tony's fortuitous reconnoitering, that the enemy will be waiting, ready to pounce the instant we appear." He glanced around again. "So how are we going to seize the initiative?"

"The same way we always have," Tristan replied. "Information is key. We share what we learn—dispositions of the enemy, their habits, their preferred strategies."

Deverell nodded. "We share tactics that work. And warn of any perceived pitfalls."

"But what we need first, more than anything," Tony cut in, "is a safe refuge. It's always the first thing we put in place when going into enemy territory."

They all paused, considered . . .

Charles grimaced. "Before your news, I would have imagined our clubs, but that clearly won't do."

"No—and our houses are not safe for similar reasons." Jack frowned. "Tony's right—we need a refuge where we can be certain we're safe, where we can meet and exchange news." His brows rose. "Who knows? There might be times when it would be to our advantage to conceal our connections with each other, at least socially."

The others nodded, exchanging glances.

Christian put their thoughts into words. "We need a club of our own. Not to live in, although we might want a few bedchambers in case of need, but a club where we can meet, and from which we can plan and conduct our campaigns in safety without having to watch our backs."

"Not a bolt-hole," Charles mused. "More a castle . . ."

"A stronghold in the heart of enemy territory." Deverell nodded, determined. "Without it, we'll be too exposed."

"And we've been away too long," Gervase growled. "The harpies will fall on us and tie us down if we waltz into the ton unprepared. We've forgotten what it's like . . . if we ever truly knew."

It was a tacit acknowledgment that they were indeed sailing into unknown and therefore dangerous waters. Not one of them had spent any meaningful time in society after the age of twenty.

Christian looked around the table. "We have five full months before we need our refuge—if we have it established by the end of February, we'll be able to return to town and slip in past the pickets, disappear whenever we wish . . ."

"My estate's in Surrey." Tristan met the others' gazes. "If we can decide on what we want as our stronghold, I can slip into town and make the arrangements without creating any ripples."

Charles's eyes narrowed; his gaze grew distant. "Someplace close to everywhere, but not too close."

"It needs to be in an area easily reachable, but not obvious." Deverell tapped the table in thought. "The fewer in the neighborhood who recognize us the better."

"A house, perhaps . . ."

They tossed around their requirements and quickly agreed that a house in one of the quieter areas outside but close to Mayfair yet away from the heart of town would serve them best. A house, with reception rooms and space enough for them all to congregate, with a room in which they could meet with ladies if necessary, but the rest of the house to be female-free, with at least three bedchambers in case of need, and kitchens and staff quarters—and a staff who understood their requirements . . .

"That's it." Jack slapped the table. "Here!" He grabbed up his tankard and raised it. "I give you Prinny and his unpopularity—if it weren't for him, we wouldn't be here today, and wouldn't have had the opportunity to make all our futures that much safer."

With wide grins, they all drank, then Charles pushed back his chair, rose, lifted his tankard. "Gentlemen—I give you our club! Our last bastion against the matchmakers of the ton, our secured base from which we'll infiltrate, identify, and isolate the lady we each want, then take the ton by storm and capture her!"

The others cheered, thumped the table, then rose.

Charles inclined his head to Christian. "I give you the bastion that will allow us to take charge of our destinies and rule our own hearths. Gentlemen!" Charles raised his tankard high. "I give you the Bastion Club!"

They all roared their approval and drank.

And the Bastion Club was born.